NEVADA RUN

The four hit men were closing in on Don Pucci's party.

Blade did the only thing he could — he suddenly crouched in front of the Don's wheelchair, aimed the Commando barrel over Pucci's right shoulder, and sighted on one of the trigger men with a pistol, the nearest one.

Blade cut loose, the Commando chattering loudly, the stock bucking against his shoulder.

The closest hit man took a burst in the chest and was flung to the carpet.

The hit man with the sawed-off shotgun let fly into the back of one of the Don's men at point-blank range, the buckshot blowing the man's chest out and sending him sprawling. Pivoting, the hit man took a bead on the Don.

Blade squeezed the trigger, stitching the shotgun-wielding killer from the crotch to the forehead.

MIAMI RUN

The Warrior's body unwound, his right hand sweeping up and over the Genie's head, his fingers locking on the man's neck and yanking the Genie forward even as his hand brought the Bowie around and up in a savage arc. The tip of the razor-honed blade penetrated the Genie's neck just below his chin, and the knife slanted upward and was buried to the hilt.

For an instant of incredulous shock, the Genie's only reaction was a widening of his eyes. He gurgled as a crimson spray gushed from his throat, then abruptly lunged, hissing, spearing the cane at the Warrior's face. There was a muted click and a five-inch sharpened metal spike popped out of the top of the cane.

ENDWORLD
DOUBLE

NEVADA RUN/
MIAMI RUN

Dedicated to Judy, Joshua, and Shane
Van and Amadon
Enoch and Elijah
and to the oldest profession of all...
the art of storytelling

Book Margins, Inc.

A BMI Edition

Published by special arrangement with Dorchester Publishing

NEVADA RUN Copyright © MCMLXXXIX by David Robbins

MIAMI RUN Copyright © MCMLXXXIX by David Robbins

Printed in the United States of America.

NEVADA RUN

PROLOGUE

Should he waste the scuzz now or later? Johnny Giorgio glanced over his right shoulder at the source of his irritation and frowned. His diamond-shaped face, with its hard, cruel features, became even more severe. A flinty narrowing of his brown eyes accompanied a bunching of his bushy black eyebrows. He lifted his left arm and swiped at the bangs of his oily black hair.

"I still say this is the craziest damn idea you ever came up with," Manzo complained for the umpteenth time. His rodentlike countenance twitched as he spoke, his dark eyes flicking over the landscape on both sides of Highway 59. His dark brown suit, unlike Giorgio's neat, black three-piece, was rumpled and in need of a washing.

Giorgio pursed his lips thoughtfully, his right hand resting on the machine gun in his lap, a Weaver Arms Nighthawk. He was tempted to order his driver to stop the jeep so he could show Manzo what happened to underlings who chronically complained, but he refrained for two reasons. First, he might need Manzo when he made the snatch. Secondly, he estimated they were within ten miles of their destination, and he didn't want anyone from the Home to hear the gunfire.

No.

He would bide his time.

Play it real smart.

And rack the son of a bitch the first chance he got!

The two green jeeps, decades ago the property of the Nevada National Guard, continued northward on 59. A new road sign appeared on the right: HALMA. FOUR MILES.

Giorgio gazed at the road sign in perplexity. What the hell was this? Was Halma inhabited? His snitch had never said nothing about Halma.

Manzo, seated in the rear of the jeep directly behind Giorgio, spotted the sign. "Look at that!"

"I see it," Giorgio said calmly.

"You know what that means?" Manzo asked belligerently.

Giorgio twisted in his seat and stared at the two men in the back, Manzo and the other trigger man, Ianozzi, who was sitting behind the driver. He focused his full attention on Manzo, composing himself so his anger was carefully concealed. "I know what it means," he said in a quiet tone.

Ianozzi, a young man of 25 wearing a blue suit and tie, gazed at Giorgio for a few seconds, then casually placed both of his hands on the Mossberg Model 500 Bullpup resting across his knees.

"Why did we have to come so far?" Manzo queried, nervously surveying the woods bordering the highway. He failed to note the expression on Giorgio's face. His fatigue and apprehension combined to make him careless. "Who cares what's in Minnesota?"

"I've explained it to you many times," Giorgio noted patiently.

Manzo scowled. "I just don't like being this far from Vegas. We could have done this another way."

"This is the best way," Giorgio assured him. "Trust me."

Manzo's weasely eyes shifted to Giorgio. "I trust you, Boss. You know that."

"Do I?" Giorgio said. "I'm beginning to wonder."

Manzo abruptly realized his mistake. He blanched and swallowed hard. "Hey, no offense meant, Boss! I was just letting off a little steam. We've been on the road for over a week, and all the muties and creeps can get to a guy. You know how it is."

"I know how it is," Giorgio said.

Manzo mustered a weak grin. "I'm a little antsy, is all. All this nature shit makes me uncomfortable. I'm used to the casinos, the broads, and the booze. Hell! I ain't been laid in over a week!"

"None of us have been laid since we left," Giorgio observed. "But you don't hear none of the other guys griping."

Manzo voiced a feeble titter. "Don't take it personal, Boss. I can't help it if I'm edgy."

"A wiseguy can't afford to get edgy," Giorgio noted. "You know the saying: If you blow your cool, you're a fool." He paused. "I don't like fools in my organization."

"It won't happen again," Manzo vowed. "I promise!"

Giorgio glanced at the other trigger man, Ianozzi. "Did you hear that, Ozzi? He says it won't happen again."

Ozzi's green eyes brightened, his thin lips curling upward. "I heard it, Boss."

The driver suddenly slammed on the brakes, causing the jeep to lurch slightly as it abruptly slowed.

Giorgio gripped the dash with his left hand for support. "What the hell are you doing, Sacks?" he demanded.

Sacks was gripping the black steering wheel tightly, his brown eyes on the highway ahead, his bulldog visage registering amazement. "Look! Up ahead!" He began to gradually accelerate.

Giorgio swiveled and faced front.

Highway 59 was awash with the bright May sunlight. Two hundred yards distant walked a quartet consisting of two men and two women, none of whom appeared to be much over 20 years old. One of the women was a blonde, the other a redhead. The blonde wore blue shorts and a faded yellow blouse; the redhead was wearing light brown pants and a green blouse. Both of the men wore jeans. One, the heftier of the pair, also wore a dark green T-shirt and carried a shotgun; the leaner of the men had on a brown shirt and was armed with a revolver in a holster on his right hip. All four were heading to the north, their backs to the approaching jeeps.

"Do we snuff 'em?" Manzo asked eagerly.

"No," Giorgio replied. "Chill out and let me do the talking."

Alerted by the roar of the jeep motors, the quartet had turned and were watching the vehicles draw ever nearer. The man with the shotgun hustled the others to the right side of the road, their expressions conveying their apprehension.

Giorgio gazed over his left shoulder and out the rear window, spying the second jeep 25 yards to the rear, the jeep containing three more of his best soldiers—Pete, Tommy, and Nicky—as well as most of their supplies, their food and water and spare gas.

"You want me to pull up next to them, then?" Sacks inquired.

Giorgio stared at his driver. Sacks was one of the old-time boys, and there were flecks of gray in his brown hair. Although Sacks was unquestionably loyal, his intellect was on a par with a turnip's. "No," Giorgio cracked, "I want you to run them over." He paused. "Of course I want you to pull up next to them! How else am I going to talk to them?"

Sacks flinched and angled the jeep to the right side of the road.

"Keep your hardware out of sight," Giorgio instructed his men. He slid the Nighthawk to the floor, then placed his right hand on the door latch. The doors on the jeeps were canvas affairs with thin plastic windows instead of glass, and the windows did not roll down. He waited until the jeep stopped approximately five yards from the quartet before opening the door and stepping out, smiling broadly.

"Hello," he greeted them.

The young men eyed him warily, the hefty one fingering the trigger of his shotgun, the lean one with his right hand on his revolver. Behind the men, the two women were clearly uneasy.

"Hello," Giorgio said again. "I hope we didn't scare you."

The second jeep was coasting to a halt behind the first.

"Who are you?" the hefty youth queried anxiously. "What do you want?"

Giorgio deliberately maintained his friendly facade. He took a step away from the door, his hands at his sides to show he was unarmed and ostensibly not a threat. "Sorry to bother you, but we're lost."

"Lost?" the hefty youth repeated skeptically.

"Yes," Giorgio lied. "We're looking for a place called the Home. Have you ever heard of it?"

The redheaded woman grinned in relief. "I'm from the Home. Who are you?"

"You're from the Home!" Giorgio stated in delight. "I can't believe my luck! We've traveled so far to get here, all the way from Nevada."

"Are the Elders expecting you?" the redhead asked.

"I don't know who the Elders are," Giorgio admitted.

"The Elders are responsible for managing the Home," the redhead disclosed. "One of them, Plato, is our Leader."

The hefty youth's brown eyes narrowed. "You came all the way from Nevada to see the Family and you don't know about the Elders?"

Giorgio resisted an impulse to smash Hefty in the chops. "I was told a little about the Family. I know they live in a thirty-acre compound on the outskirts of what was once Lake Bronson State Park. And I heard a lot about the Warriors, the ones who defend the Home and protect the Family. But I wasn't told about the Elders." He didn't add that his only interest was in the Warriors; he couldn't care less about the damn Elders.

"The Spirit is smiling on you," the redhead said. "Blade

is at the Home right now. He's the head Warrior."

Giorgio nodded. "So I heard. The Warriors have quite a reputation."

Hefty grinned. "The Warriors are the best fighters in the world! Nobody's been able to beat them—not the Trolls, the Doktor, the Technics, the Russians, nobody," he said proudly.

"Are you from the Home too?" Giorgio questioned.

"No," Hefty replied. "I live in Halma, about three miles or so to the north. My people are called the Clan. We used to live in the Twin Cities, but the Warriors saved us from the Watchers and helped us to relocate in Halma. We wanted to live close to the Family."

"I'm the only one here from the Home," the redhead chimed in.

"How nice," Giorgio said politely. "How far is it to the Home from here?"

"Three miles to Halma," the hefty youth calculated aloud, "and then another mile to the cutoff. You take a right when you come to a dirt road. It runs about five miles, right up to the Home. You can't miss it."

Giorgio grinned. The Home was nine or ten miles away, which meant no one there would be able to hear the shots and none of the Warriors could reach the scene before he was long gone. Halma was much closer, but it didn't matter if any of the Clan heard the gunfire. "This is great news," he said.

"My name is Mindy," the redhead offered. "My mother is a Warrior."

Giorgio did a double take. "She is?"

"Yes," Mindy stated.

"Why didn't you say so before?" Giorgio queried.

Hefty chuckled. "Mindy's too modest. Her mom isn't as famous as Blade, Hickok, Yama, and the others, but she's one mean momma."

"Ted!" Mindy exclaimed in protest. "Don't talk about my mom that way!"

"Well, she is," Ted insisted.

"What is your mother's name?" Giorgio asked Mindy.

"Helen," she answered.

Giorgio could scarcely suppress his excitement. Here was exactly who he needed, delivered on a golden platter! "I look forward to meeting your mother. Would you consent to drive with us to the Home?"

"I don't know. . . ." Mindy said, her blue eyes scrutinizing the jeeps.

"Come on," Giorgio urged her. "I would take it as a personal favor."

"I'd like to," Mindy said, "but I can't. Please don't be insulted, but we're taught to be very leery of strangers."

"Yeah," Ted concurred. "You haven't even told us your name yet."

"Anthony Pucci," Giorgio stated, accenting each syllable distinctly. He didn't want the kid to make a mistake. "But you can call me Tony."

"I'm sorry I can't go with you, Tony," Mindy said.

"That's perfectly okay," Giorgio assured her. "It's understandable in this day and age. You can't be too trusting."

"Why do you want to see the Family?" Ted inquired.

"That's my business," Giorgio replied, a touch testily. The shit-head was too nosy for his own good!

"Just ask for Blade or Plato when you reach the Home," Mindy advised. "The Family is always happy to see strangers if they come in peace."

Giorgio turned toward the jeep. "I'll do that. And I thank you for your time."

Ted peered into the first jeep. "Who are those guys?" he asked.

"Associates of mine," Giorgio said. He moved up to the jeep, standing with the door between the quartet and him, staring at them through the plastic window. "Say, do you like chocolate candy?"

"I've never tasted it," Ted rejoined.

Giorgio grinned. Now it was his turn to razz the shit-head. "You've never had chocolate candy?"

"No," Ted responded.

"Don't you eat sweets?" Giorgio queried.

"Sweets aren't good for the body," Mindy interjected. "The Elders teach all of the Family children about sweets. We know there was a public mania for sugar-based foods before the Big Blast. The American people downed tons of sweets each day. Many of them were addicted, which is sad when you think about it, because excessive sugar consumption disrupts our metabolism."

Giorgio shrugged. "Some candy now and then never hurt nobody." He looked at Hefty. "What about you? You're from the Clan, not the Family. Or do the Elders control the Clan too?"

"The Elders don't control anyone," Ted said stiffly. "They guide the Family and serve as teachers. We respect the Elders a lot." He paused. "As far as candy goes, where would we get it? I spent my childhood in the Twin Cities, where we had to fight for every scrap of food. There wasn't any candy to be found. Since we came to Halma, though, the Family members have taught us how to grow our own crops and to gather food from the forest. We use a lot of honey, and my mom can whip up some terrific honey treats. But we don't have any chocolate candy."

"That's too bad," Giorgio said. "You don't know what you're missing. I happen to have a box in the jeep. Would you like to taste some?"

The four exchanged glances.

"Sure," Ted declared for all of them. "Why not?"

Giorgio smiled and leaned into the jeep, bending forward and taking hold of the Weaver Arms Nighthawk. He slowly backed up, keeping the machine gun out of sight until the last possible second.

Ted had relaxed his grip on the shotgun and was saying something to Mindy. The lean youth had taken his hand from his revolver.

"If you think sweets are bad for the body," Giorgio commented casually, "wait until you see what lead does." He pivoted and leveled the Nighthawk.

The blonde screamed.

Giorgio smiled as he squeezed the trigger, shooting the first burst low and taking Ted off at the knees. The

Weaver's heavy slugs ripped into Ted's kneecaps, blowing them apart, tumbling Ted backwards and causing the shotgun to fall from his fingers.

The lean youth was clawing at his revolver.

Giorgio blasted the youth from the crotch to the chin, stitching a straight line of miniature red geysers, the impact flinging the lean one onto his back.

The blonde was still screaming, but not for long.

Sadistically, Giorgio let her have a few rounds in the face and she dropped with a strangled cry.

Mindy was gaping at Giorgio in horror, shocked to her core.

"The girl!" Giorgio snapped, and Ozzi, Sacks, and Manzo promptly emerged from the jeep. Ozzi and Sacks took hold of Mindy and started to propel her toward the vehicle.

"No!" Mindy shrieked, striving to wrench her arms free from their steely grasps.

Ozzi, holding his Bullwhip in his right hand and Mindy's right elbow in his left, unexpectedly rammed the Bullwhip barrel into her abdomen, doubling her over. "Move your ass, bitch!" he snarled.

"Don't damage the merchandise," Giorgio cautioned.

Ozzi and Sacks carted Mindy to the far side of the jeep and forced her to sit on the back seat.

Ted was on his left side, bent forward, clutching his legs above his ruined knees, whining and groaning, his eyes shut tight, in misery.

Giorgio walked up to the youth. "Open your eyes, punk!"

Ted's eyes didn't open. He trembled, breathing deeply.

Scowling, Giorgio hauled off and kicked the youth in the ribs.

Ted involuntarily cried out, tucking his right elbow against his side, his anguished brown eyes opening wide.

"That's better," Giorgio growled. He leaned down. "Listen up, punk, because I don't want you to forget any of this. Are you listening?"

Ted nodded vigorously.

"Good," Giorgio smirked. "When you see the Warriors, you tell them Anthony Pucci sends his regards. You got that?"

Tears rimming his eyes, Ted nodded.

"And I want you to give Blade a message," Giorgio directed. "I want you tell Blade we'll be waiting for him and the other Warriors. If Mindy's mom, Helen, wants to see her daughter again, then the Warriors must come to Las Vegas. They have one month. That's all. Just one month. If they don't show up by then, we whack the girl. Got that?"

Ted gulped and nodded.

"Tell Blade the girl will be waiting for them at the Golden Crown Casino. Remember that name. The Golden Crown Casino. Think you can remember that?"

Ted nodded yet again, then uttered a single word, his voice strained, his features in torment. "Why?"

Giorgio straightened. "Wouldn't you like to know," he said, and kicked the youth on the chin.

Ted's head snapped back, his teeth crunching together, and he went limp.

Someone snickered to Giorgio's rear.

"That's showing him, Boss!" Manzo said excitedly.

Giorgio turned.

Manzo stood three feet away, a Springfield Armory M1A rifle held loosely along his right side, idly gazing at the blood spurting from Ted's reputured kneecaps.

"Thanks for reminding me," Giorgio said.

Manzo looked up. "About what?"

"This," Giorgio stated, and shot Manzo in the stomach. He kept firing until all 25 rounds in the clip were expended, even after Manzo was down, and he grinned as he watched Manzo's body flopping and convulsing as it was hit again and again and again.

Ozzi was laughing.

"A good button man should be seen and not heard," Giorgio said, addressing the corpse contemptuously, then stalked to the jeep. "Let's hit the road," he announced. "We have a long ride ahead of us."

"What about Manzo's piece?" Ozzi asked.

"Leave it," Giorgio barked. "We don't need it." He slid into the jeep and glanced back at Mindy. "My plan worked like a charm."

Sacks took his seat behind the wheel. "I never doubted you for a minute, Boss," he said.

Giorgio ran his eyes up and down Mindy's attractive figure, then snickered. "Yes, sir! The trip back to Vegas is going to be a hell of a lot more interesting than the one coming out. Too bad Manzo won't be around to get a piece of the action." He cackled at his joke.

CHAPTER ONE

The giant stood on the rampart above the drawbridge situated in the center of the west wall of the Home and surveyed the cleared field beyond. His massive arms were folded across his huge chest, his muscles, even at rest, bulging in stark relief. He was wearing a black leather vest, green fatigue pants, and black combat boots. Around his waist was strapped a matched set of Bowies, one big knife on each hip. A comma of dark hair dangled over his brooding gray eyes.

He was worried.

What was he supposed to do?

The strain of living a dual life was beginning to take its toll, not on him but his marriage. His wife was miserable, and he couldn't bear to see her upset. Jenny and his son Gabe mattered more to him than anyone else in the world. He wanted to see them both happy, but Jenny could never be content with the status quo. And he couldn't blame her for her attitude because he was the reason for it. Or rather, his job was.

His two jobs.

He hadn't foreseen how difficult the task would be to juggle two positions at the same time. On the one hand, he was the head of the Warriors, pledged to safeguard the Family from any and all threats. And on the other hand, he was in charge of the Freedom Force, the elite tactical squad based in California. The Force, as it was known, had been the brainchild of the leaders of the Freedom Federation, the league of seven widespread factions devoted to preserving the fragments of civilization, to establishing order after 105 years of relative chaos. All thanks to the holocaust of World War Three.

Initially, he had moved Jenny and Gabe to California, to Los Angeles. But Jenny hated the city life. After so many years of togetherness and tranquility at the Home, she found the hustle and bustle of one of the few remaining major metropolises to be a constant source of anxiety. She also didn't like the fact he was seldom home, which essentially left her alone in a vast city of strangers.

The way he saw his problem, there were several choices. He could quit the Force or stop being the top Warrior, allowing him to spend more precious time with his wife and son. Or he could convince Jenny to return to the Home and continue his monthly trip to the compound, flying from LA to Minnesota on board one of the two VTOLs California possessed. The remarkable jets, with their vertical-take-off-and-landing capability, were utilized as a regular shuttle and courier service between the various Federation Factions. The aircraft were a godsend. What with the Family, the Clan, and the Moles in northern Minnesota, the Flathead Indians in Montana, the Cavalry in the Dakota Territory, the Civilized Zone in the Midwest, and the former state of California all comprising the Freedom Federation, they needed a means of traversing great distances rapidly and safely. Traveling overland between the factions was extremely dangerous; the barbaric Outlands were populated by savage bands of men and mutants.

So what should he . . .

There was a commotion on the rampart to his right, and

he twisted to find another Warrior jogging toward him. The newcomer was a lanky man dressed in buckskins, with long blond hair and a sweeping blond moustache, keen blue eyes, and a pair of pearl-handled Colt Python revolvers snug in their respective holsters.

"Hey, pard!" the gunman called out.

"What is it?" the giant asked, lowering his arms.

"Take a gander, Blade," the gunman directed, pointing to the west. "What do you reckon that's all about?"

Blade gazed westward. The Family diligently kept the fields surrounding their walled compound stripped of all vegetation for 150 yards to discourage any hostile attack. The 20-foot-high brick walls topped with sharp barbed wire afforded an excellent view of all approaches. No one could cross the fields without being seen. Just past the fields the dense forest began, unbroken for miles and miles except for the crude dirt road the Family and the Clan had constructed running from the Home to Highway 59.

And there on the road, barreling toward the Home at a reckless speed, stirring up a cloud of dust in the process, was an old flatbed truck.

Blade's eyes narrowed. He recognized that truck. The Clan had received the vehicle in trade with the Civilized Zone. All seven Federation factions now engaged in periodic trade and barter sessions. The Family often traded vegetables, venison jerky, buckskin clothing sewn together by the Weavers, and other items for commodities the other factions owned in abundance.

"That hombre is going like a bat out of hell," the gunfighter commented in his typical Western idiom.

"This could be trouble," Blade mentioned.

"Do you want me to sound the alarm?" the gunman asked.

Blade reflected for a moment. Why should he arouse the Family and interrupt whatever the rest of the Warriors were doing without justification? The Warriors in Beta Triad were probably still sleeping; Rikki, Yama, and Teucer had been on wall duty during the night, and it was only midmorning. "No, Hickok," Blade said. "We won't get everybody all excited until we know what's going on."

"Makes sense to me, pard," Hickok declared.

The truck was several hundred yards off, swerving and bouncing as the driver hit a series of bumps and ruts.

"We really should have made that road a mite smoother," Hickok observed. "It's murder on the kidneys."

"We did the best we could considering we don't have any heavy construction equipment," Blade remarked. He leaned out over the edge of the rampart, careful not to entangle himself in the barbed wire, and insured the draw-bridge was down so the truck could enter. The drawbridge opened outward from the brick wall, permitting access to the Home over the inner moat. The Founder of the Home, a man named Kurt Carpenter, had diverted a stream into the northwest corner of the compound and channeled the water along the inner base of all four walls, then out the southeast corner. The moat was yet another of the defenses the Founder had incorporated into the design of his sur-vivalist retreat immediately prior to the war.

"Should we mosey down and see what the fuss is all about?" Hickok inquired.

"Let's," Blade said.

"What about Geronimo?" Hickok questioned.

Blade hesitated. Together, Hickok, Geronimo, and him-self composed Alpha Triad. The Warriors were divided into triads to increase their efficiency; the three Warriors in each of the six triads became the closest of friends and functioned as supremely deadly, tight-knit teams. He knew Geronimo was patrolling the ramparts, and was most likely somewhere on the east wall. Since the walls enclosed an area 30 acres in size. Geronimo would not return for another ten minutes. "If we need him, I'll send for him," Blade said, and hurried to the stairs leading from the rampart to the inner bank of the moat. He descended quickly and crossed to the bridge, the gunman at his side.

"I just hope the cow chip doesn't run over somebody," Hickok commented.

Nearby, the Family members were busily involved in

their everyday activities. While the eastern half of the compound was preserved in a natural state for agricultural purposes, the western half contained the enormous concrete blocks the Founder had built to withstand the devastation of the war, and was where the Family generally congregated and socialized.

The flatbed was now less than a hundred yards away and closing.

"We'll meet him outside," Blade said, and hastened across the drawbridge to the field.

"How do we know it's a guy?" Hickok noted. "It could be a gal."

"Could be," Blade agreed.

Whoever was driving was pushing the vehicle to its limits. The engine was roaring and belching puffs of smoke out the exhaust.

"Maybe we should put up a Stop sign at the edge of the trees," Hickok quipped. "We don't want hot-rodders tearing up the Home."

Blade glanced at the gunfighter. "Where did you learn about hot-rodders?"

"In the library. Where else?" Hickok responded.

Kurt Carpenter had stocked one of the concrete blocks with hundreds of thousands of books. He had realized his descendants would require knowledge if they were to persevere after World War Three, and he had filled his library with volumes on every conceivable subject. The Family members prized the books as their primary means of education and as a source of entertainment. The photographic books depicting life before the Big Blast, as they referred to the war, were especially valued. Blade pondered all of this as he watched the flatbed come to a screeching stop not 15 feet away. "Let's go," he said, running up to the driver's door.

The window was down, revealing the features of the leader of the Clan. Zahner was his name, and he had fine brown hair parted on the left, blue eyes, a cleft in the middle of his upper lip, and a square jaw. He took one look at the Warriors and motioned for them to climb in.

"Hurry!" he goaded them.

"Not so fast," Blade stated. "Is the Clan under attack?"

"No," Zahner said. "But two of my people are dead and Mindy is missing. We think she's been kidnapped."

"Mindy? Kidnapped?" Blade said in disbelief. He started around the cab. "Hickock!" he ordered. "Now you can sound the alarm. Assemble all of the Warriors and man all of the walls. Don't let anyone out of the compound until you hear from me. And run a check to see if anyone besides Mindy is missing."

"Will do, pard," Hickok promised. "What do I tell Helen?"

Blade, about to open the passenger door, paused, his lips compressing. "Don't say a word to her yet. Not until we find out what's happened."

Hickok nodded his understanding, wheeled, and sprinted into the Home.

Blade climbed up into the cab and slammed the door.

"Hang on," Zahner advised, tramping on the gas and executing a tight U-turn. The flatbed raced toward Highway 59.

"Fill me in," Blade instructed the Clan leader.

"The details are still sketchy," Zahner said, bouncing on the seat as the truck struck a rut. "You'll need to talk to Ted." He frowned. "If he can talk."

"Ted? Isn't he the one Mindy's been seeing?" Blade inquired. "Helen mentioned they are getting quite serious about their intentions."

"Ted's the one," Zahner confirmed. He was wearing faded, patched jeans and a blue shirt.

"Tell me what you know," Blade reiterated.

"I was at home with Becky about an hour ago when a runner showed up at my door," Zahner detailed, keeping his eyes on the road. "As you know, not all of the Clan live within the Halma town limits. A lot of my people live outside of Halma. They've built their own homes or taken over abandoned property. Anyway, a family living south of town apparently heard some gunfire this morning.

Automatic gunfire." He swerved to avoid a bump.

"Go on," Blade said.

"The husband and his oldest son went to investigate," Zahner continued. "They found Ted barely alive and another couple, Faron and Grace, dead."

"What about Mindy?"

"Ted's parents told me Mindy had dropped by early this morning," Zahner replied. "Evidently the two couples got together and decided to go for a stroll. You know how it is when you're young and in love. But to answer your question, no, there was no sign of Mindy."

"Were they armed?" Blade asked. None of the Family members were allowed to venture outside the Home unless they were armed or escorted by a Warrior.

Zahner nodded. "Yep. Ted and Faron weren't dummies. Ted took his dad's shotgun and Faron had a revolver. Fat lot of good it did them."

"Will Ted live?"

"I don't know," Zahner said. "We don't have Healers, like your Family does, but we do have some people skilled in the herbal arts. Ted is being treated right now. They took him to the building we're using as our town hall. I jumped in the truck and took off the first chance I got."

"I appreciate it," Blade stated. "The sooner we act, the better. Do we know who shot them yet?"

"No," Zahner said. "Ted wasn't able to talk before I left. I have search parties out looking for Mindy and their attackers."

"What makes you think Mindy was kidnapped?" Blade queried.

"Ted," Zahner said.

"But you just said you weren't able to talk to him," Blade noted.

"I wasn't," Zahner explained. "But he was mumbling a lot, almost in shock. He said something about Mindy being taken."

"If someone took Mindy," Blade vowed, "they'll pay. No one attacks the Family or any of our allies with impunity."

"I just hope Ted doesn't die before he can fill us in," Zahner mentioned.

They drove in silence for a while, the truck eating up the distance between the Home and Highway 59.

"I wonder if the Russians could be behind it," Zahner commented.

"I doubt it," Blade said. The Russians controlled a large section of what was once the eastern United States, and the Reds and the Family had clashed before. Each time the Russians had lost, and they were determined to eradicate the Family at all costs.

"Why?" Zahner wanted to know. "The Russians sent a commando squad here once before, remember? Specifically to kidnap one of your Family, as I recall."

"True," Blade conceded. "But they failed, and I can't see them trying the same scheme twice. When they strike back at us, they'll come up with a bigger and better idea. Besides, why would they take Mindy? She's, what, nineteen? She wouldn't be able to give them much information."

"The Russians wouldn't know that," Zahner said, disputing the Warrior. "But even if the Russians aren't responsible, it could be any of the other enemies we've made over the years."

"You've got a point there," Blade admitted.

"Whoever did this wanted someone from the Home," Zahner observed.

"You don't know that for sure," Blade said.

"Don't I? Why were only my people shot? If whoever attacked them wanted women, why was Grace killed? Are you trying to tell me it was just coincidence that the only one left alive was Mindy? That the only one apparently kidnapped was from your Family?" Zahner countered.

Blade stared at the Clan leader, musing. Zahner might have a point, and the implications were unsettling.

"I don't see how you do it," Zahner said.

"Do what?"

"Take all the pressure," Zahner said. "I mean, here you

are, the head of the Warriors, responsible for the lives of around a hundred people at the Home, and you go and take the added responsibility of leading the Freedom Force. I just don't see how you take on all the pressure. It's rough for me sometimes, knowing so many lives depend on my judgment.''

"You have more people to look out for," Blade reminded the Clansman. "Don't you have about five hundred in the Clan?"

"Five hundred and three, to be exact," Zahner said.

"So it's a lot harder on you than it is on me," Blade stated.

"I don't care whether the number is one hundred or five hundred," Zahner said. "Being responsible for so many lives is a heavy burden. And since you're also the head of the Force, every Federation group is relying on you." He looked at the Warrior. "Don't you ever think about it? Doesn't it ever get to you?"

Blade felt like laughing but refrained. "I try not to dwell on the responsibility too much. I just take it a day at a time and do the best I can."

"All I know is I wouldn't want to be in your shoes," Zahner remarked.

The flatbed reached Highway 59 and Zahner jerked on the steering wheel, taking a left.

Blade gazed down at his combat boots. Maybe Zahner had another point. Truth was, sometimes *he* felt like he didn't want to be in his own shoes. Everyone undoubtedly felt the same way at one time or another. Learning to take the bad with the good was one of the major lessons every person had to experience.

But such was life.

CHAPTER TWO

The Clan was using a two-story brick structure as their meeting place. They had selected the building because it was centrally located in Halma and because most of the windows were still intact, a rarity in postwar structures.

Zahner brought the flatbed to an abrupt stop alongside the cracked curb and jumped out.

Blade was already out and bounding up the cement stairs to the doors. A crowd had gathered on the steps and along the walk, but they quickly parted to permit his passage. He pulled on the right-hand door and entered the cool interior. Over a dozen people lined both sides of the corridor.

Zahner came through the door behind the giant. He moved past the Warrior and headed for the second door on the right. "How is he?" he asked, addressing a portly man with a balding pate attired in green trousers and a black shirt.

The portly man frowned. "He's awake. You can talk to him, but don't stay in there long. He needs his rest."

Blade joined Zahner.

"This is Striber," the Clan leader said, introducing the

portly man. "He's the closest thing to a Healer we've got."

"I know who you are," Striber said to Blade. "Everyone knows who you are."

"What are Ted's chances?" Blade questioned.

"He'll live, if that's what you mean," Striber replied. "But he'll be on crutches for years, maybe for the rest of his life."

"Crutches?" Blade repeated quizzically.

Striber frowned. "Whoever the bastards were, they shot out his knees. Deliberately, I'd say. Ted is fortunate his legs won't need to be amputated below the knees. As it is, he may never walk again. We'll have to wait and see how he heals. You never know. With the proper rehabilitation and training he could, conceivably, regain very limited use of his legs."

"Why did you say they deliberately shot him in the knees?" Blade asked.

"Because of what they did to the other three," Striber said.

"Three?" Blade interrupted. "But Zahner said only Faron and Grace were killed?"

Striber glanced at the Clan leader. "Didn't you tell him about the stranger?"

Zahner raised his right hand and smacked his forehead. "Damn! I was so worried about Ted and Mindy, I forgot! We found another body with the rest, someone who isn't from the Clan."

"I'd like to take a look at this body after I talk to Ted," Blade stated.

"The stranger was shot to ribbons," Striber mentioned. "You'll see for yourself. A drastic case of overkill. And it was the same with Faron and Grace. But Ted was different. All they did to him was shoot him in the knees and kick him on the chin. A few of his teeth are broken, but they didn't break his jaw."

"Why did they spare Ted's life?" Blade queried.

"Ted can tell you that," Striber said, motioning toward the open door.

Blade moved to the doorway. Inside stood a couple with grayish brown hair and homespun clothing next to a couch on which was a pale, heavyset youth who was covered from his chin to his feet by a white sheet. The lower portion of his face was swollen and bruised. "Hello," Blade said, and entered.

Zahner came in behind the Warrior. "Blade, these are Dan and Agnes, Ted's parents."

Blade nodded grimly. "I'm sorry about your son."

Agnes sniffled and dabbed at her moist eyes with an old handkerchief, evidently her husband's, she was holding in her left hand.

"Why would anyone do this to my boy?" Dan asked angrily. "Ted has never hurt anyone."

"I don't know why they did it," Blade said. "But we'll find the parties responsible and they will pay for what they've done. It's small consolation, I know."

"Are you going after them?" Dan inquired.

"Yes," Blade said.

"Good! Kill the scum for me!" Dan declared.

"Dan!" Agnes exclaimed, aghast.

"Would you mind if I talked to your son in private?" Blade asked them.

Dan took his wife's elbow in his right hand. "We'll be right outside."

"I won't take long," Blade promised.

The parents silently departed, Agnes with tears streaming down her cheeks, Dan with his shoulders slumped in abject depression.

Blade squatted next to the youth. Ted's eyes were open but listless. Dried blood caked the corners of his mouth. "Ted? Can you hear me?"

Ted did not respond.

"Ted? This is Blade? I need to talk to you," Blade stated.

"Blade?" Ted said, rousing from his trauma-induced lethargy. He focused on the Warrior with an intent expression. "You're here!"

"I'm here," Blade said. He noticed the youth spoke

with great difficulty. "I'm sorry to impose at a time like this, but we must talk."

"It's all right," Ted asserted.

"I know you're in a lot of pain, but I must know what happened," Blade said, coaxing the youth.

Ted clicked his puffy lips. "Okay. Mindy, Faron, Grace, and I took a walk south of town. We were on our way back when two jeeps pulled up and a guy got out."

"Who was this guy?" Blade interjected. "Do you know?"

"He gave his name as Anthony Pucci," Ted revealed. "He was acting real nice and friendly, but I didn't like the looks of him. He claimed he needed directions to the Home. Said he'd come all the way from Nevada."

"Nevada!" Blade remarked in surprise.

"Yep," Ted went on. "He was polite at first, and he seemed very interested in Mindy after she told him her mom is a Warrior. He even offered us some candy. That's when . . ." Ted began, then stopped, torment etched in his features.

"Take it easy," Blade advised. "If you can't talk about it, I'll understand."

Ted inhaled deeply. "He shot us! For no reason at all, he shot us! He pretended to reach into his jeep for some candy, but he pulled a gun out instead. I was shot first and I didn't see the others get hit. I was in too much pain. But I dimly recall them forcing Mindy into the jeep."

"Did this Pucci say why they were taking her?" Blade questioned.

"No," Ted said sadly. "But he did tell me to give you a message."

Blade's forehead creased in bewilderment. "Me? He mentioned me by name?"

"He sure did," Ted stated. "I'll never forget his words! He wanted me to give the Warriors his regards. And he said to tell you that he'd be waiting for you and the other Warriors. He said if Helen wants to see Mindy again, then the Warriors must come to Las Vegas."

"Why Las Vegas?"

"I don't know," Ted answered. "He said if the Warriors don't show up in Las Vegas within one month, then Mindy will die."

"Was that all?" Blade asked.

"No," Ted replied. "There was one more thing. He said Mindy would be waiting for you at the Golden Crown Casino. He wanted me to be certain to remember the name. The Golden Crown Casino."

Blade was baffled. "And that was all? He didn't say anything else?"

"That was his message," Ted responded.

"Okay," Blade said. "What happened next?"

"That's when he kicked me," Ted said. "I don't remember anything else until I woke up on this couch."

Blade slowly straightened. "You said there were two jeeps. How many others were with Pucci?"

"I don't know," Ted said. "There were two or three in the first jeep, and I didn't see how many were in the second."

"What did Pucci look like?" Blade inquired.

"He was about six feet tall," Ted detailed. "His hair was black, his eyes brown. His face was kind of mean looking. I don't know how to describe it."

Blade placed his right hand on the youth's shoulder. "Why don't you get some rest? If I have any more questions I'll get back to you."

Ted's eyelids were beginning to droop. "I'll do whatever I can to help you out! We've got to save Mindy!"

"I know," Blade assured the youth. "Don't worry. We'll save her." He turned and walked into the corridor.

Dan and Agnes were waiting near the door.

"You can go on in," Blade directed them. "I'm through with Ted for now."

"Thank you," Dan responded.

Zahner stepped into the corridor and patiently waited for the parents to go into the room before he spoke. "So what did you make out of all that information?"

"I'm stumped," Blade confessed. "I don't know any Anthony Pucci. None of the Warriors have ever been to

Las Vegas, so far as I know. There doesn't seem to be any reason behind the attack."

"There has to be a reason," Zahner said. "Why else did they drive all the way here from Nevada?"

"I wish I knew," Blade stated. "Right now I'd like to see the body of the stranger."

"Follow me," Zahner said, and led the way down the corridor for another 30 feet until he stopped next to a closed door on the left. "The bodies are in here," he explained, then opened the door.

Blade strolled inside to find three long tables occupying the center of the room and a maple desk and a folding chair to his right. Each table was draped with a white sheet profiling the contours of a human figure underneath.

"This is the one with the stranger," Zahner said, moving to the table on the right. He lifted the sheet.

Blade walked to the head of the table and examined the corpse. The man's dark brown suit was soaked with blood. Someone had shot him repeatedly at point-blank range. "Why would they shoot one of their own men?" he wondered aloud.

"We found a rifle next to his body," Zahner disclosed. "It hadn't been fired."

"What do you make of his clothes?" Blade asked.

Zahner shrugged. "The suit looks new to me."

"It does," Blade agreed. "And we both know that the men in the Civilized Zone and California wear suits just like this one. It was the style the men were wearing before the war. Buckskins are the rule elsewhere, like in the Dakota Territory and in Montana. A lot of my Family wear buckskins too, because they're easy to make and they last a long time. Fabric like the material in this suit is hard to come by. Except for the Civilized Zone and California, there aren't any factories manufacturing this type of clothing. For that matter, there aren't many clothing manufacturers of any kind around, period. Which is why we must make buckskins or patch together old garments."

"Do you think there's a link between this Nevada

business and California or the Civilized Zone?'' Zahner
queried.

"Don't know," Blade said. "Maybe there's a manufacturing facility in Las Vegas." He paused. "What did
you find in his pockets?''

"His pockets?" Zahner responded, sounding surprised.

Blade looked at the Clansman. "Yes. Didn't you go
through his pockets?''

"No," Zahner said. "I had him brought here, along
with the other bodies and Ted, and then took off for the
Home. I didn't have time to search him.''

"Then let's do it," Blade declared.

Zahner tugged on the sheet and it slid to the floor.

Blade quickly examined the man's pockets. He found a
set of keys in the right front pants pocket and a wad of bills
in the left. "Here," he said, handing both to Zahner. Next
he inspected the jacket pockets. There was nothing in
either of the outside ones, but he did discover two items in
an inside left pocket. The first was a small black book, the
second a circular piece of blue plastic with the words
JOHNNY'S PALACE imprinted on both sides.

"There's two thousand dollars here," Zahner
announced, having just counted the money.

Blade paged through the small black book. On each one
was a list of names, and beside each name was an address
and a seven digit number. Some of the names were
businesses, like *Eddy's Garage*, and they were all arranged
alphabetically. Acting on a hunch he turned to the Gs and
there it was: *Golden Crown Casino. 6619 Las Vegas
Boulevard. 273-1400.*

"What have you got there?" Zahner inquired.

"Something that will come in handy when we get to Las
Vegas," Blade said, closing the book. "If we have to go
that far.''

"What do you mean?" Zahner asked.

"I want you to take me back to the Home right now,"
Blade directed. "Alpha Triad is going after the ones who
took Mindy.''

"You sure Plato will give the okay?''

"Of course," Blade said. "But even if he doesn't like the idea, there's nothing he can do about it. In times of crisis the Warriors are empowered to do whatever is necessary, and as the head Warrior I decide our course of action. Hickok, Geronimo, and I are going after these SOBs in the SEAL."

"Do you really think you can catch them?" Zahner questioned. "They've got a head start and there's no telling which route they'll take back to Las Vegas."

"I don't know if we can catch up with them before they reach Las Vegas," Blade stated. "But we've got to try for Mindy's sake. If need be, we'll go all the way to Vegas."

"I'd like to go along," Zahner proposed.

"No," Blade said flatly.

"Why not? If anyone has a right to go, it should be one of the Clan," Zahner insisted. "They killed two of us."

"I understand your feelings," Blade mentioned. "But Alpha Triad is accustomed to functioning as a team. We can't afford to be distracted by having to watch out for you or any other Clansman."

"I wouldn't get in your way," Zahner said.

"Sorry," Blade said, refusing to give in. "But the answer is no."

Zahner frowned. "Then do me a favor."

"Anything," Blade pledged.

"If you find whoever is responsible for killing Faron and Grace and shooting Ted," Zahner said angrily, "give them a taste of their own medicine."

"I'll make them regret the day they were born."

CHAPTER THREE

The SEAL had been the Founder's pride and joy. Kurt Carpenter had wisely anticipated the deterioration of civilization after World War Three. He knew society would fall apart at the seams; the government would collapse, social institutions would cease to exist, and the transportation system would crumble. Accordingly, Carpenter spent millions on a special vehicle, a prototype intended to serve his descendents in a world gone haywire. The Solar Energized Amphibious or Land Recreational Vehicle—or SEAL for short—was designed to navigate any terrain. Vanlike in build, the entire body was composed of a shatterproof and heat-resistant tinted green plastic. The floor was an impervious metal alloy. Four huge puncture-proof tires, each four feet high and two feet wide, supported the transport.

Carpenter had also incorporated armaments into the vehicle. Mercenaries had been hired at great expense. The weapons systems they had installed were activated by four toggle switches on the dash. A pair of 50-caliber machine guns were mounted in recessed compartments under each front headlight, and a miniaturized surface-to-air missile was fitted on the roof over the driver's seat. A rocket-launcher was hidden in the middle of the front grill, while a flame-thrower was situated in the center of the front fender surrounded by layers of insulation.

As its name implied, the SEAL was solar powered. The light was collected by two solar panels affixed to the roof, the energy was converted and stored in revolutionary batteries located in a lead-lined case under the vehicle. The scientists had proudly boasted the SEAL would continue to function for a thousand years provided the solar panels or the battery casings were not damaged.

All of these thoughts filtered through Blade's mind as he steered the SEAL southward along Highway 93 in northern Nevada. The highway was pitted with wide cracks and potholes, and many sections were buckled. But few were the obstacles the SEAL couldn't circumvent, and the past seven days of travel had been relatively uneventful.

A whole week on the road!

Blade was intensely disappointed they had been unable to overtake Mindy's abductors. He mentally reviewed the events of the week, speculating on what he could have done differently to achieve Mindy's rescue. Zahner had rushed him back to the Home, and he had informed the assembled Family about the tragedy. After a hasty meeting with Plato and the Elders, it had been unanimously agreed Alpha Triad should proceed after the culprits with all dispatch. The SEAL was always fully stocked and ready to go at a moment's notice. Alpha Triad, with one addition, had departed the Home within an hour of his return.

But they'd never been able to catch up to the jeeps.

Where had he gone wrong?

Blade had deduced the abductors would not dare to travel in a direct course from the Home to Las Vegas. Doing so would entail driving through the Dakota Territory, home of the Cavalry, and the Civilized Zone—both allies of the Family. The abductors would want to avoid all contact with Federation factions. Which meant the kidnappers either went due south from the

Home, hoping to bypass the Civilized Zone, and then swung to the west around Oklahoma or Texas, or else they traveled westward from Minnesota, skirting the Dakota Territory to the north, and then angled to the southwest through the northwest corner of Wyoming, avoiding the Mormons currently in control of Utah, and entering Nevada from the northeast. Blade had opted for the second route.

Acting on the theory the kidnappers would shun all large cities and towns, Blade had stuck to the secondary roads. At settlements along the way he had stopped and asked about the two jeeps. No one had seen them. Many of the inhabitants of the small towns and communities had fled at the sight of the SEAL or greeted the Warriors with unconcealed suspicion. But none of them, much to Blade's relief, had attacked his party. Twice the Warriors had seen bands of scavengers near the road, and three times they had passed mutants, but neither the scavengers or their bestial counterparts had shown any inclination to tackle the SEAL.

A voice intruded on the giant's reverie.

"How much longer before we reach Las Vegas, pard?" Hickok asked.

Blade glanced to his right. The transport was spaciously designed with two comfortable bucket seats in the front separated by a brown console. Behind the bucket seats was a single seat the width of the vehicle. The rear of the SEAL was a storage area piled high with provisions, their jerky and water and spare ammunition. In a compartment under the rear section were two spare tires and a toolbox. "I don't know how much longer," he replied. "Geronimo has the map. Ask him."

Hickok twisted in his seat and gazed at the man sitting behind him, one of the two best friends he had. "Hey, you mangy Injun! Wake up!"

Geronimo had been napping with his head resting against the window. He came instantly awake, his alert brown eyes surveying the highway ahead for any sign of trouble. Powerfully built, he was stocky with black hair and rugged features. He wore a green shirt, green pants, and moccasins. An Arminius .357 Magnum was in a shoulder holster under his right arm and a tomahawk was tucked under his deer hide belt. "What is it, O Great White Idiot?"

Blade, listening to their banter, smiled. Geronimo was rightfully proud of his Blackfoot heritage, and the Indian and the gunman constantly teased one another over their respective racial differences.

"Boy! You sure get nasty when someone interrupts your beauty sleep!" Hickok cracked.

"I'd rather wake up with my wife at my side instead of seeing your ugly puss," Geronimo observed.

"There's nothin' wrong with my face," Hickok retorted indignantly.

"Nothing a good head transplant wouldn't cure," Geronimo commented.

"Two points for Geronimo," Blade interjected, laughing, glad their light-hearted joking was alleviating the tension of the mission.

But not everyone riding in the SEAL agreed.

A harsh feminine voice intruded on their conversation. "If you morons are through clowning around, why don't we get down to business? How long before we reach Las Vegas?"

Blade looked into the rearview mirror at the speaker. She sat directly behind him, her luxurious amber hair cascading past her shoulders. Her eyes were a vivid green, her features exceptionally lovely. She wore a black leather vest similar to his, but hers was cut low in the front, displaying her ample cleavage. Tight black leather pants and boots covered her shapely legs. Around her slim waist were strapped a pair of Caspian 45-caliber automatics. And projecting above her left shoulder was the hilt of the 24-inch machete she invariably carried in a custom-designed sheath on her back, slanted between her shoulder blades. The sheath was held fast by a wide black strip of leather looped across her chest.

"Who are you callin' morons, lady?" Hickok demanded.

"If the shoe fits," Helen responded. "And don't call me lady. The name is Helen, and don't you forget it!"

"I know what your name is," Hickok snapped. "And I can understand your being upset about Mindy. But that doesn't give you call to go around insultin' people."

Helen bristled. "I'll insult you or any other *man* any time I damn well feel like it!"

"You keep it up and you'll be pickin' your teeth up from the floor," Hickok warned her. "The only ones who get to insult me on a regular basis are my missus and this crazy Injun. You've been belly-achin' ever since we left the Home. You never have a nice word for anyone. All you do is gripe. Did you treat your ex-husband like this?"

Helen's face became livid with fury. Her hands moved to her Caspians. "Why, you . . ."

"That's enough!" Blade barked, slamming on the brakes and bringing the SEAL to a grinding halt. He swiveled in his seat, glaring at Helen. "I don't ever want to see you threatening to pull your guns on a fellow Warrior again! You got that?"

"But—" Helen began.

"No buts about it!" Blade declared in annoyance. "Hickok's right! You've been a monumental pain in the butt this whole trip. I've tried to make allowances for your behavior. You've complained because you didn't think we were going fast enough, and you've complained because you didn't agree with the route I'm taking, and you've groused every time we made a rest stop. You rarely talk unless you're spoken to, and even then it's some smart-mouth reply." He paused. "I've given you the benefit of the doubt because of the turmoil you must be feeling over Mindy. But no more! I let you talk me into taking you along against my better judgment. Sure, Mindy's your daughter and you have a right to help rescue her. But you also have a wicked temper and a short fuse, not exactly ideal traits for a Warrior."

Helen seemed stung by the rebuke. "If you felt that way about me, why'd you ever accept me as a Warrior?"

"The decision wasn't up to me," Blade said. "You know the procedure for selecting a new Warrior. The candidate must be sponsored before the Elders by a Warrior of standing. Spartacus sponsored you. The Elders voted on whether to accept your candidacy or not, and they decided to appoint you as a Warrior."

"But you could have protested their decision," Helen noted. "They would have listened to you."

"I didn't think it was necessary," Blade informed her. "Your good qualities outweigh your bad. There isn't one Warrior who is perfect in every respect."

"Speak for yourself," Hickok quipped.

"To hear you talk, I didn't think I had any good qualities," Helen mentioned.

"You do," Blade assured her. "I've been following your progress ever since you were assigned to Omega Triad. You take orders well and you always do your best at whatever job you're given. You relate well with the other Warriors in your Triad. You're one of the best shots in the Family. And you believe in the ideals the Founder proclaimed. You have a lot of good qualities."

Helen visibly relaxed, her lips curling downward in self-reproach. "I'm sorry. I didn't realize I've been acting like a bitch. You were right. All I can think about is Mindy. She's all I have left in this world. If anything happens to her . . ." she said, and let the sentence trail off.

"We'll get Mindy back," Hickok told her. "Don't fret none."

"For those who might be interested," Geronimo spoke up, "I've calculated the distance to Las Vegas."

"Impossible," Hickok said. "You couldn't have."

"Why not?" Geronimo asked, puzzled.

"Because I didn't see you take off your moccasins," Hickok commented with a mischievous grin. "And I know we're more than ten miles away."

"Two points for Hickok," Blade said, accelerating.

For the first time since her daughter was kidnapped,

Helen mustered a smile.

Geronimo elected to ignore the barb. "We crossed what was once the state line not too long ago. We should be coming up soon on a small town called Contact. The map doesn't say how many people lived there before the war. It could be deserted like so many others we've seen."

"How far is it from Contact to Las Vegas?" Blade inquired.

"I estimate about four hundred and forty-six miles," Geronimo divulged. "Because of the terrible shape the highway is in, we've only been able to average forty miles an hour. At our present rate, it will take us eleven hours to reach Vegas." He consulted a watch on his left wrist. "It's ten in the morning now. So we could reach Vegas tonight if we drive straight through. It would mean driving after sunset, though."

Blade reflected for a minute. As a rule, he did not drive after dark. Spotting an ambush or other threat was next to impossible once the sun went down. He preferred to do most of his driving during the daylight hours.

"I vote we drive straight through," Hickok suggested. "The sooner we reach Las Vegas, the better. Besides, we haven't run into any trouble yet. Maybe our luck will hold until we reach Vegas."

"One thing I learned a long time ago," Blade mentioned, "is never to push your luck." He stared into the rearview mirror. "Helen, I know you probably won't agree with my decision, but I'm not going to push the SEAL to reach Vegas tonight. We don't want to waltz into a trap. They must be expecting us. So we'll take it nice and slow. Is that okay by you?"

"Whatever you say," Helen stated. "You're in charge."

"Hey! Look!" Geronimo exclaimed, leaning forward and pointing.

Blade's eyes narrowed as he saw the cluster of buildings approximately a quarter of a mile ahead.

A freshly painted billboard abruptly appeared on the right: MA'S DINER. STRAIGHT AHEAD. ALL YOU CAN EAT FOR $4.99.

"What the blazes!" Hickok declared.

"Who would open a diner in the middle of nowhere?" Geronimo asked.

"We haven't seen any other traffic since we left Wyoming," Helen remarked. "And that was a military patrol from the Civilized Zone."

"Maybe they get traffic here from time to time," Blade conjectured.

"Why don't we stop?" Hickok recommended. "I could use some home-cooked grub. Venison jerky gets a mite bland after a spell."

"I don't know . . ." Blade said doubtfully.

"Please, Blade," Helen urged. "If the kidnappers came this way, the people here might have seen them. They might know if Mindy is still alive." She paused. "Please."

Against his better judgment, Blade agreed. "Okay. We'll stop and eat our midday meal early, but I want everyone to stay on their toes."

"You're a worrywart, you know that?" Hickok declared. "This place is called Ma's Diner. What harm can a little old lady do to four Warriors, for cryin' out loud?" He snickered at the notion.

"For once I agree with Hickok," Geronimo said. "They wouldn't bother to advertise if they weren't serious about attracting customers."

"I hope you're right," Blade stated.

"Quit your worryin', pard," Hickok advised. "What could go wrong?"

CHAPTER FOUR

"Looks innocent enough to me," Hickok mentioned.

Blade kept his foot on the brake, still uncertain of the wisdom of stopping. The SEAL was idling on Highway 93 approximately 400 yards south of Contact. The town had appeared to be deserted, although several of the buildings had exhibited evidence of recent habitation; the doors and windows on three of the homes had been intact and clean, and one of the yards had sported a flower garden.

"What are we waitin' for?" Hickok queried impatiently.

Blade sighed. To their right was a gravel drive leading to a newly painted white structure. MA's DINER was painted in bold black letters on a wooden sign perched over the front entrance. Four vehicles were parked outside, prewar-model cars in surprisingly fine condition. "One of us must stay in the SEAL with the doors locked," he mentioned.

"I'll do it," Geronimo volunteered.

Blade took a right, slowly approaching the diner, thankful the SEAL's tinted plastic body enabled him to see out but prevented anyone from viewing the interior. If hostile eyes were peeking from the diner windows, they would be unable to ascertain how many were in the transport. He pulled into a parking spot between a vintage Ford on the left and a Chevy on the right, then turned off the engine.

"Are we takin' the long guns?" Hickok queried.

"Of course," Blade responded. "It doesn't pay to get too overconfident."

Hickok glanced at Geronimo. "How about passin' them up here, pard?"

Geronimo turned in his seat. On top of the pile of provisions in the rear section were four different firearms. One was a Navy Arms Henry Carbine in 44-40 caliber, Hickok's favorite rifle. Next to the Henry was Blade's machine gun, a Commando Arms Carbine, a fully automatic 45-caliber firearm with a 90-shot magazine. Also on the pile was Helen's weapon, an Armalite AR-180A Sporter Carbine. Geronimo handed each of the guns to the proper party, then took hold of his Browning BAR. All of the firearms the Warriors used came from the enormous armory the Founder had stocked in one of the concrete blocks at the Home.

"Keep the doors locked," Blade reiterated as he took hold of his door handle.

"I will," Geronimo promised. "What if you do run into trouble in there? If I hear gunfire, should I come on the run?"

"You don't budge from the SEAL no matter what," Blade directed. "The transport might be virtually impervious, but I'm not taking any chances. You stay here and guard the SEAL."

"Okay," Geronimo said reluctantly. "If I see anything suspicious while you're inside, I'll sound the horn."

"Good idea," Blade stated. He looked at Hickok and Helen. "Are you two ready?"

"I was born ready," Hickok declared.

Helen simply nodded.

Blade opened the door. "I'm leaving the keys in the ignition," he informed Geronimo. "If something does happen to us, you can drive off."

"I'm not going anywhere without you," Geronimo said.

Blade jumped out, waited for Helen to join him, then slammed the door.

Hickok closed his door and ambled around the front of the SEAL. "Do you smell what I smell?" he asked them.

The mouth-watering aroma of cooking food filled the dusty air.

"Smells like steak," Helen commented.

"We'd best be on our guard," Hickok said sarcastically. "These hombres could be fryin' a steak just to trick us, to lure us into their trap!" He chuckled.

"Keep it up," Blade admonished, and led the way up to the front entrance.

"I hear music," Helen said.

Blade heard it too. A man singing in a wailing, heart-wrenching style. He caught a few of the lyrics.

". . . your cheatin' heart . . ."

Blade grabbed the doorknob and pulled the brown wooden door wide open, then swiftly stepped inside, to the right of the doorway, flattening his broad back against the wall and leveling the Commando.

"Howdy, stranger!" a woman called out. "Welcome to Ma's!"

Blade surveyed the diner. On the opposite side of the room was a counter running the length of the one-story building. Behind the yellow counter were two people, an elderly matron with gray hair, horn-rimmed glasses, and a jowly jaw, and a tall man with black hair and a toothpick in his mouth. Both of them wore white clothes, including an apron. There were ten tables in the diner. At a table to the right sat three men dressed in ragged jeans and flannel shirts, cups of coffee before them. And at another table to the left of the door was a short, obese man in a grimy blue suit and a woman with bright red lipstick coating her thick lips and too much rouge on her cheeks. She was wearing a red dress.

None of them appeared to be armed.

"Howdy!" the matron repeated. "Come on in! Ain't no

one here going to bite you!'' She smiled in a friendly, sincere fashion.

Hickok walked through the door as if he didn't have a care in the world. He took a look around and grinned. "Yep. Definitely a trap."

"You won't need that hardware, son," the matron said, nodding at Blade's Commando. "Our muffins don't usually fight back."

Hickok laughed.

Blade slowly lowered the Commando and advanced toward the counter. The men on the right and the couple on the left watched him for a moment, then suddenly shifted their attention to the doorway. Blade looked back.

Helen had just entered the diner, her Carbine cradled in her arms. She scanned the room and followed Blade.

"Howdy," Hickok said, grinning at the couple to the left. "How's the food here?"

"Delicious," the woman answered. "Try the steak. I recommend it highly."

"Thanks. Don't mind if I do," Hickok said, stepping toward the counter.

Blade moved to within four feet of the matron. "Hello. We could use a bite to eat."

The matron beamed. "That's what I'm here for. They don't call me Ma for nothing. Tasty food and service with a smile. That's what everyone gets at my place."

Blade angled his body so he could keep an eye on the three men and the couple. "How long has your place been open?"

"Oh, about four years," Ma said. "Give or take a month."

"You get much business here?" Blade casually inquired.

"Enough," Ma replied. "We don't see much traffic heading north, but we do see a lot going toward Vegas. They're the bulk of my trade."

Hickok reached the counter and rested the Henry on top. "Howdy, Ma. Nice place you've got here."

"Why, thank you, sonny," Ma responded. "You sure are polite. What's your name?"

"The handle is Hickok," the gunman stated.

"And the big one?" Ma queried.

"That's Blade," Hickok said. "Don't mind him. His middle name is paranoia."

"And your beautiful companion?" Ma asked.

"My name is Helen," Helen said, answering for herself.

"If you don't mind my saying so, you're pretty enough to be a Vegas chorus girl," Ma mentioned appreciatively.

"What's a chorus girl?" Hickok questioned.

Ma stared at the gunman. "You mean to say you don't know what a chorus girl is? Where are you from? The moon?"

"Nope," Hickok replied.

Ma's eyes narrowed slightly. "I take it you've never been to Vegas. Anyone who's been there knows what a chorus girl is."

"Have you been to Vegas?" Blade asked.

"I was born there," Ma said.

Blade and Hickok exchanged fleeting glances.

"Do tell," the gunfighter stated. "Why don't you fix us some vittles and join us at our table? We'd like to hear all about Las Vegas."

"I'd be delighted," Ma said. "What would you like to eat?"

"How about some steaks all around," Hickok ordered. "And some milk for me, if you've got some."

"Milk?" Ma snorted. "Don't you want something stronger?"

"I never drink the hard stuff," Hickok said. "A milk will be fine."

"Milk for all of us," Blade interjected.

"It'll take about five minutes," Ma said.

"No problem," Blade told her, then walked to a table near the counter where he could command a view of Ma and the tall man behind the counter as well as the customers. He placed the Commando on the table, slid into a chair, and folded his fingers over the trigger guard.

Hickok deposited the Henry on the table, gripped the top of one of the wooden chairs and slid it to Blade's right, then reversed the chair and sat down with his arms draped over the back.

Helen took the remaining chair, sitting with her back to the front door. She leaned toward Blade. "Is it my imagination, or are these people staring at me?"

"It's not your imagination," Blade said. "They're trying not to be obvious about it, but they can't seem to take their eyes off you."

"When do you reckon they'll make their play?" Hickok asked in a hushed tone.

"What are you talking about?" Helen inquired.

Hickok lowered his voice to a whisper. "Blade was right all along. This is a trap."

Helen glanced around the room. "Are you putting me on? There's no danger here."

Blade gazed into Helen's eyes. "This is no joke. Keep your hands on your Carbine."

"How do you know this is a trap?" Helen whispered.

"Did you see the three men drinking coffee?" Blade asked.

"Of course," Helen replied.

"Did you take a look at their cups?"

"No," Helen said, and began to turn toward the men.

"Don't look at them!" Blade said hastily. "We don't want them to know we're on to them."

Helen faced the giant. "What about the coffee cups?"

"All three cups are filled to the brim, yet those men haven't taken a sip since we came in the door," Blade elaborated.

"Maybe they're not thirsty," Helen said lamely. "Maybe they've already drunk some coffee and those are their second cups. Maybe they're just waiting for their food."

"And maybe the cups are props they're usin' to try and con us," Hickok stated. "The shifty varmints!"

Helen studied the gunman for a few seconds. "I don't get you. A couple of minutes ago you were positive this diner is legit. Now you say it's a trap?"

"I knew it was a trap when I walked in the door,"

Hickok informed her.

"You didn't act like you thought it was a trap," Helen noted.

"Do you play cards?" Hickok queried.

"Cards?" Helen said, mystified. "What do cards have to do with anything?"

"A good card player never lets the other fella see his cards until it's time to put them on the table," Hickok declared.

Blade idly scanned the room. "I don't see any guns."

"They could have some stashed behind the counter," Hickok said.

Blade casually looked at the couple to the left of the door. The obese man and the woman in the red dress were simply sitting there, slight grins on their faces, their hands on top of their table, doing nothing in particular.

"You are becoming as paranoid as Blade," Helen told the gunman.

"Better paranoid than dead," Hickok retorted.

"Why don't we just walk out?" Helen proposed.

"No," Blade said. "They might let us go without any hassles, but what about the next innocent travelers who pass through Contact? What if they're not as well armed as we are?"

Helen frowned. "I don't see where this is any of our business. If you really believe it's a trap, I say we walk out and keep going. The sooner we reach Vegas, the sooner I find my daughter."

"I'm in charge," Blade reminded her. "And we're going to stay put and see what happens."

"Now what do you suppose that is all about?" Hickok asked, nodding toward the counter.

Blade turned his head, perplexed at observing Ma and the tall man embroiled in an argument. They were huddled next to a grill, speaking softly but gesturing angrily.

"Maybe they burned one of our steaks," Hickok cracked.

Blade leaned back in his chair and surveyed the room again. The "customers" were all watching the exchange between Ma and the tall man. He scrutinized their clothing, striving to detect telltale bulges that might indicate concealed firearms.

They appeared to be clean.

Ma walked to a white refrigerator and took out a pitcher of milk.

Blade abruptly realized the music had ceased minutes ago. He glanced around and found an unusual apparatus positioned against the wall six yards from the front entrance. The bottom of the machine was square, the top a golden arch. A series of bright lights rimmed the arch, reflecting off a curved glass case between the arch and the square base.

"Here we go!" Ma said happily, coming around the end of the counter with a large tray in her hands. The tray supported the pitcher and three glasses. "Here's your milk. Your steaks will be a minute or two yet."

Blade pointed at the machine with the arch. "What is that?" he inquired.

Ma set the tray on the table. "It's a jukebox. Haven't you ever seen one before?"

"No," Blade admitted.

The matron tittered. "You don't know what a chorus girl is. You don't know what a jukebox is. I've heard of pitiful, but you boys take the cake."

"You said you were born in Las Vegas," Blade remarked. "What's it like there?"

"Vegas is a tough town," Ma declared. "It's not for chumps who don't know how to take care of themselves."

"We can take care of ourselves," Hickok said, speaking up.

"You think so?" Ma rejoined.

"I know so," Hickok asserted. "Stick around. I may give you a demonstration."

"Why is Vegas a tough town?" Blade queried to get Ma back on the right track.

"Because Vegas is mob-controlled, dummy," Ma stated with a chuckle.

"You mean they have riots in the streets a lot?" Hickok asked.

Ma threw back her head and laughed. "Not that kind of a mob! I'm talking about the Families."

Blade glanced at Hickok and the gunman shrugged, signifying he didn't understand either.

The woman called Ma noticed their reaction. "Let me guess. You don't have the foggiest idea what I'm talking about, do you?"

"No," Blade answered. He was startled to learn there were other groups with the same name as the Founder's descendants.

"How do I explain it?" Ma asked herself. She stared at the giant. "Have you ever heard of Organized Crime?"

Blade reflected for a moment. The term did not ring a bell. "Never heard of it," he confessed.

Ma shook her head. "Then let me give you a refresher course. Way back when, back before the war, there were three classes of people in America. There were the ordinary slobs, rich and poor alike, who lived their lives according to the letter of the law. From cradle to grave they slaved away, basically honest jerks except for little things like cheating on their taxes and such. Oh, some of them went bad. They became drug dealers or robbed banks. But most of them were simple folks, if downright stupid." She paused and snickered. "Then there were the government types, the politicians, the most dishonest bunch of all. They stole from the people to fatten their big bellies, but they made their stealing legal. They called their system taxation. Property taxes, sales taxes, income taxes. The people were taxed to the max, and hardly complained because they trusted the politicians who were robbing them silly."

"Hold on there," Hickok interrupted. "I studied some history when I was knee-high to a grasshopper. And my teacher explained things differently. Not all politicians were crooked. There were some who cared about the people and wanted to help them. And how can you call the average folks stupid just because they obeyed the law?"

"They were stupid because they let others run their lives!" Ma replied vehemently.

Blade pursed his lips in contemplation. He had observed the woman closely as she talked. Ma wasn't the bumpkin she pretended to be, and under her seemingly friendly exterior was a heart of stone. "You mentioned there were three classes," he prompted her.

Ma smiled. "The third class was the best. They didn't pretend to be something they weren't. They knew the score. They knew there are only three things in life that matter: money, power, and loyalty. They were the organized-crime Families, and they controlled most of the action from coast to coast. The lousy politicians tried to rub the Families out, but couldn't. The Families were too strong for the government and a hell of a lot smarter. The leaders, the Dons, saw the war coming months in advance. And they decided to do something about it."

"What did they do?" Blade inquired.

"They already had a foothold in Vegas, so they decided to take the city over, lock, stock, and barrel," Ma detailed. "They flocked to Vegas right before the war began, and they were in place and ready when the crap hit the fan. When the government collapsed, it was child's play for the Families to take control. They had more soldiers in Vegas than all the law enforcement agencies combined."

"Soldiers?" Hickok said.

"Yeah. Button men. Trigger men. Hit men. They're all basically the same thing." She grinned. "So the mob has been in control of Vegas ever since. There were some rough times at first, what with the Dons unable to agree on territories and percentages. For over ten years they fought it out. The Seven Families War it's called. One Family came out on top, and their bloodline has ruled the city for seventy years. From father to son to grandson, they've passed the leadership on down the line. Their Don is the supreme Don."

"Does this Don have a name?" Blade casually asked.

Ma nodded. "The Don who runs the whole show is Don Pucci. Don Anthony Pucci."

CHAPTER FIVE

Helen's fingers gripped her Carbine until her hands started to tremble. She gritted her teeth and released the Armalite, composing her features with an effort. "Did you say Pucci?"

"Yes," Ma said. "Have you heard of him?"

Helen nodded.

Ma chuckled. "I guess everybody has heard of Don Pucci."

"What happened to the other Families?" Blade asked.

"They're still around," Ma replied. "But their Dons must take orders from Don Pucci. He makes sure they all toe the line, that they all stick to their territories and don't start any trouble."

"So the Families have divided up Vegas among them," Blade commented, pondering the implications for the mission.

Ma gazed from one Warrior to the next. "Hey! I hope nothing I've said will stop you from going to Vegas. You'll have a great time."

"We will?" Blade questioned.

"Sure," Ma stated with conviction. "Vegas is more fun

than it ever was. Thousands of people go there every year.
The casinos are open around the clock. There's gambling
and booze and floor shows, just like in the old days. You'll
love it."

"People go there all the time?" Blade inquired.

"Thousands," Ma reiterated. "They come from
Arizona, California, the Civilized Zone, everywhere. We
even had some Russian officers not too long ago."

Blade straightened. "Russians in Vegas?"

"Sounds weird, doesn't it?" Ma said. "But I guess the
Commies like a good time as much as the next person."
She leaned over the table. "Confidentially, I heard the real
reason they were in Vegas was to conduct business with
Don Pucci."

"What kind of business?" Blade asked.

Ma shrugged. "Beats me. The Don doesn't fill me in on
his private deals."

Blade was trying to analyze all of this new information.
There were so many unanswered questions. How was it he
had never heard about Vegas before? Were there really
patrons coming from as far away as California and the
Civilized Zone, two allies of the Family? If so, why hadn't
one of their many friends told them what was happening?
Surely the leaders of the Civilized Zone and California
must be aware of the situation.

"You sure know a lot about Vegas," Hickok
mentioned.

"I should," Ma said. "Like I told you, I was born there.
I spent most of my life in Vegas, and I've been around for
a long time. I'm fifty-four years old."

Blade saw the tall cook loading a tray with plates of
food: steaks, potatoes, corn, and bread. He began to
wonder if his suspicions were groundless. The three men at
the table to the right of the door were sipping at their
coffee, and the obese man and the woman in red were
talking and laughing. He decided to sit tight, finish the
meal, and if they weren't attacked, to leave without
provoking an incident.

But one of his companions wasn't so inclined.

Helen locked her green eyes on Ma. "How long ago did the jeeps come through here?" she unexpectedly demanded.

Ma blinked her eyes rapidly several times. "Jeeps?"

"Yeah," Helen stated harshly. "You heard me. Two jeeps passed this way. I want to know how many people were in them."

Ma's lips curled downward. "I haven't seen any jeeps come by here in weeks, dearie."

Helen suddenly stood, her Carbine aimed at Ma's stomach. "Don't lie to me, bitch! I don't know what your scam is, but I know you're a liar. Those jeeps stopped here. I need to know if there was a young woman with them."

Blade picked up the Commando. All of the customers had swiveled at the sound of the dispute and were watching with intent expressions. The tall man was standing behind the counter, his hands resting on the top.

"Really, dearie," Ma said soothingly. "I don't have the faintest notion what you're talking about."

Helen's eyes flashed, her voice lowering. "I'm going to count to three. If you don't tell me what I need to know by then, I'll blow you apart."

Ma glanced at the tall man, then at Helen. "Are you nuts?"

"One," Helen said, beginning her count.

Blade was tempted to intervene, but held his tongue. Helen had started this gambit; he would do what he could to back her play.

Hickok was grinning from ear to ear, his arms draped over the back of his chair.

"Two," Helen said.

Ma looked at Blade. "Aren't you going to do anything? Are you just going to sit there and let her shoot me?"

"If I were you," Blade advised, "I'd tell her what she wants to know."

Ma clenched her fists and glared at Helen. "There's only one thing I've got to say to you!" she snapped. "Go to hell!"

"Three," Helen stated somberly.

Ma abruptly performed a remarkable maneuver. She executed a dive for the floor while bawling at the top of her lungs, "Get them!"

Blade saw the tall man behind the counter bringing a shotgun up, and he threw himself backward so Hickok wouldn't be in his line of fire. He squeezed the trigger as he fell, and the Commando thundered and bucked in his brawny hands.

The tall man was caught in the chest and flung from sight.

Blade landed on his back and swiveled to find the customers producing handguns with astonishing swiftness, as if from thin air. But fast as they were, the Family's preeminent gunfighter was faster.

Hickok came up off his chair with his arms a blurred streak, drawing his Pythons with ambidextrous precision. The Colts boomed three times in succession, the shots spaced so close together they sounded as one, and the three men to the right of the front door went down, each one struck in the head, each dying soundlessly, one of them sprawling over the table while the other two toppled to the floor.

The obese man and the woman in red were taking a bead on the Warriors when Helen cut loose. Her carbine chattered, the slugs ripping into the heavyset man and doubling him over. The woman in red got off a solitary harmless round, and then she was propelled backwards by a burst to her face. She crashed onto a chair and slumped down. The obese man, gurgling and wheezing, staggered a few steps, then pitched forward.

Silence momentarily descended.

Blade leaped to his feet, scrutinizing the bodies to insure none of their foes were moving.

"A piece of cake!" Hickok declared, grinning.

"Check them," Blade ordered.

The gunman walked toward the nearest corpse to verify the man was dead.

Ma was on her hands and knees, gawking at her dead comrades in amazement.

Helen walked around the table and grabbed Ma by the right shoulder. "On your feet!" she commanded, hauling the matron erect.

Ma glanced toward the counter. "Poor Harry! He was right! I should have listened to him."

"Right about what?" Blade demanded.

Ma looked at the giant. "He said we shouldn't mess with you. He said you were trouble. He was right."

Helen jabbed her carbine barrel to within an inch of Ma's nose. "I want some answers, woman, and I want them now!"

Ma gulped. "Whatever you want, dearie."

"I want to know about the two jeeps," Helen stated.

Ma began fidgeting with her apron. "The two jeeps?"

Helen's eyes narrowed menacingly. "Don't play games with me! Two jeeps came by here recently. When?"

"Yesterday morning," Ma answered.

"Was there a young woman in one of them?" Helen queried anxiously.

"Let me see," Ma said reflectively, pursing her lips. "I seem to recall about six or seven men. They pulled in and ordered some food to go."

Helen placed the tip of the carbine barrel against Ma's forehead. "You'd better remember more than that."

Ma was wringing her hands in the apron. "Yes! I do! Now that I think about it, there was a woman with them. She used the facilities."

"Describe her!" Helen directed.

"Well, I didn't pay all that much attention," Ma said. "But I think she had red hair and was wearing a green blouse. I don't remember the color of her pants."

"Did you talk to her?" Helen inquired, lowering the carbine.

Ma shook her head. "Like I said, they pulled in and ordered some food to go. I saw them through the window, standing next to the jeeps and stretching their legs. Two of them came in and ordered the food. And two of them went with the young lady and waited outside the door while she did her business."

Hickok strolled over, his Pythons in his hands. "They're all fit for the vultures," he said.

Ma glanced at the gunman. "I've got to hand it to you, sonny. I've lived a long time, and I've seen my share of men who fancied themselves quick with a gun, but I'ver never seen anyone the likes of you."

Hickok chuckled. "Just natural aptitude, I reckon."

Blade crossed to the counter and peered over the rim. The tall man was crumpled on the floor, blood oozing from a half-dozen holes. He turned and studied the matron. "What was the setup here?"

"Setup?" Ma repeated innocently.

"Whatever it was," Hickok mentioned, "it was mighty slick. Those cow chips had their handguns taped underneath their tables."

Blade walked up to Ma. "What was the setup? Did your gang rob the customers who came through?"

Ma snorted. "I wouldn't stay in business long if I did that, now would I? Besides, I wouldn't stoop to petty robbery."

"Then what was it?" Blade snapped.

"I'm in the skin trade," Ma said.

"The what?" Blade responded.

"Oh. I keep forgetting. You don't know a thing about Vegas," Ma said. "So let me fill you in. There are dozens of casinos in Vegas. And for every casino there are five houses—"

"Houses?" Blade interrupted.

"Yeah. You know. Brothels. Whorehouses," Ma stated. "Houses of prostitution."

"Prostitu—" Blade began in astonishment.

"Yeah. Don't tell me you don't know what a prostitute is?" Ma asked.

"I've read about them," Blade admitted.

"*Read* about them?" Ma said, then laughed. "You've never visited a whorehouse?"

"No," Blade replied.

"Now I know you're from the moon!" Ma quipped.

"What do these whorehouses and the casinos have to do

with your setup?'' Blade questioned.

"I'm in the skin trade," Ma explained. "There aren't as many women around as there used to be. The houses and the casinos need women. Pretty women. Lots and lots of them. I'm in the supply business. If a real looker comes along, like your friend here, I arrange to send her to Vegas."

"How do you arrange it?" Blade probed.

Ma nodded at the tray of milk on the table. "Usually we drug their drinks. When they pass out, we grab them. Easy as pie."

"But what if there are others with them? What if they're with their family?" Blade inquired.

"They're taken care of," Ma said.

"You mean they're killed," Blade deduced.

Ma didn't respond.

Helen's lips curled downward distastefully. "You drug women and force them into a life of prostitution? How could you?"

"Don't look down your nose at me, dearie!" Ma rejoined. "Being a pro isn't as bad as all that. I should know. I worked the line once, I worked my way up to become the madam at one of the top casinos in Vegas. But there comes a time when you get put out to pasture, when you get too old for the trade. So when Don Giorgio offered me this franchise, I could hardly refuse. I make a good living here."

"Who is Don Giorgio?" Blade asked.

"He's the head of the second most powerful Family in Vegas," Ma answered.

"How long have you been doing this?" Blade queried.

"Four years," Ma said.

"So you planned to drug us and sell me into prostitution?" Helen wanted to know.

"I was going to do it," Ma admitted, "but Harry talked me out of the idea. He said you were packing too much hardware, that you looked like you could handle yourselves. He said you were professionals, that we should let you leave in peace. So I agreed. Harry was always a shrewd judge of character." She paused and snickered. "Isn't this funny? We decide not to try and snatch Helen, we don't even bother to drug your drinks, and you end up blowing most of us away!"

"It's hilarious," Blade said dryly.

"We should head on out," Helen urged. "Mindy must be in Vegas by now."

"Tell me something," Ma said to Helen. "What's this girl to you?"

Helen's features hardened. "She's my daughter."

Ma did a double take. "I didn't know."

Hickok pointed at Ma. "What are we going to do about her? If we let her live, she might find a way of lettin' the bigwigs in Vegas know we're comin'."

Ma, her hands buried in her apron, looked at Blade. "I won't rat! Honest!"

Blade stared at the matron. What *were* they going to do? If they tied her up and left her at the diner, someone was bound to come along, find her, and let her loose. Taking her with them wasn't feasible either. One of them would need to watch her at all times, and he couldn't spare anyone for the job.

The matter was suddenly taken out of his hands.

Helen absently lowered her carbine to her side, gazing at the matron with a slight grin on her face. "Now I want you to tell me something," she said.

"What's that, dearie?" Ma responded.

Helen smiled sweetly. "I'd like to know what's in that apron of yours?"

Ma stiffened. "There's nothing in my apron."

"Prove it," Helen stated.

Blade saw Ma sweep her right hand from under her apron, and he detected the metallic glint of a gun even as he brought the Commando up. But before he could squeeze the trigger, Helen fired. Her slugs slammed into the matron's neck and face, and Ma was hurled backwards to tumble over a chair.

Ma wound up on her right side, crimson spurting from

her throat and mouth, a derringer clutched in her lifeless right hand.

Helen walked over to the matron and nudged the body with her right boot. "She got what she deserved!" she snapped.

"Nice shootin'," Hickok said. "I was going to plug her myself, but I figured you should have the honor."

Helen looked at Blade. "Can we take off now?"

"In a minute," Blade told her. "We must settle some things first." He paused. "Who's in charge here?"

"You are," Helen replied promptly.

"Who decides when we will fight and when we won't?" Blade asked.

"You do," Helen said.

"Then why did you start this?" Blade demanded. "You didn't even believe this was a trap when we suggested it."

Helen gazed at Ma's corpse. "I got to thinking about the things Hickok and you said. I realized you were right. And the more I watched Ma, the more convinced I became that she knew something about Mindy. When she mentioned Don Pucci, that clinched it. I'm sorry. I was way out of line. I should have waited for your signal. It won't happen again."

"It better not," Blade cautioned. He surveyed the diner. "Let's head for Vegas before someone else shows up. They'll never know who did this if they're aren't any witnesses."

Helen hefted her Carbine. "I should be honest with you."

"How so?" Blade responded.

"I'll try to follow your orders at all times," Helen said. "But when we get to Vegas, if we find Mindy has been hurt or been forced to become a . . . a prostitute, then I intend to kill everyone responsible. With or without your permission." She stalked toward the front door.

Blade sighed in annoyance. He should have expected this attitude. Helen was too emotionally involved with the mission to function effectively. He should never have agreed to bring her along.

Hickok was reloading the spent rounds in his Pythons, smiling impishly.

"What's so funny?" Blade asked.

"Helen," Hickok replied.

"What about her?"

Hickok watched her walk out the door. "I never realized it before, but the lady is a lot like me."

"As if I didn't have enough to worry about," Blade muttered.

CHAPTER SIX

"Here he comes," Hickok announced.

Blade saw him too. Geronimo was 500 yards off, jogging up the hill toward the stand of trees and brush in which the SEAL was concealed.

"I don't know how wise it is to leave the SEAL here when we go into Vegas," Helen commented from the giant's left.

Blade glanced at her. "There you go again."

"But we'd be safer in the SEAL," Helen said. "It's bulletproof."

"It would also stand out like a sore thumb," Blade told her. "We've seen over a hundred cars and trucks enter Vegas since we pulled into these trees. But the SEAL is unique. There's nothing else like it. We'd attract too much attention if we take it into Vegas. So we'll go in on foot." He stared at the buildings to the southwest. Only an hour ago they had driven over a rise and spied the city approximately a mile distant. He had continued on until he'd spotted a suitable site to camouflage the transport, then wheeled off the road after checking to guarantee no one

was coming from either direction. Now, as he waited for
Geronimo to reach them, he double-checked the makeshift
latticework of branches and brush they had used to hide
the SEAL.

"Las Vegas is huge," Helen remarked with a touch of
trepidation. "How will we ever find Mindy in there?"

Blade adjusted a large limb over the SEAL's grill.
"We'll find her," he vowed.

"Do you have a plan?" Helen asked hopefully.

"We'll play it by ear," Blade said.

"That's a plan?" Helen retorted.

Blade gazed at her. "Do you have a better idea?"

"I sure do," Helen stated. "You said Mindy will be at
the Golden Crown Casino, right?"

"That's what Ted was told," Blade confirmed.

"Then I say we march right into the Golden Crown
Casino and get her back!" Helen declared.

"No," Blade said.

"Why not?" Helen demanded.

"Will you think with your head instead of your heart?"
Blade responded. "They will be expecting us to do exactly
like you propose. They'll be waiting for us. And what good
can we do Mindy if we walk into a trap?"

"We can't leave her in their hands!" Helen objected.

"I don't intend to leave Mindy in their hands a second
more than is absolutely necessary," Blade said. "But we'll
take it slow at first. We'll mingle, walk around, act like
everybody else, blend right in. Hopefully, we can discover
the extent of our opposition."

"Whatever you say," Helen commented halfheartedly.

Blade moved around the transport, carefully inspecting
the camouflage.

Helen's shoulders slumped as she faced Las Vegas. She
noticed Hickok was to her right, leaning against a tree,
staring at her. "What are you looking at?" she snapped.

"I'm admirin' your fortitude," the gunfighter said.

Helen studied him for a moment, trying to determine if
the gunman was serious. He was.

"I also wanted to apologize for the crack I made about

your husband," Hickok said sincerely. "It was a bone-headed thing to say, but you did get me all riled up."

"I guess I had it coming," Helen said.

"I had no right to comment on your personal life," Hickok mentioned. "I was just fed up with your gripin'."

Helen looked up at the blue morning sky. "I can't believe how I'm acting on this trip!" she remarked pensively. "I pride myself on my self-control, but I certainly haven't exhibited any."

"Who can blame you?" Hickok said. "If my son was down there, I'd go crazy."

Helen sighed. "Mindy is all I have left in this world. My parents died about six years ago. Then Andy left me for another woman. Talk about creating a scandal! We were the talk of the Home for months! Divorces are extremely rare in the Family. You know that. I'm sure you heard all the gossip."

"I heard it," Hickok said softly.

"I was heartbroken," Helen divulged. "I loved Andy. Truly loved him. I was stunned when he told me he wanted a divorce. He claimed I was stifling his manhood. Can you imagine that?" She laughed bitterly. "We appeared before the Elders, and he stood there and read a list of reasons for our marital failure, as he called it. I was too bossy. I was a dictator. I couldn't relate to him as a woman. I was immature. I was spiritually stagnant." She stopped and closed her eyes. "According to him, I was the worst woman imaginable. I suppose I shouldn't have been surprised when the Elders granted his divorce petition, but I was."

"The Elders were right to grant the petition," Hickok stated.

Helen's eyes opened and she glanced at the gunman. "Oh? So you believe Andy was telling the truth?"

"I believe Andy is a wimp," Hickok declared. "Always has been. And when you pair a wimp with a strong person in a marriage, either the wimp grows up and they learn to share as equals, or the strong person always dominates the marriage, or the wimp cracks under the pressure. The

Elders knew Andy couldn't handle the responsibility of being your hubby. If Andy had stayed with you, he would have made your life miserable. He was already foolin' around with Gladys before he even asked you for a divorce. And let's face it. Gladys is a ding-a-ling. Andy and her are perfect for each other. He wasn't mature enough for a real woman like you.''

Helen grinned. ''You missed your calling. You should have been a Counselor.''

Blade came around the transport. ''The SEAL is locked tight as a drum.'' He walked forward several yards, his eyes on Geronimo, who was now less than 20 feet away.

''About time you got here,'' Hickok declared loudly. ''Married life has made you flabby.''

Geronimo reached them and halted, breathing easily. ''The only flab around here is between your ears,'' he said to Hickok, then faced Blade.

''What did you find out?'' Blade asked.

''Anyone can come and go as they like,'' Geronimo reported. ''The road leads straight into the heart of Las Vegas. There are thousands of people everywhere.''

''Any checkpoints or security forces?'' Blade inquired.

Geronimo shook his head. ''Not a one. The city is wide open. And get this. Carrying firearms must be legal because many of the people I saw were armed. Men and women alike. I went about a quarter of a mile into the city, and I wasn't stopped or challenged once.''

''Then we go in,'' Blade stated. ''And we stay close together.''

''Are you going to carry me piggyback?'' Hickok joked.

Blade led them down the hill, angling toward the road, scanning the area for other travelers. The hill was 600 yards from the highway, and he felt supremely confident the transport would not be discovered. Nevertheless, he didn't want anyone to observe the Warriors emerging from the brush. Whenever a car or truck appeared on the road he flattened and the others followed his lead. They reached the highway without being seen, coming out near the point where the SEAL had left the road.

"Blade," Geronimo said. "Look!" He pointed at a spot ten feet off.

Blade turned and saw them: the tracks the SEAL's massive wheels had made in the field bordering the highway. The huge tires had crushed the grass and weeds.

"Should we try to cover them up?" Geronimo inquired.

Blade heard a low rumble and spied a car approaching from the southwest, leaving Las Vegas. "No. I doubt anyone will pay much attention to the tracks. They may assume someone pulled off for a rest stop. If we try to cover them, everyone driving by will see us. We'd arouse more curiosity than the tracks themselves. Let's go." He marched to the southwest. The car sped past them.

Geronimo fell in behind his giant friend.

Hickok and Helen brought up the rear.

"You must be on pins and needles," the gunman commented.

Helen managed a feeble smile. "You don't know the half of it."

"Just remember you're not in this alone," Hickok said. "We'll help you get Mindy out."

Helen stared at the buckskin-clad gunfighter. "You're not what I expected," she remarked.

"I'm not?" Hickok responded.

"Definitely not," Helen declared. "We haven't had occasion to talk together very frequently. My estimation of you was based on all the stories circulating around the Family, and the stories don't do justice to your personality."

"In what way?" Hickok inquired.

"In every way," Helen said. "According to the tales I heard, you're just about the deadliest Warrior. Your courage is indisputable, but you're also a bit of a blockhead. You have no regard for your personal safety. You'll walk into a hot spot without batting an eye, and you'll rely on your speed to bail you out if you get in over your head. Your motto is, 'Shoot first and ask questions later,' and you always go for the head. Some of the Family think you're too reckless, others believe you're the Warrior who always gets the job done, no matter what the odds might be. Personally, I don't think you're as big a blockhead as some people claim.''

"Thanks," Hickok stated. "I think."

"You're more intelligent and understanding than most give you credit for being," Helen observed. "I'm beginning to see why Sherry married you."

Hickok smirked. "She's in love with my dimples."

Geronimo glanced over his left shoulder at Helen. "Don't let him kid you. The only reason Sherry married him was because he brainwashed her. Somehow he convinced her he's an ordinary kind of guy. If I didn't know better, I'd swear he hypnotized her."

"Can I help it if the Spirit blessed me with charm, wit, and good looks?" Hickok queried lightheartedly.

"Don't forget modesty," Geronimo added.

Another car passed them, heading to the northeast.

Blade trained his eyes on the buildings ahead. Even though it was daytime, with bright sunshine, there seemed to be a lot of lights on in Vegas. Most were neon lights advertising businesses: casinos, hotels, motels, and the like. As they drew nearer he could see the throngs of people packing the sidewalks. Vehicle traffic was also surprisingly heavy.

Geronimo took two hasty strides and caught up with Blade. "See? No checkpoints, police, nothing."

"Maybe they don't need a police force," Blade speculated. "Maybe they don't want one. Ma said Organized Crime controls the entire city, and I doubt the mob would allow a police force to exist."

"But how do they keep the crowds under control?" Geronimo asked. "With all the gambling, and the drinking, and the womanizing that goes on here, there must be problems with drunks and other rowdy types. How does the mob keep them in line?"

"I imagine we'll find out," Blade said.

They reached the first buildings, sleazy motels on both sides of the highway. A wide sidewalk bordered the front of the motel nearest them.

Blade gazed across the highway and noted another sidewalk on the opposite side. The motels were doing a thriving business; vehicles were pulling in and out of the motel parking lots every few seconds. He was puzzled by the heavy traffic until he saw one of the cars pull up to a door labeled FRONT OFFICE. A lean man in a green suit stood outside the Front Office door. Whenever a vehicle pulled up alongside him, the driver would hand the man money and the man would give the driver a small white packet.

"What is that all about?" Geronimo inquired, watching yet another transaction.

"I don't know," Blade said.

"Want me to find out, pard?" Hickok offered.

"No," Blade replied. "I don't want any of us making waves. We don't want to do anything to get ourselves noticed. We have a better chance of finding Mindy if we don't draw attention to us."

They entered Las Vegas.

And three minutes later attracted exactly the attention Blade didn't want.

CHAPTER SEVEN

Blade was extremely pleased.

None of the predestrians paid any attention to the four Warriors. The hustling crowds flowed to and fro, from casino to motel or liquor store, a frenetic swirl of humanity composed of frontier types in buckskins, Las Vegas residents and tourists in shirts and slacks or shorts, and dapper sorts in three-piece suits. Machine guns, rifles, and handguns were in abundance.

The Warriors fit right in.

Blade did notice the stares Helen was receiving from many of the men. But dozens of beautiful women were strolling along the sidewalk, each one the focus of masculine interest. The women wore skimpy tops and short, short skirts, and they flaunted their sexuality with a pronounced swaying of their hips and the suggestive contours of their breasts.

"Hey! Look!" Hickok said. "That sign."

Blade halted in midstride in front of a liquor store. To the right of the entrance was a large white sign with black lettering. "Let's read it," he stated.

They crossed the parking lot and walked up to the sign.

WELCOME TO LAS VEGAS

The recreation capital of the Western Hemisphere! If we don't have it, you don't need it! All establishments are open twenty-four hours a day for your enjoyment and convenience. Precious metals and jewelry are accepted at any Exchange Center in every casino. Pre-war currency is also acceptable at the current rate of exchange. Firearms are permitted, but the killing of unarmed tourists is strictly forbidden. Las Vegas thrives on it's tourist trade. Any violations will be dealt with by the Enforcers. All questions will be courteously answered at any of the Information Booths. Thank you for vacationing in Las Vegas! We hope to see you again next year!

The Las Vegas Chamber

"Friendly folks hereabouts," Hickok remarked.

"Who are the Enforcers?" Geronimo queried.

"Your guess is as good as mine," Blade responded. "Let's keep moving."

The four Warriors turned.

Just as the front door to the liquor store opened and five men walked out. All five wore suits and three wore hats. Two of them carried Uzi submachine guns. The apparent leader was a stocky man with a pockmarked face who was wearing a blue pin-striped suit and a white hat. In his right hand was a bottle of whiskey. He started to take a swig as he headed toward a parked red sedan. His brown eyes alighted on the Warriors and he stopped. "Whoa! What have we here?"

"Uh-oh," Geronimo mumbled. "We've got trouble."

The man in the white hat cocked his head to one side, lustfully gazing at Helen. "Do you see what I see, Reggie?"

One of the men with an Uzi, a tall man in a tan suit, nodded. "I see her, Franky."

Franky took a sip of whiskey and walked toward the Warriors, flanked by his four henchmen.

Blade was standing slightly ahead of his companions. He took a stride forward, the Commando held at waist height. "Do you want something?"

Franky halted, lowering the bottle and warily studying the giant. "This doesn't concern you, buddy!"

"I think it does," Blade stated.

Franky nodded toward Helen. "I want a few words with the fox."

"About what?" Blade asked.

"That's between the broad and me!" Franky declared testily.

"What do you want?" Helen spoke up.

Franky smirked. "I want to show you a good time, gorgeous. Why don't you dump these assholes and come with me? You'll see the sights in style."

"No, thanks," Helen said politely.

Franky's eyes narrowed. "Don't you know who I am?"

"Nope," Helen replied. "And I don't care."

Franky seemed insulted. He glanced at the one named Reggie. "Tell this bimbo who I am!"

"You don't want to mess with Franky, lady," Reggie warned. "He's connected."

"Connected to what? That bottle?" Helen retorted.

Franky hissed and angrily tossed the bottle to the pavement. The bottle shattered, spraying whiskey in all directions. "I'm a made man, bitch! Does the name Giorgio mean anything to you?"

"Should it?" Helen rejoined.

Blade suddenly recalled the matron at the diner mentioning Don Giorgio. What had she said? Something about Don Giorgio being the head of the second most powerful Family in Vegas.

"Do you know who my old man is?" Franky asked belligerently.

"I do," Blade said. "And we don't want any trouble with you."

Franky grinned cockily. "Oh, really? Well, Jerkface,

you'll have more trouble than you can handle if Sweet-Cheeks doesn't come for a ride with me."

Hickok abruptly stepped to the right, slinging the Henry over his left shoulder.

The four men with Franky shifted their attention to the gunman.

Hickok's hands dropped to his sides and he grinned.

"What's so funny, Ugly?" Franky snapped.

Blade tried one more time to prevent bloodshed. "We don't want any trouble with you. Just let us walk away in peace."

Franky snorted contemptuously. "The only way you'll leave is in pieces."

Blade realized pedestrians had gathered on the sidewalk and were watching in fascination. He saw the two henchmen with Uzis fingering their weapons. The other three had swept their jackets aside to reveal pistols stuck under their belts. With a sinking feeling he knew there would be gunplay.

"So what's it going to be?" Franky demanded. "Do you hand over the vixen or do we whack you?"

"How do you do it?" Hickok unexpectedly queried.

Franky stared at the man in buckskins. "Do what, hick?"

"I've never seen anyone with your talent," Hickok mentioned.

Franky moved the right side of his jacket aside, his hand moving to within an inch of an automatic. "What the hell are you talking about?"

"I've never met anyone who could fart out of their mouth before," Hickok said. "How do you do it?"

Several seconds elapsed before Franky's alcohol-benumbed mind perceived he had been insulted. With a snarl he grabbed for this gun.

Hickok was the first to fire. The Colts flashed from their holsters and boomed, the twin shots as one.

Franky took both shots in the head, one in each eye, his cranium bursting outwards, his brains and blood gushing over the asphalt as he was flung backwards.

Hickok swiveled before Franky started to fall, planting two more shots into one of the henchmen.

Reggie swung his Uzi toward the gunfighter, but he died before he could squeeze the trigger. A burst from the giant's machine gun ripped into his abdomen and nearly tore him in half. He crumpled to the ground, the Uzi slipping from his fingers, his consciousness slowly fading, agony wracking his body. Doubled over, on his knees, shock overwhelming his senses, he saw the fight end as swiftly as it began. The giant spun and took out Lou with another skillful burst to Lou's chest, even as the Indian and the fox shot Berk and Clemens. Reggie sagged, blood spouting from his gaping mouth, his eyes glazing. A pair of moccasins appeared in his line of vision and he craned his neck upward.

"Howdy," the man in the buckskin said. "Your pards are done for. Any last words before I put you out of your misery?"

Reggie used the last of his strength to spit out, "Get screwed!"

Hickok shrugged, extending both Pythons. "I figured you might want to make your peace with your Maker." He cocked the Colts. "I reckon I was wrong." He fired, the Pythons blasting, Reggie's forehead caving inward as the two heavy slugs plowed through his brain.

Reggie toppled onto the asphalt.

Hickok glanced at his friends. "Anyone hit?"

"I'm fine," Geronimo answered.

"Ditto," Helen said.

Blade walked up to Franky's corpse. "I hope we don't run into more idiots like this one."

There was a commotion in the crowd on the sidewalk.

Blade faced the pedestrians, ready to cut loose if they displayed any hostility. To his amazement, none of the people crowding the sidewalk showed any hint of anger or resentment. The commotion was being caused by several men striving to reach the liquor store parking lot.

Were these newcomers associates of Franky's?"

The three men finally pressed through the throng and

stopped. All three wore dark-colored suits; each one was armed with a machine gun. One of them, a burly man with a black mustache and a hooked nose, walked toward the Warriors, his dark eyes surveying the five corpses gravely. "Damn!" he exclaimed when he spied Franky's body.

Hickok, Geronimo, and Helen were keeping the three men covered.

The man with the mustache looked up at Blade. "Do you know what you've done?"

"They started it," Blade said.

The man twisted toward the sidewalk. "How about it? Who saw this? Who started it?"

"Franky did," a man called out.

"Yeah," declared a woman in a red skirt. "We saw the whole thing. They told Franky they didn't want no trouble. Franky wouldn't listen."

"He finally bit off more than he could chew!" someone quipped.

"Then it was a fair and square?" the man with the mustache questioned them.

A half dozen or so nodded. A few yelled out, "Yes!"

"My name is DePetrillo," the man with the mustache stated. "I head one of the Enforcer squads. It's my job to report every killing. If it's a fair and square, there's no problem. But if it's done dirty, if unarmed civilians are shot, then a dozen Enforcers go after the guilty party." He paused and gazed at Franky, then sighed. "This is trouble, mister. What's your name?"

"George Smith," Blade lied.

"Why are you in Vegas?" DePetrillo inquired.

"We came to see the sights," Blade replied.

DePetrillo frowned. "Is this your first time in Vegas?"

"Yes," Blade admitted.

"Then let me set you straight," DePetrillo said. "Ordinarily, there's no beef over a fair and square. But one of the men you killed was Franky Giorgio. I never liked Franky much myself. He was all mouth. But he was also the son of Johnny Giorgio, and Johnny is one of the most powerful men in Vegas. I'll report this as a fair and square to Don Pucci, but even Don Pucci might not be able to keep Giorgio in line over the killing of his son. Giorgio may ask for a sanction to whack you. Do you understand me?''

"I think so," Blade said. "You're warning me that Giorgio may come after us."

DePetrillo nodded. "If I were you, I'd haul ass out of Vegas right now."

"We can't," Blade said.

"Suit yourself," DePetrillo stated. "But don't say I didn't warn you. Now get out of here before some of Giorgio's boys show up."

Blade motioned for his three fellow Warriors to follow. "Thanks," he said as he passed DePetrillo.

The Enforcer scrutinized the giant. "Don't thank me, mister. I'm just doing my job."

The crowd parted to permit the Warriors access to the sidewalk.

Blade resumed their trek into the heart of the city. He replaced the clip in his Commando.

Hickok, busily reloading his Colts, reached Blade's right side. "George Smith, huh? Now there's an original name!"

"I couldn't very well give my real name," Blade said. "Pucci is expecting the Warriors to try and rescue Mindy. But he doesn't know when. He gave us a month, remember? If I gave my real name to that Enforcer, Don Pucci would know we're in Vegas now. I want to surprise him."

"I'm partial to the direct approach," Hickok mentioned.

"I know," Blade agreed.

"So why don't we find Don Pucci, shove a gun down his throat, and give him five seconds to turn Mindy over or else?" Hickok suggested.

"Be serious," Blade said. "Don Pucci will be guarded by his button men, as Ma called them. I doubt anyone can get close to Pucci without an appointment. And I can't see him giving me an appointment."

"I still don't understand why Pucci took Mindy," Hickok remarked. "Why lure us all the way to Vegas? And why did Pucci ask for you by name?"

"I wish I knew," Blade responded.

CHAPTER EIGHT

"We're being followed," Geronimo announced.

Blade knew better than to turn around and search for their tail. "Where?" he casually inquired over his right shoulder.

"About forty yards behind us," Geronimo said. "There are two of them. They've been shadowing us for two or three minutes."

"Are they armed?" Blade queried.

"I don't see any rifles or machine guns," Geronimo responded. "But they could have handguns concealed under their jackets. They're both wearing dark suits."

"What's the plan, Big Guy?" Hickok asked.

Blade pondered their next move. He estimated they were over a mile from the liquor store. Ahead was a stretch of highway with casino after casino on both sides. Secondary streets periodically intersected the main thoroughfare. More people than ever before jammed the sidewalks, and the vehicle traffic was bumper to bumper.

"Want me to take care of them?" Hickok proposed.

"We'll do it my way," Blade said. "Come on." He

walked to the nearest intersection and waited at the curb with a crowd of pedestrians until the traffic light displayed a WALK sign.

The Warriors quickly crossed.

Blade was hoping his strategy would work. They had traversed six intersections since leaving the liquor store, and he had noticed the traffic lights never flashed the WALK sign for more than 30 seconds. Anyone wanting to cross was compelled to walk rapidly. The two men following the Warriors would be unable to catch up until the next light change. He hoped.

"They didn't make it," Geronimo confirmed, idly gazing to their rear.

Blade increased his pace, searching for the ideal spot.

Geronimo, faking an interest in the casinos, scanned the structures to the rear. "The light still hasn't changed," he mentioned.

An alley appeared to the right.

Blade slowed, noting the crates stacked at the mouth of the alley, partially obscuring the entrance. "Where are they?"

"Still waiting for the light," Geronimo said.

"Into this alley then," Blade instructed them, and took a right when he reached it. The alley was littered with refuse and lined with metal trash cans.

"Yuck!" Hickok declared. "What a smell!"

"Reminds me of you before your annual bath," Geronimo quipped.

Blade saw an open door 15 feet away. He cautiously advanced and peered inside, discovering a gloomy corridor with a closed door at the far end. "In here," he ordered, then stood aside so they could file into the hallway.

"I don't like being cooped up like this," Hickok commented.

Blade stepped inside and drew the door shut until only a crack remained, enough visibility to afford him a view of the alley mouth and the stretch up to the door.

"Are you aimin' to jump these clowns?" Hickok asked.

"I am," Blade verified, peeking through the crack.

Hickok chuckled. "This is another thing I like about Las Vegas. There's never a dull moment."

Blade watched the mouth of the alley for their shadows. Seconds later two men in dark suits, with felt hats, reached the entrance and paused uncertainly. Blade knew they were perplexed. He doubted the pair had seen the Warriors enter the alley, so they must be wondering how the Warriors could have vanished into thin air.

The two men became embroiled in a heated exchange.

Blade grinned. One of the men, the skinniest, was gesturing along the main drag, indicating he wanted to stick to the highway. But the other one was jabbing his right thumb toward the alley, apparently arguing the alley should be checked before they proceeded.

The skinny one lost.

Both men walked into the alley.

Blade slung his Commando over his broad back and drew his right Bowie. "Geronimo," he whispered. "Take the skinny one."

Geronimo nodded, then handed the Browning to Helen. He slid his tomahawk from under his belt.

Blade tensed as the second man, a pale, mousy man not over five feet tall, approached the door. He waited until the last possible instant, until the mousy mobster was reaching for the doorknob, before he lunged, ramming his powerful right shoulder into the door and sending it flying wide.

Startled, the mousy mobster was caught off guard. The door struck him in the chest and knocked him onto the ground.

Blade was on the mobster like a pouncing panther. He leaped and landed with his right knee folded, his leg hard, ramming the knee into the mobster's abdomen. The man grunted and turned red, gasping for air.

The skinny one reacted incredibly swiftly, his left hand going for a Smith and Wesson tucked in his waistband. He never pulled it.

Geronimo reached the skinny mobster in three bounds, the tomahawk glinting in the sunlight. He delivered a resounding blow to the left side of the mobster's head with the flat of his weapon, splitting the skin and staggering the mobster but leaving the skinny man alive.

Blade placed the point of his right Bowie next to the mousy mobster's left eye. "Why were you following us?" he demanded.

"Wasn't . . ." the man replied, wheezing.

Hickok and Helen moved past Blade and Geronimo to cover the alley entrance.

"I won't ask again," Blade stated harshly. "Who are you? Why were you following us?"

"I wasn't!" Mousy replied angrily.

Blade cut him. He slashed the Bowie across the man's left cheek, leaving an inch-deep slit.

Mousy started to shriek.

Blade pressed his left hand over Mousy's mouth. "Don't make a sound or you're dead!"

Mousy's brown eyes widened fearfully.

Blade looked up. Hickok and Helen were near the alley mouth, blocking the view of the passersby. Skinny was clutching the wound to his head, blood seeping over his fingers. The mobster's hat had fallen to the ground. Geronimo held the tomahawk aloft, prepared to strike again if necessary.

Perfect.

He could concentrate on his interrogation.

Blade grinned down at the small mobster. "Now you were saying? Why were you following us?" He lifted his left hand.

Mousy took a gulp of putrid alley air. "Told to!" he blurted. "Orders!"

"Orders from whom?" Blade demanded.

"Orders from Kenney," Mousy disclosed.

"And who is Kenney?" Blade queried.

"Kenney is Don Giorgio's right-hand man," Mousy explained. "We were at the casino a while ago when a call came in. Somebody whacked Giorgio's son, Franky—"

"I know," Blade interrupted. "We did."

"You admit it?" Mousy asked in astonishment. "You

must be wacko!''

"Keep talking," Blade stated.

"Kenney got a description of you guys," Mousy detailed. "He told us to tail you. We cruised the strip until I spotted you, then we parked and tailed you on foot."

"What were you supposed to do? Kill us?" Blade inquired.

"Just follow you," Mousy said.

Blade smirked. "Why don't I believe you?"

"Honest!" Mousy asserted. "We were ordered to follow you, make a note of places you stopped at and the people you talked to, and call in a report every hour."

"Does Giorgio want revenge for the death of his son?" Blade asked.

"I haven't talked to Don Giorgio," Mousy replied. "I talked to Kenney. But if you're asking my opinion, yeah. Giorgio won't stand still for the racking of Franky. He'll probably ask Don Pucci for a sanction to snuff you guys."

"We don't want to fight Don Giorgio," Blade commented.

"I'll bet you don't!" Mousy said scornfully.

"Can you tell him that?" Blade queried.

"Sure," Mousy responded. "But it won't do no good. You killed his son. Blood talks, you know."

"And there's nothing I could say or do to convince Don Giorgio to leave us alone?" Blade questioned.

"Leave you alone? Not on your life!" Mousy declared.

Blade frowned, irritated by the turn of events. As if rescuing Mindy wasn't enough of a problem, now he had to contend with a vengeful Don!

"You've got two choices," Mousy said. "You can play it smart and get the hell out of Vegas, or you can stay and die. It's that simple."

"There's one more option," Blade noted.

"What's that?" Mousy asked.

"I can kill Don Giorgio if he doesn't leave us alone," Blade stated.

Despite his wounded left cheek, Mousy laughed. "Kill Don Giorgio? You're out of your mind!"

Blade slowly stood. "Where is Giorgio's headquarters?"

"Where else? The Don hangs out at his place," Mousy divulged. "He has his own casino, just like all the other Dons."

"What's the name of Giorgio's casino?" Blade demanded.

"Johnny's Palace," Mousy answered.

Blade's eyes narrowed. "One more question. Where does Don Pucci hang out?"

"At the Golden Crown Casino, mostly," Mousy said. "Why?"

"None of your business," Blade replied. "On your feet."

Mousy complied.

Blade wagged his right Bowie in front of the mobster's eyes. "I want you to relay a message to Don Giorgio. Tell him I'm coming after him."

"You're what?" Mousy blurted in disbelief.

"Tell Giorgio I'm coming after him since he can't leave well enough alone," Blade directed. "Tell him I'll be at his Palace soon."

Mousy's mouth dropped. "You won't last three seconds."

"Just tell him," Blade snapped. "And tell him this. If he's a man and not a coward, he'll meet me one on one."

Mousy made a clucking sound. "What a jerk! I'll relay your message, and I hope I'm there when the Don creams you."

"Get out of here," Blade commanded.

Mousy turned and started from the alley. He paused next to Skinny. "What about my buddy?"

"Take him with you," Blade said.

Geronimo looked at Blade. "Awwww, gee! I was hoping I could split his head open. Can I? Huh? Can I? Pretty please?"

Blade barely supressed a laugh. "No."

"Darn!" Geronimo exclaimed wistfully.

Mousy gawked at Geronimo. "You're wacko, Indian!

All of you are flat-out crazy!''

Geronimo beamed. "You really think so?''

Mousy and Skinny moved toward the alley entrance.

Hickok suddenly blocked their path, the Henry in his hands. He aimed the barrel at Mousey's face. "Hold it!''

"What's the matter?'' Mousy queried nervously. "The guy with the knife said we could go.''

"Is that a wart on your nose?'' Hickok asked.

"A what?''

"A wart,'' Hickok reiterated. "I'm not partial to warts. I plug 'em every chance I get. If that's a wart on your nose, I'll have to shoot it off.''

Mousy gazed back at Blade and Geronimo, then stared at Helen for a second. "Lunatics! I'm surrounded by lunatics!''

"Is that a wart?'' Hickok repeated.

"There's no damn wart on my nose!'' Mousy said anxiously.

"Oh.'' Hickok lowered the Henry. "In that case, have a real nice day.'' He bowed and motioned toward the main street.

Mousy grabbed Skinny's right arm. "Come on! We're getting the hell out of here!''

The two mobsters ran from the alley and disappeared.

Helen began laughing.

Blade and Geronimo joined their colleagues.

"Were you serious about going after Don Giorgio?'' Hickok asked.

Blade replaced the right Bowie in its sheath. "Of course not. I wanted to buy us time to find Mindy. If Giorgio expects us at his Palace, he might drop the tails. We should have a few hours before he gets suspicious.''

Hickok chuckled. "By the time the cow chip realizes we're not comin', we'll be long gone with Mindy.''

"I hope,'' Blade said.

Geronimo slid the tomahawk under his belt. "So now we find Mindy,'' he remarked with determination.

"About time,'' Helen muttered.

Hickok looked up and noticed Blade was thoughtfully

chewing on his lower lip. "What's buggin' you?"

"Something is not right," Blade said.

"Like what?" Hickok questioned.

Blade frowned. "I don't know. I can't put my finger on it. There's something I'm missing."

"It'll come to you," Hickok said. "Give it time."

"I guess you're right," Blade argued. He stared at Helen. "Let's go rescue your daughter."

"And keep your eyes peeled," Hickok told Helen.

Helen gazed at the gunman quizzically. "For what?"

"Mobsters with warts. I can use some target practice," Hickok commented.

Helen simply rolled her eyes heavenward.

CHAPTER NINE

"What's that, pard?" Hickok asked.

The four Warriors stood near an intersection over a half mile from the alley.

Blade flipped through the pages of the small black book he'd removed from his right rear pocket. "I found this on the body of the stranger killed at the scene of Mindy's abduction. I'm double-checking the address for the Golden Crown Casino. That's where Pucci told Ted we'd find Mindy. And the mobster in the alley confirmed the Golden Crown Casino is Pucci's personal casino."

"We never did figure out why the stranger was killed," Geronimo mentioned.

"Maybe Pucci will tell us," Hickok said.

Blade found the address he wanted, then closed the black book and returned it to his rear pocket, slipping the book alongside the wad of two thousand dollars and the piece of blue plastic. "This is the correct boulevard. The Golden Crown Casino should be just up ahead."

Helen hefted her Carbine. "I pray she's all right."

"She will be," Hickok assured her.

"Let's go," Blade declared.

The quartet crossed the intersection.

"Any sign of a tail?" Blade inquired.

Geronimo, bringing up the rear, shook his head. "Nope. Don Giorgio must be waiting for us at his casino."

Blade scrutinized the buildings ahead as he sauntered along the sidewalk. They passed several casinos, liquor stores, one food store, and a gas station crammed with cars. He stared at the pumps, puzzled. Where did the mobsters obtain their fuel? Gasoline was a precious commodity elsewhere; the Civilized Zone and California stringently accounted for every gallon. Las Vegas, though, possessed gas in abundance. He gazed up at a flickering neon sign. There was another rarity: electrical power. The Outlands were totally devoid of such a luxury, and even California and the Civilized Zone, where generating plants were scrupulously maintained, were forced to conserve their useage, primarily supplying power to the urban centers.

The mobsters, though, were under no such limitations.

How did they do it?

Blade walked ten more yards and happened to glance at a casino sign fifty yards distant.

THE GOLDEN CROWN CASINO.

"Blade," Geronimo said, his alert eyes having already spied the sign.

"I see it," Blade stated, halting.

"See what?" Helen inquired.

Blade pointed toward the sign.

Helen took one look and started to head for it.

"Hold it," Blade directed, gripping her right wrist.

Helen angrily attempted to pull free. "Let me go! Mindy is in there!"

"We need a plan," Blade said.

"Plan, hell! I want to go to Mindy!" Helen snapped.

"Calm down!" Blade instructed her.

Helen's lips tightened, but she relaxed her arm. "Okay. What do we do?"

"We can't all go in at once," Blade said. "Pucci would

spot us too easily."

"Do you suppose he has our descriptions?" Geronimo asked.

"Could be," Blade said. "Remember, he asked for me by name. He must have some idea of how I look."

"Yeah," Hickok quipped. "It isn't every day you run into a seven-foot giant with big ears."

"His ears are no bigger than your mouth," Geronimo cracked.

"We'll go in two at a time," Blade proposed. "Geronimo and I will go in first. Hickok, give us three minutes and come in with Helen."

"I want to go in with you," Helen said to Blade.

"No."

"Why not?" Helen questioned in annoyance.

"Because I know you," Blade said. "If you spot Mindy in there, you'll start shooting every mobster in sight. I'm going in first to see if she's there."

"I'll watch over Helen," Hickok promised.

Blade inspected the Commando, insuring the safety was off. "Then let's get to it."

"Not so fast," Geronimo cautioned. "We have a problem."

"What kind of problem?" Blade asked.

Geronimo nodded at the opposite sidewalk. "See for yourself."

Blade turned, surveying the far sidewalk, perplexed until he recognized two faces in the seething crowd. "Damn!" he exclaimed.

Mousy and two other mobsters were standing on the opposite walk, and Mousy was gesturing at the Warriors and talking rapidly.

"Where'd he come from?" Hickok queried. "How'd he get here so fast?"

"He had a car, remember?" Blade reminded the gunman.

Mousy and his two companions unexpectedly began running, rudely shoving pedestrians aside, heading in the same direction as the Warriors.

"What's that all about?" Helen wanted to know.

Blade studied the casinos on the far side of the boulevard. Fifty yards away was the answer, a casino with its name in bright red letters overhead.

JOHNNY'S PALACE.

Mousy and the two mobsters were heading for the Palace as swiftly as the logjam of pedestrians permitted.

"Johnny's Palace," Geronimo said. "It's right across the street from the Golden Crown Casino!"

Blade stared from the Palace to the Golden Crown, feeling frustrated. He'd never expected this! Why were Don Giorgio's Palace and Don Pucci's Casino directly across the boulevard from one another? Was the territory on the far side of the boulevard Giorgio's? Was this side Pucci's?

"We can still find Mindy," Helen declared. "This doesn't change a thing."

"Yes, it does," Blade said, disputing her. "If we go into the Golden Crown and rescue Mindy, we'll undoubtedly have to take on Don Pucci's men to free her. And when we come out, Don Giorgio's men will be waiting for us. I don't like the odds."

"We could leave," Geronimo suggested, "then try and get inside the Golden Crown after dark. Maybe we won't be spotted by Giorgio's hit men."

"I'm not leaving!" Helen vowed.

"I have a plan," Hickok mentioned softly.

"Even if we do leave," Blade said, ignoring the gunman, "there's no guarantee we can sneak into the Golden Crown undetected after nightfall. Look at all those neon lights. This whole city must be lit up like one of those ancient Christmas trees."

"I have a plan," Hickok repeated quietly.

"Then let's march into the Golden Crown, and hang the consequences!" Geronimo advocated.

"I have a plan," Hickok said.

Blade sighed and faced the gunman. "I know I'll regret

this, but what's your plan?''

"It'll be a piece of cake," Hickok assured them. "We need to keep Don Giorgio occupied while we're savin' Mindy. So one of us should go into the Palace to keep Giorgio busy while the rest go into the Golden Crown and find Mindy.''

"I'm surprised," Geronimo remarked. "He has a good plan.''

Blade ran his left hand through his hair. Hickok's idea did make sense. With Giorgio preoccupied, three Warriors should be more than enough to quickly effect Mindy's release. "It might work," he grudgingly conceded.

"Then I reckon I'll see you yahoos later," Hickok said, and took a step toward the curb.

"Hold it," Blade said. "I'll go to the Palace.''

"Don't be a donkey," Hickok objected. "You're the brains of this outfit. If anyone can figure a way to get Mindy out of the Golden Crown, it's you. Helen should go with you because she's Mindy's mom. And Geronimo has to go with you too, because he can't hoodwink folks the way I can.''

"I can hoodwink as good as you any day!" Geronimo responded, then paused. "What's hoodwink mean, anyway?''

Hickok stared into Blade's eyes. "You can see I'm right, can't you?''

Blade reluctantly nodded. "You go.''

"Why am I so blamed brilliant all the time?" Hickok mumbled, and stepped to the curb.

"Wait!" Blade declared. "Cross at the next intersection!''

Hickok looked at each of them. "The direct approach, remember?" He winked at Geronimo. "Take care of that mangy, low-down, lyin' Injun butt of yours.''

Geronimo started to reply, but the gunman was gone.

Hickok darted into the traffic, swinging his Henry from side to side, weaving between the cars. Some of the drivers slammed on their brakes at the sight of the Warrior. Others ducked for cover when the Henry swung in their direction. There was a lot of metallic squealing and grinding intermixed with curses and screams, but the gunfighter reached the opposite side of the boulevard unscathed.

Geronimo expelled a deep breath. "I wish he wouldn't pull stunts like that."

"If he didn't," Blade commented, "he wouldn't be Hickok."

"Too bad he's married," Helen remarked.

"Hickok will give us the time we need," Blade said, heading for the Golden Crown. "Let's make sure his sacrifice is not in vain."

"Sacrifice?" Helen repeated. "You sound like you don't expect to see him again."

Blade watched the gunman wade through the stream of pedestrians on the far walk. "We may not," he said grimly, then stalked toward the Golden Crown Casino.

Don Anthony Pucci's personal casino was an imposing, stately structure 15 stories in height. Ten glass doors faced the boulevard, each with its frame painted a metallic gold. The trim on the windows was also gold. While the exterior on the upper floors was an opaque black glass, the lowest floor was a clean, white stucco. Patrons were flocking in and out of the casino constantly.

Blade walked up the three cement steps to the first door and gripped the handle. He paused long enough to glance across the boulevard at Johnny's Palace.

Hickok was just entering Giorgio's casino.

Blade opened the door and stepped inside, the Commando in his right hand.

Geronimo and Helen followed.

Blade walked several yards and stopped to get his bearings.

The lobby of the Golden Crown was opulently, tastefully furnished with plush red carpet, subdued blue walls decorated with paintings, and chandeliers to provide the illumination. Customers were everywhere.

Geronimo tapped Blade on the left arm and pointed at a sign on the nearby wall.

WELCOME!

The Golden Crown management welcomes you to the ultimate gambling experience! Exchange Centers are located throughout the casino. If you have any questions, our helpful Hostesses will gladly assist you. Enforcers are on the premises at all times to discourage disorderly behavior. The first drink is on the house. Thank you and come again!

Blade surveyed the enormous lobby, scanning the hundreds of people engaged in a variety of activities; some were seated at tables, playing cards; some were seated around a large wheel; others were at tables where cards were pulled from wooden boxes; and over two hundred were yanking levers on odd machines with flashing lights and twirling fruit emblems.

"How will we ever find Mindy in here?" Geronimo wondered aloud.

A petite brunette in a red and black outfit, her red, ruffled skirt barely covering her thighs, approached the Warriors with a wide smile. A square blue plastic tag attached to her black blouse identified her as a HOSTESS. "Hello," she greeted them. "My name is Leslie. Welcome to the Golden Crown."

"Hello," Blade said.

Leslie raked them with a critical eye. "My! You certainly are armed to the teeth! Expecting trouble?"

"You can't be too careful these days," Blade commented.

"May I help you in any way?" Leslie asked.

"We're looking for someone," Blade told her. "A young woman named Mindy."

"Is she an employee of the Golden Crown?" Leslie asked.

"We know she was brought here," Blade replied. "I don't think she would be an employee."

"Is she a guest?" Leslie inquired politely.

"She's my daughter," Helen interjected brusquely.

"I can check the casino register to see if she's a guest,"

Leslie offered. "What's her last name?"

"She doesn't have one," Helen said.

Leslie grinned. "Everyone has a last name."

Helen leaned toward the hostess, her eyes flinty. "We don't. Neither does Mindy. We know she's here. Tell Don Pucci we want her!"

The hostess blinked twice. "Don Pucci?"

"Yes," Blade stated courteously. "We're here at Don Pucci's invitation. Tell him the Warriors have arrived."

"The Warriors?" Leslie repeated quizzically.

"Do it!" Helen snapped impatiently.

Leslie's eyes widened slightly. "I'll be right back," she promised, and walked off to the left.

"Why'd you give us away?" Geronimo asked Blade.

"I didn't," Blade said, glancing at Helen. "Blabbermouth here did."

"I'm sorry," Helen said, not sounding sorry at all. "I'm tired of pussyfooting around! It's obvious we could search for weeks in a building this huge and never find Mindy. So I decided to try Hickok's method, the direct approach."

"Now we're in trouble," Geronimo said.

"Why?" Helen queried.

Geronimo gazed around the casino. "Because Hickok's method only works for Hickok. I call it the Blundering Idiot Principle."

"The harm is done," Blade stated. "We'll have to play it by ear from here on out and pray for the best."

"I'd like it better if Pucci didn't know we're here," Geronimo observed.

Blade cradled the Commando in his arms. The colossal casino would be impossible to search completely from top to bottom, so Helen's blunder was logically justified. But he was peeved at her for taking the initiative without his approval. He intended to submit her to a refresher course in the necessity for Warrior obedience after they returned to the Home.

If they returned.

"Here comes the bimbo," Helen declared.

The hostess walked up to them, smiling sweetly. "I

called the main office. They're sending someone down to see you."

"Thanks," Blade said.

"Mind if I ask you a question?" Geronimo mentioned.

"That's what I'm here for," Leslie responded.

"This is our first trip to Vegas," Geronimo revealed. "And there are some things I don't understand. For instance, why do the casinos accept prewar currency? Without the Government of the United States to back the money, isn't it worthless?"

"Prewar currency is not worthless because it's backed by the casinos," Leslie said. "Let me explain. I asked about this once, and this is what my supervisor told me. There is a lot of prewar currency floating around. Its face value is zero, but the Dons decided to use the prewar currency instead of printing their own money. All of the national mints stopped functioning during the war. No one has the capability to make money. So the Dons use the existing currency at an exchange rate of pennies on the dollar. It's cheaper for them than manufacturing their own."

"But eventually all the prewar currency will wear out," Geronimo noted. "What will they do then?"

"I don't know," Leslie said. "But they have a process for partially restoring really old bills. It will be a long time before all the prewar currency is gone."

"I have a question," Blade remarked. "How is it Las Vegas has so much gas and unlimited electricity?"

"You can get anything on the black market if you have the price," Leslie said enigmatically.

"Are you married?" Helen unexpectedly inquired.

"Yes, I am," Leslie answered. "Why?"

"How can you live in Las Vegas, you being a married woman and all?" Helen questioned.

"I don't understand," Leslie said.

"Look around you! All this gambling. Gangsters all over the place. Shootings on the streets," Helen detailed. "How can you live in such an environment?"

"What's wrong with Vegas?" Leslie responded. "Life here is good. We never have shortages of food, or clothing, or gas. The Dons protect the city from the looters and the mutants. And if you don't carry a gun, odds are you'll never be involved in a shooting. The standard of living in Vegas is higher than in most other parts of the country. The schools are excellent—"

"You have schools?" Blade interrupted.

"Of course, silly," Leslie said. "How else would we educate our children? The Dons funnel a large portion of their profits into the educational system."

"The Dons support the schools?" Blade asked in surprise.

"And the hospitals, and the utilities, and the senior centers," Leslie divulged. "Didn't you know that?"

"No," Blade confessed, "I had no idea."

"The Dons care about their people," Leslie stated affectionately.

"Will wonders never cease!" Geronimo quipped.

A lean man with black hair, a square jaw, and glasses, attired in a white suit, was walking toward the Warriors with a hurried tread. He smiled as he neared them. "Hello. My name is Mario Pileggi. I'm Don Pucci's Operations Manager." He extended his right hand to Blade.

Blade took the hand and shook, Pileggi's firm hand-shake and clear blue eyes disconcerting him. "I'm Blade. This is Helen and Geronimo." He perceived that Pileggi was an urbane, confident man.

"I was told you want to see Don Pucci?" Mario said when Blade released his hand.

"We're here at his invitation," Blade stated.

Mario studied the three Warriors for a few seconds. "This is most mystifying. Perhaps you would be kind enough to accompany me to the main office. We can sort this out there."

"What's to sort out?" Helen demanded. "I want my daughter."

"Where is your daughter?" Mario asked.

"Don't play games! You know she's here. The Don took her!" Helen said angrily.

"Hmmmm," was all Mario replied.

"We would like to get this sorted out as quickly as possible," Blade commented.

"Come with me," Mario said, and turned and headed for the far side of the lobby.

Blade kept his finger on the trigger of the Commando as he crossed the spacious floor. If Mario was leading them into a trap, he wanted to be ready. They passed a row of those odd machines with the lights and rotating pictures of fruit. "What are those?" he inquired.

Mario glanced over his right shoulder, his forehead creased. "You've never seen a slot machine before?"

"No," Blade said.

Mario halted and reached into his left front pants pocket. He withdrew a circular red plastic piece and handed it to the giant.

Blade took the piece. There was lettering on both sides. THE GOLDEN CROWN.

"It's a token," Mario mentioned. "There's a chronic shortage of coins, so we use tokens in some of the slots. This one's on the house."

"Thank you," Blade said, pocketing the token, puzzled.

Mario continued toward the far wall.

Blade was feeling uncharacteristically tense. Something was gnawing at his mind, troubling him. What *was* it? Why was he so certain he was overlooking an important factor in this mission?

A glass-enclosed elevator appeared through the crowd. Mario was heading straight for it.

Blade surveyed the patrons for any sign of Enforcers or button men, but none were in evidence.

Mario indicated the elevator when they were ten feet away. "We'll take this up to the second floor."

"Is Don Pucci's office on the second floor?" Blade queried.

"The main office is on the second floor," Mario replied.

The elevator was large enough to accommodate a dozen occupants. A sign was affixed to the glass in the middle. RESERVED. RESTRICTED USE. Two glass doors comprised the front of the elevator.

"The public elevators are over there," Mario said, pointing at four elevators 20 yards to the left.

"I was surprised to find this casino so close to Don Giorgio's," Blade absently commented.

Mario, about to reach for the gold handles in the center of the glass doors, froze and turned. "You know Don Giorgio?"

"No," Blade said.

Mario's mouth curled downwards. "Giorgio is an upstart. He deliberately built his casino across from Don Pucci's."

"Why?" Blade asked. "To increase his business?"

"Not hardly," Mario answered. "He had ulterior motives." He opened the elevator doors. "After you."

"After you," Blade said.

Mario shrugged and entered the elevator, standing next to a panel of buttons.

The Warriors stepped into the elevator.

Mario closed the doors and pushed a button marked with a 2. The elevator started upward.

"Are Don Pucci and Don Giorgio friends?" Blade questioned.

Mario laughed bitterly. "Friends isn't the word I would use."

The elevator coasted to a stop on the second floor. Below, the lobby was a jumble of bustling movement.

Mario turned. The rear of the elevator was a seemingly solid black plastic wall. He pressed a black button on the panel and the "wall" slid into a recessed slot on the right, revealing a lengthy corridor beyond.

Blade realized the glass portion only faced the lobby. Access to the corridors was through this rear door.

"Allow me," Mario said, taking the lead and exiting. He took an abrupt right.

Blade, Geronimo, and Helen stepped from the elevator.

Mario had stopped and was facing them, grinning triumphantly. The rear door to the elevator hissed shut. "Would you care to tell me the real reason you want to see the Don?"

"We've already told you," Helen responded testily. "I want my daughter."

Mario sighed and raised his right hand. "I was hoping you would cooperate." He snapped his fingers.

Doors all along the corridor suddenly opened, disgorging over a dozen somber men in suits, each armed with a machine gun. They trained their weapons on the Warriors.

"If you make a move," Mario warned in a pleasant tone, "you're dead."

CHAPTER TEN

Hickok strolled into Johnny's Palace with the Henry slung over his back and his thumbs hooked in his gunbelt. He paused just inside one of the seven glass doors, studying the layout.

Johnny's Palace was ornate, garishly decorated with an ostentatious green carpet and gaudy orange and yellow walls. Oversized chandeliers hung from the arched ceiling. The gambling was in full swing and customers crammed the joint.

A pretty blonde in a transparent, skimpy yellow dress walked up to the gunman.

"Hi there, handsome," she declared, smiling broadly. "Looking for a good time?"

Hickok noticed an orange tag imprinted with the word ESCORT pinned below her left shoulder. "Howdy, ma'am," he replied. "I'm lookin' for Don Giorgio."

The escort lost her smile. "Why do you want to see him?"

"That's personal," Hickok said.

"No one can see Don Giorgio without an appointment,"

the escort stated.

"Where would I find him?" Hickok asked.

"Didn't you hear me?" the escort responded. "You can't see him without an appointment."

Hickok lowered his voice. "Ma'am, if you don't spill the beans, right this moment, I'm afraid I'll be obliged to shoot you in the foot."

The escort did a double take. "You wouldn't dare!"

Hickok's mouth creased in a lopsided grin. "Try me."

She scrutinized him from head to toe, then stared into his blue eyes for a moment. "I just bet you'd do it too!"

"Where can I find Giorgio?" Hickok queried again.

"You're making a big mistake, mister," the escort said.

"I make 'em all the time," Hickok noted. "So what's one more? Now where is Giorgio?"

The escort turned and pointed at a wall on the opposite side of the lobby. "Do you see those doors there?"

Hickok looked. There were three wooden doors spaced about 20 yards apart visible through the crowd. "Yep."

"The middle door is Don Giorgio's office," she said.

"Is that a fact?" Hickok commented. "You wouldn't lie to me, would you?"

Her cheeks reddened. "Don't you believe me?"

"Nope," Hickok stated. "The Don isn't likely to have his office right out in the open, where anyone can mosey in anytime they feel like it. I'd imagine the Don is one cautious hombre. So where is his real office?"

The escort frowned. "Third floor. He has a suite at the end of the hall. The elevators and the stairs are to the left of those doors."

Hickok reached up and patted her on the left cheek. "Thank you, ma'am. That wasn't so hard, was it?"

"If the Don discovers I told you," she said fearfully, "he'll kill me!"

"Don't you worry," Hickok assured her. "He'll never know." He motioned at the wall to his right. "I want you to stand right there, where I can keep an eye on you, until I get across the lobby. You might be tempted to warn the Don, and I can't let you do that."

The escort walked over to the wall and stood there meekly.

"Thanks again," Hickok said cheerfully, and started toward the far side of the room. He scanned the packed patrons, noting the various games they were playing.

Out of the corner of his right eye, Hickok saw the blonde escort edging toward a wooden door 15 feet from the front entrance. He grinned, but otherwise pretended not to notice. Another minute or so and he'd have the welcoming committee he wanted.

The throng of spectators and gamblers shifted, and Hickok caught sight of three men in suits, men with countenances hardened like granite. None held weapons, but their jackets were open and each man had one hand near his waist.

"Excuse me!" a voice commanded, and Mousy appeared, shoving his way through the spectators.

Hickok grinned. "Well, if it isn't Wart-Nose," he addressed the diminutive mobster. "Long time no see!"

Mousy's beady eyes narrowed. "Don't call me Wart-Nose!"

"How about Poop-for-Brains?" Hickok quipped.

"Funny man!" Mousy snapped. "But you made the biggest mistake of your life when you waltzed into here!"

"I didn't waltz," Hickok corrected him. "I walked."

"Did you really think Don Giorgio would see you?" Mousy demanded.

"It'd be the smart thing to do," Hickok remarked.

"What do you know about smarts?" Mousy declared. "You're so dumb, it's pathetic."

"Are you going to take me to Don Giorgio?" Hickok inquired.

"Dream on!" Mousy said.

"He doesn't want to talk to me?"

Mousy snorted. "He wants to snuff you, jerk! You and all of your friends are to blame for his son's death!"

"You've got it all wrong, Wart-Nose," Hickok baited the button man.

"No, I don't!" Mousy snapped. "The big geek with the

knives told me that you guys whacked Franky!''

Hickok shook his head. "They didn't. I did."

"You killed Franky?" Mousy queried, astounded the gunman would bluntly confess.

"Yep," Hickok said. "I was the one who plugged Franky. My pards shot Franky's cronies."

Mousy glanced at his chums. "Did you hear this jerk?"

"Enough small talk," Hickok stated. "I want you to take me to Giorgio. Now."

Mousy snickered. "No way."

"Take me or die," Hickok said softly.

The spectators abruptly wanted to be somewhere else. They scrambled to put as much distance as possible between themselves and the imminent violence. All except for an elderly woman, who kept avidly sticking coins into her purse.

"Do you really think you can take on all four of us by yourself?" Mousy asked sarcastically.

"If you try and draw on me," Hickok responded, "none of you will live long enough to touch your guns."

"You smug asshole!" Mousy declared. "You're history!" He grabbed for the pistol in a concealed holster on his right hip.

The other three mobsters also went for their guns. All three were experienced Enforcers, experts at their lethal craft. Each one considered himself fast and accurate. Each one had outdrawn opponents at one time or another. But not one had ever beheld the spectacular speed of the gunfighter in buckskins.

One moment Hickok's hands were draped at his sides. The next, in a literal blur of consummate swiftness, the Pythons were out and leveled and blasting.

Mousy was hit high on the forehead by both slugs, the brutal impact catapulting him backwards into a blackjack table. He crashed onto his back, his arms outspread.

Hickok swiveled to cover the remaining three hit men. They were imitating trees, frozen in place with their limbs at odd angles, having turned to ice in the process of reaching for their weapons. Not one had managed to move their gun hand more than an inch. "What's it going to be, gents?" Hickok asked. "Do you want to die?"

Each one shook his head.

"Then unlimber your hardware, real easy like," Hickok instructed them. "One wrong twitch and I'll perforate your noggins."

The mobsters carefully eased their handguns from their holsters and ever-so-slowly set the guns on the floor.

"Now back up three steps," Hickok directed.

They obeyed.

Hickok heard a door slam and glanced at the far wall. A dozen mobsters were coming toward him, led by a tall man with a cleft chin, a beaked nose, dark eyes, and white hair, and wearing a gray suit. Many of the mobsters carried machine guns, and Hickok girded himself for a battle royal. He grinned, hoping he would acquit himself with honor.

"Don't shoot!" the man with the white hair shouted. "Don't shoot! We want to talk!"

The mobsters were over 40 yards off, but still advancing.

"That's close enough!" Hickok called out.

The man with the white hair said something to his henchmen and they halted.

"What do we have to talk about?" Hickok yelled.

"We don't want any more shooting!" the man with the white hair said. "Can I come closer?"

"Come ahead," Hickok replied.

The man with the white hair cautiously came toward the Warrior. He stared at Mousy's corpse for several seconds, then at the patrons ringing the lobby. "My name is Kenney," he said when he was within speaking range.

"You're Giorgio's right-hand man?" Hickok queried, recalling the comments Mousy made in the alley earlier.

Kenney nodded. He stopped, scrutinizing the gunfighter. "Who are you?"

"The handle is . . ." Hickok began, and paused. What name should he give? Blade had given a false name to that Enforcer because the Big Guy didn't want Don Pucci to know the Warriors were in Las Vegas. Should he do the same? If he gave his real name, would Pucci find out? Did it even matter, since Blade and the others were in the Golden Crown rescuing Mindy? Maybe he should play it safe. "Earp. Wyatt Earp."

Kenney's eyes narrowed and his forehead creased. "Mr. Earp, my boss would like to talk to you."

"Don Giorgio wants to see me?" Hickok responded skeptically.

"Yes. He sent me down to invite you up to his suite," Kenney said. "He's been watching you since Security reported you were here."

"He has?" Hickok queried.

"Yes," Kenney confirmed. "The whole casino is under constant surveillance by hidden cameras."

"Why does Giorgio want to see me?" Hickok questioned.

"You must ask him," Kenney replied. "Will you come with me?"

Hickok nodded toward the other mobsters. "What about those cow chips?"

"They'll stay down here, if such is your wish," Kenney said.

"It'd make me feel a mite more relaxed," Hickok remarked. "My trigger fingers can become awful itchy."

"You won't need your guns," Kenney commented. "No harm will come to you."

"No one is takin' my Colts," Hickok vowed.

"I simply meant you don't need to keep your revolvers in your hands," Kenney elaborated. "You can put them in your holsters."

"They'll stay right where they are," Hickok said. "You lead the way. And whatever you do, don't trip. I might accidentally blow your spine out your bellybutton."

Kenney turned and walked toward the far wall. "There won't be any trouble," he said over his left shoulder.

"For your sake, I hope not," Hickok stated. He constantly shifted his gaze from gangster to gangster, ready to gun down the first one who made a hostile move. But they and stood still, eyeing him contemptuously. What was

Giorgio up to? he wondered. Giorgio didn't sound like the forgiving sort. So why did Giorgio want to palaver all of a sudden?

And why, Hickok asked himself, did he have the feeling he was going from the frying pan into the fire?

CHAPTER ELEVEN

Blade could feel his stomach muscles tightening into a compact knot as he stared at the machine guns trained on Helen, Geronimo, and himself.

"Drop your weapons!" Mario commanded.

"Never!" Helen snapped. "Hand over my daughter!"

Mario adjusted his glasses on his nose. He gazed at the giant and spoke calmly. "I don't want any needless bloodshed."

"Neither do we," Blade assured him.

"Then drop your weapons," Mario directed. "You'll be cut down if you try to resist."

Blade glanced at the man in the white suit, gauging the distance between them as four feet. "You won't shoot if we put our weapons on the floor?" he asked.

"No. You have my personal guarantee," Mario stated.

"Okay," Blade said meekly. "We'll do it."

"I won't!" Helen objected. "No one is taking my weapons!"

Blade looked at her. "You'll do exactly as I say!" he ordered. "After I put my Commando down, you do the

same with your carbine." He deliberately accented the
word "after."

Helen frowned. "If you insist!"

Blade gazed at Geronimo. "Do you understand?"

Geronimo nodded. "I understand perfectly."

Blade faced the man in white. "Here goes. Tell your
men not to shoot."

"They won't fire unless I give the signal," Mario
disclosed.

Blade nodded. "I was hoping you would say that." He
bent over at the waist and deposited his Commando on the
red carpet. Releasing the gun, he started to straighten, and
as he did he made his move. His right hand whipped his
corresponding Bowie free of its sheath, even as he bounded
toward Mario, covering the four feet in an easy, quick
stride. Before the mobsters in the corridor could fire, he
had his left arm around Mario's shoulders and the right
Bowie pressed against the gangster's neck.

Several of the button men had swiveled, trying to bring
their machine guns to bear on the giant, but he had moved
too swiftly and was too close to Mario Pileggi to permit
them to fire.

"Freeze!" Blade barked, using Mario's body as a shield.
"If just one of you tries anything, this man is dead!"

Mario appeared stunned by the unexpected reversal.
"Don't shoot!" he shouted at his men. "Do as he says!"

"I want all of your guns on the floor! Now!" Blade
instructed them.

The hit men hesitated, collectively focused on Mario.

"Do it!" Mario yelled. "Now!"

Hesitantly, the mobsters slowly lowered their machine
guns to the floor.

"Now put your hands up and step away from your
guns!" Blade declared.

"Do it!" Mario added.

The button men moved back.

Geronimo hastily retrieved Blade's Commando while
keeping his Browning BAR trained on their foes.

Blade dug the tip of the Bowie into Mario's sweating

neck. "Now I want to see Don Pucci."

"Never!" Mario said.

"Let me have him!" Helen interjected, incensed. "I'll make him take us to Pucci!"

"Never!" Mario reiterated. "None of us will betray our Don!"

"How touching!" Helen said sarcastically. "He's being loyal to the bastard who kidnapped my daughter!"

Mario's eyes narrowed as he intently studied Helen. "You're serious!" he exclaimed.

Helen took a menacing stride toward him. "Of course I'm serious, you dimwit! What have I been telling you! The Don abducted Mindy, and I want her back now!"

Mario tried to twist his head so he could see the giant holding him, but the sharp point of the Bowie prevented him from turning. "You can release me," he said.

"Not on your life," Blade stated. "You're our ticket out of here, our insurance against interference."

"If you want to see Don Pucci, you'd better let me go," Mario advised. "I promise you I'll arrange a meeting."

"Why should we trust you?" Blade demanded.

"Because I believe your story," Mario said. "I believe this woman's daughter was abducted, and I believe you think Don Pucci is responsible. I didn't believe her before. I thought you were using the story as a ruse to get close to the Don so you could whack him."

"If he took my daughter," Helen remarked bitterly, "he's as good as dead!"

Blade glanced at Geronimo. "Cover us. I'm going to release him."

Geronimo nodded, scrutinizing the hit men.

Blade eased his Bowie away from Mario's neck and straightened. "There. Now let's see if your word is worth anything."

Mario gingerly rubbed his sore neck with his right hand, and when he withdrew his hand there was a trickle of blood on his fingers. "That's some knife you've got there," he mentioned.

Blade wiped the Bowie on his pants leg. "I'm fond of it."

"I'll escort you down to the casino," Mario said. "You can wait there until Don Pucci comes down. And don't worry. We're not about to attack you in our own casino. Business would suffer."

"What do you mean?" Blade asked.

"The casino is our drawing card, so to speak," Mario elaborated. "Our rooms on the upper floors are always filled to capacity because our customers know they can gamble here in safety. They know Don Pucci runs an honest house, unlike some of the other Dons. Whenever you have a shooting in a casino, business suffers. The customers shy away for a while. We don't want that."

Blade walked over to Geronimo and took the Commando. "We'll wait for Don Pucci, and you have my word that we won't start shooting unless you start something."

"We won't," Mario assured the giant. He moved to the wall and pressed a red button, then looked at Helen. "I'm sorry I didn't believe you. But you must understand my position. There are a lot of people who would like to see Don Pucci dead, and I would give my life to protect him. So would everyone else in his Family."

"Why did Don Pucci kidnap my daughter?" Helen asked bluntly.

"He didn't," Mario replied.

"I know better," Helen stated.

"You can talk to the Don in person," Mario said. "Then let's see how you feel."

The inner door to the elevator slid open as the elevator arrived on the second floor.

Mario entered.

The Warriors backed into the elevator, their weapons aimed at the mobsters in the corridor.

Blade breathed a slight sigh of relief when the door slid shut. He gazed down at the throngs of gamblers as the elevator descended, spying a long bar on the south side of the enormous room. Anyone approaching the bar from the gaming tables and the slot machines would need to cover 20 yards of open space. The bar was an ideal spot to await the Don.

With a scarcely perceptible jolt, the elevator stopped.

Mario exited first, standing to the right of the open doors.

"We'll be waiting at the bar," Blade said as he emerged.

"Give me ten minutes," Mario said.

"Five," Blade amended as Geronimo and Helen joined him.

Mario shook his head. "I need ten. You'll understand the reason when you see the Don."

"Ten, then," Blade said. "But one minute longer and we'll tear your casino apart."

Mario stepped into the elevator, closed the doors, and nodded at the Warriors as it climbed.

"I don't trust him!" Helen opined. "Why did you agree to this nonsense?"

"Sometimes a Warrior must rely on his or her intuition," Blade answered. "My intuition tells me to trust Mario this time."

"I pray you're right," Helen said. She scanned the patrons at the nearby tables, her features downcast. "All I want is to find Mindy and return safely to the Home. Is that too much to ask?"

"No," Blade stated. He headed in the direction of the bar, alert for an assault.

"If it's any consolation," Geronimo commented, staying abreast of Blade on the right, "I agree with you."

The Warriors skirted the gaming tables and the slot machines, winding toward the south side of the casino. The laughter, the tinkle of glasses filled with liquor, and the smiling customers were an odd contrast to the deadly mobsters running the establishment. Blade observed the patrons heartily enjoying themselves, and he remembered the words of the woman at the diner. The Organized Crime Families had controlled Las Vegas for over a century, and the citizens and tourists all seemed content with the status quo. Why? How could they allow their lives to be run by the Dons? Was it because life under the Dons was better, in a materialistic sense, than life elsewhere in the country? Was it because the Dons were no more oppressive than the government which they had supplanted? Or was it because the Dons and Las Vegas were made for each other? They both flourished in an atmosphere of permissiveness and they naturally attracted others of a similar persuasion.

The bar appeared ahead.

Blade ceased his reflection and walked up to the middle of the bar.

"I wonder how Hickok is doing," Geronimo commented.

"As soon as we finish our business here," Blade said, "we'll go get him."

"If anything happens to him," Geronimo pledged, "I won't leave Las Vegas until I settle accounts with Don Giorgio."

"Look!" Helen declared. "The elevator."

The glass elevator was descending.

"Here they come!" Helen said excitedly. "Now we'll learn where Mindy is!"

A party of men left the elevator and moved through the customers, coming toward the Warriors.

Blade's superior height enabled him to see the party clearly, and his forehead furrowed in confusion when he spotted the head of the group.

"Don Pucci better turn Mindy over to us!" Helen was saying.

Blade stared at the floor, deep in thought.

"What is it?" Geronimo inquired.

"You'll see in a moment," Blade responded.

The party of mobsters came even closer. There were ten men, eight of whom were armed with machine guns. The ninth was Mario. And the tenth was a man with gray hair, a man with a thin face and a pale complexion, a man in a beige suit with a red blanket covering his lap because he was seated in a wheelchair!

"What the hell is this?" Helen snapped.

The eight men with machine guns fanned out around

Mario and the man in the wheelchair, forming a protective semicircle.

Mario pushed the wheelchair up to the Warriors. "Allow me the honor of introducing Don Anthony Pucci."

"Hello," Blade said.

"This is the Don?" Helen inquired in shocked disbelief.

Don Pucci's piercing blue eyes belied his physical condition. He critically inspected each of the Warriors, then focused on Blade, "Mario has been telling me about you," he stated in a deep, vibrant voice. "I don't often leave my private quarters anymore, but I decided to make an exception in your case." He looked at Helen. "What is this bull about my kidnapping your daughter?"

Helen was completely confounded. "You can't be the Don!" she blurted out.

Don Pucci grinned. "I assure you I am. Ask anyone." He caught sight of one of the bartenders behind the bar, busily tending to a customer. "Hey! Arthur!"

The bartender glanced up, saw the man in the wheelchair, and instantly hastened down the bar. "Yes, sir! What would you like?"

"Arthur, would you tell this woman who I am?" Don Pucci requested.

Arthur gazed at Helen. "He's Don Pucci. Everybody knows that."

"Thank you, Arthur," the Don said. "How's the family?"

Arthur, a hefty man with a mustache, smiled. "They're fine, sir. Bobby has a birthday in a week. He'll be ten."

"Expect a little gift for him," Don Pucci stated.

Arthur beamed. "Thank you, sir! He'll really appreciate a present from you!"

"That will be all for now," Don Pucci said.

Arthur returned to his customer.

Don Pucci glanced at Mario. "Make a note. Send a gift to the kid. He'll be ten, so make it a toy fire engine. The biggest you can buy."

"Consider it done," Mario said.

Don Pucci stared at Blade. "Now to business. Out of courtesy I came down to meet you. I don't want any trouble in my casino. And I understand you believe you have a grievance against me."

"We came to see you because we believed you were responsible for abducting Helen's daughter," Blade explained. "But the man who kidnapped Mindy did not look anything like you."

Don Pucci folded his hands under his chin. "Why did you suspect me?"

"Because the man gave your name," Blade disclosed.

The Don stiffened. "He used my name?"

Blade absently stared at the crowd, striving to unravel the mystery of Mindy's abduction, to piece together the parts of the puzzle. Why would someone take Mindy and claim to be Don Pucci? He noticed four men in suits and hats casually moving through the crowd in the direction of the bar. Each man was approximately 15 to 20 yards apart, as if they were trying to convey the impression of being alone. He sensed they were working in tandem, and his Warrior's instinct sounded a siren warning in his mind.

Don Pucci's men had not noticed. Most of them were concentrating on the Warriors.

Blade was cradling the Commando in his arms. He carefully slid his trigger finger through the trigger guard.

"I want to know everything about this man," Don Pucci was saying. "But not here. I would like you to come up to my quarters."

The four men were within ten yards of the Don's party. Each man had a hand under his suit coat.

Blade knew he had mere seconds to react. If he cut loose, the Don's men would gun him down. If he did nothing, the Don would be assassinated and the Warriors would lose a potential ally in their search for Mindy. Before he could rationalize a course of action, the four men confirmed their hostile intent.

Three of them pulled pistols, the fourth a sawed-off shotgun, and in unison they charged!

CHAPTER TWELVE

Don Giorgio's suite on the third floor of his Palace was furnished much like the casino; it was tawdry and pretentious. The carpet was off-green, the walls orange and blue. All of the furniture was polished to a sheen.

Hickok cautiously followed Kenney into the Don's inner sanctum, the Pythons cocked, anticipating a trap. They crossed a large room containing only 14 empty chairs, evidently a waiting room for those with appointments to see the Don, or the room where the button men congregated to await the Don's orders. The second room they encountered, a spacious office, was likewise unoccupied.

"This is my office," Kenney commented.

They came to a closed wooden door and halted.

Kenney rapped three times. "It's me," he announced. "He has me covered."

"Come in," a gruff voice declared.

Kenney opened the door and a Python barrel touched the back of his neck.

"Go real slow," Hickok advised.

Kenney shuffled into the next room, a huge chamber

with thick carpeting, several maple chairs, a sofa, and a wide desk aligned against the opposite wall.

Hickok kept his left Colt against Kenney's neck as he vigilantly advanced into Don Giorgio's office.

Three men were already there.

Seated behind the maple desk was a man with a strikingly harsh visage. He had steely, hawkish brown eyes and exceptionally bushy brows. His mouth was a thin slit, his hair black and slicked. He wore a black suit. An aura of palpable menace enshrouded him.

This, Hickok instinctively knew, was Don Giorgio.

A youngish man in a brown suit stood to the right of the desk, his arms folded across his chest. He had green eyes and a pointed chin.

A trigger man, Hickok guessed.

The man standing to the left of the desk was older, with streaks of gray in his otherwise brown hair. His cheeks and chin sagged, as if his skin was too tired to support his face. His brown eyes nervously examined the Warrior. He was wearing a dark blue suit.

Another hit man, Hickok reasoned.

The man behind the desk extended his arms in a friendly fashion, palms outward. "There's no need for the hardware, friend! I invited you up here to talk."

Hickok gave Kenney a shove.

Kenney stumbled several feet, then caught himself and turned. "There was no need for that," he said.

Hickok motioned with his Colts to the left.

Kenney took five steps to the left.

Hickok stared at the man behind the desk. "So you want to shoot the breeze?"

"I'm Don Giorgio," the man stated haughtily.

"I know who you are," Hickok said. "But I don't know why I should let you live."

"Let me live?" Giorgio repeated in surprise. "I asked you to come here as a token of my good will, and now you want to waste me?"

Hickok pointed both Pythons at the Don.

Giorgio, to his credit, didn't so much as flinch. But the

other three tensed, the young one dropping his hands to his
sides and glaring at the gunslinger.

"I heard you aim to plug my pards and me for shootin'
your two-bit, four-flushin' son," Hickok stated.

Giorgio's face reddened and his eyes narrowed. He
seemed to wrestle with his emotions for a moment, then
was calm. "Franky always was a hothead. He was always
getting into fights over trifles. I tried to teach him not to
sweat the small stuff, but he wouldn't listen." Giorgio
paused. "The Enforcers report his death was a fair and
square. Technically, I have no right to hold his death
against you."

"Get to the point," Hickok prompted.

"The point, Mister . . ." Giorgio began, then stopped.
"What is your name, anyway?"

"He says his name is Earp," Kenney answered. "Wyatt
Earp."

Giorgio's forehead creased as he stared at the gunman.
"Mr. Earp, then. I wanted you to know I'm forgoing my
right to petition the Council for a sanction to snuff you."

"This must be my lucky day," Hickok quipped.
"Why?"

"Why look a gift horse in the mouth?" Giorgio
rejoined. "You should be grateful I'm not claiming my
blood right."

"Why?" Hickok repeated his question.

Giorgio leaned back in his chair. "It would be bad
business to whack you. By tonight everyone in Las Vegas
will have heard about Franky, and they'll know his death
was a fair and square. If I take action against you, I hurt
my own reputation. Oh, I could call for a Council of the
Dons and ask for a sanction to hit you. Every Don can ask
for a Council whenever a grievance arises. I could present
my case and demand a vote, and if the other Dons agreed
and Don Pucci okayed the decision, you would be dead by
morning. But word would get around. People would
whisper behind my back. They would say I'd done wrong
because Franky's death was a fair and square. Do you
follow me?"

"So you won't kill me because it would be bad for your reputation and your business?" Hickok queried critically.

"That's it in a nutshell," Don Giorgio said.

Hickok snickered. "So much for family devotion."

"What do you say?" Giorgio asked. "Do we shake hands and call it quits?"

"Not so fast," Hickok said. "What about the runt downstairs?"

"I didn't tell him to try and gun you down," Giorgio replied. "He did that on his own. I don't like gunplay in my casino. It affects the trade."

"Then I'm free to go?" Hickok inquired.

Giorgio nodded. "And I want you to know there's no hard feelings. In fact, I'd like you to spend time in my casino as my personal guest. All the chips and eats will be on me. What do you say?"

Hickok twirled the Colts into their holsters. "How can I refuse an offer like that?"

"Kenney will take you downstairs," Giorgio said. "He'll provide you with everything you need."

"Thanks," Hickok stated. He backed toward the door.

"Can you wait for me in the hallway?" Kenney asked the gunman. "I'll be there in a minute."

"No problem," Hickok responded. He hooked his thumbs in his gunbelt and strolled out.

Kenney moved to the door and watched until the gunfighter had passed through his office, the waiting room, and closed the hall door behind him. He faced the Don. "Before I take that clown downstairs, I need to know what's going on."

"Yeah, boss," Sacks chimed in. "I don't get none of this. How come you're letting that scumbag live after he snuffed Franky?"

Giorgio gazed at Kenney. "I want you to treat him to a good time. You know who he is, don't you?"

Kenney nodded. "I figured it out. He's one of those Warriors. Hickok, right?"

"Right," Giorgio verified. "Which means the Warriors are already in Vegas. Give him anything he wants. Find

Nadine. Tell her to hit on him. I want him to spend the night. If he leaves the Palace, I'm to be informed immediately. Understand?''

"Got you," Kenney answered. He wheeled and departed.

Sacks shook his head, clearly bemused. "I don't get none of this, boss."

"I hate to admit it," Ozzi chimed in, "but neither do I."

"Then I'll have to explain it to you," Giorgio said. "I don't want my lieutenants in the dark, so I'll spell everything out." He paused and stared at Ozzi. "Do you remember about a year ago, when that drifter lost a couple of grand at poker and couldn't pay up?"

"Sure I do," Ozzi said. "You were going to have me break his legs."

"That was the one," Giorgio confirmed. "He tried to trade information in exchange for cancelling his debt. He claimed he knew about a Federation which might pose a threat to the Dons. He said this Freedom Federation, as it's called, planned to consolidate their forces and conquer the western half of what was once the United States. He told me all about this Federation, about the different factions in it. I found his information very, very interesting, and I later verified most of it. There is a Freedom Federation, and they do have a protective association, of sorts. But they're no threat to the Dons."

"Do the other Dons know about this Federation?" Ozzi queried.

"I don't know," Giorgio replied. "I don't think so. This Federation has kept pretty much to itself, all except for one faction. They're known as the Family."

Sacks grinned and slapped his right thigh. "They're the ones in Minnesota! The ones who live at the Home!"

"Give the man a cigar!" Giorgio cracked. "Yeah. The very same. I discovered they have a heavy rep, especially their fighters, the Warriors. These Warriors have taken on the Ruskies, the Technics, even the Doktor, and they came out on top every time. The more I learned about these Warriors, the more convinced I became that they were the ones to help me snuff Pucci."

"Now you lost me," Sacks said.

"I'm not surprised," Giorgio stated dryly. "Anyway, I sent out feelers to all my sources. I learned all I could about the Warriors. I even found out some of their names: Blade, Hickok, Geronimo, Yama, Rikki, and Bertha. And I discovered a pattern."

"What kind of pattern?" Ozzi questioned.

Giorgio smiled. "Simply this. Every time the Home was attacked, or any time Family members were whacked, or kidnapped, or even just injured, the Warriors went after the party responsible. No matter what the odds, no matter how badly they were outnumbered or outgunned, the Warriors *always* made the offenders pay. They always exacted retribution," he said with sincere admiration.

"They sound like us," Sacks commented.

Giorgio snorted. "They are nothing like us. Their Family and our Families are as different as night and day. They believe in a lot of spiritual garbage, and they don't know the value of power and money. But the Warriors are as deadly a bunch of professionals as you'd ever want to meet. They're tops."

"You sound like you respect them," Ozzie remarked.

"I do," Giorgio responded. "Don't ever underestimate them."

"Even the bozo in the buckskins?" Ozzi asked.

"Especially him," Giorgio answered. "He may come across as a dummy, but I hear it's all an act. Hickok is one of the deadliest Warriors."

"He's a fast son of a bitch," Sacks mentioned. "Did you see him on the monitor when he shot Dirkson?"

"I saw him," Ozzi said.

"If you two are finished flapping your gums," Giorgio declared, "I'd like to continue."

"Sorry, boss," Sacks said.

"You didn't tell us all this before you took us to Minnesota," Ozzi noted. "You didn't tell us a thing until we were on the road, and then all you said was that we were going to make an important snatch, and that our

Family would be taking over Vegas. You kept saying the snatch was important, but you never told us the reason. How come you're coming clean now?''

"Necessity," Giorgio responded. "I didn't tell anyone about my plans to go to Minnesota except for Kenney because I didn't want a leak. I didn't want Pucci to find out what I was up to. And I had to tell Kenney because I left him in charge of my operations while I was gone." He paused. "Now, everything has changed. My plan isn't working the way I thought it would. We could be in for some rough weather, and I want my top men aware of the situation.''

"Gee, boss," Sacks interjected. "Thanks for the compliment.''

Giorgio sighed. "Anyway, I devised a scheme to use the Warriors to whack Pucci. I figured I could snatch one of the Family, pin the blame on Pucci, and the Warriors would take care of the rest. Considering their heavy rep, I knew they'd come after whoever we kidnapped. I expected them to come to Vegas, look up Pucci, and that would be that." He grinned at the deviousness of his plot.

"That would be what, boss?" Sacks wanted to know.

"The Warriors would take care of Pucci for me," Giorgio replied impatiently. "I've tried three times in the past eight years to whack that bastard, and each time I failed. The last attempt put him in a wheelchair for life, but I want him dead! I should be the top Don in Vegas, not that old prick! He doesn't deserve to rule Vegas! He's old, he's past his prime, and he should be put out to pasture. And I'm the man who's going to do it!"

"What about the Warriors?" Ozzi queried. "You said your plan isn't working.''

"Hickok is here, so some of the other Warriors must be here too. But I haven't heard anything about them making a hit on Pucci. Instead, I hear about these four strangers responsible for killing Franky. I got descriptions of the four, but I didn't put two and two together until Hickok came into the Palace," Giorgio said. "When I saw him on the monitor, I remembered the description I was given on the Warriors. Blade is supposed to be a big guy who always packs Bowies. Hickok wear buckskins and pearl-handled Colts. And one of the guys who whacked Franky's crew was a giant with knives. Then a man in buckskins shows up in my joint and uses a phony name. That clinched it!''

"He used a phony name?" Sacks interrupted.

"Wyatt Earp, remember?" Giorgio reminded him.

"Oh. Yeah. How'd you know it was phony?" Sacks inquired.

Giorgio shook his head in disgust. "Because I went to school, dummy. Wyatt Earp was one of the guys we studied in history class. He was sort of an ancient wiseguy.''

"Do you think the Warriors know you set them up to kill Pucci?" Ozzi asked. "Do you think they hit Franky on purpose?"

"No," Giorgio said. "The Enforcers and the witnesses swear Franky started it. Franky goaded them into the fight. The jackass! He was an insult to my lineage!''

"But he was your only son!" Sacks stated.

"Don't remind me!" Giorgio snapped. "I should have spent more time with him when he was a kid. He was a spoiled brat, and he didn't know what it meant to be a made man. If he'd played his cards right, he could have inherited my empire. Once I take out Pucci, I'll go after the other Dons. Everyone says the Seven Families War eighty years ago was bloody and horrible, but they haven't seen a thing yet! By the time I'm through, the Seven Families War will seem like a picnic!''

"Why haven't the Warriors snuffed Pucci yet?" Ozzi asked.

"I don't know," Giorgio admitted. "But I'm not sitting on my ass waiting for them to hit the prick! I've hired a hit squad of independents to take care of Pucci if he shows his face in the casino.''

"What about Hickok? Why is he here?" Ozzi probed.

Giorgio pondered for a moment. "He came to see if I wanted revenge for Franky."

"And do you?" Ozzi questioned.

Giorgio's mouth twisted downward. "Of course! Franky was a moron, but he was blood. I'll keep tabs on Hickok, try to find out where the rest of the Warriors are, and if they've outlived their usefulness to me, I'll have them whacked."

"Gee, boss," Sacks said. "You think of everything. If the Warriors whack Don Pucci, no one will think to blame you. You can take over Vegas without the other Dons ganging up on you."

"I'll do it one way or the other," Giorgio vowed. "Pucci's Family isn't as strong as it was eighty years ago. If the Warriors waste him, the other Dons will easily come under my thumb. But even if the Warriors blow it, Pucci *is* going down. I will be the top Don by the end of the year."

Ozzi straightened attentively. "With your indulgence, there's a matter I'd like to discuss with you."

Giorgio smirked. "As if I couldn't guess."

"I respectfully ask your permission," Ozzi said.

"I knew this was coming," Giorgio commented. "I saw the way you were looking at her all the way back from Minnesota. And I saw you threaten to rack Nicky if he laid his hands on her."

"Will you consent?" Ozzi asked.

"Why do you want her? She's an outsider," Giorgio remarked. "Why not pick one of the local girls? You could have the cream of the crop. You're a made man. A big wheel in my organization."

"I want Mindy," Ozzi stated.

"What do you see in her?" Giorgio inquired.

"I don't know how to describe my feelings," Ozzi responded. "I've never felt like this before."

Giorgio grinned. "Some call it love. I call it lust. If you want to marry her, she's yours. But there are two conditions."

"Name them," Ozzi said eagerly.

"First, you wait until this Warrior business is resolved," Giorgio directed.

"As you wish," Ozzi stated dutifully.

"Second, you convince her the marriage is in her best

interests," Giorgio said. "She's a little hellcat when she gets her temper up. I don't want one of my lieutenants dragging his betrothed down the aisle the day of the wedding. Everyone would talk."

"I'll convince her she loves me," Ozzi pledged. "Even if I must slap her around a bit. She'll get the message."

"You have the right attitude," Giorgio said approvingly. "A woman needs to be slapped around now and then to keep her in line. Sock her in the gut. That usually works for me. They don't like to be bruised, so you've got to be careful when you hit her in the face."

"Can I go see her now?" Ozzi queried.

"Go ahead."

"What about me, boss?" Sacks asked.

"I want you to go down to the casino," Giorgio directed. "Keep an eye on Hickok. Send Kenney up to me."

"Okay," Sacks said.

"I'll give the Warriors until tomorrow to off Don Pucci," Giorgio remarked. "If they don't, I can only assume they don't intend to kill him. I'll put out a contract on every Warrior in town."

Ozzi and Sacks exited the room.

Don Giorgio stared at the doorway, reflecting. Ozzi was one of his best button men, but the kid was soft in the noodle. Imagine being dumb enough to fall for the skirt from the family! Mindy was a liability, incriminating evidence. The girl had to be snuffed, and Kenney was just the man to do it. An accident could be arranged. The poor bimbo would hang herself from a light fixture. All Kenney would need to do would be arrange a scheduling snafu so the girl's room was unguarded for a while.

Ozzi would be heartbroken.

But those were the breaks!

CHAPTER THIRTEEN

The four hit men were closing in on Don Pucci's party.

Blade did the only thing he could do; he suddenly crouched in front of the Don's wheelchair, aimed the Commando barrel over Pucci's right shoulder, and sighted on one of the trigger men with a pistol, the nearest one.

Startled, the Don's eight men swung their machine guns at the giant. Afraid of hitting the Don, they held their fire.

Blade cut loose, the Commando chattering loudly, the stock bucking against his shoulder.

The closest hit man took a burst in the chest and was flung to the carpet.

Mario swung in the direction Blade had fired.

Don Pucci's hands were sliding under the red blanket in his lap. Several of his men started toward him.

The hit man with the sawed-off shotgun let fly into the back of one of the Don's men at point-blank range, the buckshot blowing the man's chest out and sending him sprawling. Pivoting, the hit man took a bead on the Don.

Blade squeezed the trigger, stitching the shotgun-wielding killer from the crotch to the forehead.

One of the two remaining hit men shot a pair of the Don's guards and aimed at the Don.

The last hit man was barreling toward the wheelchair.

Caught unawares by the abrupt assassination attempt, with their attention focused on the Warriors, none of the Don's men had fired a shot in the first three seconds of the attack. Now, as they realized the true danger was coming at them from the crowds, not the bar, they spun to confront the last two hit men. But they were too slow.

Geronimo and Helen fired simultaneously. Geronimo's Browning struck the hit man on the right in the face and he crashed onto his back. Helen's Armalite sent a half-dozen rounds into the last hit man, into the left side of his chest. He twisted and toppled over.

In the aftermath of the shooting, the casino was as quiet as a tomb.

Blade slowly stood.

Don Pucci turned his wheelchair and scrutinized the four dead hit men, then glanced at his own casualties. He gazed up at the giant. "Thanks. They nearly nailed me."

"Do you know who they were?" Blade asked.

"No," Don Pucci said. "But I'll find out. They were probably sent by Giorgio, but I'll never be able to prove it. He'd hire outside talent for a job like this. He'd never use any of his own men."

"Why does Giorgio want to kill you?" Blade queried.

"Why else?" Pucci responded. "He wants to take over Vegas. But I can't do anything about him unless I can uncover some proof. I must justify my actions to the other Dons."

"I thought you are running the show in Vegas," Blade observed. "Why must you justify your actions to them?"

"Courtesy," Don Pucci said. "If I don't show them respect, they're not about to show me any respect. All the Dons belong to the Council, our governing body. If any of us has a grievance against another Don, we bring it up in Council. If I was to hit Giorgio without a justifiable grievance and the agreement of the Council, an all-out war could result." He glanced at Mario, then nodded toward the bodies. "Clean up this mess. Discover who they were. And send ten grand to the families of each of our boys who were whacked."

Mario hurried off, barking orders to the Don's men.

The casino came alive again, gradually, the customers mingling and conversing as the gambling resumed.

"You took this calmly," Blade said, praising the Don.

Don Pucci sighed. "This has happened before. Why do you think I'm in this damn wheelchair?"

Blade stared at the body of the hit man with the shotgun. "What if they had gotten past your men?"

Don Pucci's hands came out from under the red blanket. Clutched in his right was an Eagle 357 Magnum pistol. "I'm confined to a wheelchair, but I'm not helpless."

Helen stepped up to the wheelchair. "Do you know where my daughter is?"

"I wish I did," Don Pucci replied. "I owe you for saving my life. I'll do anything I can to help." He reached up and gingerly touched his right ear, smiling at Blade. "That piece of yours almost ruptured my eardrum. I can hardly hear for all the ringing."

"Sorry," Blade said.

"Don't apologize," Pucci remarked. "I'm alive, aren't I?" He paused. "Now, about this kidnapping business. I'm not involved, but if you give me time, I will try and find out who is behind it."

Blade watched the Don's men removing the corpses. Two men in jeans and T-shirt were approaching, bearing buckets and mops to soak up the puddles of blood. He saw eight or nine people playing a row of slot machines, and he wondered how they could callously disregard the bloodshed they'd just seen. How could they become so engrossed in the slot machines so soon after witnessing the shootout? Why were the slot machines so fascinating? He recalled the token Mario had given him, the one in his left front pocket. If the opportunity arose, he intended to use the token and learn the secret of the slot machines firsthand. He . . .

The token!

Blade abruptly remembered the *other* token in his possession, the one in his back pocket, the one he had found on the corpse in Halma, the one from the man killed at the kidnapping scene. He reached into the pocket and fished out the blue token, then held it up to read the words printed on both sides: JOHNNY'S PALACE.

What a fool he'd been!

Blade suddenly perceived the reason for his previous ambiguous feelings of unease. The answer had been staring him in the face the whole time, figuratively speaking, and he'd been too dense to notice! Why would the man found dead near Halma have a token from Don Giorgio's casino *unless he frequented that casino!* He looked down at Don Pucci. "Would one of your men gamble in Giorgio's casino?"

Don Pucci snorted. "None of my men would be caught dead in Giorgio's joint. The games there are rigged."

"What about Giorgio's men?" Blade probed. "Would they gamble in *your* casino?"

Don Pucci shook his head. "Not likely. I don't trust any of Pucci's men. They rarely come in here, because if they do I have one of my boys stick with them like glue. It makes them too uncomfortable." He squinted at Blade for a moment. "Why are you asking all these questions?"

"There were three people with Helen's daughter when she was abducted," Blade detailed. "Two of them were murdered. We also found the body of a stranger. And on his body I found this." He flipped the token to the Don.

Don Pucci deftly caught it and inspected the token. His lips compressed and his nostrils flared.

"One more thing," Blade said, acting on his hunch. "What does Don Giorgio look like?"

"How should I describe him?" Don Pucci replied. "He has black hair and brown eyes. He's a heartless bastard, the meanest-looking son of a bitch you'd ever want to meet."

Ted's word came back to Blade in a rush. "His hair was black, his eyes brown. His face was kind of mean looking." He placed his right hand on his forehead and stared at the floor.

Geronimo nudged his friend's right elbow. "What's the matter?"

"Blade? What is it?" Helen added.

Blade removed his hand, his countenance set in a chiseled mask of suppressed indignation. "We were set up," he said huskily.

"What are you talking about?" Helen asked, perplexed.

"Don Pucci didn't take Mindy," Blade elaborated. "Don Giorgio did. Giorgio is using us. He probably hoped we'd barge into this casino and confront Don Pucci. Why else was Ted told we could find Mindy at the Golden Crown Casino?"

"Then Mindy isn't here?" Helen queried, distraught by the revelation.

Blade shook his head.

"Giorgio wanted us to kill Pucci for him," Geronimo deduced.

"That's my guess," Blade concurred.

"If Mindy isn't here, where is she?" Helen inquired.

"I can answer that," Don Pucci interjected. "If Giorgio took your daughter to set you up to whack me, then she's either in his joint or dead."

"Oh, no!" Helen said mournfully.

"If you take him on, if you try to locate the girl in his casino, he'll kill her for sure," Don Pucci stated. "He's not about to leave around any evidence connecting him to this caper."

Helen looked at Blade. "What do we do?"

"We need to come up with a plan," Blade replied.

"He's right," Don Pucci said. "You must play it cagey. If you rush over to the Palace, Mindy is as good as dead. If Giorgio spots any of you in his joint, he'll snuff her."

The three Warriors exchanged startled glances.

"Hickok!" Blade exclaimed.

"Who is this Hickok?" Don Pucci questioned.

"He's a Warrior, like us," Blade answered. "And he's in Giorgio's casino right this moment!"

"Then God help Mindy," the Don stated grimly.

CHAPTER FOURTEEN

"How many cards do you want, hick?" the professional gambler asked. He was holding the deck in his left hand.

Hickok glanced at the ring of spectators watching the game. Over an hour ago they had started gathering, after word of his winning streak had circulated around the casino. Initially, six players had been in the game, but one by one Hickok had eliminated them. Now only the arrogant gambler remained, and it was his turn to deal.

"Come on, hick," the gambler said, baiting the gunfighter. "I don't have all day."

Hickok deliberately stalled. How much longer, he wondered, did he need to stay in Giorgio's casino? How much time did he need to buy Blade and the others? It would be dark soon. Surely they had found Mindy by now. But if so, why hadn't one of them shown up to let him know? He glanced at the Henry, leaning against the table to his left.

"How many cards?" the gambler repeated.

Hickok gazed at his hand. Three kings, a four, and a nine. He discarded the four and the nine. "Two."

The gambler dealt two cards to the gunman.

Hickok picked up the cards and almost laughed aloud. The two of spades and the two of diamonds! He had a full house!

"Dealer takes three," the gambler said, and did so.

Hickok was beginning to worry about his friends. He had stayed in the Palace to insure he was the focus of Giorgio's attention. Sure enough, he'd been under surveillance all day. He suspected they would shadow him if he departed the casino, and he didn't want to lead Giorgio's men to his fellow Warriors. But he was growing weary of waiting, and he was extremely concerned for Blade, Geronimo, and Helen. What if they were in trouble? He decided to give them until nightfall, then go looking for them, shadows or no shadows.

"Are you playing or daydreaming?" the gambler snapped.

Hickok smiled sweetly. This varmint was going to get his, real soon! "It'll cost you to stay in the game, Big-Mouth. Five hundred." He counted out the chips and added them to the pot.

The gambler studied the man in buckskins. He was convinced the blond man was a country bumpkin, and he was determined to show the upstart how the game of poker was played by a real pro. "You're not bluffing me, mister. I'll match your five hundred."

Hickok watched the gambler slide five hundred to the center of the table.

"What do you have?" the gambler asked belligerently.

Hickok laid his cards on the table, face up. "Read 'em and weep, sucker."

The gambler looked like he was choking. He turned crimson and sputtered, then dropped his hand on the table in disgust.

Hickok reached out and claimed the pot. "Stick around. I'll give you some lessons on how to play this game." He grinned at the recollection of the many hours he'd spent playing card games at the Home. Rummy. Gin. Pinochle. Poop on Your Neighbor. Fish. Poker. Many others. The

Family members never actually gambled; they played for the sheer fun of playing. And as an avid student of the Old West, Hickok's favorite game was poker.

"Damn you!" the gambler suddenly barked. He stood, shoving his chair backwards.

The spectators scurried away from the table.

"You shouldn't gamble if you're a poor loser," Hickok remarked.

"You son of a bitch!" the gambler spat out. He swept the right flap of his coat aside, revealing a Charter Arms Bulldog revolver in a holster on his right hip. "On your feet!"

Hickok slowly rose, his hands resting on the table. "If you apologize, real nice like, you'll live to play cards again some day."

The gambler snorted contemptuously. "Apologize! You can kiss my ass first!"

"I wouldn't touch your butt with a brandin' iron," Hickok retorted.

A new voice intruded on their dispute. "Hold it right there!" Giorgio's right-hand man, Kenney, hurried up to the table. "Murphy, you've been warned about your temper before!" he admonished the gambler. "And you know the rules. No gunplay."

"Hang the rules!" Murphy declared. "This is between him and me!"

"The Don will not appreciate this," Kenney noted.

"I'm not backing down to this hick!" Murphy said angrily.

Hickok's blue eyes became flinty. "Are you going to pull your iron, or are you aimin' to insult me to death?"

Murphy went for his revolver, his right hand sweeping down and up in a practiced draw, a draw he'd employed on 14 occasions to kill a foe. He was leveling the barrel when he was shocked to see twin Colts materialize in the hick's hands.

Hickok fired both Pythons, the Magnums thundering. The heavy slugs bored into the gambler's face, making cavities of his cheeks, and blew out the rear of his cranium.

Murphy was hurled to the floor, his body landing
spread-eagled. Chunks of flesh and bits of hair dotted the
carpet around him.

Kenney gazed at the dead gambler. "Murphy had quite a
rep," he commented, then looked at the Warrior. "And
you beat him."

Hickok twirled the Pythons into their holsters. "Piece of
cake."

"You have a knack for racking up a body count,"
Kenney remarked.

"If some coyote is plannin' to perforate me," Hickok
noted, "I don't intend to oblige them."

"We'll clean up the mess," Kenney offered. "How are
you fixed? Do you want more chips?"

"No," Hickok said, glancing at the stakes he had won.
"I already have a heap." He picked up the Henry and
slung it over his back.

"Looks to me like you have over five thousand there,"
Kenney said as he scrutinized the piles on the table. "Do
you want me to cash them for you?"

Hickok shrugged. "Why not. I'll mosey around the
casino." He ambled off, heading for the slot machines.
What should he play next? He'd spent the afternoon at
various card games, capped off by his three-hour poker
match. Boredom was setting in. He couldn't understand
how folks could spend so much time gambling. Playing
cards at the Home for the sheer fun of it was one thing, but
gambling was entirely different. When a person played for
money, when valuables were at stake, the game lost its
entertaining, recreational quality. Instead, a simple,
relaxing pastime became a serious business of winning at
all costs. The gambler had epitomized such an attitude; to
Murphy, winning was everything, even at the cost of his
life.

A middle-aged couple was playing one of the slots.

Hickok stopped and watched them. He casually scanned
the casino, searching for his tail.

Fifteen yards away a young mobster in a beige suit was
gazing overhead at a chandelier as if the fixture was the

most interesting item in the universe.

Hickok grinned and walked over to the hit man. "Howdy."

The young mobster was clearly ruffled by this unexpected development. He looked at the Warrior, blinking rapidly, then up at the chandelier.

"Cat got your tongue?" Hickok asked. "I said howdy."

"Hi," the man replied. He had black hair and dark eyes.

"Would you do me a favor?" Hickok inquired. "Would you find Kenney and get some tokens for me? I'd like to play the slot machines for a spell."

The mobster stared at the gunman. "I'm not your servant."

"No, but you have been shadowin' me," Hickok said.

"I don't know what you're talking about," the man responded.

"And I was born yesterday," Hickok cracked. "Look, we both know you've been tailin' me, and you must be gettin' as bored as I am if you're admirin' the lights. Don Giorgio told me I could have anything I wanted, and I want some tokens. I promise I'll stay right here until you return."

Although no one was within ten feet of them, the mobster lowered his voice. "But you're not supposed to know I'm following you!"

"Darn! Now you tell me!" Hickok said.

"If Kenney finds out you made me, I'm in hot water," the mobster divulged.

"I won't tell if you don't," Hickok pledged. "Now what about the tokens?"

"I'm not to let you out of my sight," the mobster said.

"I'm thinkin' of payin' Don Pucci's place a visit later," Hickok commented innocently. "You certainly can't follow me over there."

"Mister, my orders are to stick with you like glue," the mobster disclosed. "Where you go, I go."

"What if I have to tinkle?" Hickok queried.

"Then I'll tinkle too," the mobster replied.

Hickok started to turn, pleased at the confirmation of

his suspicion concerning the men assigned to shadow him. They *would* tail him if he left the Palace, which meant he had to lose them before leaving. And there was one more thing he needed to know. He gazed at the mobster. "I hope I didn't do anything to get you in trouble with your head honchos," he said with sincerity. "I know they're watchin' us on hidden cameras."

The mobster glanced around nervously. "Don Giorgio and Kenney don't spend all their time watching the monitor. Internal surveillance is conducted by Security from the Security Office. There's a hookup in the Don's office which he can tap into whenever he wants. But Kenney is working the floor, and the Don might not be watching."

"Then I'd best be gettin' along," Hickok said. He walked off, observing the patrons, calculating. He doubted the cameras would be trained on him the whole time. The tails were expected to keep an eye on him. If he could shake the shadows, and if he could leave the casino and head upstairs without the cameras observing him, he stood a good chance of locating another exit from the building. The front entrance was too risky. The Don was bound to have it covered.

But how could he get upstairs without causing a ruckus?

The answer came from an unexpected source.

Hickok was walking past the blackjack tables when he saw her again. The one with the nice teeth. The one who had walked by him five times during the afternoon. Each time she had smiled seductively and given him a come-hither look, and each time he had returned her smile and gone about his business. The last such incident had been prior to the poker game. She had sashayed up to him and requested a match to light her cigarette. He'd checked his pockets, told her he didn't have any matches, and walked off, leaving her with her rosy red lips gaping.

Now there she was again, watching a blackjack game.

She was about six feet tall, and she had been blessed with a body of abundant proportions in all the right places. Her hair was a dusty gold, worn down to the small of her back.

Her eyes were blue. The front of her red dress formed a V with the point touching her navel. When she leaned forward, her breasts threatened to make a bid for freedom. Her face was oval, her lashes long and lovely.

Hickok repressed a smirk and stepped up to her. "Howdy. Remember me?"

She turned, her eyes widening slightly before she recovered her composure. "I remember you," she said huskily. "You're the man who doesn't carry matches."

"The name is Earp," Hickok fibbed once more. "Wyatt Earp."

"Mr. Earp," she said softly. "I'm Nadine."

"That's a right pretty name, ma'am," he complimented her.

"Thank you, Mr. Earp," she said.

"Call me Hi . . ." Hickok began, then caught himself. "Wyatt."

Nadine grinned. "As you wish. What can I do for you?"

"I saw you standin' here and figured we could chew the fat," Hickok replied. "I don't have any friends here and I'm a mite lonely."

Nadine's grin became a wide smile, her white teeth glistening. "How sad."

"Do you mind if we shoot the breeze?" Hickok inquired politely. "I couldn't help but notice how friendly you were earlier."

"I didn't think you'd noticed me," Nadine said.

Hickok ran his eyes up and down her body. "How could anyone not notice a beautiful woman like you?"

Nadine was clearly pleased by his attention. She cleared her throat and gazed around the room.

Out of the corner of his left eye, Hickok saw Kenney 20 feet away, regarding them intently.

Nadine's head nodded once, almost imperceptibly.

Kenney beamed.

Hickok pretended to be immersed in the blackjack game for a few moments.

"Are you hungry?" Nadine asked.

"Nope," Hickok replied.

"Me neither," Nadine said. "And if we want to talk, we won't have much privacy in the casino."

"I don't know where else we could go," Hickok remarked artlessly.

"I do," Nadine stated. "I'm on vacation. I have a suite upstairs. If you don't mind, we could go up there and talk. I have some munchies in the fridge if you do get hungry."

"I don't know. . . ." Hickok hedged. "What would your husband or boyfriend say?"

"I'm not married," Nadine answered. "And I don't have a boyfriend."

"Then I guess we can go up to your room," Hickok said, putting a nervous tinge in his voice.

Nadine looped her right arm in his left. "Don't be shy! I won't bite. We'll have fun together."

Hickok smiled at her. "I hope so."

Nadine led the gunman toward the elevators along the far wall. "Tell me about yourself," she coaxed him.

"There's not much to tell," Hickok said.

"Where are you from?"

"Oh, here and there," Hickok responded.

"What do you do for a living?" Nadine probed.

"This and that," Hickok answered.

Nadine's eyes narrowed. "I saw you tangle with Murphy," she mentioned.

"I hope it didn't shock your sensibilities," Hickok remarked decorously.

"No," Nadine said. "I've seen shootings before, but I've never seen anyone draw a gun as fast as you do." She paused. "Do you do everything so fast?"

Hickok chuckled. "Not everything."

"That's nice to hear," Nadine commented. "Some things should be done nice and slow."

"Like eatin' venison steak," Hickok said, and licked his lips.

Nadine laughed. "I was thinking of something else."

Hickok looked at her. "Oh? What?"

"I'll save it for a surprise," Nadine stated, and giggled.

"Oh, goody!" Hickok stated. "I love surprises!"

They reached the row of six elevators. Nadine pressed an UP button on the wall, and they took the first elevator which opened, the second from the right.

Nadine punched the button for the eighth floor. "I'm in 819," she mentioned.

The elevator door closed and they ascended.

Nadine squeezed Hickok's left arm playfully. "This is going to be fun!"

Hickok smiled. "You don't know the half of it."

CHAPTER FIFTEEN

Blade, Geronimo, and Helen stood quietly next to the huge windows overlooking the glittering city. Dusk enshrouded the landscape, and the nearly infinite variety of Vegas's neon lights had flared to life. To the three Warriors from the Home, where kerosene lanterns were a luxury at night, the impression was dazzling.

Blade turned and faced the doorway to the moderately sized chamber as the door opened and the Dons filed inside. The five men were a curious mixture of statures and physiques.

A large, circular wooden table filled the center of the room. Six wooden chairs ringed the table at regular intervals. Seated in his wheelchair near the windows, his hands on the table, his back to the Warriors, was Don Pucci. The token from Johnny's Palace was clenched in his left hand.

The five Dons halted when they saw the Warriors.

"What the hell is this?" demanded a portly, bald man in a white suit. "Council meetings are to be conducted in private. No soldiers. No Consiglioris. No one else."

"With your indulgence, Don Marchese," Don Pucci said. "I have called this emergency meeting of the Council, and these people are present at my invitation. Their testimony is essential to the topic we will discuss."

Another Don, a small man with brown hair and eyes, attired in an immaculate blue suit and shining, black patent leather shoes, spoke up. "What is this topic, Don Pucci?"

"We are here, Don Lansky, to discuss the danger of Las Vegas being attacked by a Federation army," Don Pucci replied.

The Dons exchanged startled glances.

"Vegas is going to be attacked?" Don Marchese queried in astonishment.

"Please," Don Pucci said, gesturing at the chairs. "Have a seat. Everything will be explained."

The Dons quickly sat down.

Don Pucci angled his wheelchair so he could see the Warriors and the table. "First, I must make the introductions." He waved his right hand at the Warriors. "These three are Warriors from a compound called the Home located in Minnesota."

With raking stares, the Dons scrutinized the newcomers.

Don Pucci went on. "Their leader is Blade, the big one. The Indian is Geronimo. The broad is Helen."

"Why are they here?" asked a man in a green suit with a ragged scar on his left cheek.

"I'm getting to that, Don Siegel," Don Pucci stated. He motioned for Blade to step over to the table.

Blade complied, the Commando slung over his shoulders, his hands on the hilts of his Bowies. "Hello, gentlemen," he said.

Don Pucci pointed at the Dons, introducing them one by one, going from right to left. "This is Don Marchese, then Don Lansky." He indicated a stocky man in brown with a bulbous nose and a sloping forehead. "Don Cuascut. Don Siegel." Next he pointed at a lean man in a gray suit. "And, finally, Don Talone."

"Wait a minute," Don Talone said in a high-pitched

voice. "Where is Don Giorgio? We can not hold a Council meeting without all of the Dons present. You know the rules."

"Don Giorgio will arrive in a half hour," Don Pucci explained. "I wanted to have thirty minutes to ourselves. You'll understand why in a few moments."

"This isn't proper," Don Talone said.

Don Pucci smiled benignly. "Don Talone, your friendship with Don Giorgio is well known and we can appreciate your loyalty. However, in this instance your loyalty is misplaced. Thanks to your friend, we are in jeopardy of having the Freedom Federation declare war on us."

"What is the Freedom Federation?" Don Lansky asked.

Don Pucci nodded at Blade. "Would you do the honors?"

"The Freedom Federation is an alliance of seven factions," Blade detailed. "Three of the factions, the Family, the Clan, and the Moles, are all located in what was once Minnesota. Our allies include the Flathead Indians in Montana and the Cavalry in the Dakota Territory. Our two largest members are the Civilized Zone and the Free State of California."

"I've heard of the Federation," Don Siegel mentioned. "Why would they want to give us any grief?"

Don Pucci frowned. "Because one of us is responsible for kidnapping a young woman from the Family," he answered.

Blade studied the expressions on the Dons. They were each digesting the news with a calm, but somber, detachment. All except for Giorgio's friend, Talone. He was biting his lower lip nervously.

"The Warriors and I spent the afternoon together," Don Pucci went on. "I am convinced their grievance is genuine. If we don't show them respect and help them, they could take their case to the Federation leaders. Do we want to risk having a Federation army sent against us?"

"Hold the phone," Don Marchese said. "We have high-ranking visitors from California and the Civilized Zone all the time. We pay them good money to insure they don't meddle in our affairs—"

"But this time *we* have meddled in *theirs*," Don Pucci said, interrupting.

Blade was hoping Don Marchese would continue. He wanted to learn about the high-ranking visitors from the Family's allies.

"What exactly is their grievance?" Don Siegel inquired.

Don Pucci looked at Blade. "Tell them about the snatch."

Blade spent five minutes describing the abduction of Mindy. None of the Dons spoke until he was finished.

"This is deplorable!" Don Lansky stated. "We have a standing rule not to involve outsiders in our affairs."

"How do we know one of us is involved?" Don Talone questioned. "The evidence is not concrete. Someone could be setting us up."

"Someone was setup, all right," Don Pucci said. "This was found on the body of the stranger found at the kidnapping scene." He tossed the token to Don Marchese.

Each of the Dons took a turn at examining the token.

Don Talone, the last to inspect it, laughed. "A token? This is your evidence? This doesn't mean a thing. Anyone can obtain a token."

"There is one more thing," Don Pucci said coldly. "Something the Warriors didn't even think of. Something I discovered when I was looking at the address book."

"What address book?" Don Marchese queried.

"The address book they found on th body of the man with the token," Don Pucci elaborated. He extended his right hand toward Blade. "May I?"

Blade reached into his right rear pocket and withdrew the small black address book. He gave it to the Don.

Don Pucci waved the book. "This is the incriminating evidence linking one of us to the kidnapping."

"A lousy address book?" Don Talone remarked sarcastically.

Don Pucci's features became rigid. "This lousy address book has the name and address of its owner written on the inside of the front cover." He slid the address book to Don

Marchese. "Enlighten all of us."

Don Marchese picked up the book and opened it. He stared at the handwriting for several seconds, his lips twitching in budding anger.

"What does it say?" Don Siegel prompted.

"Property of . . ." Don Marchese said, reading the writing. "Alberto Manzo. 6415 Roseway Avenue."

"Manzo!" Don Lansky exclaimed. "He was one of Giorgio's button men."

"This still doesn't prove Don Giorgio was involved," Don Talone said.

"It does for me," Don Pucci stated.

"The evidence is incriminating," Don Cuascut commented, "but not conclusive."

"How much more do you need?" Don Pucci asked. He surveyed the men at the table. "Do you have any idea of the gravity of the situation? We risk antagonizing a strong alliance with a powerful military force. We risk the Federation marching on Vegas. Do you want that?"

Don Talone snickered. "You're exaggerating."

"Am I?" Don Pucci rejoined. "Let me remind you of a few facts. We have several thousand soldiers, all told. We're strong, but we don't have a standing army, per se. We've survived for so long because of two conditions. First, we never meddle in the affairs of outsiders. Never. For over a century we have honored this rule. Second, we've paid off the necessary people to guarantee we're left alone. But the officials in California and the Civilized Zone on our payroll will not look kindly on having a young woman from one of their allies kidnapped by one of us."

"If she was," Don Talone interjected.

"Don Giorgio's animosity toward me is no secret," Don Pucci said. "Everyone here knows he wants to oust me. He couldn't try a direct hit with his own button men, because he knows many of you are close friends of mine and he would face your combined wrath. Someone—and let's, for the sake of argument, assume Giorgio is responsible—has hired independents to whack me. Four times, no less!"

"Four?" Don Lansky said.

"There was another attempt earlier," Don Pucci disclosed. "The Warriors saved me."

"I heard about it," Don Marchese mentioned. "I am sorry."

"The outside talent hasn't been able to do the job," Don Pucci said. "So now someone—and, again, who else but Giorgio would do it?—has attempted to instigate my death at the hands of the Warriors."

"This is all speculation," Don Talone declared. "You can't prove Don Giorgio is involved."

The door suddenly opened.

Blade looked up at the man striding into the meeting room. His mind registered the cruel visage, the oily black hair, the brown eyes, and the black suit, and he intuitively realized the new arrival was Don Giorgio.

"Don Giorgio," Don Pucci said, confirming Blade's deduction. "You are early."

Don Giorgio scanned the room, his arrogant gaze lingering on the Warriors. "You've started the meeting without me?"

"You are the topic of our meeting," Don Pucci stated. "I'd hoped to settle matters before you arrived."

Don Giorgio stared at Don Pucci. "What kind of stunt are you trying to pull?"

"Why don't you take a seat?" Don Pucci suggested. "We would like to discuss the matter of a kidnapping with you."

"Is this a meeting of the Council or an interrogation?" Don Giorgio demanded testily.

"It is both," Don Pucci answered.

"I am insulted by your lack of courtesy," Don Giorgio said to Don Pucci. "I came over to your joint in good faith, with only six of my men, as required by our agreement. And now you say you want to grill me over some kidnapping?"

"We do not intend to grill you," Don Lansky said. "We merely want to ask a few questions."

"Why should I agree to this breech of etiquette," Don Giorgio snapped.

"If you have nothing to hide, I see no reason why you can't cooperate," Don Pucci stated.

Don Giorgio stared at each of the other Dons. "Are all of you in this together?"

"Don Pucci has made serious charges against you," Don Lansky offered placatingly. "We simply want to set the record straight."

"I refuse to be treated like one of the pezzonovante," Don Giorgio said disdainfully.

Embroiled in their dispute, accustomed to conducting their business in private amongst themselves, with their attention fully focused on another, they collectively disregarded the presence of the three Warriors. The last thing they expected was to have their conference interrupted by an outsider. So they were all the more disconcerted when a disruption abruptly occurred.

Helen walked up to the table and leveled her carbine at Don Giorgio. "Where's my daughter, you bastard!"

Don Giorgio stiffened. "Who the hell are you?"

"The name is Helen," she told him icily. "You kidnapped Mindy, my daughter. Where is she?"

"I did not kidnap your daughter, bitch!" Don Giorgio growled.

Helen shot him.

The single round caught Giorgio high on the right shoulder and spun him completely around. He doubled over, his left hand pressed against the wound, blood trickling over his fingers, his face contorted in savage rage.

Without exception, the other Dons were gawking at Giorgio, dumbfounded.

"Helen!" Blade said harshly, grabbing the Armalite barrel and pushing it upwards.

Just then the door opened and button men raced into the room, each with a handgun. Each of the Dons had arrived at the meeting with six soldiers, and now those trigger men flocked to their Dons while uneasily eyeing everyone else.

Don Pucci was the first to recover. "There will be no more shooting!" he commanded sternly.

Don Giorgio straightened and examined his wound.

"It's just a scratch," he said contemptuously. "The bitch can't shoot straight."

"If I'd wanted you dead," Helen assured him, "you'd be dead!"

Blade was expecting one of the soldiers to open up at any second. They were on edge, primed to kill. All it would take to initiate a blood bath was one wrong word or hasty action.

"I did not know she would do this," Don Pucci said to Giorgio.

"You allowed outsiders to attend a supreme Council meeting," Don Giorgio declared with a sneer. "And you can't even control them! Are you a Don or a windbag?"

"This regrettable incident was completely unforeseen," Don Pucci reiterated. "You have my apology."

"I don't want your apology!" Giorgio retorted. "I want this woman! It is my right!"

"She is here as my guest," Don Pucci said. "She is under my protection."

"Are you refusing to allow my right for revenge?" Don Giorgio demanded. "I am not armed, and she put a slug through me! I have the right to snuff her!"

A deep voice stabbed the air like a knife, drawing the scrutiny of everyone in the room to the giant in the black leather vest and the fatigue pants. "Like hell you do!"

Don Giorgio, strangely enough, grinned. "The mighty Blade speaks!" he said mockingly.

"So you know who I am," Blade remarked.

"I know all about you!" Don Giorgio boasted.

Blade leaned forward, resting his fists on the table. "Then you must know I'm a man of my word. And I'm giving you one hour to turn Mindy over to us, or we're coming after her."

"You're threatening me?" Giorgio rejoined furiously.

"No," Blade said softly. "I'm promising you. If Mindy isn't freed within an hour, we'll come get her."

Giorgio gazed at each of the Warriors. "All three of you?"

"They won't be alone," Don Pucci stated.

"Are you declaring war on me?" Don Giorgio snapped.

"I would rather not," Don Pucci said.

"I am not holding this Mindy," Giorgio declared. "How can you side with these scum against me?"

"I believe you kidnapped the girl," Don Pucci observed.

Giorgio's lips curled downwards. "Are you calling me a liar?"

There were several seconds of strained silence as the mobsters apprehensively waited for Don Pucci to respond. The fate of the seven Families hung in the balance. If he answered in the affirmative, each Don and every trigger man knew war was inevitable. And a war between any two Families would adversely affect all of them.

Don Pucci straightened in his wheelchair. "Yes. You are a lying peasant."

Don Giorgio took a menacing step forward. "Why, you worthless old shit! This is the final straw! I've tolerated your meddling long enough!"

Don Pucci's eyes narrowed. "Leave now, while you still can. I invited you here under an implied pledge of neutrality, and I won't violate the sanctity of the Council."

"You pompous old fart!" Giorgio declared. "Do you really think your Family is stronger than mine? You're in for a rude awakening."

"You have ten minutes to vacate the premises," Don Pucci said.

"What about the rest of you?" Don Giorgio asked, sweeping the other Dons with an expectant gaze. "Will you side with this fossil or me?"

None of the Dons responded.

"You'd better decide soon," Giorgio informed them. "I'll remember my friends when I'm on top, but I won't be so forgiving toward those who oppose me."

"We will not be intimidated," Don Marchese stated.

"Suit yourselves," Don Giorgio said. "I don't need you. I don't need any of you." He wheeled and stalked from the Council room, his soldiers on his heels.

"Now the shit hits the fan," Don Lansky remarked.

Don Pucci looked at Helen. "That was a very foolish thing you did. There was a remote chance I could have reasoned with Giorgio to return your daughter."

"You shouldn't have let him leave," Helen said in reproach. "I could have made him tell me where Mindy is being held."

Don Pucci faced his peers. "The harm has been done. There is no turning back. You must do as your conscience dictates. If you decide to remain neutral, I will understand."

"This is not our fight," Don Cuascut commented.

"In a sense, you're right," Don Pucci said. "Giorgio has been after me for years. This is a personal conflict as well as business. But keep one thing in mind. Giorgio is merciless. He wants absolute power. If he wins this war, what is to prevent him from trying to destroy your Families?" He paused. "Where do you stand?"

Don Causcut spoke first. "I want no part of it. My Family will be neutral."

"As you wish," Don Pucci said.

"Giorgio's Family is strong," Don Lansky noted. "I'd say the two of you are evenly matched. This war could drag out for months, even years. Our tourist trade would be crippled. Our economy would suffer. I do not like the idea of diminished coffers."

"You are with me then?" Don Pucci inquired hopefully.

"Respectfully, no," Don Lansky responded. "My Family will sit this out. This is between Giorgio and yourself. You must show the upstart the error of his ways. I will, however, provide whatever hardware and ammunition you may need."

"And you?" Don Pucci asked Don Marchese.

Marchese frowned. "I love you like a brother, Tony. You know that. And as a brother, I give you this advice. You must prove yourself by defeating Giorgio. He threw down the gauntlet and you accepted. Now you must prove yourself worthy of being the leader of our Council. So long as the war is strictly between Giorgio and yourself, I will not intervene one way or the other."

Don Siegel cleared his throat. "If the others are content to allow Giorgio and you to settle this, then so am I."

Don Pucci bowed his head. He did not want his friends to see his overwhelming disappointment.

"As for me," Don Talone added, "I'm not sticking my nose in where it doesn't belong. However, if Don Lansky is willing to supply arms to the Pucci Family, I can do no less for the Giorgio Family."

Don Pucci looked up at Don Talone. "Thank you for being honest. All of you should leave before the hostilities commence."

Without saying a word, the five Dons and their soldiers departed.

Don Pucci sighed and gazed at Blade. "The lines have been drawn, Warrior. For better or for worse, Don Giorgio and I will resolve our differences permanently."

"You're not alone in this," Blade said. "We're with you all the way."

Don Pucci smiled. "I appreciate the thought, but what can three Warriors do?"

"You've never seen us in action," Blade commented.

"Besides," Geronimo chimed in, "we have an ace in the hole. Or maybe I should refer to him as a wild card."

"Who is this wild card?" Pucci asked.

"Hickok."

CHAPTER SIXTEEN

Nadine's suite was sumptuously adorned. She closed the door behind them, flicked on the lights, and indicated a huge living room. "Make yourself at home."

Hickok sauntered into the living room, admiring the luxurious accommodations. "Wow! What do you do for a living? Rob banks?"

Nadine laughed and walked toward him. "Not quite. I'm a secretary."

"You must make a heap of dough," Hickok remarked, "if you can afford to live here."

"I don't live here, silly," Nadine said. "I'm renting the suite while I'm on vacation. I saved for a whole year to be able to stay here."

"You like to gamble?" Hickok commented.

Nadine winked at him. "I like excitement."

Hickok winked back. "Me too."

Nadine glanced at a door in the center of the right-hand wall. "Do you mind if I change into something a little more comfortable?"

"Suit yourself," Hickok said.

Nadine smiled and strolled to the door. "This will just take a minute or two. Don't go away!"

"I wouldn't think of it," Hickok assured her.

Nadine entered the next room and shut the door. "Stretch out on the sofa. I'll be right there," she called out.

"Okay," Hickok replied. Instead, he unslung the Henry and leaned it against a chair, then ran to the hall door and eased it open a crack.

A tail was in the corridor, approximately 20 feet away, leaning against the wall and staring moodily at the floor.

Hickok recognized the shadow. It was not the young mobster he'd spoken to in the casino. This was the *other* youngish mobster, the one in the brown suit, the one he'd seen in Don Giorgio's office. There must have been a changing of the guard. He closed the door and returned to the living room. As he was reclining on the sofa, Nadine emerged.

"Now I'm comfortable," she declared contentedly.

She was also almost naked. Hickok averted his eyes, gazing at a nearby chair. The red negligee she was wearing did an adequate job of covering her navel, but that was the only part of her anatomy it seemed to cover.

"What's wrong?" Nadine inquired, coming around the end of the sofa.

"Nothin'," Hickok mumbled.

"Don't tell me you're shy?" Nadine asked.

Hickok quickly sat up to give her room to sit. "Me? Shy? Not in a million years."

Nadine perched herself next to the gunman. "Do I embarrass you?"

"No," Hickok said. "But maybe you should put on a robe or something. You could catch your death from pneumonia."

Nadine laughed. "I'm fine. Believe me."

Hickok stood. "I believe you." He took a step away from the sofa, keeping his back to her. He held his right hand alongside his belt buckle and clenched his fist.

"You are shy!" Nadine exclaimed. She grabbed the

fringe of his buckskin shirt. "Come on. Have a seat. Let's get to know each other."

"I can't," Hickok said. "I'm hitched."

"So what if you're married?" Nadine commented. "It doesn't make a difference to me."

"Are you sure you want me to turn around?" Hickok inquired with the utmost civility.

Nadine tugged on his shirt. "Of course," he said.

"I should warn you," Hickok advised her. "I have a surprise for you."

"What kind of surprise?" Nadine inquired. She noticed the angle of his right arm and misconstrued his intent. "Oh, you naughty thing, you!" she declared, giggling. "I love kinky men!"

Hickok's brow furrowed. What the blazes was she talking about? "So you want my surprise?" he asked, wagging his fist.

Nadine caught the movement and tittered. "Give it to me!"

Hickok shrugged. "If you insist."

Nadine was grinning in lewd anticipation when he slugged her, his wiry form whipping around in a right arc, his right fist slamming into her jaw and flattening her on the sofa.

Hickok raised his fist for another blow, but the hooker was out cold, a rivulet of blood seeping out the left corner of her shapely mouth. "It may not make a difference to you, lady," he addressed the unconscious prostitute, "but it makes a world of difference to me. I'll never cheat on my missus."

Nadine groaned.

Hickok grabbed the Henry and dashed to the hall door again. He inched the door outwards until he could see the corridor.

The tail was gone!

Or was he?

What if the turkey had shifted positions? Hickok started to gingerly open the door wider, when suddenly the door was flung all the way open.

There stood the smirking mobster with a Detonics Combat Master MK VI in his right hand. "What are you up to, asshole?" he demanded.

"About six feet," Hickok replied.

"A smartass, huh?" the mobster said. "Up with your hands."

Hickok released the Henry and casually raised his arms.

"You didn't think I saw you before, did you?" the mobster mentioned. "But you don't pull one over on Ozzi that easily."

"Your handle is Ozzi?" Hickok queried.

"What if it is?" Ozzi peered over the gunfighter's left shoulder and spied Nadine on the sofa. "What did you do to her?"

"Nothin' much," Hickok said. "I tucked her in, is all."

"I knew you were up to no good," Ozzi stated. "Okay. You're coming with me."

"Where are we going?" Hickok questioned.

"To see Don Giorgio," Ozzi disclosed. "He went over to Pucci's joint but he should be back soon."

"Why don't we grab a bite to eat first?" Hickok suggested.

"And give you the chance to make a break?" Ozzi rejoined. "Not on your life. And keep those hands in the air. Don't try to touch those Colts. I've seen you in action, and I'm not taking any unnecessary risks. I've never seen anyone as fast as you."

Hickok grinned. "Thanks for the compliment."

"All Warriors must be morons," Ozzi muttered. He backed up several feet. "Let's go. Head for the stairwell at the end of this hall. And remember, if you lower your arms by a fraction, you're dead meat."

Hickok walked from the suite and turned in the direction Ozzi was indicating, to the right. The corridor was deserted. "Where is everybody?"

"Down in the casino," Ozzi replied. "The upper floors are like a tomb during the evening."

Hickok thoughtfully studied the green door ahead, debating whether to make his move there or wait for a better opportunity. There was a small window in the door at shoulder height.

"Stop!" Ozzi barked when they were six feet from the stairwell. "Stand facing the left wall."

Hickok obeyed.

Ozzi carefully moved past the Warrior and up to the door. He was about to push it open so he could enter the stairwell first. The Warrior might be tempted to swing the door into him, or use it as a shield while drawing the Colts. By going first, he thwarted both strategies. He detected motion on the other side of the door and glanced through the window.

Kenney was hurrying up the stairs, his countenance uncharacteristically grim. He disappeared a moment later.

What the hell?

For a few seconds Ozzi was mystified. Why was Kenney heading upstairs? Normally, Kenney would be conducting his daily casino rounds, inspecting all the tables and insuring everything was running smoothly. There was nothing upstairs of any interest. Except, of course, for Mindy.

Mindy!

A hard object unexpectedly touched Ozzi's left ear.

"Guess who?" Hickok quipped.

Ozzi gulped, his eyes on the stairwell.

"Let go of the hardware," Hickok directed, his right Colt pressed against the mobster's head. He grabbed the top of the Detonics pistol.

Ozzi released the weapon.

"Smart man," Hickok said. He slid the pistol under his belt. "Now let's mosey back to Nadine's room."

Ozzi slowly turned. His mind was racing with the implications of Kenney's presence in the stairwell. Kenney never varied his routine. Never. But the man was doing so now? Why? A queasy sensation developed in Ozzi's gut. "Wait!" he blurted.

"Quit stallin'," Hickok admonished.

Ozzi looked at the gunman. "Do you know Mindy?"

Hickok was instantly all attention. "Mindy? What

about her?"

"She's the reason you're here, right?" Ozzi inquired.

Hickok nodded. "How do you know about Mindy?"

.Ozzi hesitated. What if he was wrong? The Don would never forgive him. But if he was right, then the Don must have sanctioned the killing. "Mindy is two floors up," he revealed. "I think she's in danger."

"What do you care?" Hickok asked suspiciously. "Is this your notion of a cockamamie trick?"

"No!" Ozzie responded. "I'm serious, man! She could be in danger."

"Take me to her," Hickok directed. If Mindy was really in danger, retrieving the Henry would have to wait. Every second counted.

Ozzi turned and opened the stairwell door. He took the stairs two at a stride.

Hickok stuck with the trigger man. He was puzzled by the mobster's evident sincerity, and he decided to go with his instincts. If Mindy was in the Palace, he intended to rescue her. And no passel of mangy city slickers was going to stand in his way!

Ozzi passed the landing for the ninth floor.

Hickok drew his left Colt.

As the landing for the tenth floor loomed overhead, Ozzi slowed slightly. What if he was making a fool of himself? What if Kenney was just checking on Mindy's welfare? He was behaving rashly, and a wiseguy needed a cool head at all times. What had Don Giorgio said in Minnesota? "If you blow your cool, you're a fool." His best bet was to confirm Mindy was okay on the sly, a task he could not perform with the Warrior in tow. No sooner did the realization dawn upon him than he threw himself backwards, hoping to catch the gunman unawares.

He nearly succeeded.

Hickok's lightning reflexes served him in good stead. He dodged to the left to avoid the hit man's hurtling body, but Ozzi grabbed his right arm and yanked, causing him to lose his balance and to topple backwards.

The pair tumbled down the stairwell for eight feet.

Hickok's head smacked onto the edge of one of the

concrete steps, and he wound up on his left side, dazed. He saw Ozzi come out of a roll and dive toward him, and he managed to lash out with his right foot and kick the button man in the face.

Ozzi was knocked for a loop. He landed on his back, four steps below the Warrior.

Hickok surged erect as Ozzi was rising. He took a stride and slammed the barrel of his right Python across the mobster's mouth.

Ozzi, staggered, reeled.

Hickok closed in, battering the hit man again and again. First the left Colt, then the right, then the left once more.

Ozzi, his mouth and chin a bloody, pulpy mess, sank to his knees, then collapsed.

Hickok was tempted to plug the varmint, but the shot might attract other gangsters. He holstered the Colts and glanced up the stairwell. Was Mindy really in the building, or had Ozzi fabricated the story to augment his chances of turning the tide? Hickok knew he couldn't afford to leave without verifying whether Mindy was in the Palace, whether she actually was on the tenth floor.

He jogged up the stairs.

If Ozzi had been right about everyone being down in the casino, finding an alternate exit from the Palace should be a piece of cake. A side door would suffice, or a window close to the ground.

Hickok reached the tenth floor landing and halted, peering through the window in the door.

The corridor was vacant.

Warily, his ears straining, Hickok opened the door and stepped into the hallway. He advanced slowly until he came abreast of the nearest door on the right. His right hand closed on the doorknob.

The danged thing was locked!

Hickok frowned as he surveyed the corridor. There were over a dozen rooms. Which one was Mindy in? He walked to the next door, which was on the left, and touched the knob.

A piercing, terrified scream abruptly shattered the stillness.

CHAPTER SEVENTEEN

"How did you persuade all of your customers to leave so quickly?" Blade asked.

"Would you want to be caught in the middle of a war?" Don Pucci rejoined.

Blade grinned. "I see your point."

They were in the center of the casino, watching the preparations being made by the Don's soldiers. Over three dozen armed trigger men were industriously piling furniture and wooden crates several feet from the ten glass doors, erecting a makeshift wall.

Mario approached. "The calls have all been made," he announced. "All the troops will be here within the hour."

"Weapons?" Don Pucci queried.

"All the weapons and explosives are being brought up from downstairs," Mario replied.

"What if Giorgio attacks before you're ready for him?" Blade inquired.

"He won't attack," the Don responded.

"Why not?"

"Giorgio is scum, but he's not stupid," Don Pucci said.

"Right now he's doing the same thing I'm doing, fortifying his casino and calling in his button men. This will be a war of attrition." He paused. "Constructing his casino next to mine was a stroke of genius."

"How so?" Blade probed.

"Years ago, Giorgio and I were on friendly terms. His ambition was not so obvious, but he was planning ahead, even then," Don Pucci detailed. "He asked to build his casino across the boulevard, and I assented. Now his reasons are obvious. No one will be able to enter or leave by the front doors. Our business will grind to a halt, and our financial reserves will be severely depleted the longer the war continues. If I run out of funds, I will be seriously weakened. Money talks in this town. Giorgio is in a position to keep tabs on every activity around the casino."

"But it works both ways," Blade noted. "And you'll still have the rear exits you can use."

"Unless Giorgio tries to surround the Golden Crown, to cut it off from the rest of the city," Don Pucci said. "Our provisions will not last indefinitely."

"Will you take the offensive?" Blade questioned.

"Not until I can find a weak link in Giorgio's defenses," Don Pucci responded.

Blade looked over his right shoulder at Geronimo and Helen.

Geronimo nodded.

"What if we were to weaken his defenses for you?" Blade asked, staring at the Don.

Pucci studied the giant for a moment. "I can't ask you to do that."

"Mindy and Hickok are in the Palace," Blade said. "We must go after them."

"You'll be cut down before you cross the boulevard," Don Pucci commented.

"Perhaps," Blade stated. "But if we can punch a hole in his defenses before he's ready, if we can keep him occupied, you'd have the advantage you need."

"Hmmmm," Don Pucci said thoughtfully. "Attack him now, before he's ready, before he has the opportunity to call in all of his soldiers? He'd never expect a direct assault now, because he undoubtedly assumes I'm too busy mobilizing my forces." He grinned. "It could work."

Blade looked at Mario. "You mentioned explosives. What kind do you have?"

"Name it, we have it," Mario replied. "Dynamite, grenades, plastic explosives."

"Any smoke bombs?" Blade asked.

Mario nodded. "A crate or two."

"We'll need a crate of smoke bombs and four grenades apiece," Blade stated.

Mario looked at Don Pucci, who nodded curtly. Mario hastened off.

"How do you propose to proceed?" Pucci queried the giant.

"We'll go in first," Blade said. "Hold back your men for several minutes. We want Giorgio totally unprepared for your attack. If he's involved with fighting us, he won't notice our ruse until it's too late."

"You take great risks, my friend," Don Pucci commented.

"Nothing ventured, nothing gained," Blade philosophized.

"I just pray that Mindy is still alive," Helen remarked anxiously.

"And Hickok," Geronimo added.

Blade stared at the Don. "If Giorgio loses, what happens to his Family?"

"They will be absorbed into my Family," Don Pucci answered. "They will owe their allegiance to me."

"You won't conduct reprisals?" Blade inquired.

"No. Why should I? Senseless reprisals are a waste," Don Pucci said. "The easiest way to kill a snake is to cut off its head, not chop its body into little pieces."

"With Giorgio's Family combined with your own," Blade noted, "you'll be the undisputable leader in Vegas. No one else will challenge you."

"I hope you are right," Pucci said. "But you never know. There is always someone who believes the grass is greener on the other side of the fence."

The makeshift wall was six feet high, and the mobsters had ceased piling furniture and were passing out machine guns.

Mario returned, attended by four men carrying two heavy crates. The men deposited the crates near the Warriors.

"Here you go," Mario said. "A crate of smoke bombs and a crate of grenades. Take whatever you need." He glanced at the men. "Open them."

One of the men departed, only to return moments later with a crowbar. The quartet applied themselves to prying the tops off.

"We'll need some assistance from you to get across the boulevard," Blade mentioned to the Don.

"Anything you want, you get," Don Pucci declared.

"I need a car," Blade detailed. "Can you have one running behind your casino within five minutes?"

Don Pucci snapped his fingers and Mario ran toward the rear of the casino.

"Will Don Giorgio have men watching the back?" Blade inquired.

"He might, but I doubt it," Pucci responded. "He hasn't had the time to get all his troops in place."

"What about the boulevard and the side streets? Will they be cordoned off?" Blade needed to know.

"No," Pucci said. "No one in their right mind will come near either casino. The Enforcers will keep everyone away from both joints."

"Are the Enforcers your men?" Blade questioned.

"The Enforcers are selected from every Family," Don Pucci revealed. "They take an oath of neutrality and serve for one year. After their duty, they return to their Family."

"So they won't take a part in this conflict?" Blade remarked.

"No," Don Pucci said. "Neither will the other Dons, if they stick by their word."

"Okay, then," Blade stated. "We will circle around the

Golden Crown and approach the Palace on the boulevard.
When you hear a single shot, have a dozen of your men
hurl smoke bombs out to the middle of the boulevard.
We'll do the rest."

The tops were off the crates.

Blade moved to the crate of grenades and selected four,
stuffing two into each front pocket. "Each of you take
four," he instructed Geronimo and Helen.

Geronimo hefted one of the grenades. "I just hope this
doesn't accidentally go off in my pants. My wife would be
terribly disappointed."

"I hope I get to cram one of these down Giorgio's
throat!" Helen said angrily.

Mario was running toward them. "The car is all set. It's
an antique Buick, built like a tank."

"Thanks," Blade said. He looked at the Don and
extended his right hand.

The Don, somewhat surprised, took the huge hand in his
own.

"I want your word," Blade declared. "If something
should happen to me, my friends must be permitted to
leave Vegas unharmed, no matter what else happens."

Don Pucci appeared hurt by the implication. "Need you
ask?"

"No, I guess not," Blade said. He squeezed the Don's
hand and let go.

"Let's go find that ding-a-ling in buckskins," Geronimo
remarked.

"May God be with you," the Don said to Blade. "Oh! I
almost forgot. It's important that you know Giorgio lives
on the third floor."

"Come with me," Mario directed. He turned and
jogged in the direction of a door on the left-hand side of
the rear wall.

Blade kept pace with the man in white, Geronimo and
Helen on his heels.

Behind them, Don Pucci was barking orders.

They crossed the casino, following Mario down a tiled
corridor until they came to an enormous kitchen with

white walls and sparkling utensils. Once through the kitchen, they traversed another hallway and exited the building by way of a red door. Before them was a sprawling parking lot filled with vehicles. Armed mobsters ringed the rear of the casino. Ten yards from the door was a dark blue Buick, the engine idling, three hit men standing near the grill.

"There's your car," Mario said.

They ran to the Buick.

One of the men near the grill looked at the Warriors, then at the car. "This is mine," he said sadly. "She's an antique. I've spent every spare penny I've earned to fix her up."

Mario smacked the front fender. "It's as solid as they come."

Blade opened the driver's door and slid in. The front seat was somewhat cramped for a man of his size. All the windows were down.

Geronimo and Helen walked to the other side. Helen climbed into the rear and Geronimo took the passenger side, resting the Browning barrel on the dash.

"Good luck," Mario offered, and hurried inside.

Blade closed his door and gripped the wheel.

The three mobsters had moved to one side.

"Try to keep her in one piece," the owner called sorrowfully. He looked like he was about to cry.

"I'll try," Blade said, and shifted into drive. He drove toward an exit on the northern boundary of the parking lot.

"Do you have a plan?" Geronimo asked.

"We'll use the Buick to get inside the Palace," Blade said. "Once we're there, we'll unload the grenades. After that, we wing it."

"I'm going to find Mindy," Helen vowed. "And I'll kill anyone who stands in my way."

"I hope Hickok and Mindy are okay," Geronimo commented.

"Check your weapons," Blade advised. He took a right at the exit and cruised toward the boulevard.

"Funny," Helen remarked. "I'm not nervous at all. I thought I'd have butterflies by now."

"You can have some of mine," Geronimo offered.

Blade was driving at five miles an hour. He surveyed the side street, pleased to note there wasn't a single soul anywhere. He did not want innocent bystanders harmed.

The boulevard appeared ahead.

Blade slowed until the Buick was scarcely moving. "We have to time this just right. Giorgio's men can't spot us before we reach the corner because the Golden Crown blocks their view. Once we reach the corner, they're bound to cut loose unless Pucci's men come through." He glanced at Geronimo. "When I give the word, fire one shot."

Geronimo drew his Arminius from its shoulder holster under his right arm. He cocked the revolver and poked the gun out of the window. "Ready."

Blade coasted to a stop 30 feet from the intersection. He unslung the Commando and placed the machine gun on his lap.

"I haven't seen any traffic on the boulevard," Helen mentioned.

"There shouldn't be any," Blade said. He stared at her, then Geronimo. "Take care of yourselves. And keep your eyes peeled for Hickok and Mindy."

"Say, Blade," Helen began.

"What?"

"If I don't make it, make sure Mindy reaches the Home," Helen said.

"You'll make it," Blade told her. He gazed at the boulevard and took a deep breath. "Give the signal."

Geronimo fired once.

Blade mentally counted to ten. Pucci's men should be tossing the smoke bombs into the boulevard. The smoke would disperse rapidly, enshrouding the boulevard between the two casinos in a gray haze. He was on eight when he heard the crackle of gunfire. That would be Giorgio's soldiers, belatedly firing at Pucci's men with the smoke bombs.

Nine.

Ten.

Blade tramped on the accelerator and the antique Buick surged forward. He took a sharp right at the intersection, the tires squealing, and angled the car toward the Palace. As expected, a cloaking cloud of smoke enveloped the boulevard. For several seconds he couldn't see a thing. He could only hope he was traveling in the right direction. Twice the Buick was unexpectedly jolted as it struck unseen objects.

Bodies?

The Buick bounced and bucked as it hit yet a third obstacle, and then the smoke was thinning.

Blade's hands inadvertently tightened on the steering wheel. They were on the short flight of cement steps leading up to the Palace's seven glass doors! "We're going to hit!" he cried, keeping the accelerator on the floor.

Faces were visible on the other side of the doors, astonished visages of shocked mobsters.

Blade ducked his head to spare his eyes from the flying glass.

With a resounding, thunderous crash, the Buick rammed into the center of the row of glass doors. The glass shattered, the metal frames buckling like so much paper. Beyond the doors was a hastily constructed wall of furniture and boxes similar to the barrier Don Pucci's men had erected in the Golden Crown. Its momentum hardly impeded by the doors, its engine roaring, the Buick plowed into the barricade, sending chairs and boxes and busted pieces of furniture in every direction. Several mobsters were hit by the grill and battered aside. Curses, shouts, and screams arose. And still the Buick hurtled onward.

Blade spied a group of hit men to the left and slewed the Buick toward them. They frantically attempted to evade the dreadnought, but he ruthlessly mowed them down.

Guns started firing, peppering the Buick's thick frame.

Fifteen yards off were rows of slot machines.

Blade slammed on the brakes. The Buick screeched to a jarring halt, its rear end whipping around and colliding with one of the slot machines, its front end facing the incensed mobsters. "Out!" he shouted, and shoved his door open.

The Buick's windshield dissolved in a spray of lead.

Blade vaulted from the car, rolling on his left shoulder and rising in a crouch with the Commando leveled. He squeezed the trigger, firing a burst into a charging cluster of hit men. Scrambling backwards, he reached the slot machines and ducked behind the nearest one.

Geronimo and Helen were coming around the passenger side, shooting on the run.

Blade stood, providing covering fire.

"Get them!" someone was bellowing. "Nail those sons of bitches!"

Helen took cover in back of a slot machine.

Geronimo blasted the Browning one more time, then dived for shelter.

Shots were thudding into the slot machines.

Giorgio's trigger men were assembling for a mass charge.

"Grenades!" Blade yelled, reaching into his right front pocket. He extracted one of his grenades and crouched close to the floor.

Geronimo and Helen did likewise.

Blade peeked around the edge of the slot machine. The mobsters were just starting forward, about 30 of them. "On the count of three!" he directed.

The slot machines were being struck again and again.

"Two."

There was a loud, defiant whoop from the hit men as they charged the slots.

"Three."

As one, the Warriors pulled the pins on their grenades and rose, their arms already sweeping back, then arcing around. The grenades sailed over the Buick, perfectly thrown, landing on the carpet in front of the onrushing mobsters and rolling under their pumping legs.

Blade, Geronimo, and Helen flattened.

The three concussions combined to produce an awesome

shock wave, and the floor seemed to heave upward and
settle down again.

Bits of flesh and chunks of bodies were blown across the
room. Several legs rained to the carpet.

"Oh me!" Blade commanded, heaving erect and racing
for the rear of the casino. He wanted to draw Giorgio's
men away from the front entrance. Two hit men appeared
and he killed them both.

Geronimo and Helen were pouring a lethal hail of lead
into any and all targets.

Blade noticed a door to his left. He sprinted toward it.

A mobster popped up from behind a table ten feet to the
right, a shotgun in his hands, aiming at the giant.

Blade started to whirl, knowing he would be too late,
expecting to feel the buckshot tearing through his body.

Helen saved him. Her carbine boomed, and the mobster,
hit in the face, was flung backwards.

Blade dashed to the door. He wrenched on the knob and
pulled it wide, intending to seek temporary sanctuary in
the corridor beyond.

A dozen or so trigger men were rushing down the hall
toward the door, coming to the aid of their colleagues.

"Hey! Look!" one of them shouted. "Who's he?"

Blade spun, desperately seeking somewhere they could
defend against the mobsters.

Another group of soldiers was storming across the
casino.

They were trapped!

CHAPTER EIGHTEEN

Hickok glanced to the right, in the direction of the scream. Was that Mindy? He raced along the corridor, hoping the scream would be repeated so he could pinpoint the room.

It was.

A second, subdued shriek punctuated the hall, emanating from a room to the right.

Hickok reached the door in two bounds. He tried to twist the knob, but the door was locked.

So what!

Hickok took a step back, then kicked, planting his right foot next to the doorknob.

The door held firm.

Frowning, Hickok struck with his foot twice more, and on the second kick there was a splintering crunch and the doorframe split from the base to the top. He tensed his left shoulder and slammed into the center of the door. He was elated when it swiveled inward, the lock dangling from only one screw.

Dear Spirit!

Hickok's elation turned to dismay at the sight he beheld: Kenney was straddling Mindy on a bed, striving to choke the life from her with a ragged strip of yellow bedspread.

Mindy was feebly swatting at Kenney's arms.

Kenney glanced up in shock at the Warrior. He released his grip and tried to reach a pistol under his left arm.

Hickok's reaction was instantaneous. He drew his right Colt and snapped off a shot.

The slug ripped through Kenney's right eye and out the rear of his head, the impact twisting his body to the right and knocking him to the floor.

"Mindy!" Hickok exclaimed, running to the bed and holstering his Colt.

Mindy stared at the Warrior in transparent relief. She clawed at the strip of bedspread, gasping for air.

Hickok swiftly removed the crude garrote.

"Hickok!" Mindy exclaimed, her voice raspy and hoarse. She was up and hugging him in the twinkling of an eye.

Hickok embraced her awkwardly for a moment. "There, there," he consoled her, feeling her tremble in his arms. "You're okay. You're safe. Everything is hunky-dory."

Mindy placed her face in the crook of his neck. Moist tears touched his skin. "Oh, Hickok!" she gasped.

"That's my handle. Don't wear it out," he said light-heartedly.

"Hickok!" Mindy stated again, as if his name was a tonic to her tortured emotions.

"We can't stay here," Hickok advised her.

"I'm scared," Mindy blurted. "That man almost killed me!"

"His killin' days are over," Hickok assured her.

Mindy stepped back, courageously composing herself. "Who else is with you?"

"Blade, some ornery Injun with a penchant for bull-slingin', and your mom," Hickok disclosed.

Mindy brightened. "My mom is here!"

"In the Golden Crown, across the street," Hickok said.

"We've got to find them."

Mindy rubbed her tender neck, taking deep breaths. "Give me a minute. I feel weak."

"That's to be expected," Hickok remarked, glancing at the doorway. "We really must skedaddle."

"In a second," she said. "You know, it's funny. I used to occasionally view being a Weaver at the Home as a dull vocation. But no more! I'll never gripe about my lot in life again! From now on, I—"

"Save it," Hickok said, cutting her off. He took hold of her right hand and walked toward the corridor. "I'm tickled pink that you've found your niche in life. I truly am. But this isn't the time or place for yakkin' about it. We've got to make tracks."

"Sorry," Mindy mumbled. "I'm just so happy! I feel like I could walk on air."

"I wish we could walk on air," Hickok commented. "It'd make gettin' out of here a lot easier." He stopped in the center of the hallway and gazed in both directions.

No mobsters were in sight.

"Maybe we lucked out," Hickok observed. "Maybe no one heard my shot."

"Which way?" Mindy inquired.

"The stairwell," Hickok suggested, retracing his steps. Once they were in the stairwell, he increased his pace.

"Where does this lead?" Mindy questioned.

"Whisper," he whispered.

"Where does this lead?" Mindy repeated in a hushed voice.

"Down," Hickok stated the obvious. "There might be an exit door at the bottom."

"I can't wait to see my mother again," Mindy mentioned.

Hickok abruptly halted.

"What is it?" Mindy asked apprehensively.

Hickok stared at the steps in perplexity. "The polecat is gone!" He peered over the railing.

"What polecat?" Mindy inquired.

"Later," Hickok said. They descended to the eighth

floor. He told her to wait, entered the hall, and returned in ten seconds with a rifle slung across his back. "My Henry," he explained, taking her hand once more. Down they went.

From far below came the muffled, yet unmistakable, report of an explosion. They heard the faint sound of gunfire.

"What's going on?" Mindy questioned.

"I wish I knew," Hickok muttered. He hastened ever lower, pondering the ramifications of the conflict being waged. From the sound of things, a full-fledged war had erupted. But who would be attacking Don Giorgio? And why? His friends must have come looking for him, and somehow managed to get into hot water. Leave it to those dummies to get into trouble when he had everything under control!

The noise of the shooting, intermixed with shouting and screams, grew louder and louder.

They passed landing after landing until they were between the fourth floor and the third, not ten feet from the landing door, which abruptly opened.

Hickok drew Mindy back against the stairwell wall. Her fingernails bit into the palm of his hand.

Six mobsters appeared and promptly descended the stairs. None of them bothered to look upward.

"Whew!" Mindy exclaimed. "That was close!"

"Come on." Hickok stepped down to the landing. He released Mindy's hand and cautiously approached the door. Don Giorgio's suite was on this floor. He looked through the window, verifying the hallway was vacant. "Don Giorgio was responsible for kidnapping you, wasn't he?"

"Yes," Mindy said.

"No one else?" Hickok asked.

"Just Giorgio's goons," Mindy replied. "Why?"

"Did you ever hear of a Don Pucci?" Hickok inquired.

"I heard the name mentioned," Mindy answered. "But I never met him. I was under the impression that Giorgio and Pucci are not on the best of terms."

Hickok nodded. "Everything is fallin' into place. I want you to stick close to me."

"I'm not about to wander off," Mindy promised.

"Walk directly behind me," Hickok instructed her. "If one of us is going to take a slug, I'd rather it be me."

"What do you mean by take a slug?" Mindy responded nervously.

Hickok didn't reply. He yanked the door wide and boldly proceeded along the corridor.

Mindy was about to inquire about the reason for leaving the stairwell, when a door ahead opened and two hit men emerged. They both toted machine guns, and their eyes widened as they saw the Warrior. She quickly stepped behind Hickok, but peeked around his right shoulder.

"Who are you?" one of the button men demanded.

"Where is Giorgio?" Hickok rejoined, his arms draped at his sides.

"Who the hell wants to know?" snapped the mobster.

"His executioner," Hickok replied.

The button men tried to bring their machine guns into play.

Mindy was opening her mouth to screech in mortal terror, momentarily forgetting who she was with and overlooking his reputation, certain they were both about to be shot.

But it was the other way around.

She glimpsed a blurred streak as Hickok pulled his revolvers and fired, the twin shots deafening in the corridor.

Each mobster was hit in the face just above the nose. Each one stumbled backwards and toppled over.

Hickok suddenly began walking quite rapidly toward the door at the end of the hall.

Mindy dogged him like a shadow.

A burly mobster stepped from a room on the left, a pistol in his right hand.

Hickok plugged him between the eyes, then walked even faster then before.

Mindy detected an urgency in his movements. She

marveled at the shootings she had witnessed. He had slain four men in twice as many minutes, and she wondered if she would see him kill more.

She did.

They were eight feet from the door at the end of the hall when it swung inward, framing a trigger man with a shotgun in the doorway.

Hickok shot him in the forehead.

Mindy was within an inch of the Warrior's back, craning her neck to look over his right shoulder. She intuitively sensed she was about to witness an exploit few Family members had been privileged to observe at close quarters: Hickok in action. She had heard stories of his deeds during the war against the Doktor and elsewhere, but she had never personally been an eyewitness to his prowess.

Now she was.

Hickok went through the doorway at a brisk clip, striding over the corpse blocking the door.

Mindy found herself in a large room containing a lot of chairs. On the other side of the room was a closed door, and the Warrior stalked up to it and flung it open.

A pair of trigger men were running toward them. One was armed with a machine gun, the other a pistol.

Hickok went for the most dangerous adversary first, the man with the machine gun. His right Colt cracked, and the trigger man reacted like he had been pounded in the head by an invisible sledge hammer; the mobster flipped backward onto a desk.

But even as Hickok had fired, so had the trigger man with the pistol.

Mindy saw Hickok's left shoulder jerk, and something tugged at her red hair. With a start, she realized the Warrior had been hit!

Hickok's left Python boomed, and the second mobster sprouted an extra nostril and pitched forward.

Mindy went to touch Hickok, to ask if he was okay, but he was pressing toward yet another door in their path. He was reaching for the doorknob when he did a very strange thing; he unexpectedly swept his left arm around, forcing her away from the shut door.

Not a second too soon.

The door was rocked by a machine-gun burst, the slugs bursting the wood outwards and crashing into the walls and furniture surrounding them.

Mindy flinched, covering her face with her right arm.

As abruptly as it began, the firing ceased.

And Hickok moved. He reached the door in a leaping stride and rammed his right foot into the lower half. The ravaged door swiveled inward.

Mindy, remembering his instructions to stay near him always, darted behind him in time to see a heavyset man fumbling with a mechanism on the large machine gun he was holding. He looked up, staring calmly at the Warrior, and he actually grinned.

"Wouldn't you know it," he commented pensively. "The damn thing jammed."

"Better luck next time," Hickok said, and his left Colt blasted.

The heavyset mobster stiffened as his left eye vanished and the rear of his cranium exploded, showering hair and flesh all over the thick carpet. He sagged to his knees, then fell forward.

Hickok strode into the huge chamber, glancing from left to right. "Blast!" he fumed. "Giorgio isn't here."

"But I am," said a mocking voice behind them.

Mindy, horrified, recognizing the voice, whirled.

There he was, covered with blood from his eyebrows to his waist, his nose twisted to the left, his lips split and several teeth broken, his chin and cheeks puffy and marked by welts, a machine gun in his hands, a furious gleam in his eyes.

"Ozzi!" Mindy cried.

Ozzi swept the machine-gun barrel to within a hairsbreadth of her nose. "Yes! Ozzi!"

Hickok had turned at the sound of Ozzi's voice, but his line of fire had been obstructed by Mindy. He shifted to the right.

"Don't even think it!" Ozzi growled, his finger

quivering on the trigger. "You do, and she's worm meat!"

Hickok frowned and tilted the Python barrels up at the ceiling.

"That's real smart," Ozzi said. "Now drop the revolvers!"

Hickok never hesitated. He knew he could drill Ozzi before the hit man squeezed the machine gun's trigger, and he also knew Ozzi's finger might tighten on the trigger in a reflexive death spasm. Either way, Mindy would die. Ozzi was holding a fully automatic Bushmaster.

The Colts fell to the carpet.

Ozzi beamed maliciously. "Now the Detonics and the rifle."

Hickok had forgotten about the pistol tucked under his belt. He slowly eased it loose and let go, then placed the Henry on the floor.

Ozzi glared at the Warrior, then Mindy. "Did you really think you'd get away from me?"

Mindy didn't answer.

Ozzi's eyes narrowed. "You're not so clever, bitch! I finally figured out why you turned down my marriage proposal."

Despite her revulsion and fear, Mindy responded. "Why?"

"Because you've got the hots for him," Ozzi said, leering.

"I do not!" Mindy declared, insulted at the insinuation.

Ozzi's lips curled away from his teeth. He resembled a rabid dog about to bite. "Don't lie to me! I know better!"

"You wouldn't know the truth if you tripped over it," Hickok said, hoping to draw some of the heat from Mindy.

Ozzi made a snarling noise and motioned to the right with the machine gun. "Get over there!" he barked at Mindy. "Move!"

Mindy shuffled several feet to the right.

Ozzi sneered at the Warrior. "Turn around!"

Hickok balked.

"Do it, or I'll shoot the bitch!" Ozzi roared.

Reluctantly, Hickok turned completely around.

Ozzi stepped over to the gunman and savagely rammed the barrel of his weapon into the Warrior's lower back.

Hickok gasped and clutched at the spot, lanced with agony.

Cackling, Ozzi pounded the Bushmaster across the gunfighter's head.

Hickok lurched forward, trying to pivot to protect himself.

With a cruel, primal, delight, Ozzi struck the Warrior on the left temple twice in succession.

Blood sprayed from Hickok's temple and he dropped onto his right knee, still struggling, striving to reach the mobster.

Ozzi slammed the Bushmaster's stock into the side of the Warrior's head, and Hickok finally went down. Laughing, Ozzi rotated toward Mindy. "Now it's your turn, bitch! You're going to suffer for what I've been through!"

Mindy retreated a step, panic welling within her.

"I owe you!" Ozzi declared. He gestured menacingly with the machine gun. "You'll be groveling at my feet before I'm through."

"Let us go!" Mindy pleaded. "Please!"

"Please!" Ozzi said, imitating the whine in her tone. "Kiss the world good-bye, scuzz!" He aimed at her chest.

"Wait!" commanded a new voice.

Mindy glanced at the doorway and nearly fainted. Just when she thought the situation couldn't possibly become any worse, it did.

Don Giorgio and Sacks had arrived!

CHAPTER NINETEEN

"Grenades!" Blade bellowed, tugging the second grenade from his pocket and pulling the pin as slugs smacked into the walls around him. He heaved the grenade into the corridor and dove for the floor.

Geronimo and Helen were just releasing their grenades at the group charging across the casino. Geronimo grunted and twisted to the right, then flattened. Helen followed suit.

The grenade in the corridor detonated first, and the cries of torment from the maimed and dying arose an instant later.

At the sight of the two grenades arching their way, the group in the casino frantically endeavored to disperse. They bumped into one another in their frenzy to escape the hurtling doom, and they were largely unsuccessful. A mere handful survived. The grenades went off in their midst— *Whomp! Whomp!*—and literally blew them to shredded pieces.

Blade crawled into the corridor, the Commando in front of him. Five or six trigger men were alive and closing. He fired, sweeping the Commando from side to side, stopping the mobsters with a withering wall of lead. As the last one fell, he jumped to his feet. "Oh me!"

Helen darted into the corridor.

Geronimo joined them, his right hand pressed against his side, grimacing. "I'm hit," he mentioned.

"How bad?" Blade asked.

"It creased my side," Geronimo said. "I can manage. Let's move!"

Blade raced for a door at the far end of the hallway. He could hear his companions pounding after him. They wound past the bodies of the dead mobsters, past unattached, ruptured limbs and contorted torsos. Once he almost slipped in a puddle of gore. Some of the trigger men were groaning piteously.

One of the soldiers, a man with a gaping hole in his abdomen, clutched at Helen's legs. She tripped, righted herself, and shot him in the mouth.

Blade was beginning to believe they would reach the door without further incident, but he was wrong. They were less than 15 feet from their goal when gunfire broke out to their rear.

The Warriors whirled, dropping to their knees.

Seven mobsters from the casino were in hot pursuit, firing as they ran.

Geronimo went prone, sighting the Browning and squeezing the trigger with a practiced economy of movement, the BAR thundering.

The leader of the pursuing pack dropped.

Helen lifted the Armalite and aimed at the next mobster. His life was momentarily spared when the carbine clicked instead of discharging. "Empty!" she cried, discarding the Armalite and drawing her .45-caliber Caspians. She fired both automatics simultaneously, and her original target tumbled to the floor.

Blade removed his third grenade, slipping it from his left front pocket and yanking on the pin. He spied one of the mobsters doing the same thing, and he tossed his before Giorgio's man could let fly. "Grenade!" he yelled, and sprawled onto his stomach.

The five remaining gangsters were virtually obliterated. They were packed together when both grenades exploded, one after the other. The corridor heaved and shook, plaster falling from the ceiling, dust permeating the air and obscuring the grisly remnants of the mobsters.

Blade was up and jogging to the door before the dust could settle. He distinctly heard shots from the casino, and he wondered if Don Pucci's men were assaulting the Palace. He reached the door and wrenched it wide, finding a stairwell on the other side.

Geronimo and Helen ran to the door. Geronimo was reloading the Browning. Helen had replaced the Caspians and was slapping a fresh clip into the Armalite.

"Ready?" Blade queried.

They nodded grimly.

Blade darted into the stairwell without bothering to establish whether Giorgio's men were already there, and he immediately regretted his foolhardiness.

Six well-armed trigger men were rounding a bend in the stairs above, halfway between the doorway and the next landing. They opened up the second they saw him.

Blade hit the floor and rolled alongside the stairs, effectively screening his body from view from above.

Geronimo and Helen, still in the corridor, provided covering fire.

The mobsters were compelled to retreat up the stairs to the landing.

All firing abruptly stopped.

Blade risked a hasty glance upward. The trigger men were not in sight. Were they hiding on the landing, waiting for the Warriors to ascend, or had they fled? Giorgio's men did not impress him as the craven type.

A minute elapsed.

Blade rose to a crouch and moved to the base of the stairs, his eyes on the landing.

Nothing.

Geronimo and Helen were waiting at the doorway, one on either side.

With his Commando angled upward, Blade cautiously advanced to the halfway point.

Still nothing.

Blade hesitated, chafing at the delay. Reaching the third floor swiftly was imperative. Don Giorgio's termination was essential if Don Pucci was to triumph. Every second the Warriors dallied increased the likelihood of Giorgio escaping.

Giorgio must *not* get away!

His lips a compressed line, Blade moved higher. In four strides he could see the landing clearly.

The mobsters were gone.

Geronimo and Helen were waiting at the bottom of the steps.

Blade motioned for them to join him, and while they climbed the steps he inserted a new magazine into the Commando, even though the one he replaced still contained over a dozen rounds.

"Where did they go?" Geronimo whispered.

"Beats me," Blade replied quietly.

"Do you hear all the gunshots coming from the casino?" Helen inquired.

Blade nodded. "Don Pucci's men, I bet. Which means Giorgio's soldiers in the casino will be preoccupied for a while. There could be more of his trigger men scattered throughout the building. If there are any on this next floor, I don't care. We'll leave them for Pucci's men to mop up. I say we're going directly to the third floor. Odds are, that's where we'll find Giorgio."

"Then what are we waiting for?" Helen asked sharply. "I want to get my hands on that bastard!"

"Let's go." Blade took off up the stairwell, alertly scanning the stairs overhead for any sign of the six trigger men. They passed the landing and kept going, and only when they were almost to the next bend did he realize his blatant error.

The six mobsters had not fled. They had gone into the corridor and crouched low against the walls, waiting for their foes to open the landing door so they could gun the

giant and the other two down. Their ambush was thwarted
when the three continued upward, but the mobsters were
equally pleased. They simply waited for the giant, the
woman, and the Indian to climb a little higher, and
without any warning the trigger men spilled onto the
landing and blasted away.

Blade heard the landing door opening, and he tried to
spin, knowing he had committed a grave mistake.
Geronimo and Helen were also in motion, but they were all
too late.

All three Warriors were hit.

Blade felt a searing, burning sensation in his right side.
He winced, forcing his mind to disregard the pain as he
returned the mobsters' fire.

Geronimo took a slug in the left thigh. He stumbled
backwards and fell, landing on his right side. Twisting, he
brought the Browning to bear and squeezed the trigger.

Helen, her body at an angle, trying to reach the cover of
the bend as she sighted on the trigger men, was struck
twice. The first shot dug a bloody furrow in her right
cheek. The second shot tore through her right shoulder just
under the bone. She was bowled over by the impact,
stunned for several seconds.

Blade saw two of the trigger men go down. The
remainder ducked into the corridor. He could guess their
strategy; they would regroup and reload, and in a minute
or so they would try another sneak attack. With Geronimo
and Helen both down, he couldn't afford to wage a
running firefight. He couldn't allow the trigger men to
harass them. With the realization came action, a maneuver
the mobsters would not be expecting. Instead of assisting
Geronimo and Helen, instead of helping them to reach the
bend, he opted for, as Hickok would say, the direct
approach.

He charged the landing.

One of the trigger men was at the slightly open landing
door, and he shouted a warning to his fellows as the giant
bounded down the steps four at a leap. He poked his
shotgun through the opening.

Blade saw the shotgun barrel and fired from the hip, his
burst striking the edge of the landing door, splintering and
chipping the wood.

There was a gurgling screech from the far side, and the
shotgun barrel disappeared.

Blade never missed a beat. He vaulted onto the landing
and grabbed the doorknob, flinging the door wide.

The trigger man with the shotgun was on the floor,
writhing and convulsing, miniature crimson geysers
spouting from his neck and chest, the shotgun lying across
his legs.

Three mobsters were left. One, on his knees, was coolly
reloading a Marlin. The other two were armed with
machine guns, and they automatically swung their
weapons toward the doorway as the giant materialized.

Blade fired first.

The pair with machine guns were both stitched across
the chest, their bodies propelled backwards to collapse on
the hall floor.

Blade pivoted and lowered the Commando barrel to bag
the trigger man with the Marlin.

The mobster possessed incredible reflexes. He had
dropped the Marlin and sprang toward the giant in a flying
tackle as his two associates were mowed down.

Blade never got off a shot. He felt strong arms encircle
his legs below the knees and he was knocked backwards,
losing his balance and falling, landing hard on his back.

The mobster, a powerful man with dark hair and green
eyes, wearing a grey suit, released the giant's legs and
lunged, grasping the Commando.

Blade tried to jerk the Commando free, and for several
seconds the two men thrashed on the landing, wrestling for
control of the gun.

The mobster broke the deadlock by kneeing the giant in
the nuts.

A spasm of pain caused Blade to bend forward, his
privates twinging, as the man in gray rolled to the left. He
saw the mobster's right hand vanish under the gray jacket
and reappear holding a 14-inch survival knife. With a

monumental effort, his teeth gritting, perspiration beading his forehead, Blade heaved to his feet.

Not expecting the giant to recover so quickly, the mobster had not immediately pressed his advantage. Now he crouched, the survival knife gleaming, his wary eyes on the Commando barrel which was pointing directly at him.

Blade took a deep breath, feeling his privates returning to normal. He noted the look of defiance in the mobster's eyes, and he admired the man's courage.

Several seconds elapsed.

Already perplexed by the giant's hesitation in shooting, the mobster was positively stupefied when the giant unexpectedly placed the Commando on the landing and drew the right Bowie.

"Are you any good with that toothpick of yours?" Blade asked, baiting him.

For an answer, the mobster came in fast and low, swinging the survival knife in a glistening arc.

Blade blocked the blow with a swipe of his Bowie, the two knives clanging as they struck. He backpedaled to avoid another swing, his movements slightly awkward due to lingering discomfort in his groin.

The mobster, noticing, pressed his attack.

Blade parried and evaded a skillful series of feints and jabs. He allowed himself to be forced to the railing, letting the mobster's confidence grow. Overconfidence bred carelessness, an adage proven time and again.

Like now.

Believing he was the superior knifeman, the mobster tried to end the fray quickly by feinting a stab at the giant's stomach, expecting the giant to counter by lowering the Bowie and leaving his neck exposed. So the mobster feinted, then arced his survival knife upward at the giant's throat.

Only the giant wasn't there.

Blade *had* lowered the Bowie to protect his stomach, but he had *also* shifted to the right at the same instant. As the mobster's arm swept the survival knife up, leaving the trigger man's midriff completely unprotected, Blade drove his Bowie into the man's abdomen to the hilt, then twisted.

With a strangled wheeze, the mobster stiffened and started to sag.

His enormous arms bulging, Blade used both hands to slice the Bowie from the mobster's stomach to the sternum. He yanked the Bowie out and stepped aside.

The mobster's eyes were wide and unfocused. His intestines and organs were bulging through the abdominal wound. He tottered forward into the railing and clutched at the top rail for support, but he couldn't seem to get a grip on it. Slowly, so slowly, he limply sagged over the top rail, his arms flailing weakly. With a pathetic whimper he pitched over the railing.

Blade wiped his Bowie on his pants and faced the stairs leading upward. He stopped and retrieved the Commando.

Geronimo was sitting on the step below the bend, the Browning in his lap, his legs drawn inward, staunching the flow of blood from his injured left thigh with a strip of cloth torn from his shirt. He grinned. "It's nice to see you haven't lost your touch."

Blade dashed up the stairs. "Can you walk?"

"I can hobble," Geronimo responded. "But I won't be running any marathons for a while."

"Maybe Helen can . . ." Blade began, then stopped, his eyes narrowing and searching the stairs above. "Where *is* Helen?"

Geronimo jerked his right thumb upward. "She went after Mindy."

"What?"

"She took off for the third floor while you were using that mobster for carving practice," Geronimo explained.

"Damn!" Blade snapped in annoyance. "She's not supposed to make a move without any orders."

"She's a woman, isn't she?" Geronimo remarked.

"What does that have to do with anything?" Blade demanded.

Geronimo chuckled. "How can you be married and ask such a ridiculous question?" he rejoined.

"We've got to go after her," Blade stated. "Here. I'll

give you a hand." He extended his right arm.

"No," Geronimo said. "I'll slow you down. Go on alone. I'll wait here."

"You're coming with me," Blade declared, "and that's final!"

"Fine by me," Geronimo agreed, taking Blade's arm and rising. He stared at his friend for a moment, then grinned. "Has anyone ever told you that your cheeks twitch when you're mad?"

CHAPTER TWENTY

"Don Giorgio!" Ozzi blurted out.

Don Giorgio entered the chamber, Sacks right behind him. The Don carried his Weaver Arms Nighthawk in his left hand. Sacks was armed with a pump shotgun.

Giorgio gazed at Ozzi's face. "What the hell happened to you? You look like you lost a collision with a cement truck."

Ozzi wagged his Bushmaster at the Warrior on the floor. "Hickok," he said simply.

Giorgio frowned as he looked at the Warrior. "Is he dead?"

"No," Ozzi said. "Just unconscious."

"Then we'll finish the son of a bitch off before we leave," the Don stated. He shifted his attention to Mindy. "I want her alive."

"I want to waste her!" Ozzi protested.

"We need her alive," Don Giorgio reiterated. "She's our ticket out of here. Don Pucci's men are in the casino. They'll be here before too long. We're leaving while the leaving is good."

"Where will we go, boss?" Sacks inquired.

"I have hideouts Pucci doesn't know about," Don Giorgio replied. "He hasn't won yet! I'll reorganize and throw everything I have at him."

"Where can Kenney be?" Sacks asked.

"We'll worry about him later," Giorgio said. "Right now, I need to grab my papers from my safe. You two stay put." He walked to a door on the left side of the chamber and went into the next room.

Ozzi glanced at Sacks. "I want the honor of snuffing the Warrior."

Sacks shrugged. "Suit yourself. He means nothing to me."

Mindy gazed from one hit man to the other. "You two are despicable!"

"Listen to who's talking!" Ozzi retorted.

"I hope I'm around when Blade catches up with you," Mindy taunted Ozzi. "I want to see the look on your face."

"Shut up!" Ozzi barked.

Mindy's loathing and resentment supplanted her caution. "Big, tough man, huh?"

"I said shut up!" Ozzi growled.

"We have babies at the Home who are more manly than you'll ever be!" she mocked him.

Ozzi took a step toward her, scowling in fury. "Keep it up, bitch!"

"Ozz!" Sacks said. "The Don needs her alive."

"But he didn't say I couldn't rearrange her face a bit," Ozzi hissed. He jabbed the Bushmaster stock at her face.

Mindy instinctively raised her hands to screen her head.

Which was the reaction Ozzi wanted. He smirked as he rammed the stock into her stomach instead.

Gasping, Mindy doubled over.

Ozzi laughed. "Want some more, scuzz?"

Mindy looked up through tears of anguish. She saw Ozzi cackling, and near the doorway Sacks was staring in disapproval at the younger button man. Sacks started to open his mouth, to say something, but the words never came out.

There was a swishing noise from behind Sacks, and a scintillating, streaking, metallic object swept into the rear of his head.

Sacks arched his back and uttered a choking, inarticulate, panting sound. His eyes bulged, his arms dropping loosely to his sides, the shotgun falling to the floor.

"Sacks?" Ozzi said in surprise.

Sacks took a single step, then keeled over, his head bending downward as he fell, revealing the rear of his cranium; his head was split open from neck to crown.

Mindy straightened in amazement as her gaze alighted on the person responsible for Sacks's demise. "Mom!" she cried.

Helen stood in a martial-arts stance, jodan-no-kamae, her bloody machete held in the same manner as the traditional katana. Her amber hair was disheveled, her black leather vest and pants spattered with gore. Blood caked her right cheek and chin, and her right shoulder was awash in crimson.

"She's your mom?" Ozzi blurted out, and tried to swing the Bushmaster around.

Helen was faster. She closed on the hit man and swung the machete, her blade deflecting the Bushmaster barrel to the right. With the deadly proficiency born of years of practice, she employed a reverse strike, slashing the machete across Ozzi's chest, the keen edge cleaving several inches into his flesh.

Ozzi screamed and frantically tried to back away.

Helen wouldn't let him. She took a measured stride and swung the machete with all her strength, catching the hit man in the throat and nearly decapitating him.

Ozzi was dead on his feet. His head flopped to the left as blood gushed from his ravaged neck, and he sank to the floor in lifeless silence.

Helen glared at the mobster for a second, then moved to Mindy.

"You're hurt!" Mindy exclaimed in alarm.

"It's nothing," Helen said. "A scratch."

For a moment mother and daughter gazed into each other's eyes in mutual love and devotion, and then they embraced in a hug.

"Oh, Mom," Mindy said, sniffling.

"It's over," Helen stated. "You're safe. No one will hurt you now."

"I wouldn't be so sure of that," commented a sarcastic, gruff voice.

Helen spun in the direction of the voice, putting herself between Mindy and the man in black six feet away. She raised the katana.

"I wouldn't, if I were you," the man remarked, pointing his Nighthawk at Helen.

"Don Giorgio!" Mindy declared in stark terror.

"How nice of you to remember me," Giorgio mentioned bitterly. He held the Nighthawk in both hands. On the floor to his right was a brown leather briefcase.

"You're the one who kidnapped Mindy!" Helen stated.

"Give the woman a prize," Don Giorgio taunted her. He looked at Sacks and Ozzi. "You Warriors are more trouble than you're worth."

Helen took a step toward him. "You deserve to die!"

Giorgio's grip on the Nighthawk tightened. "Don't be stupid, woman! You'll be cut to ribbons before you can get within two feet of me."

"You're going to kill us anyway," Helen noted.

Don Giorgio grinned. "True. So which one of you wants it first? Mother or daughter?"

Helen was girding herself for a desperate lunge.

"No answer?" Giorgio scoffed. "Well, then, I'll kill both of you together. What can be more appropriate?"

"How about if you go first, cow chip?" interjected someone in a distinctly familiar Western accent.

Mindy glanced to her right.

Hickok was lying on his stomach on the floor, the Henry snug against his shoulder, sighting down the barrel. He was smiling, his left temple coated with blood.

Don Giorgio froze, the Nighthawk still trained on Helen. He knew Hickok would drill him if he so much as blinked.

"Go ahead," Hickok said. "Make my year!"

Giorgio released the Nighthawk and the gun fell to the carpet. "I'm not an idiot."

"You could have fooled me!" Hickok retorted.

Smiling smugly, Giorgio held his arms up, palms outward. "I know all about you Warriors. You're real spiritual types. You live by some asinine code of honor." He chuckled. "You would never shoot an unarmed man."

"Do you know something?" Hickok asked, raising his chin from the Henry.

"What's that?" Giorgio responded arrogantly.

Hickok's features became an iron mask. "You're wrong."

In a startling flash of insight, Don Johnny Giorgio recognized he was staring death in the face. He took a step backward, fear flooding through him. "No!"

"Yes," Hickok said, and fired.

The heavy slug from the 44-40 lifted Giorgio from his feet and hurled him over a yard to crash onto his back. He pushed himself into a sitting posture and gawked at a gaping hole in the center of his chest. Whining in despair, he stared at the gunfighter.

"Say hello to oblivion for me," Hickok said softly, and squeezed the trigger.

Mindy heard the deafening retort of the Henry even as the top of Don Giorgio's head exploded over the carpet and he was knocked flat. This time Giorgio didn't move.

Hickok slowly stood and walked over to the Don.

"Is he dead?" Mindy queried hopefully.

"They don't come any deader."

EPILOGUE

"Are you positive I can't convince you to stay longer?" Don Pucci asked.

"Thank you for your kindness," Blade responded, "but we've stayed too long as it is. We must return to the Home."

They were standing on the front steps of the Golden Crown Casino. Pedestrians passed on the sidewalk, and the boulevard was filled with traffic.

"Peace has been restored to the city, thanks to you," Don Pucci remarked.

Blade gazed across the boulevard at the Palace. The front entrance was boarded over. "Will you reopen Giorgio's casino?"

"Eventually," Don Pucci said. "I think I'll have Mario run it."

"He's a competent man," Blade remarked.

Loud laughter sounded behind them.

Blade glanced over his right shoulder, smiling at the sight of Hickok, Geronimo, Helen, and Mindy emerging from the Golden Crown. Hickok sported a white bandage on his head, courtesy of the staff at a nearby hospital. Geronimo's right side was bandaged under his shirt, and his left thigh was wrapped tight with a white dressing. He had refused a crutch, and was walking with a pronounced limp. Helen's right cheek had required seven stitches, and her right shoulder was covered by a white binding. Blade reached down and gingerly touched his vest above the area on his right side wounded during the battle. The dressing was itching terribly.

"I tell you, pard!" Hickok declared. "These casinos are great ideas! How about if we try and convince the Elders to build one at the Home?"

"I doubt they'd consent," Blade replied.

"They don't know what they're missing!" Hickok said.

"I know someone who is probably missing you," Blade mentioned. "Your wife. We've been here a week. It's time to hit the road."

Helen walked up to Don Pucci. "Thank you for your hospitality. If you ever get up our way . . ."

"I'll keep the thought in mind," Pucci commented.

"What about the proposal I made?" Blade inquired. "We can always use another member in the Freedom Federation."

"Thanks, but no," Don Pucci said. "We have survived for over a century because we have scrupulously avoided all entanglements. We must uphold our neutrality."

"I understand," Blade commented.

Don Pucci gazed at the giant thoughtfully for several seconds. "There is some information I must pass on to you," he said. "But I must qualify my remarks. As you can imagine, with the thousands and thousands of visitors to Vegas every year, we hear a lot of stories, a lot of rumors. Most of it is worthless hearsay. Exaggerated tales. Inebriated rambling. But we do glean important information from some of our customers. They may mention a fact to a hostess, or to a bartender, or one of the pros. And if the information is considered to be of any merit, it is passed up the chain of command to me." He paused.

"Did you hear something about us?" Hickok asked.

"Was someone blabbin' about Blade's snorin' again?"

Pucci shook his head. "This is most serious. A man passed through Vegas several weeks ago. He spent several nights with one of the pros, and he talked a lot. She didn't think much of it at the time, because the man was a heavy drinker. But everyone in Vegas now knows we are in your debt. And when she realized you are the ones this man was talking about, she came to see me."

"What did this man say?" Blade questioned, his curoisity aroused.

"He told her about this group living in Minnesota," Don Pucci related. "He said his masters—that was the word he used—were planning to eradicate this group known as the Family."

The Warriors exchanged glances.

"Anything else?" Blade probed.

"This man mentioned the name of his masters," Don Pucci divulged. "They are called the Dragons." He frowned. "I have heard of these Dragons, Blade. I don't know a lot about them, but I do know they are based in the former state of Florida. And I know they have a reputation for viciousness unmatched by anyone else."

"Why would these Dragons want to take on the Family?" Hickok interjected. "We've never tangled with them."

"Again," Don Pucci emphasized, "I can't vouch for the reliability of this information. But I thought you should know."

"Thanks," Blade said. "We'll report it to our Leader."

"Is there anything you need before you depart?" Don Pucci inquired.

Blade thought of the SEAL, parked in the lot behind the Golden Crown. Mario had driven him from the city four days before so he could reclaim the transport. "No, thanks. We're fully provisioned and ready to go."

The giant Warrior and the Don shook hands.

"I hope we meet again some day," Don Pucci said.

"Take care," Blade stated. He turned and walked to the sidewalk, bearing to the left, intending to stroll around the

Golden Crown to the rear parking lot.

Hickok, Geronimo, Helen, and Mindy followed him.

"Say, pard," Hickok said, catching up with Blade. "I'd appreciate it if you wouldn't say anything to my missus about me spendin' a week gambling. She might not cotton to the idea."

"I won't lie for you," Blade remarked.

"Who's askin' you to lie?" Hickok queried. "I just don't want to get in trouble."

"You don't need to worry about Blade telling your wife," Geronimo spoke up.

Hickok looked back. "I don't?"

"Nope," Geronimo said, grinning. "Because I will."

"What did I ever do to you?" Hickok demanded.

"Do you want me to list everything?" Geronimo inquired. "There was the time when we were six years old, and you convinced me to take a bath in a mud puddle with my clothes on. Remember that? You claimed everyone did it, and my mother wouldn't mind. She did."

Hickok chuckled. "I'd plumb forgotten all about that."

"And there was the time when we were ten," Geronimo went on. "You persuaded me to stick a frog down Emily's dress. You claimed she loved frogs. She didn't."

Hickok snickered.

"And how about the time when we were fifteen?" Geronimo continued. "We went on a double date, remember? You suggested we should all go skinny-dipping in the moat. We were supposed to each get undressed separately, behind the bushes, then come out and go swimming. But when I stepped out in the open, I was the only one naked."

"I thought the girls would bust a gut laughing," Hickok recalled, and laughed.

"And you have the gall to ask about my reason for telling your wife?" Geronimo asked in amazement.

Hickok sighed and glanced at Blade. "It's pitiful."

"What is?" Blade responded.

"This mangy Injun is one of my best friends," Hickok muttered.

"I know. So?" Blade said.

"So with friends like him, is it any wonder I'm always in hot water?" Hickok lamented his fate.

Blade smiled. "Look at it from our perspective."

"What do you mean?" Hickok inquired.

"With a friend like you around," Blade said, "there's never a dull moment."

MIAMI RUN

Prologue

The night was perfect for a sacrifice.

A brilliant full moon illuminated the Everglades as the party of 13 robed figures and the woman in the blue dress threaded a path toward the grove on the island 50 yards ahead. A cool, moist breeze stirred the red robes of the 13 and caused the woman to shiver. Her fearful green eyes locked on the island and she stumbled.

The scarlet-robed figure to her rear stepped in close and gripped her left arm to prevent her from falling.

She regained her balance, but she recoiled defiantly at his touch, jerking her arms from his grasp. Her wrists were already hurting from the tight coils of rope binding them behind her back. "Don't touch me!" she snapped.

"We wouldn't want you to fall," the figure responded, his features enshrouded in the hood of his robe.

"I didn't know you cared!" she stated sarcastically.

"We care, Carmen," the figure said. "We care about keeping you clean for the Masters."

"Stuff the Masters!"

The red-robed figure sighed. "Such a childish attitude will only make it worse."

"What could be worse than dying?" Carmen retorted.

"You have no one to blame but yourself," the figure noted. "You deliberately violated the Precepts of Dealership. The consequences are inevitable."

Carmen glanced at the grove of trees and began chewing nervously on her lower lip as they moved nearer.

"You always were too smart for your own good," the figure commented. "You thought you were better than everybody else."

"I was," Carmen replied. "I was the best damn Dealer in the Dragons, and you know it!"

"Your distribution network was superbly organized," the figure conceded. "And your enforcement procedures were carried out to the letter. You had everything worth living for. Wealth. Power. Prestige. And you blew it."

"I was framed!" Carmen declared.

"You were stupid," the figure responded. "You weren't satisfied. How did you expect to get away with cutting your own deal? Did you really think the Masters wouldn't learn about your deception? The Masters know everything."

Carmen snorted. "They don't know crap!"

"They know you were cheating them," the figure said. "They know you were diluting the Powder of Life, then selling the watered-down bags at full market value. You were skimming some of the Powder to sell on the side and make yourself richer." He paused. "You were greedy."

"Lies! It's all a bunch of lies!" Carmen insisted.

"Please," the man said. "Don't insult my intelligence. Your hearing was fair and square. The evidence against you was overwhelming."

"What evidence?" Carmen retorted. "You took the word of a low-life junkie over mine!"

"Four complaints were lodged against you," the figure mentioned. "Three were from middle-echelon distributors. Only one was from a street junkie."

"That damn Harlan!" Carmen muttered.

"Harlan did the right thing. He knew he wasn't getting his money's worth, and every customer is granted the right to petition the Directors for a hearing."

"I was framed!" Carmen repeated.

"Suit yourself," the figure said. "But the thirteen of us listened to all of the evidence and rendered the only possible verdict. The Masters had advised us to keep—"

"They what?" Carmen interrupted.

"The Masters knew of your deception before Harlan and the others brought their formal complaints," he detailed. "The Directors were advised to keep an eye on your activities."

"You were?" Carmen asked in disbelief.

"We were," the robed man confirmed.

"But how?" Carmen queried.

"The Masters have their ways," he replied.

Carmen looked to the right and the left, gauging her chances of escaping. They were nil. The path to the island was the only solid strip of ground for hundreds of yards, surrounded by the mucky, peat-filled, treacherous soil of the Everglades submerged under a foot or more of water.

"Don't even think about it," the man advised, as if he could read her mind.

The party reached the eastern edge of the island and started up a slight incline. Wax myrtles and willows lined the path.

Carmen gazed toward the top of the rise. "I thought we were friends, Arlo," she commented.

"That's a cheap shot," Arlo said.

"You can get me off the hook with the Masters," Carmen stated. "They'd listen to you."

"Be serious."

Carmen licked her lips. "I am. Talk to them for me. Intercede in my behalf."

"I can't, and you know it."

"Please!"

"Don't beg," Arlo said. "It doesn't become you."

They climbed steadily higher.

"Tell them I'll straighten up my act," Carmen said. "Tell them I'll turn over a new leaf."

"Are you finally admitting your guilt?" Arlo questioned.

Carmen's slim shoulders slumped and she expelled the breath in her lungs. "All right," she declared. "I admit it. I wasn't framed."

"Surprise, surprise," Arlo said dryly.

"What if I make a full confession?"

"It wouldn't do any good," Arlo told her. "The execution verdict is final."

"I can always try," Carmen said.

"I expected better from you."

Carmen glanced over her left shoulder. All she could see was the tip of Arlo's angular chin and his nose protruding from his hood. "What else can I do? What would you do if you were in my shoes?''

"I would never allow my ego to supplant my better judgment," Arlo remarked.

"I don't want to die!" Carmen declared bluntly.

"Who does?"

Carmen faced the path, a feeling of utter helplessness welling up within her. Her resolve faltered and her courage flagged. A sensation of weakness engulfed her legs and she slowed.

"Don't drag your heels," Arlo admonished.

Carmen looked at him and mustered a feeble smile. "We've been through a lot together."

Arlo didn't respond.

"We organized our distributorships at the same time," Carmen mentioned. "We rose through the ranks together. Hell, we were even appointed as Dealers on the same day."

"It won't work," Arlo said. "You can't expect me to change my mind by recalling the good old days. Those days are long gone. We've been out of touch in recent years, and the fault wasn't mine. You set yourself up as a queen in your district. You lorded it over everybody. Where are all your other old friends? I'll tell you. They don't want to have anything to do with you. You alienated everyone with your ambition, Carmen.''

"I always treated you with respect.''

"Only because you had to," Arlo stated. "As a fellow Dealer, I was your equal.''

"And now you're more than my equal," Carmen said bitterly. "You were selected to become a Director. I was overlooked.''

"You would have been selected as a Director someday," Arlo observed.

"Someday! When?" Carmen demanded. "I was tired of waiting! You became a Director over four years ago. Why wasn't I given a Directorship? My qualifications were as good as yours.''

"The Masters didn't think so.''

"The Masters have had it in for me since the beginning," Carmen maintained.

"Have you been snorting your own sneeze?" Arlo inquired.

"Up yours!"

They reached the rim, the 13 forms in red fanning out. Arlo took Carmen by the right shoulder and led her toward the middle of the large clearing crowning the island.

Carmen gasped. "Please! No!"

"Be brave," he advised.

The clearing was man-made, 20 yards in diameter, and bathed in the additional glow of a half-dozen braziers positioned at regular intervals around the edge. Flickering embers drifted skyward from the metal receptacles. Flat, knee-high granite pedestals encircled a low marble slab situated in the center.

Carmen tensed and halted.

"There's no resisting," Arlo stated, pulling her toward the marble slab.

"This can't be happening to me!" Carmen mumbled in a daze.

A pair of red-robed forms walked over to assist Arlo, one taking Carmen's left arm, the other her right, and as Arlo stepped aside they dragged her to the slab.

"Please!" she whined. "I'm begging you!"

"Save you breath," Arlo said, following them. "You'll need it."

Each of the figures in red was stepping onto one of the kneehigh, square granite pedestals. The pair holding Carmen stood her upright next to the slab, then turned and dutifully climbed onto their pedestals. Every pedestal was spaced a precise distance of seven feet from the marble. Only one was left unoccupied, the pedestal to Arlo's rear. He stood to the right of Carmen, his hood facing the slab.

Carmen began to tremble. "Please, Arlo!"

"Stop it!" he barked. "You've sealed your fate! Now have the decency to meet it with dignity!"

"I could make a deal," Carmen said hopefully.

"You have nothing to deal with," Arlo assured her.

The wind was picking up and shaking the leaves on the

willows and the other trees.

Carmen stared to the north. "How many do you think will come?" she asked with a tremor in her voice.

"I don't know," Arlo said.

"I hope Radnor isn't one of them," she commented. "He's the worst of them."

"You cannot judge the Masters by our standards," Arlo stated. "They are as different from us as night and day."

"Or mutants from humans," Carmen noted.

"Mutants will be with us forever," Arlo opined. "World War Three saw to that."

"Maybe so," Carmen said. "But how many humans serve mutant Masters? How many kiss mutant ass for a living?"

"You're being petty," Arlo remarked stiffly. "You were willing to serve the Masters while it suited your purposes." He paused, his hood swiveling toward her. "I once thought you had a good head on your shoulders, but I see now that you can't accept reality. You can't accept the world as it really is. You still mistakenly believe humans are the dominant species."

"We are," Carmen said.

"Oh? Is that why you served the Masters for eleven years?"

"I wanted power," Carmen admitted. "And the Masters reward those who serve them efficiently with ever-increasing power."

"You attained a position of power," Arlo said, "but you abused your trust. You failed to place your position in its proper perspective. You were a servant, Carmen. A Dealer, true, but still a servant. And that's as it should be. Eventually, all humankind will serve mutant rulers."

"You're crazy," Carmen mentioned.

"Am I?" Arlo rejoined. "Take a good look at our world. World War Three unleashed incalculable amounts of radiation on the environment. The entire biological chain was affected. And radiation, old friend, inevitably causes mutations in living things. Scientists knew this. They experimented with deliberately producing mutant strains in their laboratories, both by genetic engineering and through controlled radiation exposure. One of the first mutants they created was a hairless cat—"

"A hairless cat?"

"That's right. It cooed like a pigeon, wagged its tail just like a dog, and ate like a horse. Even its body temperature was higher than a normal feline. The scientists went on from there, of course, to develop many other mutations. And again, this was before the war." Arlo stared at the moon. "World War Three transformed the planet into a mutant breeding ground. Whereas prior to the war a mutation might occur naturally in a species every one hundred thousand generations or so, the radiation unleashed by the nuclear weapons caused mutations in every species immediately after the war. Think of it! Every species was drastically affected simultaneously! And the mutations have been appearing ever since."

"One day the humans will wipe the mutants out," Carmen said.

"Never happen," Arlo said, disagreeing. "There are too many mutants now. Both the wild ones—the two-headed bears and the six-legged alligators and the like—and the mutants stemming from human ancestry will be with us always."

"Were the Masters human once?"

"No," Arlo replied. "But ninety-four years ago the first Master was born to human parents. The parents must have consumed tainted radioactive substances, and the result was the formation of an embryo unlike any other ever known." He chuckled.

"You sound like you're happy about it."

"I owe everything I am to the Masters," Arlo said. "The birth of the first one was a monumental occasion."

Carmen scrutinized the trees lining the north side of the clearing and shuddered. "Where did the other six come from?"

"The first Master's human parents gave birth to a daughter a year later," Arlo detailed.

"Jarita?"

Arlo nodded. "Jarita. She and Orm mated."

"Orm was the firstborn?"

"Yes."

"Somehow I received the impression Radnor was the oldest," Carmen commented. She was feeling grateful for the conversation. *Anything* was better than contemplating her inpending fate.

"Radnor is the oldest son," Arlo explained. "Then came Dimitri, Sapphira, Quartus, and Marva."

"I never knew," Carmen said. "It's impossible to guess their age by their appearance." She glanced at Arlo. "You seem to know everything about them."

"Orm trusts me," Arlo stated proudly. "Physically, they're different from us. But they have the same emotional needs. They can be our friends."

Carmen snorted. "Now who's not facing reality?"

"You simply don't understand them," Arlo said. "You never did. Look at what they've accomplished. A handful of mutants have subjugated the southern third of what was once the state of Florida. Seven mutants rule a hundred thousand humans! Amazing!"

"Why are there only seven? Why didn't they breed more?"

"They tried," Arlo answered. "But that's the trouble with mutations, especially those created by excessive radiation. The mutants have difficulty procreating. Most of their offspring are stillborn. Even when they do give birth, the infants might be deformed or mutated more than the parents. Orm and Jarita were able to have five children. That was all. And Radnor and the others have been unable to continue the line. Orm once considered the idea of mating with humans, but they decided against it."

"Thank God," Carmen remarked.

Arlo straightened. "They will be coming soon."

Carmen pursed her lips. "Why did Orm's parents let him live? If I had a child like him, I'd drown it."

"You would," Arlo said testily. "Fortunately, Orm's human parents couldn't bring themselves to slay him. He must have been an adorable baby."

"Adorable!" Carmen declared, then laughed. "You're

worse than crazy! You're really sick in the head! How can you call something like him adorable?"

"You wouldn't understand."

"Try me."

"The Masters are the pinnacle of mutant evolution. They're more intelligent than humans, they're stronger, and they're more adaptable. We should feel privileged to serve them," Arlo stated earnestly.

Carmen stared at the marble slab and blanched. "I always thought they picked a strange name for their organization."

"The Dragons? What could be more appropriate?"

There was a loud splashing from the north side of the island.

Carmen jumped. "What was that?"

"A fish or a gator," Arlo said. "Maybe a turtle. Who knows?"

Carmen tried to relax, an impossibility given the circumstances. She wiggled her fingers and flexed her arms to keep her circulation flowing. "Any chance of being untied?"

"The Masters will untie you when the time comes," Arlo said. His hood bobbed up and down as he studied her. "Since we're being so honest with each other, maybe you'd see fit to set me straight."

"About what?"

"Why, Carmen?" Arlo queried. "Why'd you do it?"

Carmen frowned. "You hit the nail on the head earlier. I did it for wealth and power."

"But you already had wealth and power," Arlo observed. "You were a Dealer in a prime district."

"It wasn't enough," Carmen said. "Once a person gets a taste of genuine power, they always want more. Power is addictive. I wasn't satisfied. I wanted to be appointed to the inner circle, to become a Director. When they made you one, and not me, I realized I would have to increase my power base myself. That's why I took the initiative and contacted Don Giorgio in Las Vegas."

"You did what?"

Carmen laughed, a brittle sound. "Do you mean to tell

me the Masters didn't let you know about my Vegas activities? I thought they know everything.''

"You overstepped your bounds," Arlo said. "No one except the masters may negotiate distribution contracts. Besides, Las Vegas is already part of our distribution net work.''

"But the Vegas market is far from saturated," Carmen noted. "And they pay for their Powder of Life in gold and silver.''

Arlo suddenly raised his right hand and snapped his fingers. "So that's it! You diluted the Powder you were sending down the line on your network, then shipped the skimmings to Don Giorgio for him to sell there. What kind of split did you arrange?''

"Fifty-fifty," Carmen confessed.

"I'm surprised Don Giorgio went along with your scheme," Arlo mentioned. "He knows the consequences of violating a contract with the Dragons.''

Carmen bowed her head. "Giorgio is dead.''

"What?''

"He planned to use his share of the profits to finance his war against the other Dons," Carmen elaborated. "Giorgio wanted to take over Vegas.''

"The other Dons found out and had him killed?" Arlo speculated.

Carmen shook her head. "The Warriors killed him.''

Arlo's robed figure visibly stiffened. "The Warriors? How did they get involved?''

"I'm not sure," Carmen said. "My regular runner to Vegas couldn't find out.''

"The damn Warriors again!" Arlo snapped. "They pop up all over the place! The Masters will want to hear this news.''

"Do you think the Masters will step up their timetable for destroying the Family?''

"I wouldn't doubt it," Arlo said. "They—''

A muted hum sounded in the distance, from the north.

"Oh, God!" Carmen exclaimed in alarm.

The hum grew in violence, becoming a distinct, peculiar buzzing.

"Your hour of reckoning has arrived," Arlo commented.

Carmen started to back away from the marble slab, but he grabbed her right arm.

"You're not going anywhere."

"Let go of me!" Carmen cried, vainly striving to break free.

"Be still."

Carmen listened as the buzzing grew louder and louder. "I'll pay you!" she blurted.

"Pay me?" Arlo repeated.

"Yes! I have over two million in gold in a secret stash!" Carmen said. "No one knows about it! It's all yours if you'll let me go!"

"Two million, huh?" Arlo remarked.

"That's right! And it would all be yours!" She glanced at the ring of robed figures. "All of you! You could split it!"

"What good would the gold do us if we're dead?" Arlo asked.

"The Masters don't need to know!" Carmen stated. "You could lie! You could say I fled Florida and you weren't able to apprehend me!"

"Do you really expect to be able to buy us off?" Arlo inquired. "The Directors of the Dragons don't need your paltry two million." His head shook back and forth. "You don't understand at all."

"What's there to understand?"

Arlo gestured at the robed forms on the granite pedestals. "Why do you think we were selected as Directors? Why do you think you were denied promotion to Director rank?"

"I never—" Carmen began.

"I'll tell you!" Arlo said, cutting her off. "You pathetic bitch! We were chosen because we owe our exclusive allegiance to the Masters. We don't care about money, or power, or all the rest of the trappings that go with our posts. All we care about is serving the Masters. Nothing else. Which explains the reason you weren't promoted, why you would never have risen higher than a

Dealer. The Masters aren't fools! They evaluate us according to our loyalties and promote us accordingly. They knew where your loyalties were.''

The humming now resembled an odd, pronounced whirring.

"They're almost here!" Carmen cried, and tried to bolt.

Arlo held on tight. He motioned at the pair who had assisted him previously, and they promptly jumped from their pedestals and hurried to Carmen. They seized her arms.

"No!" Carmen wailed.

The whirring reached a crescendo, then abruptly ceased.

Carmen felt her stomach muscles tighten. She gazed at the north side of the clearing with baited breath. The trees were engulfed in inky shadows, and a minute elapsed before she spied the dark, lean shapes moving toward the clearing, their tall bodies rising and falling with their unearthly rolling gait.

"The Masters," Arlo said happily.

Carmen wrenched her body backwards, frantically attempting to flee, her face a mask of stark terror.

Seven alien forms materialized at the edge of the clearing and halted.

Arlo bowed, his hands clasped at waist height. "Masters!"

The seven advanced toward the marble slab.

"No!" Carmen shrieked, bucking and heaving. She kicked the red-robed form to her left, but he ignored the blow.

One of the seven, the tallest, bounded forward. It reached the marble slab and rounded the end, coming for Carmen.

She threw back her head and screamed.

The tall Master clamped its right hand on her neck, its left grasping the fabric of her dress over her breasts, and lifted her into the air with supreme ease. "Greetings, Carmen,'' it said in a guttural voice. "Long-time-no-see.''

Carmen gurgled and thrashed.

"Be patient," the Master advised coldly. "We're not about to rush the proceedings on your account. You should be grateful for the unique experience you're about to undergo. Not many humans have ever been skinned alive!"

The steely grip on her neck slackened just a bit, and Carmen screamed even louder.

CHAPTER ONE

"Did you hear that?"

"I heard it. Was it thunder?"

"Thunder don't sound like that. Besides, there ain't a cloud in the sky."

"Then what was it?"

"I don't rightly know."

The twins studied the sky to the west, the bright sun making them squint.

"Let's go have a look-see," suggested the boy.

"No way!" objected his sister.

"Come on!" he goaded her. "I think I saw somethin' over there a ways."

"Poppa would blister our butts, and you know it, Leo."

"Come on, Ernestine! Don't be such a candy-ass!" Leo said. He placed the bundle of sugar cane he was carrying on the ground.

"What are you doing?" Ernestine demanded.

"What does it look like?" Leo retorted. He wiped the sweat from his forehead with the back of his right hand.

"We can't just leave the cane here!" Ernestine protested.

"What's gonna happen to it?" Leo asked.

Ernestine gazed to the west, frowning. "We'll get in trouble for sure."

"It won't take but ten minutes," Leo assured her. "We got to go see what it was."

Never one to deny her brother for long, Ernestine deposited her bundle of cane beside his.

"All right!" Leo declared. "That's more like it!"

"You lead," Ernestine said. "And we'd best not run into anything!"

"Don't worry," Leo said. He patted the machete in its sheath on his right hip. "I can take care of us."

"Big talk for a fourteen-year-old," Ernestine remarked.

"Poppa says I'm a man now," Leo said. "And don't you forget it!"

"Men do their duties. They don't go chasing noises and funny lights," Ernestine mentioned.

"Then you saw the lights too?" Leo asked.

Ernestine nodded.

"What do you think they was?"

"I don't know," Ernestine replied.

"It looked like the sun was reflectin' off of somethin' shiny," Leo guessed. He hastened to the west.

"Slow down!" Ernestine complained.

"You're the one who's worried about gettin' our butts blistered," Leo reminded her.

Ernestine walked faster, sticking to her brother's heels, watching the sweat trickle from under his Afro. The scorching July heat caked her faded jeans and yellow blouse to her trim body. Leo's jeans and brown shirt were stained with sweat marks. She glanced down at her grungy sneakers, at the holes exposing her toes, thankful for the ventilation.

"It can't be more than a mile," Leo said.

"I ain't going no mile."

"A mile's not far."

"The hell it ain't," Ernestine declared. "We're in the bush, you idiot!"

Leo skirted a dense cluster of shoulder-high bushes. "So?"

"So there's *mutants* in the bush," Ernestine stated.

"There ain't many mutants in these parts," Leo said.

"One is enough to waste your black butt," Ernestine commented.

"All you do is gripe."

"Let's just get this over with," Ernestine advised.

They trekked westward, staying in the open areas where possible. Once they startled a marsh rabbit, distinguished by its short, broad ears. It took off from a clump of weeds in their path and zigzagged to the west, its small gray and brown tail bouncing with each leap.

"There must be water hereabouts," Leo remarked.

Ernestine felt her skin crawl. She didn't like the idea of being near water. Water meant a swamp or a marsh. Water meant a lot of wildlife. Water meant possible mutants. "Let's go back," she recommended.

"Not yet."

"Come on! This is stupid!"

"Just a ways yet," Leo insisted.

They hiked for several hundred yards.

"This is stupid," Ernestine reiterated, peeved.

Leo didn't reply. He angled to the left, heading up a low hill.

"What are you doing?" Ernestine asked impatiently.

"We'll see good from this hill," Leo said.

They reached the crest of the hill and halted. To the west stretched a swampy tangle of lush vegetation.

"This is it!" Ernestine announced. "I ain't going no farther!"

"We could go a little ways," Leo urged.

"Not into no swamp!" Ernestine stated. "You know better."

Leo sighed. "I guess you're right." He sauntered down the hill toward a wide pool of brackish water.

"What are you doing?" Ernestine questioned, following. "I said this is it!"

"Just to the edge of the water."

"What difference does it make?" Ernestine snapped.

Leo disregarded her protest, walking to the bank bordering the pool.

"Leo! I want to go home! Now!" Ernestine stepped to his left.

"Hold your horses," Leo responded. He knelt at the edge of the bank and dipped his left hand into the water.

"Don't drink that!" Ernestine warned.

"How dumb do you think I am?" Leo asked. He cupped water in his left hand and splashed the cool liquid on his face.

Ernestine hesitated for a moment, then joined him. "This feels nice," she commented, swirling her right arm in the pool. She imitated her brother, feeling a sense of relief as the water trickled down her cheeks, over her chin, and moistened her neck.

Leo rose. "Okay. Let's go."

"Not so fast," Ernestine said, reaching for another handful of water. As she did, her left foot slipped, throwing her off balance to the left.

The motion saved her life.

An alligator surged from under the water, its mouth opening wide, its broad, rounded snout tilted upwards, its teeth exposed. The gator's jaws closed within an inch of Ernestine, who screeched and scrambled backwards.

Leo gripped her by the armpits and hauled her from the bank.

The alligator came after them, a huge specimen over 12 feet in length, its powerful, squat legs propelling it up and over the bank at a speed belying its bulk. The beast snapped at Ernestine's feet, missing her heels by a hairsbreadth.

"Leo!" Ernestine squealed.

Leo jerked her upright, twisted, and shoved, sending her stumbling. "Run!" he shouted. He took a stride.

Her eyes riveted on the gator, terrified to her core, Ernestine saw the massive reptile lunge forward. She screamed as its maw closed on her brother's right leg with a sickening crunch.

Leo stiffened, his brown eyes bulging, and shrieked.

The alligator twisted its head, upending its victim.

"Leo!" Ernestine cried.

Her brother was flat on his back, his face contorted in severe agony, desperately striving to draw his machete.

Ernestine froze.

The gator began to move backwards, dragging Leo, intending to savor its meal in the pool. With slow, measured steps, it slid toward the water.

"Leo!" Ernestine yelled, her fear for his safety eclipsing her instinctive sense of self-preservation. She darted to the left, past Leo, and up to the gator's head.

"Run!" Leo shouted, pulling the machete.

Ernestine kicked at the reptile's protruding right eye, but missed. "Let go of him!" she wailed.

The alligator abruptly shifted position, bending its body in half, whipping its heavily armored tail in a tight arc while keeping its teeth imbedded in its prey's leg.

Ernestine felt something slam into her left side, and then she was sailing through the air to crash onto her back on the hard ground. Dazed by the impact, she forced herself to roll over and faced the pool.

The lower third of the gator's serrated tail was already in the water.

Leo swung the machete, landing a blow on the reptile's snout.

The beast's eyes blinked, but that was the only reaction as it continued to ease backwards into the water.

"Leo!" Ernestine shouted in dismay. The alligator would drag her brother under the surface! Leo would drown! She pushed to her knees.

Half the reptile's tail was immersed.

"Leo!"

A loud pounding unexpectedly sounded to Ernestine's rear. A hurtling figure flashed past her, a giant of a man in a black leather vest, green fatigue pants, and black boots. She gaped at the newcomer in astonishment as he launched himself in a flying dive *onto the alligator*! Mesmerized, she saw the man swing his legs around as he landed on top of the reptile. His left arm looped under the alligator's thick neck as his right arm swept aloft. Clutched in his right hand was a gleaming knife.

Leo, about to swing the machete again, froze.

Ernestine couldn't believe her own eyes! The giant was the biggest man she'd ever seen, at least seven feet in height, and his body rippled with layer upon layer of bulging muscle. His hair was dark, hanging above his gray eyes. She glimpsed his features in the fraction of a second before he went into action.

The giant's right hand plunged downward, burying his large knife in the gator's head between the eyes.

Ernestine saw the alligator respond in a fury, releasing

her brother and swiveling its head toward the giant. It snapped at the man with the knife, unable to get a grip. The newcomer's knife sank into the gator's head again and again. With an enraged hiss, the reptile suddenly scrambled backwards into the pool, and no sooner was it in the water than the gator rolled, seeking to dislodge its foe.

The water became a wild whirlpool of thrashing forms, the reptile spinning over and over as the man hung onto its neck and repeatedly stabbed his knife into the gator's head.

Ernestine was filled with awe at the white giant's daring. But how could any man, even someone with his incredible physique, hope to kill a 12-foot gator with just a knife?

More pounding came from behind her. Two men raced to the edge of the pool and halted. One was a lanky man dressed in buckskins and moccasins. His hair and sweeping mustache were both blond. Around his slim waist were strapped a pair of pearl-handled revolvers. A camouflage backpack rested between his shoulder blades, and a rifle was slung over his left shoulder. He stood six feet tall, an easy head and shoulders above his smaller companion. The second man was dressed all in black, a glimmering sword held in his hands. His features were Oriental, his hair dark. Like the man in buckskins, the man in black had a backpack. An M-16 was slung over the Oriental's right shoulder.

For a second or two Ernestine was distracted by the arrival of the two men. She glanced at the pool again to find the gator on its side, struggling feebly, as the giant continued to ram his knife into the beast.

The man in buckskins took a step into the pool, but the wiry man in black grabbed the blond's left arm.

"It's not necessary," the man in black said. "The alligator is finished."

"I reckon," the one clad in buckskins responded uncertainly. His hands hovered near his pearl-handled revolvers.

The short man in black turned and studied Leo for a

moment. He replaced his sword in a black scabbard slanted under his black belt above his left hip, then walked to Leo. "I'll tend your injury," he offered in a soft tone.

Leo appeared to be in a state of shock. He simply nodded, his mouth slack.

Ernestine slowly stood.

The alligator was limp, all except for the sluggish twitching of its tail. A punctured mess of flesh, spurting blood, was all that remained of the creature's upper head.

Ernestine watched as the giant straightened, the water reaching above his waist. He stared at the gator, evidently insuring the reptile was no longer a threat. Satisfied, he looked at the man in buckskins and smiled.

"You're lucky it was just a little one," the man in buckskins quipped.

"You call this little?" the giant retorted, moving toward the bank.

Ernestine saw the alligator abruptly turn upright, its wicked maw swooping at the giant's back. She went to yell a warning, but the man in the buckskins was faster. His hands were twin streaks as his revolvers cleared leather, and both guns boomed simultaneously.

The gator's eyes exploded.

Perhaps sensing his danger, the giant had started to pivot to confront the reptile. He watched as the great body sagged and was partially submerged, then he headed for shore again. "Thanks," he said to the blond man.

The gunman chuckled and twirled his revolvers into their holsters. "It was a piece of cake, pard."

"For you maybe," the giant said. "But try killing an alligator with a Bowie knife sometime. It isn't easy."

"It gave you an excuse to take your annual bath," the gunman remarked. "Besides, you like doing things the hard way."

The giant placed his Bowie knife in a sheath on his right hip.

Ernestine realized the giant was carrying an identical

Bowie on his left hip, and for the first time she noted the two ammo belts crisscrossing his broad chest.

"Do you think that critter might have a hubby hereabouts?" the gunman asked as his enormous friend stepped onto the bank.

"Maybe," the giant answered. He glanced at the carcass. "What makes you think that one was female?"

"Anything that contrary had to be," the gunman joked.

"And you talk about me being lucky," the giant muttered.

"What's that supposed to mean?"

"It means you're the lucky one," the giant said. "If Sherry wasn't such an understanding wife, she would have booted you out the door years ago."

The gunman elected to change the topic. He faced Ernestine and smiled. "Howdy, ma'am. The handle is Hickok," he disclosed, crossing to her and extending his right hand.

Ernestine gazed up into a pair of alert blue eyes. "Hello," she responded, shaking.

"The Spirit smiled on you today," Hickok remarked, nodding at her brother.

Leo was lying on his back, grimacing, his right forearm on his forehead.

The short man in black had deposited his backpack on the dirt and removed a brown leather pouch. Having lifted Leo's shredded pant material to one side, he was administering a greenish powder to the deep lacerations.

The giant walked over to the man in black. "How is he, Rikki?"

The one called Rikki looked at the man with the Bowies. "I believe the leg is broken," he replied. "He requires stitches in two of the gashes. The rest is not as serious." He paused. "The herbs will prevent an infection, but the leg should be set and the wounds cleansed with hot water as soon as possible."

"We could start a fire here," the giant proposed.

"Our cabin!" Ernestine blurted. "Bring him to our cabin!"

"Is your cabin nearby?" the giant inquired.

"It's five miles or so that way," Ernestine said, pointing to the east.

"The cabin would be better," Rikki mentioned.

"Then the cabin it is," the giant stated. "I'll carry the boy. Hickok, you bring the girl. Rikki, my gear." He nodded at a point behind Ernestine.

She turned and discovered another camouflage backpack and an automatic rifle ten feet to her rear. The giant must have dropped them when he came to their rescue. She began to rotate toward the giant, and was startled when a strong arm encircled her waist and another scooped her up by the knees. "What?" she exclaimed.

"Don't fret none," Hickok advised, holding her close to his chest.

Ernestine could see the giant lifting Leo with extreme care. "Put me down! I can walk!"

"It will be quicker this way," Hickok told her.

"I can walk!" Ernestine protested.

"You've just been through a nasty ordeal," Hickok observed. "You rest and leave the runnin' to us." He jogged to the east, heading up the hill.

The giant was following with Leo.

Rikki was donning his backpack.

"But it's five miles!" Ernestine emphasized.

"So?" Hickok responded.

"You can't carry me five miles," Ernestine assured him. "It's too far."

"This is nothin'. I once had to lug *him*," Hickok said, indicating the giant with a jerk of his head. "It about near gave me a hernia."

CHAPTER TWO

"Where the devil can those children be?"

"I don't know, Clara," the man responded, his brow furrowed with worry.

"Go look for them, Ted," Clara urged.

Ted stepped from the wooden porch to the ground and placed his brawny hands on his hips. His stocky frame was clothed in a patched blue shirt and ragged jeans. "I swear. Sometimes those youngsters are more bother than they're worth!"

"The good Lord blessed us with healthy, normal children," Clara stated. "We should be grateful."

Ted nodded. "At least their minds haven't been turned to mush."

"Go find them," Clara reiterated.

Ted sighed and began walking across the cleared expanse in front of their small cabin. "Those twins!" he declared, then stopped, shocked.

"Ted!" Clara exclaimed, looking out across the clearing.

"I see them," Ted confirmed. He wheeled and stalked toward the open cabin door.

"Ted?" Clara said, wringing her hands in the fabric of her pink dress.

"I'm getting the gun," he announced as he reached the porch.

"Ted Butler! You'll do no such thing!" Clara rebuked him sharply.

Ted hesitated, staring to the west. "But they're white."

"They've got Leo and Ernestine," Clara said.

Ted disappeared into the cabin.

"Ted! No!" Clara objected. She gazed at the figures, now 40 yards distant and closing at a dogtrot, and perceived they were well-armed.

Her husband emerged with their ancient double-barreled shotgun cradled in his arms.

"Put that away!" Clara stated.

"No."

"You don't even know if it'll work!" Clara reminded him. "Those men are armed to the teeth!"

"No," Ted said with finality. He moved to the edge of the porch, interposing himself between the approaching threesome and his wife.

"Leo looks hurt!" Clara cried.

Ted gritted his teeth and leveled the shotgun.

The three strangers never slowed. They fearlessly crossed the yard and halted ten feet from the porch.

"That's far enough!" Ted warned needlessly.

"Howdy," said a blond man in buckskins.

Ted glanced at his children, his eyes narrowing as he saw Leo's right leg.

"Your son requires prompt medical attention," the short man in black stated.

"We come in peace," added the giant bearing Leo.

"Put down my kids," Ted directed.

"You're not being very neighborly," commented the one in buckskins.

"Put down my kids!" Ted repeated.

"Suit yourself, mister," the blond man said, and gently lowered Ernestine to the grass. He moved a pace to her right, his hands dropping to his sides.

Ted could see the sunlight glinting off the man's pearl-handled revolvers.

"We just toted your young'uns five miles," the man in buckskins mentioned. "Your boy here needs help. Now."

"Hickok!" the giant interjected.

The gunman glanced at his companion. "We don't have time for this, pard." He looked at Ted. "Put down that shotgun."

Ted wagged the barrel. "I've got you covered."

Hickock smiled. "I don't mean to brag, you understand, but if you tried to shoot one of us, I'd plug you before you so much as moved a muscle. I'm askin' you nice. Put down the gun."

"Poppa!" Ernestine exclaimed. "Do it! These men are our friends!"

Ted balked.

"Please, Poppa!" Ernestine prompted. "I've seen Hickok draw. You wouldn't stand a chance! He'd kill you!"

The gunman glanced at her. "Kill him? Are you loco? I might shoot him in the foot for being such an obstinate cuss, but I'm not about to kill your pa."

"Put down the damn gun!" Clara snapped.

Surprised at his wife's rare use of profanity and the tone in her voice, Ted slowly lowered the shotgun.

"Thanks," Hickok said, beaming. "I hate pluggin' folks in the foot. It's a pitiful waste of toes."

The giant walked up the porch, his gray eyes scrutinizing Ted. "Your son was attacked by an alligator. He needs a Healer."

Ted reached out and touched his son's forehead. "A Healer? There's Doc Stone, but he lives fifteen miles from here."

"I am not a Healer," the small man in black remarked. "But I do possess some small skill at treating injuries. With your permission, I will tend to your son. You can send for the physician after his condition is stabilized."

Ted glanced at Clara, who nodded.

Leo appeared to be woozy. His eyeslids fluttered as he grinned at his parents. "They saved my life, Poppa, Momma. I was a goner."

Ted looked into the giant's gray eyes. "Thank you. Come in." He motioned at the doorway. "My name is Ted Butler. This is my wife, Clara."

"I'm Blade," the giant said. He nodded at the gunman. "That's Hickok—"

"Right pleased to meet you folks," the gunman stated.

"—and that's Rikki-Tikki-Tavi," Blade said, nodding at the man in black.

"Let's get inside," Clara suggested.

"I'll stand watch out here a spell," Hickok offered.

Ernestine watched her parents, Blade, and Rikki enter the cabin. She gazed at the gunman in frank fascination.

Hickok hooked his thumbs in his gunbelt and smiled at her. "Shouldn't you be inside with your family?"

Ernestine shrugged. "There's not much I could do. Leo will be okay."

"You think so, huh?"

"I know it, Mister Hickok," Ernestine assured him.

"Drop the mister," Hickok instructed. "And what makes you so blamed sure of yourself? You're not much more than a sprout."

"I know Leo will be okay," Ernestine explained. "We're twins, you know. We're like two peas in a pod. Sometimes we even have the same thoughts at the same time. Ain't that spooky?"

"Not really," Hickok responded, his voice momentarily losing its decided western twang. "Biological twins, as Plato once said, enjoy a mental rapport."

"What?"

Hickok chuckled. "Oops. Sorry. I plumb forgot myself. Yeah, you're right. It is downright spooky."

"You talk funny," Ernestine told him.

"No one's ever noticed it before," Hickok said with a smile.

"Who's Plato?"

"He's the leader at the place I come from," Hickok replied, scanning the yard and the fields beyond.

"Where's that?"

"It's called the Home," Hickok said.

"Your people have a name?"

Hickok nodded. "The Family. We were named by the hombre who started the Home right before the war."

"Is it far to your Home?"

"Far," Hickok stated, grinning at her. "You sure are a bundle of questions."

"Am I botherin' you?"

"No," Hickok said. "I'm hitched."

"Hitched?"

"Yeah. I'm married."

"I don't get it," Ernestine commented.

"You will after you're married," Hickok mentioned.

Ernestine seated herself on the edge of the porch and rubbed her left side.

"Are you all right?" the gunman inquired.

"A little sore."

"We should have Rikki check you after he's done with Leo," Hickok suggested.

"I'm fine," Ernestine insisted.

Hickok inspected their cabin, noting the craftsmanship displayed in the meticulous construction. "Did your pa build this?"

"Yep."

"He did a right smart job," Hickok said.

"Thanks."

"But why'd he build it out here? Why are you folks livin' in the middle of nowhere?"

Ernestine frowned. "We came here about four years ago to get away from the city."

Miami?"

"Yeah. Miami. It's about twenty miles southeast of here," Ernestine said.

"I know. That's where my pards and I are headed."

Ernestine's eyes narrowed. "You'd best be real careful there. Miami is a bad place. Momma says its evil."

"Did you like it there?"

"No way! Ernestine declared. "It was terrible! All those pushers after you to get stoned! Everybody on their own little trip. It was a real bummer. Being straight was out."

The gunman's forehead furrowed in perplexity. "What the dickens are you talkin' about?"

"Don't they have pushers at your Home?" Ernestine asked.

"The Family doesn't go in for pushin' folks around," Hickok answered. "And if anyone tries pushin' us, they're in for a world of hurt. The Warriors don't take kindly to anyone messin' with the Family."

Now it was Ernestine's turn to be confused. "No. That ain't what I meant." She paused. "Are you a Warrior?"

"Yep."

"Your friends too?"

Hickok nodded. "The big dummy, Blade, is the head Warrior. Rikki and I are under him."

"How many Warriors do you got at this Home of yours?"

"Let me see," Hickok said thoughtfully. "Sometimes it seems like we're addin' new members every time the wind changes. We had five Triads with three Warriors apiece, and then we added the mutant Triad—"

"Mutant!" Ernestine exclaimed.

"Yep. Two furry runts and another ding-a-ling. They were created by a scientist, a genetic engineer. Anyway, that gives us eighteen Warriors," Hickok detailed.

"Mutants!" Ernestine said again, astounded.

"You don't like mutants?"

Ernestine shuddered. "Who does? Some of the Dragons are mutants, you know."

Hickoks blue eyes locked on hers. "What do you know about the Dragons?"

"Everybody knows about the Dragons," Ernestine said. "Poppa says they practically own everything and everyone."

"And some of 'em are mutants?"

"The ones at the top. Just ask Poppa."

"I will."

Ernestine glanced at the cabin door. "I don't hear no yellin'. Leo's takin' it like a man," she said proudly.

"Your brother and you are real close," Hickok noted.

"Sure are," Ernestine conceded. "Do you have any kids?"

The gunman's chest puffed up. "Yep. A little bucka-roo named Ringo. He's a chip off the old block."

"Do you let him get stoned?"

"There you go again," Hickok said. "Listen. Anybody throws stones at my son, and they're liable to wind up addin' some lead to their diet. If you get my drift."

"I ain't talkin' about the kind of stones you throw," Ernestine stated. "I mean the—"

Blade walked from the cabin. "Leo will be fine," he informed them. "Rikki has washed the wounds and is preparing to set the leg. Leo is fortunate. It's a clean break."

Ernestine stood. "I never did thank you proper for savin' us."

"We happened to be in the right place at the right time," Blade mentioned. "I heard your scream."

"What were you doing out there near that swamp?" Hickok inquired.

"We heard this noise like thunder," Ernestine answered. "And we saw this funny light in the sky."

"That was us," Blade said.

"You?"

"The noise and the light were caused by the Hurricane," Blade stated.

Ernestine gazed at the blue sky. "There ain't no hurricane in these parts."

Blade grinned. "Not a storm. The Hurricane I'm referring to is an aircraft, a jet with VTOL capabilities. It brought us here."

"I ain't never seen no jet."

Hickok cleared his throat. "How long are we stayin', pard?"

"We've been invited to supper," Blade said. "We'll stay until morning. I want to learn all we can about Miami."

"You're stayin' the night?" Ernestine asked, excited. "Good!"

There was a cry of pain from within the cabin.

"Rikki must be settin' the leg," Hickok commented.

Ernestine ran inside.

"Sweet kid," the gunman remarked.

Blade surveyed the fields to the west. "Why don't you take a walk?"

"Is it my breath?" Hickok rejoined.

"Conduct a perimeter sweep," Blade directed.

The gunman sighed and strolled to the west. "I doubt the Dragons know we're here."

"Better safe than sorry," Blade philosophized.

"Be back in a bit," Hickok said.

"Just don't get bit by a gator," Blade commented.

Hickok looked back, grinning. "I didn't know you cared!"

"We've already killed one alligator," Blade noted with a straight face. "Giving another one food poisoning would be irresponsible."

"Ouch."

CHAPTER THREE

"You're a humdinger of a cook, ma'am," Hickok said, complimenting Clara Butler.

Clara smiled self-consciously and shrugged. "It was a little something I threw together."

"Feeding you was the least we could do," Ted remarked. "We're in your debt."

The three Warriors and their hosts were sitting on the front porch, the Warriors to the right of the doorway, Ted and Clara to the left. A strikingly beautiful sunset emblazoned the western horizon. Bird and insect sounds provided a natural melody.

"I'm beginnin' to see why you folks settled here," Hickok said, admiring the resplendent hues in the sky.

"This was just part of the reason," Ted said, then frowned. "We wanted out of Miami."

"Tell us about it," Blade coaxed. "We studied the old maps in our library and read all we could on the city, but our information is outdated. The Founder of our compound assembled the hundreds of thousands of books we own prior to the war. All of our maps were accurate one hundred and five years ago, but things are bound to have changed since then."

"I have no way of knowing how it was before the war," Ted said. "But it had to be better than it is now, what with everybody wearin' guns and doin' drugs. Miami ain't fit for decent people."

"How do you mean?" Blade probed.

"The Dragons control Miami," Ted stated.

"Ernestine mentioned the Dragons," Hickok brought up. "She said the head honchos are mutants."

Ted nodded, his lips compressing.

"Only the leaders of the Dragons are mutants?" Blade stressed.

"That's what everyone says," Ted replied. "But very few have ever seen them. They're called the Masters, and they formed the Dragons about four decades ago."

"How many Masters are there?" Blade queried.

"I don't know," Ted said. "Only the top Dragons have contact with the Masters. No one else meets them and lives."

"Go on about the Dragons," Blade prompted. "You said they control Miami. How?"

"Drugs mainly," Ted said.

"Drugs?"

"Yeah. You know. Grass. Coke. Other hard stuff like heroin, opium, and morphine. You name it, the Dragons supply it. Getting high is a way of life nowadays. Everyone does dope," Ted disclosed.

"Not everyone," Clara amended bitterly.

"We didn't want our children to have their minds destroyed by the drugs," Ted said. "So we up and left Miami and homesteaded this place. It's been rough, but we're making a go of it."

"I'm puzzled," Rikki-Tikki-Tavi interjected. "These drugs you mention. Why do so many people use them?"

"Like I said. They do it to get high."

Rikki gazed skyward. "High?"

"Yeah, man. High means to feel good. To get a buzz on. To pack up all your cares and woes," Ted elaborated.

"I still don't understand," Rikki said.

"Have you ever used drugs?" Clara inquired, staring at each of the Warriors.

Blade shook his head. "The only drugs we know are those used by the Family Healers, and they're all medicinal herbs."

"Do your people drink alcohol?" Ted questioned.

"The Tillers concoct a home brew for special occasions," Blade answered. "But no one in the Family drinks on a regular basis, if that's what you mean. The Elders would not tolerate alcoholism."

"Well, that ain't the way it is in Miami," Ted revealed.

"Those who don't do drugs do the booze. Findin' a sober person is next to impossible."

"You're exaggerating," Blade said.

"A little," Ted admitted. "But not by much. You haven't been there. The rotten pushers are everywhere, and every pusher is a Dragon."

"What's a pusher?" Hickok wanted to know.

Ted did a double take. "A pusher pushes the dope."

"They sell the drugs," Clara clarified.

"How many pushers are there?" Blade asked.

"Thousands," Ted replied. "And they're just the lower-level Dragons. There's a whole chain of command from the pushers to the Masters."

"Do you know how many Dragons there are, all told?" Blade inquired.

"No," Ted admitted. "But if you wanted a guess, I'd say there's seven thousand Dragons, maybe more."

Hickok whistled. "Whew! That's a heap of opposition."

"We're not here to deal with the lower-level Dragons," Blade said. "The pushers are none of our concern. We're after the Masters."

"If you want my advice," Ted offered, "I'd say go home. Go back to where you came from. There's no way you can take on the Dragons. Not with just three of you."

"We've tackled tough odds before," Hickok observed.

"Are there others like yourselves?" Blade queried. "People who don't like the Dragons, who don't like the drugs?"

"Some," Ted responded. "But not a whole lot. Most of the decent people left ages ago."

"What about the authorities?" Blade asked. "Doesn't Miami have a police force?"

"Yeah," Ted said, his lips curling downward. "The Narcs."

"How effective are these Narcs against the Dragons?" Blade asked.

Ted snorted. "Effective? You've got to be kidding! The Narcs are in league with the Dragons."

"How can the police force be in league with the Dragons?"

"I might be able to answer that," Clara said. "It all goes back to the war. An aunt of mine told me the story when I was a young girl. The federal government, as you probably know, resettled in the Midwest after evacuating a lot of folks from the east. The state governments fell apart. Florida was no different than the rest. With the government gone, the police and the sheriff departments broke down. Miami was a wide-open city. There was no one in control. The drug gangs took over."

"Where did these drug gangs come from?" Blade inquired.

"They were always around," Clara said. "Even before the war. The drug business in the United States was a big operation. A lot of the drug smugglers used Florida as the entry point for the drugs they brought in from other countries. Miami was a hot spot of drug activity. But before the war, at least, the authorities kept a lid on it."

"And after the war, with the collapse of the government, the drug organizations moved in to fill the vacuum," Blade deduced.

Clara nodded. "You've got it. For forty years after the war, according to my aunt, there were three or four major drug dealers fighting for the upper hand. And then the Masters showed up."

"From where?"

"No one knows," Clara said. "The Masters took over the largest drug gang in Miami, and within a couple of years they had wiped out all their opposition. They named themselves the Dragons, and they've ruled Miami ever since."

"The Dragons control all of the land from Fort Lauderdale south," Ted added. "Alligator Alley is their boundary line."

"Alligator Alley?" Blade repeated.

"The Everglades Parkway," Ted explained. "It runs from Naples in the west to Fort Lauderdale in the east. Anything south of the Parkway is in Dragon territory."

"And they rule it with an iron fist," Clara went on.

"They pass laws. They appoint people to posts like mayor or councilperson. And they set up their own police force, the Narcs."

Ted laughed bitterly.

"What's so funny?" Blade questioned.

"The Narcs," Ted responded. "The Masters have a warped sense of humor. You see, before the war, back in the days when there really was law enforcement, the Narcs were the police who went after the pushers and the dealers. The Narcs were the tough officers who put the drug-runners out of business." He paused. "But after the Dragons took over, they made drugs legal. All drugs. They set up a system of big-time dealers and thousands of pushers. And they made it illegal for anyone to interfere with the drug trade. If a pusher tried to sell crack or smack to Leo or Ernestine, and if I tried to stop it, I'd be arrested by the Narcs. They're the so-called official police force, hand-picked by the Dragons. And the Masters must have named them Narcs as a play on words."

Rikki-Tikki-Tavi, who had been listening attentively, gazed at Ted. "What did you mean earlier about getting high? What is this 'high' you speak of?"

"Getting high. Getting stoned. It's all the same," Ted said. "The drugs do things to your head, to your body. They make some people feel good, but there's always a price to pay. The drugs can destroy the mind and the body. They mess up your head. The strong stuff makes you hallucinate. You can go off the deep end just like that." He snapped his fingers.

"Why do people use drugs?" Rikki asked.

Ted shrugged. "They like the buzz they get. They like to escape from reality."

"This is most bewildering," Rikki confessed. "Why would anyone want to escape from reality? Attuning our souls to cosmic reality is one of the purposes of our very existence."

"You're a weird one," Ted remarked.

"Ted!" Clara said.

"Our souls should be devoted to perceiving the nature of spirit reality," Rikki elaborated. "Without a spirit anchor, our lives are like a piece of dead wood floating on a pond, tossed every which way by the currents and the wind, without direction, without purpose.''

"Are you a preacher of some kind?" Ted inquired.

"I am a martial artist," Rikki answered. "A perfecting swordmaster. I have devoted my life to the principles of Zen and the Circles."

"What in the world is Zen?"

"Zen is the art of finding your true spirit center," Rikki detailed. "Through Zen, we attain a state of intuitive enlightment."

Ted shook his head. "I never heard of it."

"We believe in the Bible," Clara mentioned. "Do all of you practice this Zen?"

"No," Blade replied. "The Family Elders encourage each one of us to seek our own spiritual path. We are not forced to follow any one religion. We have Christians, Moslems, Buddhists, and others. Many follow the teachings of the three blue Circles. Rikki happens to prefer Zen."

"Do you mind if I ask you a question?" Ted said.

"No."

"You haven't told us exactly where you're from," Ted noted. "And I can understand the reason. The less we know, the better. But why are you here? Why are you after the Masters?"

"Because the Masters are after us," Blade divulged.

"You've had a run-in with the Masters?" Ted queried in surprise.

"Not yet," Blade said. "Let me explain. A while back we were in Las Vegas. We became embroiled in a mob war. And before we left, we heard a story, a very interesting story, about the Dragons. We were told that the Dragons intend to eradicate our Family. After the Elders were informed, they decided to send three Warriors to Florida to see if the story was true. If so, we're to prevent the Dragons from carrying out their threat."

"We're gonna kick us some butt," Hickok said, grinning.

"How did you know the Dragons were based in Florida?" Ted questioned.

"We'd heard about the Dragons several times before," Blade disclosed. "They have a formidable reputation. From what you've told me, I suspect their drug dealings extend to other areas of the country. Some of the rumors we heard were incorrect. For instance, I was told that all of the Dragons are mutants, but now we know that's not the case."

"Why are the Dragons after your Family?" Clara asked.

"We don't know," Blade said, his tone lowering, "but we'll find out."

Clara studied the trio for a moment. "Do the three of you always work together?"

"Sometimes we go on runs together," Blade said. "The Warriors are divided into Triads, and Hickok and I usually work with a friend named Geronimo. But Geronimo is overseeing the Warriors in our absence to give him the added experience."

Hickok chuckled. "That was my idea. Since I've been picked to head the Warriors whenever the Big Guy is in California, I figured Geronimo should be my second-in-command. He didn't like the notion of being left behind."

"Rikki has been with us to Denver, St. Louis, and Seattle," Blade mentioned. "He knows the score."

"It sounds like you've been everywhere," Ted commented.

"We get around."

Ted leaned forward. "What's it like out there? We never hear much about the outside."

"The country is divided up into factions," Blade expounded. "As Clara pointed out, the government of the United States reorganized in the midwest and became known as the Civilized Zone. It's one of the largest factions in terms of area. The Civilized Zone includes the former states of Colorado, Wyoming, Nebraska, Kansas, Oklahoma, the northern half of Texas, New Mexico, and portions of Arizona. Denver, Colorado, is the capital."

"What about the other factions?"

"The state of California survived the war intact," Blade said. "California has a standing army and a navy. They've been able to protect themselves from the scavengers, raiders, and looters. In fact, the governor of California proposed the formation of the Freedom Force."

"What's that?" Ted asked.

"The Force is the special strike squad set up to deal with threats to the Freedom Federation."

"The what?"

"Maybe I'd better back up a bit," Blade stated. "The Civilized Zone, California, and five other factions have banded together into the Freedom Federation."

"What five other factions?" came from Clara.

"There are the Flathead Indians in Montana, the Cavalry in the Dakota Territory, and three groups from Minnesota—the Clan, the Moles, and the Family."

"So you're from Minnesota?"

"Now you know," Blade said. "Anyway, as the head of the Warriors and the head of the Force, I spend my time bouncing back and forth between Minnesota and California."

"And when he's not at the Home, I handle runnin' the Warriors," Hickok interjected.

"Lucky us," Rikki-Tikki-Tavi quipped.

"What about the rest of the country?" Ted inquired.

Blade sighed. "It's a mess. Barbaric. Savage. The Russians control a corridor in the eastern half, sort of a belt from the Atlantic Ocean to the Mississippi River. Chicago is under an autocratic group called the Technics. St. Louis is the territory of a biker gang, the Leather Knights. And Houston is run by androids."

"Androids?"

"Artificial men and women," Blade divulged. "They treat humans as inferior life-forms."

"Incredible," Ted commented.

"I don't know about the rest of what was once America," Blade said. "Any area not under the control of a faction is designated as part of the Outlands. And as far as the rest of the world is concerned, all we have to go on are a few rumors."

"There's something I don't understand," Clara observed.

"What?"

"If you heard about the Dragons in—where was it?"

"Las Vegas, Nevada."

"Yes. Why didn't your Federation just send in an army to take care of the Dragons? Why are only the three of you here?"

"Good question," Blade said. "There are several reasons. First, I didn't inform the other Federation members about the threat from the Dragons."

"Why not?"

"The threat was directed against the Family. I relayed the information to the Family Elders, and they agreed we should deal with the situation ourselves. The Federation has enough problems to deal with. Secondly, we couldn't be sure the report was legitimate. We had to confirm the Dragons existed. Third, the Warriors are pledged to defend the Family and the Home from all danger. This is rightfully our job."

Clara nodded.

"So we were dropped off by one of the Hurricanes," Blade concluded, "and here we are."

"What's a Hurricane?" Ted queried.

"It's a jet with the ability to take off and land like a helicopter," Blade detailed. "California owns a pair. They're at my disposal as head of the Force, and I use one of them to shuttle to the Home at least once a month."

"I've always wanted to fly," Ted commented.

"So what's your next move?" Clara asked.

"Tomorrow we go into Miami."

Clara frowned. "You don't know what you're getting yourselves into."

"There's no turning back," Blade said. "We have a week before we rendezvous with the Hurricane at our pickup point. Thanks to you, we've verified the Dragons exist. Now we need to find out why they want to destroy our Family. We have to track down the Masters."

"And then?"

Hickok answered for the Warriors by grinning and placing his hands on his Colt Python revolvers. "We teach these critters the error of their ways."

CHAPTER FOUR

"What do you make of it, pard?"

"I don't know," Blade responded.

"Should we intervene?" Rikki asked.

"Not yet. Let's listen and see what's going on," Blade directed. He stared over the rusted chain-link fence at the dilapidated, weed-choked playground bordering the alley.

"Why are they chasin' him?" Hickok wondered aloud.

Blade's eyes narrowed as he watched the gang of ten youths pursue a solitary boy of ten or twelve around the playground. No one else was in sight. The gang consisted of older youths, 16 and up. They were attired in black leather clothing, some with miniature metal spikes adorning their shoulders and sleeves. Their hair was invariably past their shoulders and dyed different colors. One female member sported hair arranged with alternate stripes of purple, orange, and yellow.

Hickok had noticed her too. "Do you see that one? It looks like she was stirrin' paint with her head."

The gang was laughing and taunting the younger boy, circling him and shoving him, preventing him from fleeing.

"What's the matter, Stevey?" declared a hefty youth with a Mohawk haircut as he stepped in front of the panting boy.

Stevey halted, breathing deeply, obviously afraid.

"Didn't you hear me, Stevey?" Mohawk demanded. The gang formed a loose line enclosing the boy.

"Let me go!" Stevey blurted out.

Mohawk laughed. "Did you hear Stevey? He wants us to let him go."

As if it was a great joke, the gang cackled.

Mohawk poked Stevey in the chest with the index finger of his right hand. "You ain't going nowhere, chump!"

"Please!" Stevey cried. He was a skinny boy who barely filled his tattered jeans and green shirt.

"Please!" Mohawk mimicked the boy.

"I want to go home!"

"You want to run to Daddy and Mommy!" Mohawk snapped. "Well, your ass is ours!"

"I haven't done nothin'!"

"Oh?" Mohawk gazed at his peers. "He says he ain't done nothin'!"

Some of the gang snickered.

Mohawk grabbed the front of Stevey's shirt. "Who are you tryin' to kid? You've insulted us."

"I did not!"

"You won't buy our shit."

"I don't want any!"

Mohawk made a smacking noise with his lips and released the boy. "You just don't understand the facts of life, Stevey. I'll do you a favor. I'll tell you how it is." He paused, then tapped his chest. "I'm a registered pusher, dude. I make my bread by hustlin' smack, bennies, weed, and anything else you need—"

"But I don't need it!" Stevey interrupted.

Mohawk slapped the boy across the mouth. "Shut your face when I'm talkin' to you!"

Stevey's legs nearly buckled.

"I'm beginnin' to think you're a real lowlife," Mohawk told the boy. "Haven't I offered you a ten-percent discount? Who else would give you a deal like that?"

Stevey didn't answer.

"But if that's not good enough for you, then how about a fifteen-percent discount?" Mohawk asked. "Just for the first three months."

"No," Stevey said.

"What?"

"I don't want any drugs."

Mohawk frowned. "He doesn't want any drugs!"

"He's a goody-two-shoes!" cracked one of the other

gang members.

"Mommy's boy!" mocked another.

"The little turd!" declared a third.

"What are we going to do with you?" Mohawk asked.

"Let me go!" Stevey pleaded.

"No can do," Mohawk said. "You're givin' my reputation a bad mark. If I don't sell to you, then some of the others might get it into their heads not to buy. I can't allow that. This is my assigned turf, man. I have a quota to meet. My commission money don't grow on trees."

"What if I buy just a little?"

"And then what? Flush it down the john? I know you, you chickenshit bastard. You won't use it."

"No one would know."

"*I'd* know!"

Stevey gazed at the ring of harsh faces and gulped. "What are you going to do?"

"What do you think, nerd?" Mohawk responded. He reached into the right front pocket of his leather jacket.

Stevey's eyes widened. "No!"

"Yes." Mohawk's hand emerged holding a closed knife. His thumb moved, there was a loud click, and a six-inch blade snapped out.

"No!" Stevey repeated, taking a step backwards.

"If it was up to me," Mohawk said, "I'd cut you a few times and be done with it. But I know you'd run to your folks and blow the whistle, and they'd probably file a formal complaint with my Dealer. Technically, I'm not supposed to force my business on anyone." He shrugged and grinned. "But you know how it goes. We all have to eat." He wagged the knife.

Stevey seemed frozen in place.

"Stand still," Mohawk advised. "I'll make this short and sweet." He drew back his right hand.

"Release the boy!"

Mohawk whirled at the sound of the low, firm voice coming from his rear. He did a double take at the sight of the small man in black ten yards away, immediately noting that the man was armed with an automatic rifle and a sword. But the rifle was slung over the man's right shoulder, and the sword was in a scabbard on his left hip. The man's hands were empty, dangling at his sides. "Who the hell are you?"

"Release the boy," the man in black repeated.

Mohawk motioned with his left hand, and within seconds the man in black was surrounded by the entire gang. Three members produced knives, one a pair of brass knuckles, one a blackjack, and another slid a footlong metal rod from his left sleeve.

The man in black remained motionless.

"I asked you who you are?" Mohawk reiterated angrily.

"If this boy does not want his body polluted by your drugs," the man in black stated, "you will not sell them to him."

Mohawk glowered. "Mister, you've got one hell of a nerve talkin' to me like that! Do you know who I am?"

"Someone whose sense of self-importance is greatly exaggerated," the man replied.

"What the hell does that mean?"

"It means the boy and I will depart without interference."

"You think so, huh?" Mohawk asked, and snickered.

"I know so."

Mohawk's brown eyes narrowed. The stranger had yet to make a move for his weapons. The chump was just asking for it! "Take him!" he ordered.

They tried.

Three of the gang members closed in on the diminutive figure in black, two of them with their knives extended.

The man in black uttered a peculiar, catlike noise, his body dropping into a squat and his hands rising. One moment he was perfectly still; the next he was a black blur as he executed a series of spinning roundhouse kicks. Once. Twice. Three times in all. And with each kick, with each devastating spin, a gang member was sent sailing through the air to crash onto the cracked playground asphalt.

"Get him!" Mohawk bellowed.

The burly youth with the brass knuckles tried to deliver an uppercut to the stranger's chin. Instead, the palm of the man's right hand slammed into *his* chin, snapping his head back, and he crumpled.

"I'l get this prick!" declared the one with the metal rod, taking two quick strides and swinging the bar.

With consummate ease, the man in black deftly ducked under the blow, then spun his body in a coiled arc, his left leg whipping outward, his left foot driving into the youth's midsection and knocking the gang member over six feet to sprawl onto the ground.

"Get the bastard!" Mohawk screamed.

The man in black suddenly moved even faster, taking the offensive, his legs flashing up and around, his feet landing off decisive blows in half as many seconds.

Mohawk abruptly found himself the only one left, with the man in black three feet off, in a crouching stance.

"It is over."

"Suck on this!" Mohawk snapped, and charged, whipping his switchblade toward the man's face.

Stevey, an astonished witness to the squence of events, gaped as the man in black easily blocked the knife, then retaliated with an open-hand blow to his foe's nose.

Mohawk screeched as his nostrils were crushed. He felt an agonizing pain in his forehead, then tumbled, gurgling and spraying blood.

"Are you all right?" the man asked Stevey.

Stevey nodded vigorously. "Thanks," he blurted.

The man in black smiled and walked up to the boy. He placed his right hand on Stevey's shoulder. "You were very brave. A person must be true to their convicions. These others had no right to force you to take drugs."

Stevey watched several of the gang thrashing in anguish. "I never saw anyone move like you."

The man's smile broadened. "Practice." He glanced at the alley to the west. "I must leave. May the Spirit guide you at all times." He turned and jogged toward the alley.

"Hey! Wait!" Stevey called.

He stopped and turned.

"What's your name? I need to know your name!"

"I am called Rikki."

Stevey nodded, grinned, then ran to the south.

Rikki-Tikki-Tavi watched the boy for several seconds, then resumed his sprint to the alley. He slowed slightly as he reached the chain-link fence, his hands flicking out and grabbing the top metal rail, and with a light-footed spring he vaulted into the alley, clearing the four-foot-high fence with a foot to spare. His companions were waiting.

"Well done," Blade said, complimenting the martial artist.

"I thought it was a mite sloppy myself," Hickok remarked.

"They lacked skill," Rikki said.

"You should have let all of us tackle those yahoos," Hickok commented.

"We don't want to draw any more attention to ourselves than necessary," Blade responded. "Rikki took care of them with a minimum of fuss."

"So what now?" Hickok inquired.

"We keep going," Blade stated, and led them to the south. "We're in a residential suburb northwest of downtown Miami. We'll stick to the alleys and side streets for the next few miles."

"I'm gettin' tired of all this skulkin' around," Hickok declared. "Let's find a bigwig and force the cow chip to take us to the Masters."

"Easier said than done," Blade noted. "We need a plan."

"And you have one?"

Blade nodded.

"Mind fillin' us in?"

"We find a bigwig and force him, or her, to take us to the Masters."

Hickok made a show of gazing around the alley. "There's a blamed echo around here."

"Locating the right person won't be simple," Blade said. "We need to learn more about the Dragons, about their chain of command."

"Then why didn't we question the leader of that gang?"

"He's strictly small potatoes," Blade replied. "We need someone higher up the ladder."

They came to the end of the alley and found a busy avenue running from east to west. Pedestrians jammed the sidewalk. Many of the men and women wore side arms, and a few carried rifles.

"The folks here sure look like a friendly bunch," Hickok quipped.

None of the pedestrians paid the slightest attention to the Warriors; they were too involved in the hustle and bustle of their daily lives.

"Why are the citizens permitted to bear firearms?" Rikki inquired. "Before the war, doing so was against the law."

"The Dragons make the laws now," Blade speculated. "I would expect that all of their Dealers and pushers go around armed. The Dragons wouldn't want the bearing of firearms to be illegal."

"My kind of city," Hickok said.

"Which way?" Rikki asked.

"Left," Blade said, and merged into the flow of pedestrians. He scanned the avenue and the buildings on both sides. Although the avenue contained cracks and potholes, and a majority of the stores and residences were grimy and in need of a fresh coat of paint, Miami was in better shape than some of the other cities he'd visited. Lost in thought, he absently adjusted the shoulder strap on the F.N.-LAR Paratrooper slung over his right arm. So here he was again! About two thousand miles from the Home! Two thousand miles from his beloved wife and precious son, Jenny and Gabe. And his soul was troubled.

Jenny had pleaded with him not to make the run. Her lovely green eyes had been moist with tears when he'd explained the necessity of the trip. She had sat at their kitchen table, her back to him, and cried silently, her blonde hair bobbing, her slim shoulders rising and falling. Thank the Spirit that Gabe had been asleep! Jenny was becoming increasingly distraught over his prolonged absences, and who could blame her? With his duties as the head of the Force and as leader of the Warriors, he was constantly away from his family. The emotional strain was beginning to tell. A resentment was gradually growing inside him, increasing with each mission. The Federation leaders had no right to expect him to relegate his family to a secondary status in his life. The Elders taught every Family member to revere and cherish his or her loved ones. Jenny and Gabe were the core of his life; they gave meaning to his existence. Their happiness should come first, yet their happiness would continue to suffer for as long as he held down two posts.

What should he do?

Give up one of his positions?

Which one?

His train of thought was interrupted by the sight of a couple up ahead. What was this? He saw the man hand a packet of white powder to the neatly dressed woman. She gave the man a handful of silver coins. They both laughed at some private joke, then parted company. Was the man a pusher? Had he just sold the woman drugs? What type of currency were they using in Miami? Old coins? He decided to trail the man, a portly, balding individual dressed in a light brown suit and black shoes. If they could—

"We are being followed," Rikki abruptly announced.

Blade glanced over his left shoulder at his friends.

Rikki nodded at the avenue.

A black and white sedan was slowly cruising on the other side of the street, traveling in the same direction as the Warriors. The uniformed driver's window was rolled down, and the driver was not trying to conceal the fact he was staring at them. On the driver's door, in large, bold, red letters, was a single word: NARC.

CHAPTER FIVE

"Want me to plug the varmint?" Hickok asked, his left hand on the strap to his Navy Arms Henry Carbine.

"Be serious," Blade said.

"I am. I can always use the target practice," Hickok stated impishly.

Blade gazed to the east and spied an intersection 30 yards distant.

The Narc vehicle unexpectedly accelerated, driving to the intersection and taking a left, then pulling over to the curb. Two men in blue uniforms and caps climbed out and crossed to the near side, then halted, waiting.

Blade knew the Narcs were waiting for the Warriors. He casually placed his hands near his Bowies and looked at Hickok and Rikki. "Let me do the talking."

Hickok grinned. "Fine by me. But if you decide to plug 'em, I get first dibs."

"We want to avoid a confrontation," Blade said.

"What a party-pooper."

Blade faced the intersection with an expression of feigned innocence. He pretended to be interested in a grocery store across the avenue as he neared the intersection. Out of the corner of his left eye, he saw the pair of Narcs coming toward him.

The men in blue positioned themselves directly in the giant's path. Both wore revolvers on their right hips.

"Hello, citizen," said the tallest of the two.

Blade stopped and smiled. "Hello."

Hickok moved to Blade's right, Rikki the left. Both stood calmly, Rikki with a slight grin, Hickok beaming like an idiot.

"Howdy!" the gunman declared.

The tall Narc glanced at the gunfighter, then at the short

man in black. "These two friends of yours?"

"Two of the best," Blade admitted. "How may we help you?"

"We received a call a couple of minutes ago," the tall Narc disclosed, raking the Warriors with a probing gaze. "There's been a report of a 10-69."

"A what?" Blade questioned.

"A 10-69. Restraint of trade by intereference with a pusher in the exercise of his or her rights," the tall Narc elaborated.

Hickok looked at Blade with a shocked countenance. "Do you mean that uncouth character was a pusher? I didn't know that!"

"What uncouth character?" The Narc demanded.

"We had a minor disagreement with a young gentleman who tried to force us to buy drugs from him," Blade answered.

"Then it was you," the Narc said. "You three fit the descriptions."

"Are we in any trouble?" Blade inquired.

"That depends," the Narc said. "Do you live in Miami?"

"We're visiting," Blade replied.

"From where?"

Blade mentally reviewed the map of Florida he'd studied. "Jerome," he responded quickly.

"Why are you here?" the Narc interrogated them.

"We're on vacation," Blade said. "Thought we'd come to the Big City. Have some fun. Live it up." He paused and frowned. "We didn't expect to be jumped by a gang of wet-nosed delinquents."

"That damn Fowler!" the Narc muttered.

"Fowler?"

"Yeah. He's a lower-echelon pusher. We've received a few complaints about him before. Seems he likes to strong-arm his sales. But there's never been a case we could prove. Do you want to file a formal complaint with his Dealer?"

Blade's forehead creased, as if he was pondering the matter. "I don't want to make waves," he remarked.

The Narc shrugged. "It's your choice, mister. But if it was up to me, I'd file the complaint. Assholes like Fowler only spoil the trade for the law-abiding, hard-working pushers."

"How would I go about filing a complaint?" Blade queried.

"I'll see that Admin gets the proper forms to you," the Narc said, reaching into the top right pocket of his uniform shirt. "But I'll need your names and the place where you're staying." He pulled a small notepad and a pen from the pocket.

"We just arrived," Blade stated. "We haven't decided where to stay."

"Try Hotel Row," the Narc suggested.

"What's that?"

The Narc cocked his head at an angle and stared at the giant. "Jerome must be in the boonies. Hotel Row is another name for Miami Beach. It's an island to the east of Miami, about two and a half miles across Biscayne Bay. You can take any of the causeways over on a shuttle bus. From where we're at, I'd say take the Kennedy Causeway or the Julia Tuttle Causeway. Both will get you there. And if you're looking to live it up, Miami Beach is the place you want."

"Thanks for the advice," Blade said.

"Tell you want I'll do," the Narc offered. "I'll have the forms delivered to the Ocean View. It's not the ritziest joint, but it should suit you just fine."

"I don't want to put you to any trouble," Blade remarked.

"It's no trouble," the Narc insisted. "Besides, if you do file the complaint, and if the Dealer decides Fowler did try to stiff you, then I get a bonus. Every little bit helps."

"You get a bonus?" Blade mentioned in surprise.

"Sure. The Dealers don't like the pushers to overstep their bounds. Most of the pushers know how to toe the line, but a shithead like Fowler can give all of them a bad name. Which is why the Dealers like to know about incidents like this. They want the bad seeds weeded out.

Any Narc who helps get rid of the driftwood receives a bonus. After all, the last thing the Dealers want is to jeopardize the tourist trade.''

"Understandable," Blade commented.

"Your going to Miami Beach will make filing your complaint a lot easier," the Narc observed.

"It will?"

"Sure. The Dealers all have their assigned territories in the Greater Miami metro area. The whole city is divided among them. North Miami. Hialeah. Coral Gables. You name it, a Dealer controls it. But not Miami Beach. That's neutral territory. No one Dealer can claim it, and that's where most of them hang out. Practically all the Dealers have suites there."

"Fowler's Dealer too?"

"Yeah," The Narc confirmed. "But I can't think of the name of his hotel. I'll have the forms and the info sent to the desk at the Ocean View. All you have to do is complete the paperwork, then drop it in the mail. Easy as pie."

"You have mail service?" Nickok asked.

The Narc snickered. "Yep. You're definitely country boys. Of course we have mail service! It's only in the Greater Miami area, and delivery is slow sometimes, but the mail gets through."

"I appreciate your effort on our behalf," Blade said courteously.

"No problem. Now I need your names."

"John Clayton," Blade answered.

"And you?" the Narc asked, looking at Hickok.

The gunman grinned. "William Cody."

"And you?" the Narc inquired of Rikki.

"Bruce Lee."

The Narc dutifully scribbled the names in his notepad. "Okay. Thanks for your cooperation." He nodded at them, wheeled, and strolled off with his fellow officer.

"Most mystifying," Rikki mentioned.

"Not really," Blade said.

"Then maybe you can explain it to me, pard," Hickok chimed in. "Why the dickens was that hombre so blamed nice to us? Why didn't he haul us in?"

"Checks and balances," Blade stated. "The Masters have set up a system of keeping everyone in their organization in line. I didn't realize it before, but the tourist trade must be critically important. They wouldn't want the pushers to endanger it."

"Where do these tourists come from?" Hickok asked.

"The southern U.S.," Blade guessed. "Probably else- where. Maybe Central or South America. The Dragons must have trade relations with someone able to supply the fuel for their vehicles."

"What's this business about checks and balances?" the gunman questioned.

"The Narcs serve a two-fold purpose," Blade said. "They insure no one interferes with the drug trade, but they also keep an eye on the pushers to make sure none of them step out of line. That Narc said he gets a bonus for turning in pushers gone bad. The idea is brilliant. The pushers are continually monitored by the so-called police force created to protect the drug trade."

"I'm glad you're impressed," Hickok stated.

"We can't underestimate the Masters," Blade warned.

"I don't intend to estimate 'em," Hickok said. "All I want to do is plug 'em full of holes."

"Are we going to Miami Beach?" Rikki inquired.

"We are," Blade replied. "Let's go." He headed to the east.

The next hour passed uneventfully as they meandered into the heart of the metropolis. Both the pedestrian and vehicle traffic increased the farther east and south they went. Guns were in evidence everywhere, but the citizenry appeared to take the presence of the firearms in stride. Miami's population was a cosmopolitan mix of ethnic groups. Some neighborhoods consisted of predominantly Hispanic or black residents, while others were racially integrated. Gangs were in abundance. Every six blocks or so, there would be an average of ten youths lounging on the steps of a tenement or hanging out on a street corner. Their faces were invariably hard and challenging, and black leather was obviously the preferred style of clothing.

If the gangs and the guns were common, the drug use was universal. Deals were conducted openly. Hundreds of people the Warriors passed were smoking odd, stubby cigarettes that gave off a pungent odor. Popping pills or capsules was also a favorite pastime. A large number of the gang members bore needle marks on their arms. Street vendors, urchins mainly, hawked their wares brazenly. The result of all this drug use was reflected in the customers; heavy users weaved as they walked, or gazed at the world with blank expressions, or talked to themselves. Totally wasted men and women were a frequent sight, their personalities shattered, their clothing mere rags, filthy and beyond reclamation.

"Remind me to never take a vacation here," Hickok said at one point.

"Same here," Rikki said. "Why would anyone come to Miami as a tourist?"

"Why else?" Blade responded. "For drugs. Miami could well be the drug capital of the Western Hemisphere, for all we know. When that Narc talked about tourists, he wasn't referring to the old-fashioned kind who took their families on trips to amusement parks once a year. He was talking about drug-users. Think of it. An entire tourist industry catering to drug-users. Every drug a person could imagine, right here at their fingertips."

"People come here from all over merely for drugs?" Rikki commented in disgust.

"That's the way I read it," Blade replied.

Hickok spotted an emaciated man, naked from the waist up, to their left. The man's arms were discolored and dotted with needle tracks. "This is sick."

The buildings were becoming taller, more stately. Dozens of skyscrapers appeared to the southeast.

Blade made for them. He spied a Narc car patrolling the adjacent street, and realized dozens had driven by during their trek. The Narcs must need to maintain a high profile to keep a lid on the city.

A boy of six or seven, wearing jeans and a green shirt,

ran up to the Warrior and tugged at his left leg. "Hey, mister?"

Blade halted and glanced down. "What?"

"Can you spare some coin?"

"I don't have any coins," Blade told him.

"Please, mister," the boy said. "My dad needs a dime bag bad."

"You need money for your dad to buy drugs?" Blade asked.

The boy nodded.

"I can't help you," Blade said sadly.

Frowning, the boy ran off.

"How could these folks do this to themselves?" Hickok wondered aloud.

"I don't know," Blade admitted.

They entered the heart of Miami, the downtown section with its towering skyscrapers, with predominantly antiquated cars and trucks bumper to bumper, and with a seething wave of pedestrians on every sidewalk.

Blade drifted with the crowds, enthralled by the spectacle. He was in no hurry to reach Miami Beach. Studying enemy terrain was essential to the success of any mission, and he was familiarizing himself with the landmarks, noting the tallest skyscrapers and other distinctive structures.

"Does the air smell funny to you two?" Hickok inquired. "Sort of tangy?"

"We might be near the ocean," Blade guessed.

They traveled in an easterly direction. A sign materialized ahead: BAYFRONT PARK. Water was visible to the east and south.

"We'll take a break in the park," Blade suggested.

They followed the sidewalk until they came to a beautifully landscaped strip of land, a garden of tropical foliage. Dozens of people were lounging on the green grass. Others were engaged in games or conversation. Skimpy attire was the order of the day.

"At last!" Hickok remarked. "Breathin' space."

The Warriors mingled with the crowd, moving at random, observing.

"What the blazes is that guy doing?" Hickok asked.

Two men and two women were sitting on a blue blanket under a tree. In the center of the blanket was a small folding table, not more than six inches high. On one side of the table was a pile of packets of white powder. On the other side, one of the men was opening packets and arranging the white powder in straight lines.

The Warriors halted, perplexed.

One of the women leaned forward over the table, pressed the first finger of her left hand against her left nostril, then lowered her right nostril to the white powder. She started inhaling loudly.

"She's suckin' that gunk up her nose!" Hickok declared in amazement.

One of the men heard the remark and looked up, smiling. "Hi. Care to join us? There's plenty to go around."

"What are you doing?" Hickok asked.

"Getin' high, dude. What else?"

"What is that stuff?"

The man stared at the Warrior as if he was from another planet. "Coke, man. We're snortin' a little. You sure you don't want some?"

Hickok shook his head. "No thanks. I don't even stick a finger up my nose unless it's a serious emergency."

The man shrugged and returned his attention to the small table.

"Cow chips," Hickok muttered. "The whole blamed city is full of cow chips."

The Warriors continued walking.

"We have company," Rikki stated, nodding to their right.

Blade glanced around.

Seven men, ranging in age from their twenties to the late thirties, were standing in a compact group 15 yards away. All seven were eyeing the Warriors with intense interest. And all seven were armed, four with revolvers, two with rifles over their shoulders, and one with a pump shotgun. Their attire was a mix of jeans, boots, and leather shirts and jackets. One of them, a man about six feet tall with a neatly trimmed beard and mustache, motioned with his left arm. The seven strolled toward the Warriors.

Hickok sighed. "Here we go again."

"I'll handle this," Blade said.

The seven approached to within three yards and stopped. Their apparent leader, the man with the beard, grinned. "*Buenas tardes, señor,*" he said to Blade.

"Hello," the Warrior responded.

"*¿Habla español?*"

"What?"

"Do you speak Spanish, *señor*?"

"No," Blade admitted.

The man nodded slowly. "English then. I am Pedro."

"What can we do for you?"

Pedro tilted his head, inspecting the portion of the Paratrooper visible above the giant's right shoulder. "We couldn't help but notice, eh? Your guns."

"What about them?"

"They are nice guns, no?"

"They get the job done," Blade replied.

Pedro patted the Smith and Wesson on his right hip. "Our guns are not so new as yours. Ours are old guns."

"Ours were manufactured before the war," Blade said. "We take good care of them."

Pedro nodded. "So I see, eh? Real good care."

Blade waited for the man to come to the point.

"Would you like to sell them?" Pedro asked.

"No."

"Just one or two."

"No."

The corners of Pedro's mouth curled downward slightly. "Please, *señor*. You don't understand. We will buy some of your guns. We won't cheat you on the price. You name it."

"Our guns are not for sale," Blade stated firmly.

Pedro sighed and gazed at his companions, then back at the three strangers. "*Por favor, señor*. Guns like yours are important to us. Good guns are hard to come by. They can mean life or death. You see?"

"I see. But the guns are not for sale."

Pedro surveyed the park, his lips pursed.

Blade tensed. He realized the man was checking for Narcs. "Don't do something you'll regret."

"One last time, *señor*," Pedro said. "Will you sell us some of your guns?"

"No."

"Then we will take them."

The seven sprang forward.

CHAPTER SIX

Blade was about to whip the Bowies from their sheaths when he perceived that the seven gang members were not relying on their weapons; not one was reaching for a revolver or bringing a rifle into play. Before he could reflect on this, Pedro was on him.

The gang leader aimed a vicious kick at the giant's genitals.

Blade twisted to the right, dodging the blow, and grabbed Pedros' leg in midair. Gripping the ankle with his left hand and thigh with his right, Blade rammed his right knee into the underside of Pedro's leg directly below the kneecap.

There was a distinct popping noise.

Pedro screeched and fell as the giant released his leg.

The tough with the shotgun swung the stock at the giant's head.

Blade ducked under the swing, then slammed his right fist onto the tip of the man's jaw. There was no time to gauge the effect of the punch, because another gang member was already hurtling toward him. Blade side-stepped to the left, then lashed out with his right leg, catching the charging man in the gut and doubling him over. As the man gurgled and wheezed, Blade swept his left knee into the gang member's face.

The remaining four had separated, two going for the man in black, and two attacking the man in buckskins. Neither pair succeeded.

Blade spun in time to see Rikki-Tikki-Tavi leap into the air, a piercing kiai bursting from the martial artist's lips. Rikki's legs flicked outward, each foot connecting with the head of one of the men asaulting him. Both gang members went down.

Which left the two rushing Hickok. They were both within a stride of the gunman, who had not moved a muscle, when his hands became a literal blur. Both gang members drew up short, gawking, as each one found himself staring down the barrel of a Colt Python .357.

"You boys are being a mite inhospitable," the gunfighter remarked. His voice hardened. "It's not nice to be inhospitable."

Blade stared at Pedro. The gang leader was clutching his knee and groaning, his face contorted in agony.

"What should we do with these turnips?" Hickok asked. "Turn 'em over to the Narcs?"

Blade scanned their vicinity. Many people were standing and watching, but none seemed inclined to interfere. There was no sign of any Narcs. "No," he replied. "They might want us to fill out an official report, or take us to their headquarters. Let's get out of here."

Hickok winked at the pair in front of him. "Don't so much as twitch until we're out of sight, or I'll ventilate your noggins. Savvy?"

Neither man responded or moved a muscle.

The Warriors slowly backed off.

"They didn't go for their hardware," Hickok remarked.

"They probably didn't want to get the Narcs after them," Blade deduced. "Carrying firearms may be legal, but I doubt that the Narcs allow random gunplay."

Hickok twirled the Pythons into their holsters. "What now?"

For an answer, Blade turned and jogged in the direction of a nearby avenue.

"I've been thinkin'," Hickok commented as he kept pace with Blade.

"Uh-oh," Rikki said.

Hickok ignored the martial artist. "I'm serious. Let's suppose we find these Masters. Let's suppose we terminate them."

"If they're a threat to the Family, they'll be terminated," Blade guaranteed. He spotted a row of buses parked near a monument and angled toward it.

"Will killin' the Masters stop the drugs?" Hickok queried.

Blade glanced at his friend. "Stop the drugs?"

"Yeah. Do you think blowin' the Masters away will put an end to the drug use?"

"I doubt it," Blade said. "Someone, or some group, will take over the operation."

Hickok frowned. "That's what I figured. Pity."

"This drug business has you upset, doesn't it?" Rikki interjected.

"Yep," Hickok acknowledged. "I keep thinkin' of what drugs could do to Ringo."

"Your son is safe," Rikki assured him. "The Home is drug free."

"Only because we keep it that way," Hickok mentioned. "The Elders teach us to enjoy life naturally, to value our health. As parents, we're expected to set an example for our young'uns. We have to show 'em that pollutin' their bodies is the worst thing they could possibly do."

Rikki nodded. "Any type of addiction hampers our spiritual communion. Chemical poisons prevent us from enjoying a fuller contact with the Spirit."

"We know that," Hickok said. "And we try to pass on our values to our young'uns. But what about that boy we saw earlier? The one who asked Blade for some money?" He paused. "That kid is learnin' to use drugs from his own parents. He'll be hooked before he's ten. What kind of life is that?"

"There's nothing we can do about it," Blade said.

"I know," Hickok reluctantly agreed. "I was just thinkin', is all."

Blade studied the gunman for a moment. Hickok was genuinely perturbed, and rarely did the Family's preeminent gunfighter become disturbed over anything. "You don't need to worry about Ringo," he assured him.

"I pray I don't," Hickok said.

Blade slowed to a casual walk, heading for the buses.

He stared at the monument, a curved wall with the words THE TORCH OF FRIENDSHIP near the top. In front of the wall was a solitary pillar. A man was playing a guitar a few yards from the pillar, a metal cup at his feet. Five people were listening to him, and one of them deposited several coins in the cup.

Blade halted.

The guitarist finished his song and the five listeners dispersed, two of them adding coins to the cup.

"What's up, pard?" Hickok asked.

"We need money," Blade noted.

Hickok looked at the musician. "Got you." He marched toward the guitarist ten feet away.

"Wait—" Blade began, but the gunman kept going.

Hickok stepped up to the musician with his thumbs hooked in his gunbelt. "Howdy."

The guitarist, in the act of tuning his instrument by ear, glanced up. "Hey, man, how's it going?"

"Just dandy," Hickok said.

"Do you have a request?" the guitarist inquired.

"Do you use drugs?"

The man's green eyes narrowed and he ran his right hand through his shoulder-length brown hair. "Say what?"

"Do you use drugs?"

"What kind of question is that?"

"Answer it."

"Yeah, I do drugs. Doesn't everybody?"

"I figured you'd say that."

The musician lowered his guitar. "What's the big deal? Do you want to hear a request or not?"

"Yep."

"What's it called, dude?"

"Do you know This Is a Stickup?"

The guitarist pondered for several seconds. "No. Can't say as I do. How does it go?"

Hickok leaned forward. "It goes like this. You hand over your money, and I let you live."

The musician grinned. "Are you puttin' me on, dude?"

Hickok's voice became flinty. "Do I sound like I'm puttin' you on, you peckerwood? And if you call me 'dude' again, I'm gonna gram my Python barrels up your nose and see what happens when I pull the triggers."

The guitarist blinked rapidly. "You're not puttin' me on!"

"You must have all the intellect in your family," Hickok quipped.

"You're really stealin' my bread!" the man exclaimed in astonishment.

"Keep your voice down!" Hickok warned. "I couldn't care less about your bread. I want your *money*. Now."

The guitarist blanched, his lips quivering. "Like, this is for real!"

"The money," Hickok prompted, his hands inching toward his Colts.

The musician noticed the movement and swallowed hard. "Take it! It's all yours!"

"Be a nice . . . dude . . . and hand it to me," Hickok directed.

With supreme care, the guitarist leaned over, retrieved the metal cup, and straightened. "Here. Just don't shoot me!"

"I wouldn't think of wastin' the bullet," Hickok commented, taking the cup in his left hand. It was two-thirds full.

"Like, this is a cosmic injustice!" the man stated belligerently.

"Get me riled and you'll see an injustice," Hickok said.

"I'm an artiste!"

"You're a dipshit," Hickok countered. "You're lettin' drugs mess up your head and cramp your talent."

The guitarist snorted derisively. "You're crazy! What do you know? Drugs expand my mind, dude. They make me more creative."

"That's why you're standin' here playin' for small change?" Hickok retorted.

"I need my smack, man."

"Smack?"

"The Big H."

"Can you speak English?"

"Heroin, man. It chills me out. If I don't get my fix, I freak out."

Hickok gazed into the musician's slightly disoriented eyes, recognizing the reflection of commingled craving and fear. He extended the cup. "Here."

The man gawked at the cup. "What?"

"Here. Take it. You need this more than we do." Hickok wagged the cup and heard the coins jingle.

"You're givin' it back?" the man asked in disbelief.

"Take the damn cup!" Hickok snapped. He suddenly became aware of someone standing behind him and looked over his right shoulder.

Blade and Rikki were a foot away.

"What, *exactly*, are you doing?" Blade calmly inquired.

Hickok mustered a feeble grin. "Who? Me?"

The guitarist, unaware that the guy in buckskins, the giant, and the man in black were together, took a step toward the giant. "Stop him! He's tryin' to rob me!"

Blade glanced from the musician to the gunman. "Is that right? You're robbing him in broad daylight in the middle of a park?"

"You said we need money," Hickok responded.

"But I didn't intend for you to steal it," Blade said.

The guitarist stared from the giant to the guy in buckskins. "You two know each other?"

"How else will we get the money?" Hickok asked Blade.

"You two know each other!" the musician reiterated.

"We'll find a way," Blade stated. "First, we see if one of these buses goes to Miami Beach. Then we'll find out how much it will cost for the three of us. After we know how much we'll need, we'll find a way to get it."

"You want to take the bus to Miami Beach?" the guitarist questioned in astonishment.

"I figured this yahoo could spare a few coins," Hickok commented.

The musician's face was turning a light shade of crimson. His eyes glared from one to the other. "All this over the lousy bus?" He snatched the cup. "You morons!"

Hickok looked at the guitarist. "What's eatin' you?"

"What's eatin' me?" the musician exploded. "I'll tell you what's eatin' me! You scared me half to death over a lousy bus fare! You threatened to blow out my brains for a bus ride!"

"I was only joshin' you," Hickok said.

The guitarist became madder. He leaned his guitar against his left leg and began sorting through the coins in the cup. "Of all the dumbass, screwball, wacked-out things I've ever heard—"

"I don't see why you're being so touchy," Hickok remarked. "You're still in one piece."

The musician's mouth moved, but no words came out. He held three large silver coins in his left hand and jabbed his arm at the gunman. "Here!"

"What are they?" Hickok asked.

"What do they look like?" the guitarist retorted. "They're your bus fare."

"What?"

"You heard me!" the musician snapped. "It costs a buck to ride the shuttle bus from here to Miami Beach. There's three bucks here. Enough for all three of you."

"We don't want your money," Hickok stated.

"Take it."

"No. You keep it."

"Take the damn money!" the guitarist shouted.

"We'll take it," Blade said, stepping up and palming the coins. "And thank you."

"Don't thank me!" the musician barked. "I don't want your gratitude! I just want you out of my life!"

"We're going," Blade assured him.

"And take this lunatic with you!" the guitarist demanded, nodding at the gunman.

"Who are you callin' a lunatic?" Hickok responded.

"Get him out of here!"

Blade tugged on the gunfighter's right arm. "Come on."

Hickok shook his head and turned toward the buses. "Some people have no sense of humor."

CHAPTER SEVEN

"May I help you?"

Blade smiled at the elderly desk clerk, then scrutinized the dozens of small wooden boxes on the wall to the rear of the front desk. "Yes. My name is John Clayton. I believe some forms were dropped off for me."

"Forms?" the desk clerk said, turning toward the boxes. His balding pate was nonetheless slicked and combed, his cerulean suit immaculate. "No one mentioned any forms—"

"The Narcs were supposed to leave them here for me," Blade explained.

The desk clerk wheeled. "The Narcs! So you're the gentleman!"

"Yes."

The desk clerk stepped to the boxes and removed several folded sheets of paper from a box on the lower left. "It isn't every day the Narcs drop off something."

"I hope it wasn't an inconvenience."

"Inconvenience?" the desk clerk repeated, sounding shocked at the suggestion. "Helping the Narcs is an honor!" He placed the papers on the counter.

"Thanks," Blade said, taking them and starting to leave.

"Will you be staying the night?" the desk clerk inquired hopefully. "I can reserve a suite for you right now."

"I'll think it over," Blade said. He walked to the front entrance to the Ocean View and pushed through the glass doors.

Rikki and Hickok were waiting on the top step.

"Did they leave the papers?" Rikki asked.

Blade nodded, unfolding the three sheets.

"I don't see why we're diddlin' around with this nonsense," Hickok remarked. "Are you plannin' to file a formal complaint?"

"No," Blade said.

"I know you," Hickok stated. "You don't do nothin' without a reason. What gives?"

"Your great plan, remember?"

"My plan?"

"To find a bigwig and force whoever it is to take us to the Masters," Blade reminded the gunfighter.

"How's this tie in?"

Blade examined the top sheet, a white piece of paper entitled FORM 1073 CITIZEN COMPLAINT. The second sheet, another white paper, bore a bold, black PAGE TWO at the top. He checked the third and final sheet and smiled. This one was a yellow paper, and hand-written in the middle of the page was the information he wanted. "Bingo."

"What is it?" Hickok questioned.

"The name of Fowler's Dealer and his address," Blade replied.

Hickok grinned. "Now I get it."

"The Narc wanted us to fill out the forms and drop them in the mail," Blade said. "We'll go him one better. We'll deliver the forms personally."

"So where does this big-time Dealer live?" Hickok inquired.

Blade read from the paper. "The Oasis Resort Hotel. It's on Collins Avenue."

"We're on Ocean Drive now, right?" Hickok brought up.

"Yeah," Blade said.

"How far is Collins Avenue from here?" Rikki queried.

"Let's find out the same way we found this place," Blade responded. "Ask."

The Warriors descended the half-dozen concrete steps to the street.

"Miami Beach sure comes alive at night," Hickok commented.

Blade was thinking the same thing. The avenues and streets had been much less crowded two and a half hours ago when the shuttle bus from Bayfront Park had deposited them on Dade Boulevard after crossing the Venetian Causeway. The late afternoon heat had instilled a lethargy in the inhabitants, a sluggishness promptly dispelled by the enveloping shroud of darkness. Now, with a few stars faintly discernible in the inky sky, Miami Beach was a vibrant, hustling hub of activity. People thronged to the sidewalks. Vehicles packed the thoroughfares. And there was a distinct difference evident, as if those who roamed Miami Beach at night were a breed apart from the daytime dwellers. The clothing worn by the passersby consisted more of tailored suits and dresses instead of black leather and jeans. Even the cars prowling from block to block betrayed the meticulous care they received by their shiny paint jobs and gleaming bumpers and chrome strips.

A pair of women approached the Warriors, one in a sheer black dress, the second in a yellow blouse and short red skirt. Their hair was stylishly coiffured, their nails painted red, their lips a striking scarlet.

Hickok nodded at them and smiled. "Howdy."

They stopped. The brunette in the red skirt raked the Warrior with a critical gaze. "Howdy yourself, handsome."

"We need some help," Hickok told her.

The woman laughed and nudged her friend. "I'll bet you do, lover!"

"We're open to anything except S and M," the woman in the black dress added.

"S and M?" Hickok repeated quizzically.

"Yeah," the brunette stated. "We don't do the kinky stuff. A working girl has to draw the line somewhere."

"It's nice to know you ladies are holdin' down jobs," Hickok remarked. "and we really can use your help. Which way is it to Collins Avenue?"

The brunette's brown eyes narrowed. "Is that all you want? Directions?"

"We're lookin' for the Oasis Resort Hotel," Hickok

elaborated. "Do you know it?"

"Yeah, we know it," responded the one in the black dress.

"How do we get there?" Hickok inquired.

"Is that *really* all you want?" the brunette demanded.

"That's it," Hickok said. "We'd be in your debt."

"You don't want to turn a trick?" asked the brunette.

"This isn't a blamed trick!" Hickok declared.

The women exchanged bemused glances.

"Are there many like you at home?" the brunette asked.

"Nope," Hickok said. "I'm one of a kind."

"Figures," the brunette stated. "So you need directions to the Oasis?"

"That's the general idea."

"Go north three blocks," she instructed them. "Then take a left. The next drag you'll come to is Collins. Take a right. Go about a half-mile. The Oasis is on the right. You can't miss it."

Hickok grinned. "Thanks. Hope you ladies have a fun night."

"Business before pleasure," the brunette said, and they walked off.

"What did she mean by that?" Hickok queried.

"They must work the night shift," Rikki speculated.

"Let's go," Blade directed, leading them to the north. He folded the papers and slid them into his right front pants pocket.

"What if this Dealer doesn't want to take us to the Masters?" Hickok asked.

"He'll take us," Blade stated.

They traveled the three blocks to the appropriate intersection, then turned to the left. Their progress was slow, hampered by the press of the lively crowds.

"Will you look at that!" Hickok marveled.

A tall black woman was drawing near. She wore black, high-heeled shoes, a lavender skirt scarcely covering her shapely thighs, and a pair of silver cups constructed from a pliable material over her large breasts. Purple tassels dangled from the tips of the cups.

"The womenfolk hereabouts sure don't believe in modesty," Hickok observed.

The Warriors reached Collins Avenue and took a right. The volume of pedestrian and vehicle traffic was twice that of Ocean Drive.

"I'm glad I don't live in a city on a regular basis," Hickok remarked. "Give me the wide-open spaces any day."

"Millions, maybe billions, lived like this before the war," Blade mentioned pensively. "Overpopulation was a serious problem for most of the countries in the world."

"No wonder they went off the deep end and tried to blow themselves sky-high," Hickok said.

Blade glanced at Rikki. "Why are you so quiet?"

"Something is amiss," the martial artist answered.

"Like what?"

Rikki's thin lips tightened. "I don't know. But I feel that something is wrong."

Blade scanned the avenue in all directions. "I don't see anything."

Rikki shrugged. "I could be mistaken. My intuition is not infallible."

Blade looked at Hickok. "Do you feel anything?"

"Hungry."

"You're a big help," Blade muttered. He threaded his way to the north, bothered by Rikki's revelation. The martial artist was not prone to needless worry or flights of fancy. Rikki was always levelheaded, even if the Zen he practiced did imbue him with a mystical air. If Rikki's senses were telling him that something was wrong, then something was wrong.

But what?

What had they overlooked?

"It's all this sea air," Hickok quipped. "Everything seems fishy."

Blade couldn't help but grin. He searched the avenue for someone who might be tailing them or watching them surreptitiously.

Nothing.

Maybe Hickok was right.

They proceeded a quarter of a mile.

Blade was almost to an intersection when there was a tug on his right arm. He turned to find a thin man with a sparse mustache attired in a natty white suit and carrying a cane. "Yes?"

The man in white beamed. "I couldn't help but notice you boys. I bet you're from out of town, right?"

"Is it that obvious?" Blade responded.

"Your threads have a lot to do with it," the man said.

Hickok looked down at himself. "Threads?"

"What can we do for you?" Blade inquired.

"You've got it backwards, friend," the man said. "It's what I can do for you."

"For us?"

"You name it, I can supply it," the man boasted. "You want broads? I have a stable of the finest in Miami. You want to connect, I'm your source. Crack, smack, ludes, weed, whatever you want, the Genie can get."

"Are you the Genie?" Blade questioned.

The man in white bowed. "At your service, sir! I don't mean to brag, but my rep is as heavy as they come! I supply the tourists with the stuff dreams are made of. I—"

A young girl, not much over 15, abruptly materialized to the Genie's left. She was wearing a lacy red dress and red shoes. Her hair was blonde, her face caked with makeup. Her arms were folded across her chest and she was shivering. "Genie?"

He stared at her in disapproval. "Not now. Can't you see that I'm busy?"

"Please," she said, fidgeting with the strap to her brown purse.

Before the Warriors could intervene, the Genie slapped the girl on the mouth.

"You know better than to interrupt when I'm making a sale!"

Tears welled in the girl's eyes. "I can't help it! I need a fix."

"Work for it like everyone else."

The girl glanced at Blade. "How about you, mister?"

"Me?" the Warrior responded.

"Yeah. I'll get you off for twenty. Please. I need the bread."

Blade studied her for several seconds. His features seemed to ripple in the glare of the streetlight, hardening for a fraction of a instant before inexplicably relaxing as he smiled at the girl. "I may be dense, but I'm not stupid."

"What?" the girl asked.

"Nothing," Blade said. He gazed at the man in white. "You've impressed me. I'd like to do business with you."

The Genie snickered. "A man of class! What what will it be? Coke? Grass?"

"Grass will be fine."

"How much do you want?"

"A handful should be enough."

The Genie blinked twice, then cackled. "I like your style, my man. You can buy it by the joint, the lid, whatever. If you've got the green, you can buy a whole key."

"We'll take three keys."

Hickok and Rikki looked at one another and Hickok shrugged.

The Genie's mouth slackened. "Three keys? Are you putting me on?"

"No."

"Three keys is a lot of bread, man," the Genie said. "You have that much on you?"

Blade patted his right front pocket. "I have it on me."

"You wouldn't be trying to stick it to me, would you?" the Genie queried suspiciously.

"I want to do the honorable thing," Blade said.

The Genie hesitated, his dark eyes roving over the Paragrooper on the giant's right shoulder and the Bowies in their sheaths. "I don't know—"

"Suit yourself," Blade stated, and started to turn.

"Wait!"

Blade faced the Genie.

"All right. We've got a deal," the man in white

declared.

Blade began to reach into his right front pocket. "Do you want the money now?"

"No!" the Genie replied hastily. "Don't go flashing that much bread! Some of these hit-and-run types might see it!"

Blade removed his hand. "Where then?"

The Genie jerked his head to the rear. "My wheels, man. They're parked down the block. I've got the stuff in the trunk."

"After you," Blade said.

"What about me?" the girl asked.

"You stay put, bitch!" the Genie snapped. "I'll.deal with you later."

Blade looked at his companions. "You two stay here. I'll be right back."

"You sure, pard?" Hickok responded.

Blade nodded.

"Follow me," the Genie directed, and hurried down the block.

Blade warily followed, deliberately holding his hands away from his Bowies. He spotted a row of flashy cars parked along the curb.

The Genie hastened toward an enormous automobile notable for its sparkling golden finish and more chrome per square inch than any other vehicle in sight. "I knew this was my lucky night!" he declared excitedly over his right shoulder.

"Mine too."

"You never can tell," the Genie went on. "If there's one thing I've learned in this business, it's never to judge a book by its cover. You never now how much bread a customer will have."

The front passenger door on the gold car suddenly opened and a huge black in a black suit climbed out. His head was bald, his expression tainted with a cruel edge.

"This is Hugo," the Genie said, introducing his henchman as he halted next to the front fender.

Blade stopped and nodded.

Huge said nothing, his eyes radiating distrust.

"This gentleman wants to buy three keys," the Genie stated. "Open the trunk. Give him a peek at our goodies."

Huge moved to the rear of the car, withdrew a key ring from his left front pocket, and unlocked the trunk.

"See for yourself," the Genie said, walking to the rear and motioning for Blade to join him.

The Warrior moved to within a foot of the trunk.

"Open it," the Genie said.

Hugo slowly raised the lid.

Blade's eyes narrowed as he beheld the bewildering collection of drugs and drug paraphernalia. The trunk was filled to the brim.

"I'm as good as my word," the Genie declared. He reached into the trunk and patted three large bundles. "Three keys. Just what you want. Now I need to see the color of your money."

Blade reached for his right pocket.

"Wait a second," the Genie said. "Why don't we do this right? Step into my parlor. We can have a drink while we finalize the deal." He stepped to the rear door and threw it wide. "After you."

Blade leaned over and peered into the spacious, indulgently furnished interior. The back seat was covered with a lustrous brown leather, and the floor was a rich, thick, green carpet. A handsome wooden cabinet was positioned behind the front seat.

"Slide on in," the Genie urged.

Blade hunched his broad shoulders and eased into the plush vehicle. He looked out the rear window to see Hugo standing next to the trunk.

"Close it," the Genie ordered, then bent down to enter the car.

Blade was in the middle of the seat, his buttocks resting on the edge, his body slightly twisted to the left, his right hand touching the wooden cabinet, his left on his left Bowie.

The Genie was halfway inside, the cane in his right hand.

Blade tensed and watched as Hugo walked to the rear

and was momentarily obscured by the trunk lid.

Now!

The Warrior's body unwound, his right hand sweepig up and over the Genie's head, his fingers locking on the man's neck and yanking the Genie forward even as his left hand brought the Bowie around and up in a savage arc. The tip of the razor-honed blade penetrated the Genie's neck just below his chin, and the knife slanted upwards and was buried to the hilt.

For an instant of incredulous shock, the Genie's only reaction was a widening of his eyes. He gurgled as a crimson spray gushed from his throat, then abruptly lunged, hissing, spearing the cane at the giant's face. There was a muted click and a five-inch sharpened metal spike popped out the top of the cane.

Blade jerked his head aside, but the spike dug a red groove in his left cheek. He tightened his hold on the Genie's neck and slammed the man to the seat.

The trunk lid closed with a thump.

Blade kept his eyes on Hugo as the black came around the driver's side. His arms bulged as he held the Genie flush with the seat, and he felt the spurting blood spatter his left forearm. Would Hugo look inside first or simply open the driver's side door? Blade gritted his teeth as the Genie thrashed and heaved, the cane swinging wildly.

Hugo reached for the rear door.

The Genie uttered a strangled gasp and went limp.

Blade yanked his left Bowie free as the door on the driver's side opened. He spun, the Bowie going straight out, knowing he had to take Hugo down without attracting the attention of anyone outside.

Hugo was leaning down when the Bowie sliced through his trousers and into his groin. Totally stunned, racked by torment, he inadvertently doubled over and clutched at his genitals.

Blade clamped his right arm on the bodyguard's throat and hauled Hugo inside, onto the floor. The small oval overhead bulb cast a garish yellow glow on the black's stupefied expression.

Hugo brought his bloody hands up, clawing at the Warrior.

Blade wrenched the Bowie out, then sank the knife in Hugo's chest.

Hugo stiffened, his lips moving formlessly, then sank back, his eyes open but unfocused. He expelled a lingering breath and was still.

Blade glanced at the avenue. Cars and other vehicles were passing, but not one appeared to have noticed the struggle. He pulled his Bowie from Hugo's body, wiped the blade on Hugo's jacket, and replaced the knife in its sheath. Working quickly, he closed the driver's side door, then reached for the passenger door.

And froze.

The Genie's black shoes were protruding from the passenger side.

Staring at those shoes, not two feet from the car, was the young girl in the lacy red dress.

Blade prepared to pounce, expecting her to scream.

Instead, she looked him in the eyes, her features composed and licked her lips. "I get half or I'll roll over to the Narcs."

"What?"

She moved closer. "Don't try and scam me, turkey! I want half!"

"Half of what?"

She put her hands on her hips. "You know damn well what I'm talking about! What's it going to be? Fifty-fifty, or the Narcs?"

"I don't want the Narcs involved," Blade admitted.

She slapped the Genie's shoes. "Dump his ass on the floor."

Confounded, Blade rolled the man in white on top of Hugo.

"Keep your hands away from your knives," she warned as she slid in.

"Close your door," Blade said.

"Do I look stupid?" she countered. "The door stays open!" She reached for the wooden cabinet and jerked on a gold knob. "Fifty-fifty is fair," she commented nervously.

Blade did a double take as his gray eyes alighted on the contents of the cabinet. Under a shelf containing liquor bottles and glasses was another shelf piled high with stacks of bills and rolls of gold and silver coins bound by plastic bands.

"Look at it!" the girl said in awe.

"You want to split this fifty-fifty?" Blade asked.

The girl stared at him defiantly. "Damn straight! Unless you want me to go to the Narcs!"

"You seem more concerned about the money than the Genie," Blade commented.

She glanced at the corpse in white, scowling. "Who the hell cares about that bastard? I can always get me a new pimp. Young fluff is always in demand. Know what I mean?"

"Fluff?"

She nodded at the cabinet. "Look! Enough stalling! Do we split this or not?"

Blade studied her for several seconds, then sighed. "Take as much as you want."

"What?"

"I don't need half of it," Blade told her. He removed two half-inch stacks of bills and two rolls of coins. "The rest is yours."

She looked like she was going to lay an egg. "Are you for real?"

Blade stuffed the bills into his left front pocket, then placed the coins in his left rear pocket.

"Are you for real?" she repeated.

The Warrior gestured at the cabinet. "Help yourself."

She laughed and opened her purse. "I may never have to hustle again!"

"You could start a new life," Blade suggested.

She grabbed stacks of bills and crammed them into her purse. "You don't know the half of it!"

"You could give up the drugs."

Her hand paused in midair. "Why would I want to do that?" She laughed and resumed filling her purse.

"You like using drugs?"

"Sure. Doesn't everybody?" She giggled. "With this, I can get a buzz on like you wouldn't believe."

"Why not do something constructive with your life? Why not find a mate and settle down? Why not rear a family?"

She gazed at him in surprise. "Get real, man! You sound like my grandmother. Those old ways are for nerds! Number one is all that counts, and I intend to look out for number one."

Blade waited as she finished stuffing her purse.

"That's it!" she exclaimed happily, looking at him. "Thanks. I'll never forget you!"

Blade said nothing.

"Are you sure you wouldn't like a freebie? I feel like I owe you. How about a quickie right here?"

"No," Blade responded softly.

"What's the matter with you? A big hunk like you, and you don't want to make it? Why not?"

"I doubt that you'd understand."

"Try me," she prompted.

"For one thing, I'm married—"

"So? Three-fourths of my johns are married."

"For another, sex should be an expression of love, not lust."

The girl laughed. "You're weird! Do you know that?"

"We should leave before someone looks inside," Blade advised.

She glanced at the sidewalk, at the people hustling past. "I guess you're right. If I had the time, I'd snatch some of the trunk stash. But we're pushing our luck as it is."

"May you know true happiness someday."

The girl laughed and climbed out. "Ta-ta, lover!" she said in parting, and dashed to the south.

Blade emerged from the car and closed the door. He spotted a man in a brown suit standing a few yards away, watching him. "Do you want something?" he demanded.

The man shook his head and blended in with the throng.

Blade turned to the north.

"Havin' fun, pard?"

"We could have helped you."

Hickok and Rikki were near the front fender, their bodies positioned so that anyone walking past would need to swing wide of the vehicle.

"Let's find the Oasis Resort Hotel," Blade said.

Hickok nodded at the car. "What was that all about?"

Blade frowned. "I don't know if I could explain it."

"Yeah," Hickok said thoughtfully, surveying their surroundings. "This city is gettin' to me too."

Blade headed north.

CHAPTER EIGHT

"Can I be of service?"

Blade stared at the middle-aged desk clerk in the blue suit. "I hope so. The Narcs sent me to the Oasis."

The desk clerk was suddenly all attention. "The Narcs? Whatever about?"

"I'm to deliver some papers to a man staying here," Blade detailed.

"Who is the gentleman?"

The Warrior reached into his right front pocket and extracted the three folded sheets. He deposited them on the counter and read the name written on the yellow paper. "Tom Barbish."

"Mr. Barbish!" the desk clerk exclaimed.

"Do you know him?"

"Of course! Everyone knows Mr. Barbish!"

"We need to see him."

The desk clerk glancced at the giant's two associates and his nose crinkled. "What about?"

"That's between Mr. Barbish and us," Blade stated.

"Mr. Barbish is one of our top tenants," the desk clerk said. "He occupies the Presidential Suite, and has for years. I'm not about to risk interrupting him over a trifle."

"This is important," Blade persisted.

"So *you* say."

"All right," Blade said in feigned resignation. "But I'll need your name."

"My name?"

"To tell the Narcs," Blade explained. "They'll want to know the reason Mr. Barbish didn't receive the forms."

"I don't see why I should be involved," the clerk said defensively.

Blade shrugged. "You know the Narcs."

"I don't want the Narcs on my case."

"I don't blame you." Blade folded the forms again and took a step from the front desk."

"Hold it," the clerk stated.

Blade looked back.

"I can phone Mr. Barbish's suite for you. If he consents, you can go up."

"That's fair," Blade said. "We'll wait."

The desk clerk moved to a white telephone on the wall behind the desk.

Hickok leaned toward Blade. "I don't see why we didn't just mosey upstairs and tend to Barbish."

"Take a look at the elevators," Blade advised.

Hickok glanced to the right at the row of four elevators. Three were set off by themselves and were being used by the general public. The fourth, though, isolated by itself in the corner, was distinguished by a large sign above it with the word PRIVATE, and by the pair of guards blocking the elevator door.

"I want you to stay in the lobby," Blade directed the gunman. "Keep your eyes on those guards. If an alarm sounds, take them out."

"Piece of cake," Hickok pledged.

The desk clerk returned to the counter. "You're fortunate that Mr. Barbish is in and has consented to see you." He pointed at the isolated elevator. "Take Mr. Barbish's private elevator to the penthouse on the eighteenth floor."

"Thank you," Blade said. He led Rikki through the crowded lobby to the far wall.

The two guards straightened, their hands hovering near their belts.

"You want something?" the burliest of the duo demanded.

"Mr. Barbish wants to see us," Blade replied. "The desk clerk said we can go up."

The guard glanced at the desk clerk, who nodded. "Okay. But the hardware stays here."

"We can't take our weapons?"

"Not if you want to see Mr. Barbish. No ones goes up armed. That's the rule. No exceptions," the guard stated.

Blade unslung the Paratrooper and leaned the automatic rifle in the corner. He hesitated before drawing his Bowies. "These had better be here when I come back down."

"No one is going to steal your hardware," the guard assured him. "What do you think we're standing here for? Our health?"

Blade rested the Bowies on the carpeted floor.

Rikki-Tikki-Tavi rested his katana and M-16 in the corner.

The second guard pressed a button to the left of the elevator and the door hissed wide.

Blade moved toward it.

"Not so fast," the burly guard said. "Leave the backpacks."

The two Warriors removed their backpacks and dropped them next to their weapons.

"Anything else?" Blade asked impatiently.

"I've got to frisk you."

Blade frowned.

"Don't blame me, buddy," the guard said. "I'm just doing my job." He stepped in close to the giant and expertly ran his hands over all potential spots where a weapon could be concealed. "You're clean," he declared.

Rikki raised his arms from his sides.

The guard frisked the martial artist. He was running his fingers around Rikki's back when he froze. "What's this on the back of your belt?"

"My pouch."

"What's in it?"

"My kyoketsu-shogei, four shuriken, and a yawara."

"What? Show me?" The guard stepped back.

Rikki opened the pouch and withdrew the weapons, holding them in his palms.

"What the hell!" the burly guard declared. He picked up a metal star and inspected its sharp edges. "What's this thing?"

"A shuriken."

"What do you do with it?"

"Throw it."

The guard snickered. "You use this dingy thing as a weapon? Give me a .357 any day!" He tapped a black round piece of metal an inch in diameter and six inches long. "And what's this one?"

"The yawara."

"What do you do? Poke people with it?"

"Something like that."

His eyes narrowing, the guard inspected the last item, a doubled edged, five-inch knife attached to a length of cord with a metal ring at the end. "And what the hell is that?"

"My kyoketsu-shogei."

"How's it work?"

"Perhaps one day I can give you a demonstration."

"Mr. Barbish is waiting for us," Blade noted.

"Okay," the guard said. "Put your stuff in the corner," he instructed Rikki, handing over the shuriken. "I'll keep a real good eye on it. I wouldn't want anyone to walk off with your deadly arsenal."

Both guards laughed.

Blade entered the elevator and waited for Rikki to join him. He spied Hickok in the lobby, nonchalantly leaning against an ornate white column.

The gunman smiled and winked.

"You'll be searched again upstairs," the guard informed them as he pressed the button on the wall.

The elevator door closed and the cage ascended.

"Orders?" Rikki inquired.

"They'll be waiting for us upstairs," Blade said. "We'll play it by ear. Watch me. If I nod, you know what to do."

Rikki nodded.

The elevator climbed swiftly to the penthouse and coasted to a smooth stop, and a second later the door opened. Four men in suits were standing outside the elevator, two of whom were armed with machine guns, M.A.C. 10s. They stood slightly to the side of the doorway, one to the right, the other to the left. Two more men, neither holding a firearm, were directly in front of the elevator.

"Hello," said the tallest of the duo, a man in a blue suit. "Step out and raise your arms."

Blade and Rikki complied, with Blade deliberately taking a shuffling stride to the right. He scanned the plush, spacious living room beyond and spotted a sole figure seated on a large sofa. The man's back was to the elevator, and all Blade could see was a thatch of gray hair and slim shoulders. Was it Barbish? The man was gazing out an enormous window at the Miami Beach skyline.

The tall bodyguard stepped up to Blade as his unarmed companion did the same to Rikki.

"This will just take a moment," the tall one said to Blade.

Blade smiled, looked at Rikki, and nodded, and even as he nodded he was whipping his body to the right, his massive fist clenched, delivering a pile-driver blow to the guard with the M.A.C. 10, his knuckles crunching on the guard's nose and sending the man flying backwards.

As Blade attacked, so did Rikki. Lacking the giant Warrior's extended reach, Rikki was compelled to compensate with his skill and speed. There was no way he could reach the second bodyguard packing a M.A.C. 10 before the man could fire. So he grabbed the guard about to frisk him by the lapels, whirled, and shoved, flinging the startled man into his colleague. Both men stumbled backwards, and Rikki was on them in two bounds. He deflected the M.A.C. 10 with his left forearm, then delivered a slashing leopard-paw strike to the bodyguard's throat, crushing the larynx. The frisker was clawing for a pistol on his left hip. Rikki kicked the guard on the right kneecap and heard a cracking sound, and as the man buckled, opening his mouth to scream, Rikki used a sword-hand blow and chopped the man across the throat. The Warrior pivoted.

Blade had already dispatched the tall guard and was holding a Browning automatic pistol in his right hand, trained on the figure on the sofa.

The man in the living room had not budged.

Blade glanced at the pair Rikki had dispatched, then pointed at the machine gun the bodyguard had dropped.

Rikki retrieved the M.A.C. 10.

The figure on the sofa still hadn't moved.

Blade's forehead creased as he advanced into the living room, the thick, green carpet muffling his footsteps. He aimed the Browning at the rear of the gray-haired man's cranium. Slowly, cautiously, he skirted the end of the sofa, then stopped.

The man was asleep! He was dozing on the sofa, his chin slumped forward, breathing regularly. His gray hair was streaked with white, and he wore a tan suit. Wrinkles lined his weathered features.

Blade walked up to the man and nudged him with the Browning.

The sleeper abruptly awakened, his head swiveling to the left, his green eyes widening at the sight of the giant. He turned, spying the man in black cradling a M.A.C. 10 six feet from the sofa, and then looked at the four forms on the floor near the elevator. Instead of registering fear or shock, the gray-haired man recovered his composure and stared up at the giant. "Congratulations. No one has ever taken Casper down before. You must be good."

"Are you Tom Barbish?" Blade asked.

"One and the same," Barbish replied. "And you?"

"My name is unimportant," Blade said.

"Are you here to kill me?" Barbish inquired coolly.

"That depends on you," Blade stated.

Barbish studied the giant for a moment. "You're from the outside."

Blade surveyed the living room, bothered by the dealer's calm demeanor.

"You are, aren't you?" Barbish asked.

"I'll ask the questions," Blade told him.

Barbish shrugged. "Suit yourself. But I know I'm right."

"You do, huh?"

The dealer smiled. "When you've been around as long as I have, young man, you learn a thing or two. You're not from Miami. You're not from Dragon territory."

"Would you believe I'm from Jerome?"

Barbish chuckled. "Is that what you're telling everyone? No, you're not from Jerome."

"How can you be so sure?"

The dealer looked fearlessly at Blade. "Elementary, young man. Jerome is a small town approximately twenty miles from the Gulf, as the crow flies. Not many people live there now. My travels have taken me through Jerome several times, and I never saw you there. And face it. You'd stand out like the proverbial sore thumb." He paused. "Don't try to convince me you live on the outskirts of Jerome either. You're not the type to spend his days raising sugar cane or trapping alligators for a living. No, you have the air of a leader about you."

"Where are the Masters?" Blade demanded bluntly.

Barbish was taken by surprise by the unexpected question. "The Masters?"

"You heard me. I need to find the Masters."

"Is that what this is all about?" Barbish asked, then laughed.

"What's so funny?"

Barbish laughed louder and slapped his left thigh.

Blade glanced at Rikki, who shrugged.

"You went to all this trouble for nothing!" Barbish stated. "I can't help you!"

"You'll help us," Blade directed, leaning down, "or else."

"Please, young man!" Barbish said, smiling. "There is no need to be so melodramatic. I'm not a fool. I don't want to die. If I could assist you, I would. But I can't, because I have no idea where the Masters can be found."

"Don't lie to me."

Barbish held his hands out, palms up. "I'm not lying! I have had very little contact with the Masters."

Blade wagged the Browning. "You're a Dealer. You're one of the top men in the Dragons. And the Masters head the Dragons."

"I'm a Dealer," Barbish confessed. "But I'm two levels removed from the top of the Dragons."

"Explain," Blade ordered.

"The Masters run the show. At the bottom of the barrel are the pushers, who receive their wares from the middle-echelon distributors. Dealers like myself comprise the next level up. We insure our merchandise is alloted properly to our distributors, and through our network we keep tabs on our pushers to ensure they don't cheat us. We're responsible for all the people under us, and we're held accountable for the quality of the dope we sell. But we're also held to account by those above us," Barbish detailed.

"Above you?" Blade repeated.

Barbish nodded. "The Directors. There are thirteen of them, and each one is personally selected by the Masters. The Directors get together with the Masters on a regular basis, not the Dealers. Once a year the Masters hold a meeting in Miami with us." Barbish grinned. "So if you came here hoping I would take you to the Masters, I'm afraid you're in for a disappointment."

Blade scrutinized the Dealer, striving to determine if Barbish was being truthful. Reluctantly, he decided the man was sincere. "Do you report to one of these Directors?"

"Yes," Barbish answered. "Each Director is responsible for the oversight of six Dealers." He sighed wistfully. "Most of the street people look up to the Dealers. They think we have all this power, all this prestige. Most of them don't even know about the Directors."

"The Directors are the only ones who know where to find the Masters?" Blade requested confirmation.

"You've got it," Barbish said. "I don't know why you're after the Masters, but I do know you'll never find them."

"We'll locate them," Blade stated, "with your help."

"My help?"

"You're going to take us to your Director," Blade directed.

Barbish tensed. "I can't do that."

"You have no choice."

"If I take you to my Director, the Masters will have me killed."

Blade grinned as he reached out and tapped the Browning on the Dealer's nose. "And what do you think I'll do if you don't take us?"

"I'll take my chances with you," Barbish said.

"Your mistake," Blade declared, and rammed the Browning barrel into the Dealer's stomach.

Barbish doubled over, wheezing, his face reddening.

The Warrior gouged the barrel into the side of the Dealer's neck. "Are you paying attention?" he asked gruffly.

His face flushed, his eyes wide, gasping for air, Barbish nodded vigorously.

"Good. Because if you don't do exactly as I say, when I say it, you're dead," Blade stated. "Understand?"

Barbish nodded again.

"I've seen this city," Blade went on. "I've seen what's happened to the people here. The drugs have ruined their lives, turned their values upside down. They've become slaves to their addictions. And the Dragons are to blame. Since you're one of the major Dealers, you're largely responsible for the conditions here. You're more guilty than most." He paused, his tone lowering. "I think you're scum, Barbish. You're the human equivalent of garbage. And if you don't cooperate, I'll squash you like the bug you are!"

"The Dealer trembled.

"Now on your feet!" Blade commanded, stepping back.

Barbish slowly stood, his right hand holding his abdomen.

"We're leaving," Blade said. "You're taking us to your Director. If you try any tricks, you'll be dead before we are."

Rikki moved toward the elevator.

"Let's go!" Blade snapped, hefting the Browning. He backed across the living room with the Dealer following meekly. "What's the name of your Director?"

"Arlo," Barbish answered in a barely audible tone.

"Arlo what?"

"Arlo Paolucci."

"And where do we find Mr. Paolucci?"

"He has an estate west of Miami," Barbish disclosed.

"How far west?"

"About fifteen miles west of the city limits on Highway 41."

Blade reached Rikki's side and halted. "Okay. We're going down. You'd better pray that your men downstairs don't start something, because you may be caught in the cross fire."

"They'll know something's up," Barbish said. "They'll try and stop you."

"Then you'll buy us a few seconds," Blade stated. "Talk to them. Tell them anything. Stall them." He glanced at Rikki. "Take them out quietly."

Rikki-Tikki-Tavi nodded.

Blade waved the Browning at the elevator. "Inside," he said.

The Dealer walked past the Warriors and entered the cage.

Blade and Rikki stepped inside. Blade scrutinized the side panels to the door. "Where's the button?"

Barbish nodded at the doorway. "On the outer wall, to the right. It's a security precaution. The elevator can only be operated by someone standing outside, by one of my guards."

"That's easily remedied," Blade declared, leaning out the doorway and looking to the right. The black button was positioned just beyond the reach of a normal-sized man, but he wasn't normal-sized. He reached out and easily stabbed the button, then withdrew before the door could shut.

The elevator began its descent.

Blade tucked the Browning in the small of his back. "Stall them or you're dead."

Rikki placed the M.A.C. 10 in a corner and straightened.

Barbish swallowed hard, his eyes flicking nervously from Warrior to Warrior.

"Don't do anything stupid," Blade cautioned.

The elevator passed floor after floor.

Sweat broke out on the Dealer's face.

Blade pushed Barbish up to the door. "Remember what I've said."

The Dealer took a deep breath as the elevator glided to a rest at the bottom of the shaft.

Rikki was waiting to the right of the doorway.

With a protracted hiss, the door slid wide.

Both guards were facing the elevator, their hands at their sides. Both displayed surprise when their gaze alighted on the Dealer.

"Mr. Barbish!" the burly one exclaimed. "Where's Casper?"

"Upstairs," Barbish answered. "I wanted to see these gentlemen out by myself."

The burly guard's eyes narrowed. "Is everything okay?"

Barbish stepped from the elevator. "Of course."

Rikki exited, smiling at the guards as he walked to his pile of weapons and crouched.

The burly guard eyed the Warrior suspiciously. "I don't know about this," he said, his right hand drifting under his jacket.

"Believe me," Barbish assured him. "Everything is fine."

Both guards glanced at their boss.

And Rikki uncoiled with the dazzling quickness of a striking cobra. He spun around, a shuriken in his left hand, the kyoketsu-shogei in his right. His left arm arced up and out, and the gleaming shuriken streaked straight into the second guard's forehead, the razor teeth biting deep. Powered by Rikki's steely sinews, the shuriken sank over half its width inward. The guard tottered backwards, his right hand gripping the shuriken and tugging, but all he succeeded in doing was slicing his hand and three fingers. Crimson flowed over his face.

The burly guard was drawing a pistol.

Rikki released the kyoketsu-shogei in an underhand motion, the last two fingers on his right hand retaining a hold on the metal ring as his thumb and first two fingers sent the five-inch knife into the burly guard's throat. The man grabbed for the double-edged knife in sheer reflex. Before his foe could snatch the weapon, Rikki wrenched on the metal ring connected by the leather cord to the knife hilt. The knife was yanked free, its trajectory marked by a geyser of spurting blood.

Pressing his slippery, crimson-coated hands over the hole in his neck, the burly guard fell to his knees.

The guard struck by the shuriken collapsed onto his back.

Rikki scooped up the yawara and stepped up close to the burly guard. He delivered a roundhouse blow to the side of the man's head with the tip.

With a loud groan, the guard sprawled onto his face.

Rikki crouched and began reclaiming his gear.

Blade hastily joined him. "Stay right where you're at!" he said to Barbish.

The Dealer appeared pale, his eyes on his dead men.

Blade replaced his Bowies first, then aligned the backpack between his shoulder blades. He lifted the Paratrooper.

"You'll get yours, bastards!" Barbish snapped.

Blade stepped up to the Dealer. "Keep your mouth closed." He glanced at Rikki.

The martial artist had put the kyoketsu-shogei, the yawara, and his three other shuriken in his belt pouch. He was donning the backpack, his eyes on the lobby, when he suddenly dived for the M-16 while shouting, "Look out!"

Blade whirled.

Three men in suits were charging the two Warriors. All three held pistols. Two of the trio already had a bead on the giant; the third was sighting on the diminutive man in black.

Blade tried to bring the Paratrooper into play, realizing he was way too late, expecting to hear the boom of their guns and feel their slugs tear through his body. Out of the corner of his left eye he caught a motion.

Hickok. Crouching and drawing his right Python, his

arm nearly invisible, the gunfighter fired three times from the hip, the shots thundering in the lobby, unerringly on target.

The three charging bodyguards died on their feet; not one managed to squeeze the trigger. They tumbled to the carpet, head-shot, brain dead.

Hickok sprinted to his friends, pulling his left Python on the fly. "We'd best skedaddle."

Blade nodded, then shoved Barbish toward the front entrance. "Move it!"

Rikki slid his katana under his belt and brought up the rear.

"You'll never get out of here alive!" the Dealer taunted them.

Hickok took the lead, his revolvers sweeping from side to side, covering the people in the lobby.

Blade realized there were over two dozen men and women surrounding them. How many were in the Dealer's employ? Would Barbish plant men in the—

A man in a dark brown suit burst from behind a column to their left, an Uzi in his hands.

Hickok's Pythons cracked.

His eyes rupturing as they were perforated by the slugs, the man in brown was catapulted onto his back by the impact.

Hickok walked faster, his blue eyes darting every which way.

Barbish was dragging his feet, moving as slowly as he could.

Blade gave the Dealer a brutal push, and Barbish stumbled forward, cursing under his breath.

Hickok was within eight feet of the entrance.

A brunette in a green dress, standing to the left of the glass doors, suddenly whipped a revolver from her black leather purse.

The gunfighter shot her in the forehead.

Blade covered a group to their right. So much for abducting the Dealer without attracting attention! Every Dragon in the city would be on the lookout for them! Which meant they had to get out of the city as quickly as possible. But how?

A portly man with a shotgun abruptly jumped up from concealment behind the front desk, his appearance accompanied by the instantaneous, simultaneous discharge of a pair of pearl-handled .357 Magnums. He dropped from sight.

Hickok reached the glass doors and stood to the right, his Pythons trained on the lobby.

No one else seemed disposed to dispute the Warriors.

Blade grasped Barbish's left shoulder and propelled the Dealer outside.

They'd made it!

Or had they?

A pair of Narc patrol cars, their sirens wailing, their lights flashing, took the nearest intersection to the south at 50 miles an hour and roared toward the Oasis.

CHAPTER NINE

Blade was fuming. His simple plan had gone awry with potentially disastrous consequences. The last thing he'd wanted to do was draw the Narcs into the conflict. The Narcs were, after all, the legal arm of the law in Miami, even if they were allied with the Dragons and the drug trade. But now, as he watched the two patrol cars screech to a halt at the base of the concrete steps leading into the Oasis, he knew he could no longer afford the luxury of minimizing conflicts with the Dragons *or* the Narcs.

Two officers piled from each cruiser. All four were armed with revolvers. They started to train their weapons on the giant at the top of the stairs. "Freeze!" one of them bellowed. "You're under arrest!"

Blade fired from the right hip, sweeping the Paratrooper in a semicircle.

A pair of Narcs were stitched across their chests and flung to the tarmacadam.

The pedestrians on the sidewalk between the concrete steps and Collins Avenue, many of whom had stopped to stare at the Narc cruisers, panicked. Screaming and shouting, they frantically endeavored to remove themselves from the line of fire. Some were trampled in the process. The flow of traffic on Collins was disrupted by drivers slamming on their brakes. Horns blared. Bedlam ensued.

Hickok and Rikki came through the glass doors.

The surviving pair of Narcs took cover in the shelter of their patrol car. One of them jumped up and fired a hurried shot. He missed.

Hickok didn't. His right Python blasted, the slug boring through the Narc's skull and knocking the officer backwards.

"On me!" Blade barked, running to the south, his left hand clamped on Barbish's arm.

Hickok jogged after them.

The last Narc tried to shoot the gunman in the back, rising and placing his gun hand on the roof of the cruiser to steady his aim. He glimpsed another man on the concrete steps to his left, a man in black, and perceived that he'd miscalculated. Drastically.

Rikki-Tikki-Tavi fired the M-16 from a distance of less than 20 feet.

The final Narc twisted and fell, his head riddled.

Rikki took off.

The people crowding the sidewalk were scrambling to get out of the path of the Warriors. Many ran into the avenue, causing cars to brake abruptly, adding to the mass confusion. More sirens pierced the night, drawing ever closer to the Oasis.

Blade slowed, waiting for Hickok and Rikki to catch up. He swept the Paratrooper back and forth, clearing the sidewalk as everyone in front of him moved aside. Footsteps pounded behind him.

"Where we headin', pard?" Hickok asked, his eyes on Collins Avenue. He saw a car rear-end another.

"We've got to get out of Miami," Blade stated.

Rikki raced up to them. "Clear to our rear," he declared.

Blade nodded and pressed forward, peering to the south. How far was it? A quarter of a mile? Less? Would it still be there, or had the Narcs found it?

"You've done it now, prick!" Barbish commented.

Blade ignored the Dealer, scanning the cars parked adjacent to the curb. Where *was* it?

"You've killed Narcs," Barbish said. "No one kills a Narc and gets away with it! They have a fraternal spirit. Do something to any one of them, and you wind up with every one of them on your case." He snorted. "They'll hunt you down."

Blade increased his pace, concerned by the growling volume of sirens. Most of the Narcs in the city must be converging on the Oasis!

"I wouldn't want to be in your shoes!" Barbish remarked.

"Can I plug this varmint?" Hickok asked. "His prattle is startin' to get to me."

"We need him," Blade said.

"Can I shoot him when we're done with him?"

"Be my guest," Blade offered.

"Thanks, pard."

Barbish clammed up.

Blade spied several Narc patrol cars speeding toward them from the south. He could see their lights flaring, and he judged the cruisers were less than two blocks off. And he'd also noticed something else. The farther south the Warriors proceeded from the Oasis, the fewer frightened pedestrians they encountered. The actual witnesses to the fight with the Narcs were lingering in the vicinity of the Oasis. None had dared follow the Warriors. The people directly ahead had no way of knowing the Warriors were the reason for the turmoil. Blade forced himself to walk at a normal rate. He threaded through a crowd watching the approaching cruisers.

"Why'd you slow down, pard?" Hickok queried.

"Act innocent," Blade said.

"What?"

"The Pythons."

Hickok looked at his Colts, at the crowd, then at the fast-coming patrol cars. He grinned and twirled the Pythons into their holsters.

Rikki slung the M-16 over his left shoulder.

The Narc vehicles were under a block off.

Hickok clasped his hands behind his back and started whistling a random tune.

Blade lowered the Paratrooper alongside his right leg. His left hand closed in a vise on the Dealer's arm.

"You're hurting me!" Barbish hissed.

The patrol cars raced north on Collins Avenue.

Blade speeded up again with the Dealer struggling to match his lengthy stride. The avenue was well lit by the streetlights, and he knew he'd have no difficulty recognizing the car when he saw it. Provided it was there. As he covered more and more ground, traversing four more blocks, he seriously doubted he would locate the vehicle. But a few minutes later, as he was crossing an intersection, he discerned the golden finish on the car in question and smiled.

Hickok's keen eyes saw the vehicle too. "Isn't that the buggy—" he began.

"It is," Blade verified.

"Are you thinkin' what I think you're thinkin'?" Hickok questioned.

"I am," Blade confirmed.

"Can I drive?" Hickok asked excitedly.

"We'll see," Blade said. He neared the car cautiously, puzzled. Someone, either on Collins Avenue or on the sidewalk, *had* to have seen him dispatch the Genie and Hugo. And if someone did, then logic dictated that that person would report the deaths to the Narcs. The Narcs would send a patrol car to check the story. But there was no sign of the Narcs in the immediate vicinity. The big gold and chrome vehicle was exactly as he'd left it: parked at the curb, with all the doors closed. None of the passersby were paying any excessive attention to it.

Was it possible no one had seen the Genie and Hugo die?

Or had there been a witness, but the witness had preferred to remain silent? Was it natural for a citizen in Miami to automatically report a crime? Did the populace trust and rely upon the Narcs, or did they resort to contacting the police only under extreme circumstances?

He didn't know.

And he wasn't about to look a gift horse in the mouth.

Blade walked up to the rear door on the passenger side and opened it. "Inside," he directed the Dealer.

Barbish bent over at the waist and started to climb in. His body tensed and he gasped when he observed the pair of corpses. "What the hell!" he blurted.

Blade prodded the Dealer with the Paratrooper. "Inside! We'll dispose of them later."

Barbish sat down on the driver's side. He was forced to

rest his legs on the bodies.

"You drive," Blade told the gunman. "Rikki, you get in front. I'll keep our friend company." He slid in and slammed the door.

"Who are these guys?" Barbish asked, nodding at the corpses.

"They dealt in drugs," Blade responded acidly.

"Pushers?" Barbish said, aghast.

Hickok and Rikki entered the car.

The gunman studied the instrument panel for a moment. "Where the blazes is the key?"

Blade glanced at the Dealer. "Search Hugo."

"Who?"

Blade tapped the bodyguard's bald pate. "Hugo. Search his pockets. He was carrying the keys."

Barbish scrunched up his nose. "You want me to *touch* him?"

"Unless you're adept at telekinesis," Blade quipped.

"Tele-what?"

"Find the car keys," Blade directed.

Barbish leaned over the bodies and reached his arms under the Genie. He started and jerked his right arm up, his hand coated with blood.

"Squeamish son of a gun, isn't he?" Hickok remarked.

"Keep looking," Blade ordered.

Barbish hesitated, then applied himself to the task once again. He ran his fingers over the black's body, feeling for pockets. Locating a pants pocket, he plunged his left hand inside, awash with relief as his fingers closed on a key ring. About to extract the keys, his right hand bumped against a hard object attached to the black's belt above the hip. He traced the outline of the object and suppressed a surge of elation at his discovery: a derringer. "I can't seem to find any keys," he remarked casually. His torso was bent over the corpses, screening his arms and hands from the bastards holding him. Here was his chance to gain the upper hand! He could get the drop on them! The thought made him tingle! He owed these sons of bitches! *How* he owed them! He would personally officiate at their torture.

"You haven't found them yet?" Blade asked skeptically.

Barbish shook his head. "No. Not . . ." he said, then pretended to grope the corpse. "Wait! Here they are!" His right hand eased the derringer from its small leather holster, and he grinned triumphantly as he straightened, bringing the derringer up. Expecting to take his captors unawares, he was all the more shocked to behold a Paratrooper, M-16, and a pair of Colt Python revolvers trained on his head.

"Drop the derringer," Blade commanded.

"And do it quick," Hickok added. "My trigger fingers are a mite itchy."

Barbish allowed the derringer to fall to the seat.

Hickok made a smacking noise. "Tisk! Tisk! Didn't your Ma ever teach you any manners?" He holstered his Magnums.

Blade picked up the derringer, examined it, then placed the gun in his left rear pocket. "The keys. Now!"

Barbish frowned as he reached his left hand down to the appropriate pocket again and withdrew the key ring. He held the ring aloft. "Here," he said bitterly.

"Thanks," Hickok said, taking the keys in his right hand and turning.

"Can you drive this thing?" Blade asked.

"Piece of cake," the gunman responded. "It's an automatic, just like the SEAL."

Blade nodded. The SEAL was the impervious, vanlike vehicle constructed by the Family's Founder prior to World War Three as a prototype. Solar powered, outfitted with deadly armaments, and capable of traversing any terrain, the SEAL was employed by the Warriors on most of their trips into the Outlands or elsewhere. The Solar-Energized, Amphibious or Land Vehicle was unlike any other in existence.

Hickok inspected the key ring, found one he felt would fit, and inserted it in the ignition. He twisted the key and the car's engine rumbled to life. "Which way are we headin'?" he asked.

Blade looked at the Dealer. "You heard the man."

"You can either drive north until we reach Dade Boulevard," Barbish stated, "and then take the Venetian Causeway across Biscayne Bay to Miami, or you can make a U-turn and go south and take the General MacArthur Causeway."

"How many Causeways are there?" Blade inquired.

"Four," Barbish replied. "The Kennedy is fartherest north, then the Tuttle, the Venetian, and the MacArthur."

Blade recalled the Narc mentioning the first two. Of course, the Warriors had been in northwest Miami at the time, then drifted to the south, eventually taking the Venetian Causeway by bus.

"Which way should I go?" Hickok queried.

Blade debated for a moment. If they went north toward the Venetian again, they would have to pass the Oasis Resort Hotel. The hotel was undoubtedly swarming with Narcs and Dragons, and he didn't relish the idea of driving past and risking detection. "Make a U-turn," he instructed. "We'll take the General MacArthur Causeway."

Hickok shifted into Drive, turned the steering wheel sharply to the left, and tromped on the gas.

"Take it slow!" Blade said, but his advice came a second tardy.

The car barreled out of the parking space and shot across Collins Avenue, its tires screeching. Oncoming traffic was thrown into confusion; brakes squealed, drivers shouted obscenities, and vehicles slewed to abrupt stops.

"What a bunch of lousy drivers!" Hickok remarked, grinning as he wheeled the gold car south on Collins.

"Don't attract attention," Blade declared.

"Too late," Rikki mentioned, gazing out the rear window.

Blade glanced over his left shoulder, his eyes narrowing as he spotted a Narc cruiser bearing down on them with its lights and siren on.

Hickok looked into the rearview mirror. "Are they

after us?''

Barbish unexpectedly laughed. ''Oh! Did I forget to tell you?''

''Tell us what?'' Blade responded.

''That U-turns are illegal on Collins Avenue,'' Barbish said with relish. ''Too much traffic, you know.''

Blade's mouth curled downwards. ''You told us to make a U-turn on purpose, hoping it would attract one of the patrol cars.''

''Who? Me?'' Barbish said, the picture of innocence.

''What do I do?'' Hickok asked. ''Stop or keep going?''

The cruiser was a block to their rear, moving fast.

''If we pull over,'' Rikki noted, ''they will see the bodies.''

''Not to mention Barbish,'' Blade said.

''Do we outrun the coyotes?'' Hickok questioned eagerly.

''You can't outrun a Narc car,'' Barbish informed them. ''Their vehicles have high-performance engines. They're souped up. You wouldn't get two blocks.''

Blade felt his frustration mounting. He wanted to get out of Miami Beach swiftly, but they were being thwarted at every turn.

The Narc cruiser roared toward them.

''Roll down your window,'' Blade directed the Dealer.

Barbish balked. ''Why?''

Blade rammed the Paratrooper into the Dealer's ribs. ''Do it!''

Barbish grunted, then hastily complied.

''Lean back,'' Blade snapped. He rested the tip of the Paratrooper barrel on the door, his finger on the trigger.

With a harsh blare of its sirens, its lights spinning, the Narc vehicle pulled abreast of their car. A Narc on the passenger side had his window down, and he waved at them to veer to the curb.

Blade fired instead, his initial burst catching the Narc in the head and flinging him backwards. He kept firing as the Narc vehicle started to slow, his rounds punching into the patrol car's windshield, shattering the glass and riddling the driver.

The Narc cruiser angled to the left, into the opposite lane, narrowly missing a station wagon. Its speed still over 60, the patrol car plowed into a red sedan parked at the curb, the impact thrusting the sedan onto the sidewalk. Both vehicles flattened a number of pedestrians.

Blade looked back to see a fireball envelop the Narc cruiser.

"You bastards!" Barbish said.

"You're the one who tried to get us caught," Blade mentioned. "Try it again and I'll shoot you in the knee. Consider this your last warning."

Barbish started to say something, but thought better of the idea. If his abductors wanted to go to his Director's estate, fine. He would take them. Once there, though, they were in for an unpleasant surprise. He suppressed an impulse to smile. There was no sense in giving away his ace in the hole.

One thing was for sure.

He would piss on their graves!

CHAPTER TEN

"So where is it?"

"It's just up ahead."

"That's what you said a mile ago," Blade noted.

"Cut me some slack!" Barbish retorted. "The cutoff isn't easy to see in broad daylight, let alone at night! Just look for a dirt road on the left. The road leads south to Paolucci's estate."

The gold car was heading west on Highway 41, its headlights illuminating the trees and other vegetation lining both sides. Traffic during the hours preceding the dawn was sparse.

"Any sign of a turnoff?" Blade asked Hickok.

The gunman shook his head. "Not yet, pard." He was driving at 30 miles an hour, hunched over the steering wheel, his gaze riveted to the left side of the highway.

Blade stared at the Dealer, wondering if the man was leading them on a wild-goose chase. He doubted Barbish would be that stupid. Perhaps the cutoff was genuinely hard to spot at night. In any event, he—

"Blast!" Hickok muttered, applying the brakes. "Missed it."

Blade looked out the rear window, spying a break in the vegetation, a lighter patch of gravel.

Hickok executed a tight U-turn and drove to the turnoff, then braked. The gravel road receded into the distance without any trace of a light or indication of habitation.

"I don't see an estate," Blade remarked.

"We have about ten miles to go," Barbish said. "Arlo lives in the middle of nowhere, on forty acres surrounded by swamp. He likes his privacy."

"Keep driving," Blade instructed the gunman.

Hickok shrugged and accelerated. The gravel road was
bumpy, filled with shallow ruts, causing the car to
bounce and vibrate with each bump and jar.

"Arlo had this road built," Barbish commented. "One
day he may get around to blacktopping it."

"Does every Director live out in the country?" Blade
inquired.

"Some live in Miami," Barbish replied. "Some, like
Arlo, prefer the rural life."

"How many guards protect his estate?"

"I don't know," Barbish said.

Blade sighed and placed his right hand on the Paratrooper in his lap.

"I don't know!" Barbish insisted. "I've never counted
them! I've seen a dozen or so, but there are probably
more."

"Describe the estate."

"Most of it, up to the edges of the swamp, is wooded,"
Barbish detailed. "An eight-foot-high brick wall encloses
five acres, the main area. There's a house to the north, a
barn to the east—"

"A barn?"

"Arlo raises horses," Barbish said. "He likes the
races. The gate to the compound is located in the north
wall."

"What about quarters for the guards?"

Barbish grinned. "Did I forget to mention that? Their
quarters consists of a barrackslike building on the west
side."

"And the southern section of the five acres?"

"Gardens," Barbish said. "Arlo fancies himself a
horticulturist, another reason he lives in the country."

"Do the guards make regular rounds?"

"Yes," Barbish responded. "But I don't know their
schedule."

Blade peered out the window at the darkened
landscape, reflecting. He estimated there were three
hours until dawn, ample time to reach the estate and
penetrate it before sunrise. The predawn assault would
give the Warriors a decided advantage; any guards awake

would be sluggish, either just waking up to start their day or closing out a night shift and ready to hit the hay. The delays in Miami had not proven too costly. He recalled the ride across the General MacArthur Causeway, and dumping the bodies of the Genie and Hugo in the first alley they'd found. They had driven to the southwest, staying under the posted speed limits, doubling back on themselves repeatedly to insure they weren't being tailed.

"What the heck!" Hickok abruptly exclaimed, slamming on the brakes.

Blade looked ahead.

Not 15 yards away, vividly revealed by the car's headlights, was an enormous alligator crossing the road. The reptile lumbered from left to right, ignoring the vehicle.

"Where the blazes did that critter come from?" Hickok asked.

"Ever hear of the Everglades?" Barbish responded.

Blade thought of the century-old map. "Aren't the Everglades southwest of here?"

"You're thinking of the Everglades National Park, as it was once known," Barbish said. "The Park covered a million and half acres on the southwest tip of the peninsula. But the Park was a small part of the total Everglades. You're on the eastern edge of the Everglades right now. Five thousand square miles of swamp. Nothing but water, gators, and snakes for miles and miles and miles."

"Snakes?" Hickok said.

Blade watched the alligator disappear in the brush on the right side of the road. "Let's go?"

"Snakes?" Hickok said again, driving forward.

"The Everglades are a haven for snakes," Barbish elaborated. "Swamp snakes, brown snakes, ribbon snakes, garter snakes. And they're the harmless ones. Poisonous varieties abound in the Everglades. There are the coral snakes, the cottonmouths, and the rattlers, of course, as well as the exotic types, like the cobras."

"Who are you tryin' to kid?" Hickok demanded. "Cobras live in India and Africa, not Florida."

"That was true once," Barbish said. "But not

anymore. You see, a lot of people imported exotic species into Florida before the war. Cobras. Piranhas. Others. And some escaped or were deliberately let loose by their owners. The climate in Florida was ideal for breeding. The cobras and piranhas multiplied, despite the best efforts of the authorities to eradicate them. Don't believe me if you want, but I assure you that there are cobras in the Everglades. One of Arlo's men was bitten by a cobra a few years ago.''

"What happened to him?'' Hickok asked.

"What else? He died.''

Blade remembered a schooling class on Florida and voiced a question. "What about the alligators? There seem to be a lot of them, and yet I read that they were almost exterminated before the war.''

"Not quite true,'' Barbish answered. "The alligators made a comeback before World War Three. They were protected by law, and they reproduced so fast that special hunting seasons were set up. After the war, of course, with so few hunters and poachers to reduce their ranks, the gators made like rabbits. Now the damn things are everywhere.''

"I don't reckon I'll retire in Florida,'' Hickok joked.

"The gators and the snakes aren't the worst of it,'' Barbish went on. "There are other—things.''

"What kind of things?'' Blade queried.

"Mutant things,'' Barbish said. "Huge things.'' His tone changed, becoming filled with awe. "I saw one once, from the south dock on Arlo's estate. It was splashing in the swamp, heading from east to west. The moon was out, and we could see it fairly well.''

"What did it look like?'' Blade probed.

"How can I describe it?'' Barbish responded. "It was like a dinosaur. Think of an alligator fifty feet long, only with spikes on its back and a head like a frog. It was bizarre.''

The mention of mutants had stimulated Blade's curiosity. He stared at the Dealer. "And the Masters?''

"What about them?''

"They're mutants. What do they look like?''

"Only two of the Masters have attended the annual Dealer meetings," Barbish said. "Orm and Radnor. How can I describe them? Walking nightmares? And," he emphasized, "they never revealed where their base was."

"Weren't you ever curious? Didn't you ask Arlo questions?"

Barbish snorted. "It's not healthy to ask too many questions of your superiors in my line of work. Yes, I was curious. Yes, I tried to gather as much information as I could on the sly. But I didn't learn much."

"How much?"

The Dealer looked at the giant for a moment. "Perceptive, aren't you? All right. What harm can it do? I learned there are seven Masters, and they're all part of the same family."

"They're all related?"

"So I was told," Barbish confirmed. "But I don't know the specifics."

"And that was it?"

"Trying to discover more would have cost me my life," Barbish stated.

"So working for mutant Masters never bothered you?"

"Maybe a little," Barbish said. "But the benefits outweighed any qualms of conscience."

"So you sold countless souls into a life of drug addiction to line your own pocket and please the Masters," Blade commented scornfully.

"We all have to look out for number one."

Blade frowned. "That's twice I've heard the same stupid statement. It's so selfish, it's disgusting. We're not put on this planet just to look out for number one, just to think of ourselves first all the time. We're put here to learn to care for others, to learn the meaning of love and sharing—"

Barbish laughed. "Where did you ever hear nonsense like that?"

"Our Elders taught us the importance of possessing fundamental values."

"Your Elders? Where are you from?"

"Never mind."

"Your philosophy on life is all backwards," Barbish commented. "It's a dog-eat-dog world. Only the strong survive, by any means necessary. If you want something out of life, you have to take it. Love is an illusion. Power is what counts. Power and wealth. And by rising through the ranks of the Dragons, by becoming a Dealer for the Powder of Life, I'm living proof of what I say."

"What is the Powder of Life?" Blade asked.

"Cocaine. The Masters refer to coke as the Powder of Life. They like the Dealers to encourage the pushers to push coke over the other drugs," Barbish replied.

"Why?"

"The profit potential is greater, for one thing," Barbish said. "Smaller quantities bring bigger profits. Coke is easy to handle, easy to measure and packet. Plus the addiction factor is incredible."

"The addiction factor?"

"Yes. The addiction factor is a primary concern for every Dealer and pusher. If we want to maximize our profits, to increase our pool of repeat customers, we must get them hooked on the hard stuff. Coke is ideal. It has fewer side effects than, say, heroin, and it gives a high like you wouldn't believe. Coke is the mainstay of the Dragons' business."

"Where do the Masters obtain their coke?"

"I was never told," Barbish said. "I suspect they get it from a cartel in South America. I accidentally saw some vouchers once dealing with planeloads of dope coming down the pipeline from Colombia."

"Someone should have put the Dragons out of business a long time ago," Blade remarked.

Barbish snickered. "Like who, young man? The police? They are paid by the Dragons. They're in our employ. The same with the politicos. The people think they get a real choice at election time, but every candidate is on the Dragon payroll. We allow elections for mayor and council seats to give the citizens the illusion of freedom. But it's all a farce, and the people are too stupid to realize it."

"Are they stupid, or drugged out of their minds?" Blade asked. "Their entire perception of reality is off."

"No one forces them to use our products."

"Products? Don't you mean poisons?"

"Call it whatever you want."

"Someday, someone will come down here and mop up the Dragons," Blade predicted.

"Never happen," Barbish responded.

They drove in silence for over five minutes.

"Hey!" Hickok declared. "Look!"

Blade stared through the windshield. A cluster of lights had appeared far in the distance.

"The estate, you figure?" Hickok inquired.

"Must be," Blade said.

"It's the estate," Barbish verified.

"Kill our headlights," Blade advised.

Hickok promptly complied, slowing down as he did so. "How the dickens am I going to drive? There's no moon tonight."

"Perhaps we should walk from here," Rikki suggested.

"Drive another mile or so," Blade directed. "We want to get as close as we can, but not so close that they'll hear our engine."

Hickok leaned forward, reducing their speed to under 20 miles an hour. "I just hope we don't bump into one of those mutant things."

Barbish glanced at the lights and grinned, then quickly wiped the grin from his face.

The swampy land bordering the gravel road was enshrouded in an inky gloom. A breeze rustled the intermittent stands of trees. Insect sounds filled the night accompanied by a chorus of frogs and other creatures.

"What was all that big grass I was seein' before we killed the headlights?" Hickok asked.

"That's sawgrass," Barbish disclosed. "It's all over the Everglades. Grows over twelve feet high in some places."

"I'll bet a lot of snakes could hide in it," Hickok remarked.

"You don't sound like you're very fond of snakes,"
Barbish noted.

"Let me put it this way," Hickok said. "There are a
heap of critters on this planet, and I think I understand
the reason the Spirit put a few of 'em here." He paused.
"But snakes aren't one of them."

"He was attacked by a mutated snake when he was
twelve," Blade detailed. "The snake was over eight feet
long and had two heads. Ever since then, he hasn't liked
snakes very much."

"The only way to conquer a fear is to face it," Rikki
said to the gunman.

Hickok glanced at the martial artist. "Are you sayin'
I'm afraid of snakes?"

"No," Rikki respnded. "But you may be afraid of
being afraid of snakes."

"One of these bumps must have rattled your noggin',"
Hickok mentioned. "I'm not afraid of anything, least of
all a passel of creepy, crawly reptiles."

"I'm not fond of snakes either," Barbish said.
"Which is why I've seldom visited Arlo unless it was
unavoidable. Being situated in the Everglades like it is,
there are snakes everywhere."

"Just what I wanted to hear," Hickok muttered.

"Enough about snakes," Blade said. "Look for a spot
to pull over."

Hickok slowed slightly and gazed from side to side.
The narrow, cramped road, rimmed by the prolific
vegetation, afforded few parking places. He proceeded
several hundred yards. "What if I drive this buggy off the
road into the brush?"

"That 'brush' could be swampland," Barbish
cautioned. "The car could sink."

"Just dandy," Hickok said.

Blade rested his right arm on the top of the front seat
and peered into the night.

"Do you see those trees?" Rikki inquired, pointing
ahead and to the right.

A stand of tall trees was silhouetted against the sky 50
yards in front of them.

"Trees require solid soil," Rikki observed.

"He's right," Barbish agreed. "The Everglades are dotted with tree islands, clumps of higher ground where myrtles, bays, and willows grow. There are also a lot of islands and scattered sections of firm ground, like Arlo's forty-acre plot."

Hickok braked when the car drew alongside the trees.

"I'll check it out," Rikki offered, looking at Blade.

The Warrior leader nodded. "Be careful."

Rikki opened his door and vanished into the dark.

"We should have about a mile and a half to walk from here," Blade calculated.

"Just so we don't step on any snakes," Hickok said.

Blade looked at the Dealer. "You'll be coming with us. But not a peep out of you, or else."

"What? You're not going to tie me up and cram me in the trunk?" Barbish retorted sarcastically.

"The idea occurred to me," Blade said. "But we can use you once we reach the estate."

"Does this estate have a name?" Hickok asked.

Barbish chuckled. "Yes. As a matter of fact, it does. Arlo calls it Happy Acres."

"You're joshin'," Hickok said.

"I kid you not," Barbish stated.

Rikki-Tikki-Tavi materialized at the door. "Twenty yards up ahead is a flat, clear area between the trees. You can park the car there." He climbed in and closed his door.

"Did you see any snakes?" Hickok inquired as he drove forward slowly.

"No," Rikki said. "But I did hear a ferocious-sounding killer cricket."

"You're gettin' worse than Geronimo," Hickok cracked. "Where's this clear spot?"

"Right there," Rikki replied, pointing at a break in the foliage.

Hickok turned the wheel, moving the vehicle at a snail's pace, angling the car between the trees and parking on a level stretch of firm turf. He switched off the ignition, and as the muted rumble of the motor died,

the nocturnal sounds of the wildlife in the swamp
hummed, buzzed, and thrummed to a crescendo. "Noisy
bunch of critters," he remarked.

A high-pitched cry, a y-eonk, y-eonk, y-eonk,
punctuated the general din.

"What was that?" Hickok queried.

"A young gator," Barbish answered.

"How do you know it's a young one?" Hickok asked.

"The big ones *roar*," Barbish said.

"Oh."

"Okay. So much for our class in Everglade zoology,"
Blade interjected. "Let's get moving. Check your
weapons."

Each Warrior dutifully insured his firearms were
loaded. Barbish watched them with a scornful stare.

"Out," Blade directed, and they exited the car. He
glanced in at the Dealer. "That means you too."

Barbish sighed and opened his door. He stepped onto
the ground and stretched. "The air here is always so
fresh."

"Should I bring the keys?" Hickok questioned.

"Leave them under the front seat," Blade said. "If we
get separated, one of us might make it back."

The gunman nodded, then tossed the key ring under
the driver's side. He closed the door quietly.

Blade and Rikki shut the other doors.

Hickok walked up to the Dealer. "You must be feelin'
a bit frustrated right about now."

"Not in the least," Barbish declared.

"Won't you get in hot water for bringin' us to the
estate?" Hickok questioned.

"Time will tell," Barbish said enigmatically.

"Hickok, keep him covered," Blade instructed. "I'll
take the point. Rikki, the rear. Five-yard spread." He
moved toward the road, his boots swishing in the grass,
enjoying the invigorating, cool breath of air on his skin.
His nostrils detected a musty, earthy odor. The pale
gravel outlined the road distinctly, and moments later the
small stones and pebbles were crunching underfoot. He
turned to the south, the Paratrooper cradled in his arms.

Barbish's behavior was troubling him. Why was the Dealer being so congenial? Why wasn't Barbish terrified at the prospect of betraying his Director and the masters? At the Oasis, Barbish had been petrified by the mere thought. So what was the reason for the Dealer's changed attitude? What did Barbish know that they didn't?

They covered over five hundred yards in tense expectation.

Blade glanced over his left shoulder. Barbish was five yards to his rear, with Hickok's Henry unslung and pointed at his back. Rikki was almost invisible five yards beyond the gunfighter; his black clothing blended with the night, accenting his facial features and hands.

A frog croaked to the right.

Blade faced front and continued toward the lights. He recognized the lights were arranged in the shape of a square, apparently aligned along the wall enclosing the five-acre living area. What was the power source? he wondered. A generator? Or a line from the metropolis? Did the utility company run lines out this far? If so, it was underground. There was no evidence of utility poles.

"Pssssst!"

Blade halted and pivoted, thinking Hickok had signaled him, but he was mistaken.

Rikki had done the whispering.

The martial artist dashed up to Hickok and the Dealer. "We are being followed," he declared in a hushed voice.

Hickok looked to their rear. "What? Are you sure?"

"Something is after us," Rikki asserted.

Blade walked to them. "Something?"

"Listen," Rikki said.

"I don't hear nothin'," Hickok commented.

"Listen," Rikki reiterated.

Blade cocked his head to one side, straining his ears, hearing only the sounds of the swamp. He was surprised Rikki would be susceptible to a case of overwrought nerves.

"I don't—" Hickok began, then froze.

Blade heard it then too. A deep, heavy sort of

breathing, as if a gigantic animal was on their back trail, expelling its breath in wheezing sighs.

"It's comin' after us," Hickok said.

"What the hell is it?" Barbish asked fearfully.

"We're not sticking around to find out," Blade stated. "Run!"

And run they did, sprinting to the south, their feet pounding on the gravel, swirls of dust rising from the road.

Blade intentionally refrained from reaching full speed. His companions could not hope to match his lengthy strides, and he was not about to outdistance them in a crisis. If whatever was chasing them caught up with them, he would make a stand with his friends.

Which just might be the case.

Because the thing was gaining.

CHAPTER ELEVEN

The three Warriors and the Dealer raced down the gravel road two abreast, with Hickok and Barbish a few feet in front of Rikki and Blade. From their rear came the measured thump-thump-thump of their colossal pursuer.

Blade could hear the breathing grow louder and louder. He racked his mind, speculating on its identity, and reached an inescapable conclusion. Only one type of creature achieved such awesome prorptions; only a genetic deviate, a hybrid or a unique new specimen, fit the bill; only a mutant could be after them. A gust of warm air suddenly struck the nape of his neck, and a fetid stench assailed his nose.

The thing was so close it was breathing on him!

Blade risked a glance over his right shoulder, his eyes discerning the bulk profile of a lizard-like beast with a gaping maw rimmed by white teeth. The creature's head was eight feet behind him and twice that distance above the gravel road.

Damn!

What was the word Barbish had used?

Dinosaur?

It fit.

Involved with keeping his eyes on the gargantuan, carnivorous brute, Blade did not realize that Barbish was on the verge of collapsing until the Dealer abruptly cried out, clutched his chest, and toppled forward. Blade looked around in time to see Barbish go down onto his knees, but he did not have enough time to react. The Dealer was directly in his path, and he tried to throw himself to the left to avoid a collision. His legs crashed into Barbish and he was upended, tumbling to the gravel and landing on his right shoulder. He rolled onto his back, bringing the Paratrooper up.

The creature reared above them.

Blade could see the beast swiveling its huge head, gazing from Barbish to himself.

The Dealer was on his hands and knees, taking deep gulps of air and groaning.

Blade waited for the thing to lower its head. He wanted a better line of fire at the mutant's eyes.

Barbish unexpectedly rose on his knees, swaying unsteadily, his arm flapping weakly. "My chest!" he cried. "My chest!"

The movement and the outcry attracted the creature's attention. Its head tilted downward as its eerie, light green eyes appraised the human below it.

Barbish caught sight of Blade. "Help me! It hurts!"

Blade went to warn the Dealer to keep quiet, but the harm had already been done.

The beast's head swooped low, its maw wide, attacking with astonishing rapidity for an animal so huge. Its mouth closed on the Dealer, its jaws locking fast, taking in Barbish's head and shoulders in one bite. There was a muffled scream as Barbish was lifted into the air, his arms and legs flapping wildly. Without a moment's hesitation, the creature turned to the west and plowed into the vegetation. Loud splintering and crackling attended its progress through the undergrowth, terminated by a monstrous splash. Then all was still.

"Are you lyin' down on the job again?"

Blade craned his head backwards.

Hickok and Rikki were a yard away, their weapons trained on the west side of the road.

"I thought you kept going," Blade remarked as he rose.

"You know better than that, pard," Hickok said.

"We would never desert you," Rikki added.

Blade gazed to the west, listening for more sounds of the creature's passage. Everything was quiet.

"What the blazes was that critter?" Hickok asked.

"A mutant would be my guess," Blade said.

"What happened to Barbish?" the gunman queried. "It looked to me like the cow chip had a heart attack."

"Same here," Blade concurred. "He wasn't in the best of shape. Maybe he didn't exercise regularly. Maybe the strain was too much for him."

"That critter will probably get indigestion," Hickok joked.

"Perhaps Barbish will not satisfy the creature's appetite," Rikki commented.

Hickok glanced at the martial artist. "What?"

"Perhaps it will return for a second helping," Rikki said.

"We'd best vamoose," Hickok suggested.

"Let's go," Blade stated, jogging to the south.

Hickok and Rikki flanked the giant.

"Do you think they heard Barbish yell at the estate?" Hickok questioned.

"I doubt it," Blade replied. "We have about a mile to go yet."

They ran a quarter of a mile, constantly glancing to their rear, alert for the return of the beast.

"What's the plan once we get to Happy Acres?" the gunman inquired.

"We'll go in over the wall," Blade said. "We'll find this Arlo Paolucci and force him to take us to the Masters."

"Then we can wrap this up and head for the rendezvous site," Hickok mentioned.

"We have plenty of time before the Hurricane returns to pick us up," Blade noted. "The VTOL won't be at the site for five days."

"There's something I've been wondering about," Rikki mentioned. "What's the maximum range of the Hurricanes?"

"The Hurricanes were constructed right before the Big Blast," Blade answered, using the colloquial term the Family employed for World War Three. "They were designed to ferry combat troops, strike squads, over vast distances. With greater fuel efficiency than previous models, with their state-of-the-art technology, and with their six fuel tanks each filled with five hundred gallons, they have a maximum one-way range of approximately three thousand miles."

Rikki performed a few mental calculations. "The Hurricane that dropped us off won't have enough fuel to return to the Home."

"It's flying to Denver, not the Home," Blade said.

"Denver?" Rikki repeated. "It still won't have enough fuel."

"It will once it's been refueled en route," Blade divulged.

"What are you talkin' about?" Hickok inquired. "They can refuel those contraptions in midair?"

"Yes," Blade replied. "Refueling in flight was a common procedure before the war. California owns eight tanker aircraft, and the governor has loaned a pair to the Civilized zone. They're being housed at Stapleton Airport in Denver. If necessary, they can fly out to meet the Hurricanes and refuel the VTOLs." He paused. "Do you remember when we left the Home to come to Florida? We flew a wide loop to the southwest."

"I remember," Hickok said. "I figured the pilot was gettin' his bearings."

"He flew the southwest loop so he could radio Stapleton and arrange to be refueled on his return flight from Florida," Blade explained.

"So the Hurricanes can go anywhere in the country," Rikki remarked.

"And out of it," Blade added.

They were now within a half mile of the estate. The insect sounds, mixed with the calls of other wildlife, emanated from everywhere.

Blade noticed more and more trees as they drew near to the lights, and he realized they were on the estate, on the 40 acres of dry land Barbish had mentioned as comprising the Director's domain. Ahead was the walled, five-acre compound. If it wasn't for the thin ribbon of gravel connecting Happy Acres to Highway 41, the swamp would enclose the 40 acres entirely. If Arlo had

financed the construction of the gravel road, merely to
link his compound to the rest of the world, then the
Director must be a man of staggering wealth and
influence. All of which substantiated his status as a top
kingpin in the Dragons.

The Warriors advanced cautiously until they were
within 40 yards of the brick wall.

Blade stood behind a tree and studied the layout. As
the Dealer had related, the wall was eight feet high, but
Barbish had failed to disclose a pertinent fact: The wall
was crowned with strands of barbed wire. The gravel
road went straight up to the closed metal gate in the
center of the north wall. Floodlights were positioned just
inside the wall at 20-yard intervals. The vegetation for 30
yards from the walls had been stripped to the ground,
affording the guards an unobstructed view. Two guards
were standing inside the gate, conversing idly. Another
guard, armed with a machine gun, was patrolling the top
of the brick wall. Evidently there was ample walking
space between the strands of barbed wire and the inner
edge.

"How will we play this?" Hickok whispered from a
tree on Blade's right.

Blade motioned for his companions to withdraw
deeper into the undergrowth. They retreated 15 yards and
crouched down. "We're going to circle around the
compound," he informed them.

"I wouldn't want to trip and give us away," Hickok
commented. "Any chance of you carryin' me
piggyback?"

Blade straightened and headed eastward.

"I guess not," Hickok said to himself.

The Warriors wound between the trees, moving as
shadows, their consummate stealth a testimony to their
skill at their lethal trade. They angled to within a few
yards of the cleared strip bordering the walls, never once
exposing themselves to the men on guard duty. A hush
enveloped the compound, the lull before the dawn.

Blade knew they had to work quickly if they were to
gain access to the compound and locate Arlo Paolucci

before daylight. He surveyed the walls intently, searching for a weak spot in the defenses. But there wasn't one on the north wall, nor the east. Only when they were skirting the compound to the south did they hit pay dirt.

They found a door.

Blade halted under the spreading limbs of a willow and stared at the small wooden door situated in the middle of the south wall. What was its purpose? Why have a narrow door on the opposite side from the gravel road? Was it an exit in case of an emergency? Not likely. Who would dare attack a Director of the Dragons? There was a trail in the grass, leading from the door toward the south side of the estate. Where did the trail lead?

A finger tapped him on the right side.

Blade looked around.

Rikki pointed at the south wall. "Where is the guard?"

The guard? Blade gazed at the wall again, his forehead creasing as he noted the absence of a sentry. Strange. There had been a guard on the rampart on both the north and east walls. Why wasn't there one on the south side?

"Let's go for it," Hickok urged from Blade's left.

"I don't like it," Blade said.

"What's not to like?" Hickok responded. "They don't know we're here, so this can't be a trap. Maybe the guard is takin' a leak. Why don't we give it a shot?"

Blade looked at Rikki.

The martial artist shrugged. "When the time has come for action, the moment must be quickly seized," he quoted.

"More Zen?" Blade asked, smiling.

"The *I Ching*," Rikki said.

"Sounds like my kind of book," Hickok commented. "I've always said that the direct approach is the best."

"You should read it sometime," Rikki suggested.

"Does it have any gunfights in it?"

"No."

"Any mangy Injuns tryin' to scalp thievin', fork-tongued whites?"

"No."

"Any damsels in distress?"

"No."

"I'll reckon I'll stick with Zane Grey."

"Are you two done with your literary discussion?" Blade demanded.

"You sure are touchy this trip, pard," Hickok whispered. "Is your missus makin' you sleep on the couch again?"

Blade sighed and moved toward the wall, using every tree and bush as a screen, his gray eyes sweeping the wall again and again, insuring the guard was really absent. He stopped in the shelter of the last tree before the cleared section and crouched.

Hickok and Rikki were right behind him.

"Rikki," Blade ordered. "You stay here and cover us. I'll signal if the coast is clear."

"If I see the guard, I'll whistle," Rikki said.

"Whistle? What kind of warning is that?" Hickok asked. "If you see the guard, pretend you're a hoot owl."

"A hoot owl?"

"Yep. Like this." Hickok placed his right hand on the side of his mouth and uttered a realistic imitation of an owl's "Whooo?"

Rikki glanced at Blade. "Which do you prefer? The whistle or the hoot owl?"

"Blow a trumpet, why don't you?" Blade answered.

Hickok and Rikki stared at the ground.

"I want you two bozos to remind me of something after we return to the Home," Blade said.

"What's that?" Hickok inquired.

"To bring Geronimo and Yama the next time I make a run," Blade said, and eased forward.

Hickok leaned toward Rikki. "Don't take it personal. He has these cranky moods now and then." He grinned and tailed after his giant friend.

Blade checked the wall once again, then took a deep breath and bolted from under the willow's limbs, racing across the open stretch, anticipating a verbal challenge or the blast of gunfire at any moment. Amazingly, he reached the wall to the right of the door without incident.

Hickok ran to the left of the door and flattened his back against the wall, his Henry in his hands.

So far, so good, Blade thought. He glanced at the vegetation, pleased Rikki was completely hidden. Now for the door. Gingerly, he reached for the brass knob and twisted it.

The door wasn't locked!

Blade frowned as the door swung inward on well-oiled hinges. His intuition was nagging at his mind, but he couldn't pinpoint the reason. What could be wrong? Hickok was right. The Dragons didn't know the Warriors were at Happy Acres. Still, his intuition blared.

Hickok was waiting.

Annoyed at his indecision, Blade slid inside, keeping his back to the wall, stepping to the right away from the doorway and pausing with the Paratrooper level.

The gunfighter came through the doorway, stepping to the left and standing in front of the door.

The Warriors found themselves in a 20-foot grassy space between the wall and a waist-high hedge. Beyond the hedge flourished the gardens, with an astounding array of diverse plant life; flowers, shrubs, herbs, and other ornamental greenery grew in profusion. The floodlights illuminated the gardens as brightly as if it were daylight.

Blade was about to take a step when he heard the metallic click. He tensed, glancing at Hickok, and for a second their eyes touched.

And over a dozen men in camouflage outfits, each armed with a machine gun or an automatic rifle, rose from concealment behind the hedge, their weapons pointing at the pair of Warriors.

Blade held his fire, knowing to do otherwise would be suicide, hoping the impetuous gunman would do the same.

He didn't.

Hickok's Henry boomed twice, and with each shot one of the gunmen was hurled backwards to drop from view. He managed a stride toward the doorway before the inevitable transpired.

The tallest of the men behind the hedge, an M-16 already pressed to his shoulder, fired once.

Hickok grunted as he was struck, the impact wrenching him to the right and bringing him down.

Blade turned toward the gunman.

"Don't move!" barked the tall man. "Drop your gun!"

Blade hesitated, his gaze on Hickok. The gunfighter was sprawled face down, eyes closed, with a bullet hole rimmed by blood above his right shoulder blade, next to his backpack.

"Look above you, *señor*!" the tall man declared.

Blade gazed up at the wall, stunned to discover ten more men in camouflage clothing, ten more barrels centered on him.

"I will not tell you again!" the tall man stated. "Drop your weapon!"

Gritting his teeth in resentment at his stupidity, and shaken by what it had done to Hickok, Blade reluctantly released the Paratrooper.

"*Excelente*," the tall man said.

The men in camouflage filed through a six-food-wide gap in the hedge, the tall one in the lead. He radiated an aura of power, of strength. His black hair was curly, and a dark mustache framed his upper lip. With a measured stride he crossed the grass.

Blade took a step toward Hickok.

In one light-footed bound, the tall man reached the giant's side and pressed the barrel of his M-16 against Blade's temple. "Are you prepared to die, *señor*?"

CHAPTER TWELVE

Blade felt his abdominal muscles tighten into a knot. Immobile, his right arm outstretched in the act of reaching for the gunman, he forced himself to project an air of indifference to the tall man's threat. "You won't shoot me."

"What makes you so sure?"

"If you'd wanted me dead," Blade said, "I'd be dead by now. You wanted both of us alive."

Chuckling, the man with the mustache lowered the M-16. "A man of courage and insight. I like that. Yes, we were under orders to take both of you alive. Your friend was most *impetuoso*, yes? And most *tonto*."

"*Tonto*?"

"Foolish."

Twelve hardened figures now hemmed in the Warrior.

Blade stared at the obviously professional squad, then up at the ten on the wall.

The man in charge noticed the giant's gaze. "They were on the wall the whole time, lying flat next to the wire. You couldn't see them from the ground. The top of the wall is a yard across."

Blade frowned. "We walked right into it," he said in self-reproach.

The tall man nodded. "We were waiting for you most of the night." He paused and extended his right hand. "I am called El Gato. The Cat."

Surprised at Cat's seemingly authentic friendliness, Blade shook. "I must examine my friend."

"We will take care of him, *señor*," Cat said. He motioned to two of his men, and the pair promptly slung their weapons over their shoulders and lifted the gunfighter by the arms. "Take him to the infirmary," he ordered.

"You have an infirmary here?" Blade asked.

"*Si*," Cat replied. "Mr. Paolucci provides for all of our needs. There are accidents from time to time, snakebites and such, and occasional sickness. We need a doctor on the premises. The medicos in the city are too far away."

The pair of guards lifted Hickok by the arms and draped him between them. They hurried to the north.

"And now, Señor Blade," Cat said, "I will have your Bowies."

Blade's mouth slackened in astonishment.

Cat laughed. "*Si*. I know your name."

"But how?" Blade blurted.

"Señor Paolucci will explain everything to you," Cat stated. "But first—" He looked up at the men on the wall. "Gehret."

A stocky man with blond hair and an Uzi snapped to attention. "Yes, sir?"

"Take eight men with you and go find the third one," Cat directed. "The one in black. Leave Webster on the wall."

Gehret saluted. "Yes, sir."

El Gato gestured at the Bowies. "And now, Blade, your knives. Don't forget the gun behind your back, the derringer, and the backpack." He raised his left hand and his men sighted on the Warrior.

Inwardly seething, Blade nonetheless smiled placidly. El Gato was a pro; he'd detected the Browning and the derringer's outline easily. The Warrior removed the backpack, Cat snapped his fingers, and one of the guards stepped forward to take the gear.

"Your men are well trained," Blade remarked.

"Yes," Cat agreed. "But they are not my men. They are the Director's men, Mr. Paolucci's men. I am but a captain."

"Mr. Paolucci has his own little army," Blade deduced.

"He needs one," Cat said, nodding toward the break in the hedge. "After you."

Blade walked into the gardens.

"Go straight," Cat declared, staying on the giant's right.

The lush collection of plants was more impressive close up. Every conceivable variety appeared to be represented.

Blade glanced over his right shoulder. Gehret and eight others were descending the wall using a narrow flight of stairs 20 feet to the east of the south door.

"They will have your friend in custody within fifteen minutes," Cat predicted.

"I wouldn't count on it," Blade responded.

"Mr. Paolucci hires only the best mercenaries," Cat stated. "Your friend in black is as good as captured."

"You don't know my friend," Blade said. "I hope your men are expendable."

Cat laughed. "I like you, *gringo*."

"Oh?" Blade commented skeptically. He followed a worn path to the north, inhaling the heady fragrance of the myriad of flowers.

"I am sincere, *señor*," Cat insisted. "Call it professional courtesy, from one man of reputation to another."

"I have a reputation?"

"You are playing games with me," Cat said. "The fame of the Warriors has spread far and wide. We have even heard of you here."

Blade's brow creased in confusion. What else did Cat know?

Cat observed the giant's expression and chuckled. "So many questions, eh?"

"This is an unexpected development," Blade admitted.

"Be patient. Mr. Paolucci will answer everything. He has been looking forward to your arrival."

Blade caught sight of buildings. A large red barn appeared to the east, and to the north loomed a four-story, sprawling, magnificent house with a portico supported by marble columns. "Where is the infirmary?'' he asked.

Cat pointed to the west.

Blade gazed in that direction and discovered another structure, the barracks Barbish had told them about, a low wooden building with several doors and a green roof. Of course, the Dealer had conveniently lied about the size of the guard contingent. A large sign imprinted in red with the word INFIRMARY was attached above the northernmost door. The door was open, and the two guards responsible for conveying Hickok were standing outside, conversing.

''They will bring word as soon as your friend has been examined,'' Cat said. ''What is his name anyway?''

''Hickok.''

''So that was Hickok?'' Cat remarked. ''I did not expect him to be so rash.''

''You've heard of Hickok too?''

''*Si*.''

''How many Warriors do you know by name?''

Cat Grinned. ''Mr. Paolucci has talked about four of you by name. Hickok, an Indian named Geronimo, the hombre they call the Dispenser of Death—Yama, and yourself.'' He paused. ''There was an unconfirmed report concerning a small man in black, but his name was unknown.''

''Where did this report come from?''

''You must ask Mr. Paolucci.''

Blade looked over his left shoulder at the mercenaries. One was carrying his Bowies, the Browning, and the derringer, and a second was bearing the Paratrooper, the Henry, and the backpack.

''They say you are quite skilled with your knives,'' Cat commented.

Blade said nothing.

''Perhaps we will have the chance to test your mettle,'' Cat stated. ''You and I, eh? *Mano a mano*. One on one.''

''You sound like you'd enjoy it.''

''*Si*, Blade. I would,'' Cat confessed. ''There is very little action at Happy Acres.'' He spoke the last two words contemptuously. ''A man of my expertise, my caliber, needs challenges. Without action, what use are the talents we have? When Mr. Paolucci told us you were coming, I was overjoyed. This is the first action I've seen in two years. No one else would have the *cojones* to take on the Dragons. You have my respect, *amigo*."

Blade stared into Cat's dark eyes, only four inches lower than his own. He perceived that the mercenary was sincere.

"Yes," Cat went on. "I will be glad when my contract is up. Another six months and I can return to Colombia."

"You're from South America?"

"*Si*. Why do you sound so surprised?"

"I suppose I expected you to be from Miami."

Cat snorted. "That sewer? Give me the green hills of Colombia any day!"

"How did South America fare during the war?"

"There were not any nuclear strikes on South American soil," Cat replied. "But most of the governments fell apart. The winds brought a lot of radiation, and there was much sickness and death."

"And now?"

"Colombia is ruled by the Cartel," Cat disclosed. His eyes narrowed as he gazed ahead.

Blade faced the house.

A man was awaiting them on the bottom step of the portico, a stately individual attired in an immaculate white suit and matching shoes. His hair was black, tinged with gray at the ears. Frank blue eyes watched the Warrior approach. The man's face was leonine in aspect. Here was a man accustomed to giving orders and being obeyed. Here was a man of power.

Cat stepped in front of the Warrior and saluted. "Here he is, Mr. Paolucci. Just as you wanted."

Paolucci raked Blade from head to toe with a critical gaze. "I heard shooting."

"Hickok tried to resist. He's in the infirmary," Cat detailed.

"And the third one?"

"Sergeant Gehret is out after him as we speak," Cat

said.

Paolucci smiled at El Gato. "Well done." He walked up to the Warrior and offered his right hand. "I am delighted to make your acquaintance, Blade. My name is Arlo Paolucci."

Blade shook the Director's hand. "I know."

"Ahhh. Yes. Tom Barbish. Where is Mr. Barbish? I expected him to arrive with you."

Blade slashed his right forefinger across his throat.

"Really? You?"

"No," Blade said. "I can't claim the credit. A mutant made a snack out of your Dealer friend."

"Barbish was a business associate," Paolucci said. "Not a close friend. His betrayal necessitated his termination, and I'm happy the mutant has saved me the trouble." He moved to the east, nodding at a white table ringed by four white chairs. "Why don't we take a seat and continue our discussion in a civilized vein?"

El Gato nodded at the men toting the weapons, and the duo hurried to the table and deposited their loads. At a jerk of Cat's right arm, the mercenaries fanned out around the table.

"Simply a precaution, you understand," Paolucci said to the Warrior.

Blade nodded. He took a chair on the south side of the table.

The Director stepped to the chair on the opposite side. As he sat down, a petite, dark-haired woman in a white blouse, white skirt, and a white apron hastened to him.

"Refreshments, *señor*?"

"Yes, Maria," Paolucci said. He looked at Blade. "What would you like? We have tea, coffee, milk, fruit juice, water, or any liquor you can name."

"Do you have raspberry juice?" Blade asked.

Paolucci looked at Maria, who shook her head. The Director's mouth curled downward. "I apologize for the oversight."

"No big deal," Blade said. "Raspberry juice is my favorite, but I can live with grape juice, *if* you have any."

"We do, *señor*," Maria assured him.

Paolucci waved his right hand, and Maria took off for the house at a run.

"Are you always up at this time of the night?" Blade inquired.

The Director smiled. "My business activities demand unusual hours. But no, I would have been asleep tonight, if it wasn't for your arrival. I wanted to be up, to greet you in person, to bid you welcome."

"How kind of you," Blade said sarcastically.

"There's no need to be nasty," Paolucci stated. "Crudity from a man of your stature insults both of us."

The light from a floodlight at the eastern corner of the house cast a glimmering reflection on the weapons piled on the table. Blade glanced at the Paratrooper, estimating his chances of successfully making a bid for freedom. With the table encircled by mercenaries, and El Gato standing four feet to his right, any precipitous movement on his part would be met by a hail of lead. Wisdom dictated sitting tight, biding his time. He stared to his left at the infirmary 50 yards distant, suppressing his anxiety over Hickok. Why had the gunfighter pulled such an inane stunt? Hickok was impetuous, true, but the gunman wasn't an idiot; his gambit at the south door made no sense.

"I was quite surprised to learn of your presence in Miami," the Director commented.

"How did you find out?"

"I was called by one of Barbish's people fifteen minutes after you took him from the Oasis," Paolucci divulged. "It wasn't terribly difficult to put two and two together. When my caller described the three men responsible for the abduction, I remembered the descriptions I'd been given of yourself and a few of your colleagues."

"But how did you know it was me?"

The Director smiled. "How many seven-foot men with Bowie knives are traipsing around the country?"

"That's not what I meant," Blade said. "How did you know about me, about the Warriors? Where did you hear about us?"

"From the Masters," Paolucci answered.

"How did they learn about the Warriors?"

"You'll need to ask them," the Director said.

"They didn't tell you?"

"No," Paolucci said. "And I'm not about to pry into their affairs. As a Director, my job is to carry out their wishes, not to pry into their sources."

"How much were you told?"

Paolucci leaned back in his chair. "The Masters held a conclave with all of the Directors in attendance. We were told about this group in Minnesota, the Family, and provided with convincing evidence of the Family's threat to our operation."

"What are you talking about?" Blade demanded. "How can the Family be a threat when our Home is located over two thousand miles from Miami?"

"If the Masters see your Family as a threat, then you're a threat," Paolucci maintained.

"What else did they inform you of?"

"We were provided with a brief description of your administrative organization," the Director said. "We learned about the Elders, about your Leader, Plato, and about the Warriors."

"And did the Masters happen to reveal their plans for the Family?"

Paolucci nodded. "Complete eradication."

"Then the report we heard was true," Blade commented.

"Now it's my turn," the Director stated. "I've answered all of your questions, and I expect you to extend the same courtesy." He paused as Maria approached with a silver tray containing liquid refreshments. She placed the tray on the table, picked up a glass filled with grape juice, and handed the drink to the Warrior.

"Your grape juice, *señor*."

"Thank you," Blade said.

"That will be all, Maria," Paolucci stated stiffly.

Maria glanced nervously at the Director, then departed.

"I'll talk to her about the raspberry juice," Paolucci commented.

"Talk to her?" Blade repeated, and took a sip.

"I pride myself on running an orderly household," the Director said. "My servants perform their duties impeccably, or they don't work for me very long." His tone lowered ominously. "I despise imperfection."

"So what if you're out of raspberry juice," Blade responded. "It's not worth getting upset about."

"To you," Paolucci said sternly. He abruptly smiled. "But enough of this. Where were we? I believe you were going to answer my questions."

"I never said I'd answer anything."

"But I answered all of yours," the Director declared.

"That doesn't make us best friends," Blade quipped.

Paolucci's lips compressed. To cover his chagrin, he reached for a pitcher of red juice. "Tomato juice," he explained. "*My* favorite." He poured the tomato juice into an empty glass, set down the pitcher, and reached for the glass. His fingers were an inch away when the predawn quietude was shattered by the blast of gunfire.

From the infirmary.

CHAPTER THIRTEEN

Sergeant Ambrose Gehret hustled his men across the cleared strip and into the trees to the south of the compound. He stopped under the willow, the same willow he'd seen the giant and the guy in buckskins dart from when they'd approached the wall. As he expected, the man in black was gone.

"We're after one man, Sarge?" asked a tanned, experienced soldier to his rear.

Gehret nodded.

"We won't even work up a sweat," Stanz remarked.

Gehret turned to his men. "Listen up!" He recalled an episode earlier that night. Shooting the breeze with El Gato near the barn, both of them had been surprised to see the Director running toward them from the house. The Director, displaying an uncharacteristic uneasiness, had told them about Barbish's abduction, about his belief that the Warriors were involved. Gehret had been secretly amused at the Director's ill-concealed anxiety. Paolucci had expressed his belief that the Warriors were on their way to Happy Acres, based on the assumption the Warriors would not go to all the trouble to snatch the Dealer alive without a specific purpose. And what better reason than to compel the Dealer to take them to Barbish's superior in the Dragons? Gehret had to hand it to Paolucci. The Director had been right on the money.

"In case you didn't hear, we're after a Warrior." He said the name scornfully.

"What's a Warrior?" Stanz asked.

"They're supposed to be real hotshots," Gehret replied. "The one we're after is dressed in black. He must know his pals have been caught. I doubt he'll go very far. We'll divide up into three teams. Stanz, take two men with you and sweep to the west, then north. Check under every tree and behind every bush.''

Corporal Stanz nodded. He looked at two of the mercenaries and wagged his right thumb westward. The trio hurried off.

Sergeant Gehret glanced at one of his men. '' Weber, take two men with you,'' he directed. ''Go east, all the way around the compound until you join up with Stanz.''

Private Weber selected a pair of men and off they went.

''Right,'' Gehret said, staring at the remaining duo. ''The south side is all ours. Let's go.'' He advanced into the undergrowth, his men flanking him.

The mercenaries dispersed in three directions of the compass, and as their stealthy footfalls faded, a lithe, pantherish form dropped from the overspreading limbs of the willow to the ground.

The hunted was now the hunter.

Sergeant Gehret was becoming increasingly annoyed at the minutes elapsed without a sign of the Warrior. No trace at all! Not one of the other search parties had signaled, not so much as a single shot had been fired.

Where the hell was the guy in black?

Gehret paused on a low mound and surveyed the terrain. In front of him was a 15-foot incline covered with weeds, and then a sea of sawgrass. They were nearly to the southern edge of the estate; beyond was the reptile-infested swamp. Dawn was streaking the eastern horizon, the increasing sunlight lending the murky water a golden hue. He turned to the west, intending to head for the airboat dock.

''Sarge!'' one of his men exclaimed, pointing to the north, at a tree 20 yards distant.

Gehret swiveled, doing a double take when he saw the cause of the man's alarm.

There he was!

The son of a bitch was standing next to the tree, just watching them, an M-16 slung over his left shoulder, his hands empty!

Gehret recovered from his amazement and raised his Uzi, his finger on the trigger.

With startling swiftness, the man in black stepped behind the trunk and was screened from view.

"Damn!" declared the first man.

"He must be crazy!" said the second.

Gehret motioned with his left arm. "Take him from both sides," he commanded.

Moving with practiced precision, the three mercenaries closed on the tree, their weapons at the ready.

Gehret fixed his gaze on that tree. The nearest brush was five yards from the trunk! The guy had trapped himself! There was no way the man in black could reach the brush without being cut down. Gehret smiled in expectation.

One of the other mercenaries was moving cautiously to the right, the second to the left.

Sergeant Gehret halted a yard from the three-foot-wide trunk and crouched. He glanced at his men and nodded, and all three hurled themselves forward. Gehret rounded the trunk on the left and swiveled, prepared to blast away.

But there was no one to blast.

The Warrior was gone.

"Where'd he go?" asked the private on the right.

"I don't know!" Gehret snapped. "Fan out. Find the bastard!" He watched them enter the undergrowth, his brow knit in puzzlement. No one could up and vanish. No one ordinary, that is. But Gehret had lived as a professional mercenary for two decades. Before being hired by the Dragons, he'd worked for seven years in the Far East. In Japan he'd encountered certain men capable of astounding feats, men known as Ninja. Oddly enough, the Oriental in black reminded him of those Ninja. In the brief glimpse he'd had, he'd recognized the same aura of supreme confidence in the man in black as he recollected observing in the Ninja. Was it possible? he started to think, when a strangled gurgle sounded from the vegetation to his left.

"Anders?" Gehret said softly but urgently.

There was no response.

"Anders?"

Still no answer.

Gehret took a stride toward the undergrowth, looking to the right as he did so. "Wilson!" he hissed.

"Yeah, Sarge?" came a reply from the other side of a dense thicket.

"Get back here! On the double!"

"On my way."

Gehret heard the muffled footfalls as Wilson started to obey, and an instant later there was a loud crash. Then silence.

"Wilson?"

Wilson did not reply.

Discarding prudence, concerned for his men, Gehret plunged into the woods, weaving to minimize the target he posed, skirting the dense thicket. The morning light cast the vegetation in a deep green tint. His combat boots bumped an object in his path and he looked down, a chill washing over him.

Private Wilson was on his back, his mouth open, his tongue protruding out the left corner. His head was almost severed from his shoulders; only a few inches of flesh and the spinal column had not been sliced clean through.

Sergeant Gehret licked his lips. He'd seen this kind of handiwork before, and a word flashed into his mind unbidden, a word with supremely lethal connotations: katana.

The Oriental had a katana.

Gehret scanned the vegetation. He vaguely remembered seeing something long and thin slanted under the Warrior's belt. The katana? He wanted to kick himself for underestimating the man in black. Now his men were dead, and El Gato would have his hide! He decided to head to the west and locate Corporate Stanz, and he took several steps. As he did, the short hairs on the nape of his neck tingled.

No!

Sergeant Gehret whirled, his Uzi tucked against his

right side.

The Warrior was a foot away in the Kokutsu-tachi, the back stance. His M-16 was still over his left shoulder, and his katana was angled over his left hip. As the mercenary turned, the Warrior slid in close, his left hand in the Nukite, the piercing hand, position, his right in the Shotei. A slash to his left hand deflected the Uzi barrel aside. He uttered a sharp kiai and drove his right hand in a palm heel thrust into the mercenary's side, hemorrhaging the spleen underneath. Another Shotei blow to the sergeant's chin snapped the soldier's head back.

Gehret saw pinwheeling lights explode before his eyes. Dazed, he tried to stagger backwards, to clear his head. But the Warrior wouldn't let him.

The man in black rammed his right elbow into the mercenary's jaw.

Gehret felt his teeth crunch together. His world spun and danced and he sagged forward.

The Warrior yanked the Uzi free and tossed it aside. He stood above the mercenary as Gehret landed on his knees, struggling to focus.

This couldn't be happening!

Gehret felt steely fingers lock on his throat. He gasped and grabbed the arm holding him.

"You have captured my friends," the man in black stated harshly. "Now you are going to tell me everything there is to know about Happy Acres." To emphasize his point, he raised his right arm aloft, his fingers taut, ready to use a Crane strike to the eyes.

Gehret blinked and gulped.

CHAPTER FOURTEEN

Dear Spirit!

His shoulder hurt like the dickens!

Hickok kept his eyes closed, listening to the conversation between the doctor and the nurse.

"Will you operate?" the nurse asked.

The doctor had removed the backpack, then used a scalpel to cut a line in the gunman's buckskin shirt from the right shoulder to the neck. He'd peeled the strong, pliable leather down to expose the wound. Now, as he probed at the hole with his instruments, he voiced a contemplative "Hmmmmm."

What the blazes did that mean? Hickok resisted an urge to cry out as the doctor's probe hit a sensitive spot. He didn't want the physician to know he was awake and he had been the whole time.

So far his plan had worked to perfection.

Sort of.

When those coyotes had popped up from behind the blasted hedge, springing their ambush, he'd believed he and Blade were going to cash in their chips. But when the men hadn't fired, in that split second when he'd realized they were about to be taken prisoner instead of perforated with dozens of rounds, he'd attempted to get through the doorway, hoping the varmints would hesitate just long enough.

Wouldn't you know it.

The dipsticks hadn't.

The shot had knocked him for a loop. Surprisingly, the pain had been slight at first, then grew progressively worse. He'd retained consciousness all the while the two guards were lugging him to the infirmary and making snide comments about his level of intelligence.

What did those cow patties know?

"Most remarkable," the doctor remarked.

"What is?" the nurse prompted.

"The wound isn't life threatening," the doctor said. "The bullet missed the clavicle, the subclavian artery, and the subclavian vein. Except for damange to the trapezius muscle—and the entry and exit holes, of course —this man is fine. Remarkable," he repeated.

"What should I tell the two outside?"

"Tell them we'll need to clean and bandage the shoulder," the doctor directed. "It shouldn't take more than five minutes."

Hickok heard the nurse walk off.

This was his chance.

He opened his lids a fraction and studied his surroundings. The doctor was a man of 30 or so, attired in a white smock and gray trousers. As Hickok watched, the physician walked to a cabinet and opened the glass door. Medical instruments were everywhere, and the ten-by-twelve-foot room was spotlessly clean. A door was visible six feet from the foot of the metal table Hickok was on. Through the doorway he could see a smaller room, and on the far side was another door, this one to the outside. The nurse, an attractive redhead, was framed in the doorway. Beyond her were two men in camouflage uniforms, the same pair, evidently, who had carried him to the infirmary.

The doctor began humming to himself.

Hickok closed his eyes and debated his next move. His Henry was gone, but the dummies had neglected to take his Colts. Since Blade had managed to get himself captured, his first priority was to rescue the Big Guy.

There was the sound of footsteps at the foot of the table.

"What did they say?" the doctor inquired.

"They said they'll wait," the nurse responded. "Mr. Paolucci wants to see him as soon as possible."

"Do they know who he is?"

"They don't know his name. But El Gato said

something about expecting Warriors to attack Happy Acres. He must be a Warrior.''

"What's a Warrior?"

"Beats me."

Hickok heard the swishing noise of running water.

"You'd better wash up," the doctor directed.

The nurse shuffled to the right. "What do you think Mr. Paolucci will do to him?"

"Your guess is as good as mine."

"They captured another one," the nurse mentioned. "I saw him from the front door. He's a big one."

"I hope I don't go to all the trouble of bandaging this man," the physician commented, "only to have the good Director execute him."

"Don't talk like that," the nurse cautioned. "Someone may hear you."

"I am not one of the Director's hired flunkies," the doctor said. "I'll voice my opinion any time I desire."

"It's dangerous to anger Mr. Paolucci."

"Paolucci is not God."

"At Happy Acres he's the next best thing."

The water was turned off.

"Prep the patient," the doctor directed.

Hickok breathed deeply, simulating unconsciousness. Soft, gentle fingers began washing the blood from his shoulder. Perfume stimulated his nostrils.

"This guy is good looking," the nurse remarked.

"Behave yourself, Norma."

"I was just making an observation."

The doctor chuckled.

Hickok's nose started to itch.

"So tell me," the doctor said. "How's things going between Sergeant Gehret and you?"

"I don't know what you're talking about?"

"Oh. That's funny. You know how gossip spreads around the estate. Yesterday I treated someone who told me Gehret and you are an item."

"Who?"

"You know I won't tell you."

"Why not?"

"Because you'd punch their lights out."

The nurse laughed. "I would not!"

Hickok's nose twitched as the itching intensified.

"I'm done," the nurse announced.

"Allow me," the doctor stated.

Not now! Hickok felt a growing impulse to sneeze and tried to suppress it.

The physician began probing at the wound again. "Would you get the gauze?" he asked the nurse.

"Certainly."

Hickok was unable to control the urge. The sneeze exploded from him, and as his head snapped forward he sat up and opened his eyes.

The doctor, standing next to the table with a long, thin silver instrument in his right hand, took a step backwards, startled. To the left of the table, her hand on the knob of a white cabinet, the nurse shifted her hand to her widening mouth.

Hickok pulled his left Python. "Howdy," he said with a smile.

"You're awake!" the nurse blurted.

"And rarin' to go," Hickok said, glancing at the doorway. He spied the guards through the outer door, both standing with their backs to the infirmary, talking. "Close this door," he instructed them, nodding at the entrance to the room.

Neither the doctor or the nurse moved.

"You'd best hop to it," Hickok suggested. "If those guards see me, there's liable to be gunplay. You'd be caught in the cross fire."

"Close the door, Norma," the doctor said.

The nurse moved tentatively to the door and eased it shut.

Hickok motioned with the Python at a far corner. "Why don't you mosey on over there where I can keep my eyes on you, ma'am?"

Norma complied hastily.

"Now, Doc, you can bandage my shoulder," Hickok directed.

"I should administer anesthetic," the physician remarked.

"No anesthetic."

"It will cause some discomfort."

"No anesthetic."

The doctor shrugged. "As you wish."

Hickok bore the dressing of his wound stoically despite intermittent twinges of severe pain. He held the Python in his lap, his thumb on the hammer.

"You know," the physician commented as he wrapped up the bandaging, "there's only one way out of the infirmary."

"No windows?"

"There is a window in the waiting room," the doctor disclosed. "On the north side."

Hickok smiled. "Thanks, Doc."

"This will suffice temporarily," the doctor said, stepping back and examining his handiwork. "But you should avoid excessive activity."

"I'll keep it in mind," Hickok quipped. He slid to the left, placing his moccasins on the white-tiled floor. "I want you two to stay put until I'm out of here. You'll stay a lot healthier if you do."

"We won't budge," the doctor promised.

Hickok walked to the door and opened it a crack. Peeking through the narrow slit, he observed the guards still engaged in conversation and still facing away from the infirmary. This was a golden opportunity. He quickly opened the door, sidled into the waiting room, and quietly closed the door.

Neither guard looked in his direction.

The gunman moved to the north wall and examined the narrow window. The inner pane was already up; all that separated him from freedom was a screen. He touched the screen with his right hand, grimacing at the soreness. How would he get through the screen? Find a knife?

A boot scuffled the floor to his rear.

Hickok spun, the Colt tight in his left hand.

One of the guards was a yard inside the waiting room, slack-jawed in amazement. A machine gun was cradled in his left arm.

"Howdy," Hickok said with a grin. "Are you here for your lobotomy?"

Recovering from his initial shock, the mercenary pivoted and endeavored to level his weapon.

Hickok's left Colt boomed, the slug slamming into the guard's forehead and knocking him backward. There was no time to lose. The gunman stepped hurriedly to the doorway, and there was the second mercenary, unslinging his M-16, about to enter. Hickok shot the man in the right eye, then dashed outside.

Now what?

The gunfighter glanced to the east, relief engulfing him at the sight of Blade seated at a white table. Unfortunately, his friend was ringed by ten or eleven mercenaries.

Those mercenaries abruptly raced toward the infirmary.

Hickok swiveled to the right, frowning as he beheld three guards exiting a barracks door. He thumbed the hammer three times, and with each shot a mercenary dropped. But more would be coming. It was time for Mama Hickok's pride and joy to skedaddle. He turned to the left, to the north, spying the closed front gate and a pair of guards. Another mercenary was on the brick wall to the west of the gate. All three were staring at him.

So much for subterfuge.

Hickok bolted toward the gate. With a clipped wing, and without the range provided by the Henry, the odds were stacked too high against him. His best bet was to reach the woods, then rescue Blade later.

Easier said than done.

Several of the mercenaries charging from the east opened up, their rounds narrowly missing the sprinting gunman.

Hickok's right shoulder was throbbing. He saw the pair at the gate run in his direction, and the mercenary on the wall was aiming a machine gun.

When outnumbered, do the unexpected.

The gunfighter stopped, extending and elevating his left arm, and fired once.

With his arms flung wide, the sentry on the wall staggered to the inner rim and plummeted over the edge.

Hickok resumed speeding toward the gate. The layout of the compound worked in his favor; he could make a beeline for the gate from the infirmary, but the mercenaries pursuing him were thwarted by having the house between themselves and the north wall. They had to run all the way around the Director's huge residence. Now, with less than 30 yards to go, and with the pack of mercenaries obstructed by the intervening mansion, he pumped his legs for all he was worth.

The pair of gate guards had halted ten feet from the gate and were sighting on the Warrior.

Hickok threw himself to the left, to the ground, jarring his left side. The left Colt was empty, and reloading was out of the question.

Would his right arm work?

The gunfighter rolled to his knees as the gate guards fired. He grunted as he drew his right Python, his shoulder lancing with agonizing protest. Steady! he mentally warned himself.

Slugs smacked into the turf in front of him.

Hickok fired twice, each shot planted dead center, a slug tearing into each guard's head and dropping them in their tracks.

Move! his mind screamed.

The gunman rose and darted for the gate, looking over his left shoulder. The pack had not yet appeared. He might make it after all. He holstered the left Python and studied the gate ahead. Six-foot-high metal bars, spaced at one-foot intervals, formed the core of the framework, braced by heavy bars at the top and the bottom. A heavy chain was looped around the central bars and secured by a large padlock. He slowed as he neared the pair of dead guards, intending to search their pockets for the key.

A loud shout sounded behind him.

Hickok looked over his right shoulder to see the pack of mercenaries rounding the northwest corner of the house. They were hard in pursuit, and several of them yelled with excitement as they spied their quarry.

Blast!

He could forget the key.

Hickok spun and ran to the gate, sliding the right
Python in its holster. He didn't slow or stop. Instead, he
took a leap and grabbed the middle bars, holding on with
all of his strength, his right shoulder twitching in
excruciating torture. He resisted the waves of pain and
climbed higher, hand over hand, using his left arm to
bear most of his weight and shimmying upward with his
legs.

The chatter of automatic fire greeted his maneuver.

Hickok heard slugs thud into the brick wall, and a few
rounds pinged off the metal bars. His neck muscles
bulged, his face becoming crimson, as he scaled the gate
to the top horizontal bar.

Something tugged at his left leg.

Hickok draped his left arm over the top bar, girded his
shoulders, and surged up and over the heavy bar. For a
moment he hung suspended by his left arm alone, his
right too racked with torment to use.

A stinging sensation lanced his right cheek.

He dropped to the gravel road, landing and almost
losing his balance. But he recovered and headed for the
vegetation to the north, his sore right shoulder impeding
his speed.

A moment later, the mercenaries pounded up to the
gate and cut loose at the twisting, dodging figure in
buckskins making for the shelter of the trees.

"Get the son of a bitch!"

CHAPTER FIFTEEN

In terms of experience and expertise, Rikki-Tikki-Tavi was acknowledged by the Family as one of the more deadly Warriors. Rikki practiced his martial arts skills daily. He would spend hours honing his ability to throw shuriken into logs positioned upright as makeshift targets. He continuously worked at increasing his mastery of the katana, his favorite weapon. Calloused and hardened by constant striking of hard surfaces, his hands and feet were employed in unarmed contests with other Warriors, friendly affairs with a lethal undertone. Only two Warriors could hold their own against Rikki in hand-to-hand combat: Blade and Yama. Devoted to attaining the spiritual state of a perfected swordmaster, Rikki honed his reflexes ceaselessly. He recognized the critical importance of sharpening his reflexes to a razor readiness. When on a run, if he slacked off for just a second, it could mean the difference between life and death. Warriors had to guard against being taken by surprise. Their reflexes must be equal to the unexpected developments of any given moment. Yet despite this fundamental knowledge, Rikki knew the impossibility of maintaining a perpetual state of hypersensitivity to imminent danger. Invariably, inadvertently, when a Warrior least expected it, his guard would falter for a crucial interval. This happened to every Warrior at one time or another.

And now it happened to Rikki.

The martial artist was listening to his prisoner describe the interior of the compound, when from the north erupted the crack of gunfire. Rikki should have kept his eyes on the mercenary. He knew to do otherwise was a major blunder. He had trained and trained for just such a contingency. But the gunshots sounded familiar despite the distance. Countless times he had heard Hickok fire the Pythons, and eventually, after years of familiarity, his ears could register the subtle difference between a Colt Python revolver and other firearms. So when he heard the gunshots, and when he realized that Hickok could be doing the firing, he carelessly, automatically, looked up, gazing to the north.

In that moment Sergeant Gehret struck.

The mercenary had babbled to save his life, supplying the details the man in black requested. Gradually, the intense pangs in his side and jaw had subsided to a tolerable level. His arms at his sides, he had meekly complied with the Warrior's demands for information. But he was still, first and foremost, a seasoned, professional soldier, a mercenary of outstanding ability. He was not a man to permit an opportunity to pass untaken. And when he saw the Warrior glance to the north, he reacted with all the speed and efficiency at his command. He drove his right fist into the Warrior's groin.

Rikki-Tikki-Tavi doubled over, gasping, his genitals afire. Any normal man would have clutched his privates and been oblivious to all else. But Rikki was not normal; his self control, his inner discipline were supreme. Instead of allowing the agony to control him, he controlled it. Instead of wheezing for air, at the mercy of his foe, he threw himself backwards to put distance between them, tottering, every iota of his concentration devoted to regaining domination of his body.

Sergeant Gehret pushed to his feet and closed on the Warrior, performing a side thrust kick to his opponent's midsection.

Rikki stepped to the right, evading the kick, his fluidity reduced to a mere shuffle.

Eager to press the initiative, Gehret delivered a sweep kick at the Warrior's legs.

The blow was telegraphed by the mercenary's stance and muscle movement, and Rikki skipped out of range. His legs were responding better to his mental commands.

Gehret made a mistake of his own. He stepped back

and assumed a fighting stance, and then he violated the cardinal rule of martial combat: He spoke. "I'm going to stomp you into the ground, little man!"

Rikki said nothing. He tensed his muscles, gauging his recovery, waiting.

"I've got to hand it to you," Gehret said. "You're good. But I'm better." So saying, he attempted to connect with a front rising kick to the Warrior's head.

Rikki-Tikki-Tavi was not so easily taken. His left forearm blocked the blow and he rotated, whipping his left elbow in nearly a full circle, adding the momentum of the swing to his inherent power. His elbow caught the mercenary on the nose and crushed the cartilage, flattening the nostrils.

Gehret tottered backwards, blood pouring from his nose.

Eager to aid Hickok and Blade, Rikki wanted to end the fight promptly. He flicked his left foot in a side kick, his heel jamming into the mercenary's right kneecap.

Gehret stiffened and cried out as his kneecap was shattered. He hobbled to the left and tripped over a log, going down on his left side at the crest of a four-foot-high drop off, the eroded vestige of a low mound.

Rikki pressed his advantage, moving to the mercenary's right, seeking an opening.

The realization that he was hopelessly outclassed goaded Gehret to a desperate measure. He scrambled onto his good knee, his hands in front of his torso in a defensive posture. An unorthodox ploy was called for, a strategem the Warrior wouldn't expect. But what? What was the one tactic the man in black would never anticipate? He riveted his eyes on the Warrior as the martial artist circled him, and an insane idea gave him a straw at which to clutch. He glanced at a stretch of sandy earth below the drop-off. The ground appeared slightly soggy and ideal for his purpose.

Rikki neared the edge of the drop-off to his enemy's right.

It could work. Gehret told himself. He shifted his body to keep the Warrior in front of him, then used his uninjured knee as a crutch and retreated a yard.

The Warrior stepped along the rim of the drop-off, his back to the sandy patch below.

Gehret waited until the man in black was at the midpoint of the rim, then put his scheme into operation. He heaved erect and started to turn, pretending to flee, hoping the Warrior would take the bait.

Rikki, believing the mercenary was foolishly striving to get away, took a stride after his foe and lowered his guard slightly.

Which was precisely the reaction Gehret was counting on. He spun on his left leg and dived, his arms outstretched, tackling the Warrior, gripping the man in black about the ankles and propelling them both toward the rim.

And over the edge.

Gehret had planned it this way. He wanted them to fall to the ground below with him on top, pinning the Warrior beneath him. But he had failed to account for the Warrior's reflexes.

Rikki-Tikki-Tavi flipped his body to the right in midair, and both men landed on their sides. Rikki was surprised to feel the earth yield to the impact, to feel the dirt give out under his body. The soft ground absorbed the force of the drop, and a moist, sticky substance clung to his right ear and cheek. Although he was puzzled, he knew better than to take his eyes from the mercenary. And so it was that he observed a remarkable occurrence.

As his left shoulder sank into the sandy turf, Gehret's eyes showed stark fear. He twisted and tried to push up, but his arms sank to the elbows in the mushy soil. "No!" he cried.

Bewildered by the sight of the mercenary sinking, Rikki remained motionless, trying to comprehend what he was seeing.

Gehret endeavored to sit up, but the motion only contributed to his rate of submersion. His arms disappeared to the shoulders, his legs to his knees. Frantic, he wrenched on his arms, his blood-stained face contorted in horror. He was sinking even faster. "No!" he shouted, looking at the Warrior with an expression of pathetic despair. "Help me!" he yelled. "It's quicksand!"

At last Rikki understood.

Even as the damp sand touched his nose.

CHAPTER SIXTEEN

"Don't move, *señor!*"

Blade had risen as he spied Hickok exiting the infirmary, but he stopped, his body poised to run.

El Gato was covering him with the M-16. "Stay right where you are, Blade." He waved his right arm at the infirmary. "Get Hickok!"

The ten mercenaries took off in pursuit of the gunfighter.

Blade reluctantly sat down, watching the tableau unfold. He saw Hickok shoot three guards, and then the gunman wheeled and ran to the north. Where was Hickok heading? Blade thought of the front gate and smiled.

"What is so humorous about the death of one of your fellow Warriors?" Paolucci asked.

"Hickok isn't dead yet."

"He will be soon," Paolucci vowed.

Blade listened to the gunshots coming from the north side of the house. He could distinguish between the boom of Hickok's revolvers and the lighter, more metallic chatter of the mercenaries' automatic weapons.

"And for that matter, so will you," Paolucci said.

Distracted by the noise of the running gun battle, Blade wasn't certain he'd heard correctly. "What?" he asked belatedly.

"Your demise is at hand."

With a conscious effort, Blade faced the Director. "What do you have in mind? A firing squad?"

Paolucci smiled. "Nothing so prosaic."

"You're going to feed me to the alligators?"

"Now there's an idea!" Paolucci stated. "But, sorry to

say, no. To tell you the truth, the manner of your death is not my decision to make."

"Then whose is it?"

"Guess."

Boom. Boom.

Hickok was still alive and kicking! Blade focused on the Director, reflecting. Insight struck him seconds later. "The Masters want to attend to my death personally?"

Paolucci nodded.

"Why am I receiving special treatment?" Blade queried. "Or do the Masters dispose of all of your enemies?"

"The Masters only involve themselves in the exceptional cases," the Director said. "You're receiving quite an honor."

"How so?"

"The Masters will sacrifice you."

"They make sacrifices?"

"Yes."

Blade tensed as the automatic gunfire attained a crescendo. He envisioned Hickok being hit by a storm of slugs, and he shook his head to dispel the image.

Paolucci misinterpreted the movement. "You don't believe me? I'm offended. I have no reason to lie to you. And I know whereof I speak, because I have personally attended fourteen sacrifices."

"You stood by and watched the Masters sacrifice humans?" Blade asked in disgust. Out of the corner of his right eye he noticed El Gato frowning.

"Most of the sacrifices were Dealers gone bad," Paolucci detailed. "The rest were troublemakers, people who couldn't appreciate the essential social service provided by the Dragons."

"In other words, they were against the Dragons and everything you stand for. They opposed your drug-dealing."

"They were fools."

"You're the fool, if you think you can continue to control the people of Miami with drugs," Blade said.

Paolucci did a double take, genuine amazement flickering across his features. "My compliments. Your perception is remarkable."

"What's so remarkable about the obvious?"

"You're wrong, though," the Director said. "The Dragons have controlled southern Florida for sixty-five years. We will control this area, and much more, long after your bones are bleached white by the sun."

"You think so?"

"I know so," Paolucci asserted. "Your problem is that you fail to understand the nature of the human condition. Most people are sheep, content to be led by anyone with the strength to assume command. All the average person cares about are the basics. Where is the next meal coming from? Where will the money come from to put clothes on their backs and keep a roof over their heads? And there's one more consideration." He paused. "What can help them forget all their cares and woes? What can alleviate the pain, if only for a little while? What can give them the illusion of being on top of the world, when in reality they're in the gutter?" He smiled. "That's where the Dragons come in. By feeding this need to feel happy in a world of suffering and sickness, by fostering their illusions, we supply an essential social service. And therein lies the source of our power."

"You're sick in the head," Blade stated. "And your philosophy is perverted."

Paolucci shrugged. "Perverted or not, the Dragons *do* control Miami and the rest of southern Florida. And soon we will extend our control to other areas."

"Not if the Family can help it."

The Director smirked. "But the Family can't."

Blade stared into Paolucci's eyes. "Sooner or later, someone will come along and lead the people in a revolt against your manipulation. I know there have already been a lot who have moved away from Miami, rather than live under the influence of a drug-dominated culture. Not everyone is gullible enough to stupidly believe that pleasure is the only pursuit in life that matters. There are those who believe in higher values, in spiritual values of love and faith—"

Slapping the table in mirth, the Director laughed uproariously. "Love and faith? You don't actually believe that nonsense?"

Blade's eyes became flinty.

"You're too idealistic, my friend," Paolucci declared patronizingly. "The world is not governed by love and faith. It's dominated by greed, lust, and power. Nothing else counts."

A sole mercenary was approaching the table at a trot.

Blade gazed at the guard apprehensively, worried about Hickok.

"Report!" El Gato barked.

The mercenary halted and saluted. "Hickok escaped."

"How?"

"Over the gate."

"And our casualties?" Cat questioned.

The mercenary averted his eyes. "Eight dead."

"Eight!" El Gato snapped. "One man killed eight of our men!"

The mercenary did not respond.

"Where are the others?" Cat queried angrily.

"Hickok ran into the woods to the north," the mercenary answered. "Corporal Kingsley is leading a search sweep right this minute."

"Tell Kingsley to track Hickok down," El Gato stated, "or not to show his face in the command again. Understand?"

The mercenary nodded.

"Why are you still here?" Cat demanded.

After a brisk salute, the mercenary pivoted and raced away.

"Now where were we?" Paolucci asked, leaning back in his chair. "Oh, yes. You were indulging in whimsy."

Blade said nothing.

The Director looked at El Gato. "Do you know what we have here?"

"No, *señor.*"

"What we have, Cat, is a throwback to an earlier age, an age when so-called decent types believed in basic values like the importance of the home and family life." Paolucci chuckled. "Blade is archaic and doesn't even know it. He's out of step with the times. And he would have been out of step with the society existing before the war."

"How do you figure?" Blade was prompted to ask.

"Study history," Paolucci said. "Take note of the conditions just before World War Three. Crime was rampant, social diseases proliferated, corruption in government was commonplace, and the average turkey on the street was either an addict, a couch potato, or a vain mental midget."

"I don't share your low opinion of them," Blade stated.

"Then you're denying reality again," the Director said. "I'll cite one example I read about in a library in Miami. Did you know that the educational system was in complete disarray? That the students achieved lower and lower grades on aptitude tests each year? The students just didn't care. And who can blame them? When they had a choice between studying a stuffy old book and partying with their friends, between acquiring knowledge or living it up, the book would lose every time."

"What's your point?"

Paolucci smiled condescendingly. "My point, Warrior, is that no one gave a damn about the values you honor. No one cared then, and no one cares now. Oh, there are a few misguided souls around. But Miami is living proof of my point. If people are given a choice between their own selfish interests and the common good, they will pick their selfish pursuits every time."

Blade pursued his lips, contemplating.

El Gato stared at the Warrior with a strange expression.

"I'll hand it to you," Blade said after a minute. "Even with your warped perspective, you're more intelligent than I'd expected. But you're totally wrong. People are not inherently selfish, and if you give them half a chance, they'll prove it. The Elders teach us that a lot depends on the leaders of a society. If there isn't wise leadership, the society will suffer. And many of the leaders before the war were . . ." He paused. "How shall I say it?"

The Director grinned. "They had their heads up their butts."

"They lacked wisdom," Blade amended. "And worse, they were more concerned with lining their own pockets than with public service. They tried to promote a system without values, and such systems produce people without values. They saw everything as a shade of gray, when reality is a contrast of white and black. They prided themselves on a neutral educational system, not realizing that neutral systems breed neutered citizens."

Paolucci slowly rose, smiling. "Fascinating! Everything I was told about you is true. The Warrior with an intellect. What a pity you must be terminated!"

"When?"

The Director stared at the rising sun. "You have about six hours to live. You see, I radioed the Masters last night after I received the call about Barbish. They ordered me to contact them again at sunrise with an update." He smirked. "They are quite interested in learning the reason for your presence in Miami. An emergency session of the Directors has been called for noon. I imagine the Masters will interrogate you personally, and no one ever survives an interrogation."

"The Masters are coming to Happy Acres?"

"No," Paolucci said. "The other Directors will come here, then we'll travel by airboats to the Shrine."

"The Shrine?"

"You'll see for yourself, soon enough," Paulucci commented. He glanced at El Gato. "Keep him covered while I make my calls and change."

"He will be here," Cat promised.

The Director strolled toward the portico.

Blade looked at Cat. "How can you live with yourself working for a man like that?"

El Gato's mustache curved downward. "I suggest, *amigo*, that you keep your mouth closed until the

Director returns.''

Blade started to speak.

''Unless, of course, you do not want to enjoy the six or seven hours of life left to you.'' So saying, Cat aimed the M-16 at the Warrior's head.

Blade shifted in his seat and stared at the fiery orb in the eastern sky.

CHAPTER SEVENTEEN

"Oh, God! Help me!"

Rikki-Tikki-Tavi could do nothing to aid the hapless mercenary. Any sudden motion would result in sinking faster; accordingly, he stayed as immobile as possible, lying on his right side and watching his foe flounder.

Gehret was immersed in the quicksand almost to the neck. Only his right shoulder and head were above the clinging, slippery ooze. His eyes were saucer-shaped from stark terror, and his breathing was ragged. He glanced at the side of the drop-off a mere three feet distant. The firm ground might as well have been on the moon. The quicksand extended for yards in every other direction. He frantically sought salvation in the form of a trailing vine or a projecting log, but such a deliverance was to be denied him. The mercenary whined.

Inhaling and exhaling slowly, shallowly, Rikki still had three-fourths of his body above the quicksand. The sand had not yet seeped into his nostrils, but it was only a matter of time. The nearest terra firma was the drop-off. But how could he reach it? He suddenly realized that the mercenary was looking at him.

Gehret was measuring the space separating them, an estimation he pegged at three feet, maybe less. He girded his muscles and raised his right arm high overhead, about to implement a wild design intended to extricate himself from his smothering grave.

Rikki saw the reckless set of the mercenary's features, he saw his adversary's uplifted arm, and he guessed what was coming next. The mercenary was going to try and grab hold of him and use his body to stay afloat!

Sergeant Gehret took a deep breath, then rose as far as he could and lunged at the Warrior. And missed. The man in black flipped onto his back as Gehret's hand descended, and the mercenary, unable to check his swing, was horrified as his arm sank into the quicksand up to his elbow. He attempted to jerk his arm free; instead, the sandy substance enclosed him to his chin.

The Warrior turned his head to the right.

Gehret gazed into the martial artist's eyes, his own conveying his overwhelming desperation. "I don't want to die," he said plaintively.

"We are all called to the higher mansions eventually," Rikki said softly.

The quicksand was rising toward Gehret's lower lip. He mustered a halfhearted grin. "I never thought it would be like this, you know?"

Rikki did not respond.

Inexorably, the quicksand reached Gehret's lower lip and he sputtered. For the last time his eyes locked on the man in black. "Life is so damn unfair!" he stated, and went under.

Rikki observed the quicksand swirl and roil as the mercenary fought his fate to the end. A grimy hand poked from the ooze, its fingers stiffening, clawing at the sky as if the very air could somehow provide support. For a moment the hand waved back and forth, and then the fingers went limp and the arm was claimed by the primeval muck.

Somewhere, a bird was greeting the new day with a cheery song.

Somewhere, crickets were chirping.

Somewhere, a frog croaked.

Flat on his back on the surface of the quicksand pool, Rikki-Tikki-Tavi suddenly felt very, very alone. He gazed at the steadily brightening sky, at the arrival of the new day, and he wondered if he would be alive to see the sun set. Such a morbid thought disturbed him. A Warrior must maintain a positive attitude; anything less could result in the Warrior's premature demise.

A beautiful yellow and black butterfly flitted over the pool, passing within several inches of the Warrior's nose. Rikki admired the insect's delicate structure and the beating of its frail wings. Life could be so sublimely glorious, so full of promise and marvels. He was not yet ready to interrupt his quest for perfection by passing to the other side. He would not forsake life while a breath remained.

But how was he to escape the quicksand?

Rikki's feet were nearer to the drop-off than his head. He tilted his chin, tucking it against his chest, and peered between the black shoes especially constructed for him by the Family Weavers at the earthen slope. His only hope lay in reaching that four-foot-high drop-off.

A bee buzzed past his head.

What were his options? Simply surging to his knees and diving was out of the question; the quicksand would not bear his weight and his doom would be sealed. Wriggling toward it was an attractive idea, but he ran the risk of working his body lower into the mire before he reached the drop-off and becoming inextricably trapped. What was left? Swimming? Ridiculous.

There was movement to his right.

Rikki glanced in that direction and spotted a small green snake moving across the quicksand to the far side. The snake's negligible weight was insufficient to cause it to sink, and lacking appendages or limbs to be sucked under the surface, it traversed the pool with indifferent ease.

What was the lesson learned?

Rikki stared at the drop-off again, pondering the significance of the snake's safe passage. As he'd learned from his study of Zen, enlightenment was a state of being attained by blending the soul with the cosmos. And life's lessons were learned by a scrupulous attention to details; even the smallest, most inconsequential happening could be fraught with import.

So what had the snake taught him?

Stay flat. Keep the head up. Keep the arms close to the body and the legs tucked tight together. Distribute the weight as evenly as possible. And don't stop. Not for a second.

What about technique?

Should he wiggle toward the drop-off or roll? Rolling would bury his shoulders in the quicksand. Therefore, wiggling was the only alternative. He hunched his shoulders, tightened his superbly muscled abdomen, and tentatively slid his legs toward the drop-off. The soles of his shoes crept less than an inch closer. He relaxed, breathing regularly. At this rate, hours would be encompassed in the effort.

A red-shouldered hawk winged above the landscape.

Rikki recalled a comment Geronimo had once made: "My ancestors saw signs in everything. They viewed the sighting of a hawk as a particularly good omen." He hoped Geronimo was right.

The drop-off beckoned.

With the focused determination of a skilled martial artist, Rikki-Tikki-Tavi applied himself to the task at hand. The technique was always the same: a barely perceptible compacting of his slim shoulders, then a bunching of his stomach, followed by stretching his legs as far as they would go. Over and over and over he repeated the procedure. Sweat coated the pores of his face and neck.

The minutes lengthened into hours.

Three times he paused to rest and gather his strength. His abdomen became sore, and his shoulder muscles periodically cramped. He resisted the discomfort, concentrating on the drop-off.

Hour succeeded hour.

The sun angled toward the meridian.

Rikki narrowed the gap to ten inches. He halted, taking a brief break.

Muffled footsteps sounded from the north, the tread of someone advancing stealthily through the undergrowth.

Alarmed, the Warrior craned his head. The footsteps were drawing ever closer to the pool. If the mercenaries found him stuck in the quicksand, rendered powerless, they wouldn't hesitate to finish him off.

He had to hurry.

Rikki renewed his effort, moving twice the speed as

before. The ache in his stomach became increasingly severe. Earlier he'd aligned the katana and the M-16 along his left leg. The strain of insuring they were held horizontal and not allowed to dip into the quicksand was taking an acute toll on his left arm.

Nine inches separated him from the drop-off.

Eight inches.

Seven.

Rikki scanned the underbrush bordering the quicksand to the north.

The footsteps slowed, then seemed to cease.

So close, and yet so far!

Rikki stared at the drop-off, calculating. If he stayed where he was, he risked being slaughtered. He was near enough now to justify a gamble, a move that would either succeed in liberating him from the muck or result in a decidedly distasteful outcome. The quicksand gave the impression of being firmer near the bank, augmenting his chances.

A twig snapped in the woods to the west. Had the mercenaries changed direction?

Further delay could prove fatal.

Rikki-Tikki-Tavi launched himself toward the drop-off, elevating his body from the waist up and lunging, his arms at full extension. His fingers dug into the yielding soil, but even as they did, his legs were sucked under, the sandy ooze enveloping him to the waist. He struggled to get a firm grip on the drop-off, but his hands were slipping through the dirt.

The quicksand was pulling him down.

Rikki employed all of his strength, his fingers buried in the earth to the knuckles.

With the irresistible force of gravity on its side, the quicksand was winning the elemental battle. The sand rose to the Warrior's arms.

A heightened resolve flooded over the martial artist, and he released his right handhold and speared his arm upward, trying for a higher grip.

As if the quicksand was a living entity endowed with a malevolent will, the suction intensified at that precise moment.

Rikki felt himself sliding under, and the grainy sand was up to his neck, his arms above his head, when a hand clamped on his right wrist, arresting his descent. He looked up.

"You Zen types sure are loco," commented the figure in buckskins above him.

"Hickok!"

"You were expecting maybe the tooth fairy?" the gunman retorted. He was lying flat, his right hand gripping Rikki, his left arm looped over the edge of the drop-off.

Rikki's elation changed to dismay as he beheld the gun-fighter's bandaged right shoulder. Blood was seeping from the bandages, and Hickok's face was distorted in profound pain.

The gunman grunted as he hauled on Rikki's arm, straining to the maximum.

Rikki, the focus of the tug of war between the gun-fighter and the quicksand, racked his brain for something he could do to aid his friend. The lighter the load, the easier it would be for Hickok to pull him out. With the idea came action; he used his left hand to unsling his M-16 and allowed the rifle to drop into the mire.

Hickok's neck muscles were quivering and his face was beet red. He closed his eyes and gritted his teeth. "And I thought Blade was overweight," he muttered.

There was one more item he could discard. Rikki used his left hand and drew his katana, his arm protesting the sharp angle required to draw the sword straight up. Once the blade was clear of the scabbard, he glanced over his left shoulder at the backpack strap. Working swiftly, he slid the katana under the strap, pressed the razor edge against the fabric and sliced. The strap parted, the backpack dangling from his right side. He gazed over his right shoulder, locating the strap, then bent his left arm behind his head as he slanted the blade under it.

Two seconds later the backpack fell into the quick-sand.

"Your katana!" Hickok exclaimed.

"Never!" Rikki responded.

Hickok grunted once more as he nodded at the bank. "The katana!" he repeated urgently.

And Rikki abruptly understood. He brought his left arm back and drove the sword into the drop-off, all the way to the hilt. The katana held fast, and Rikki had the added leverage he needed to combine his strength with the gunman's.

Together, the Warriors achieved the success denied them singly. Inch by laborious inch, with the quicksand resisting every gain, Rikki's body came clear of the sandy ooze. Once his elbows were out, he dug them into the ground and arced his hips upward. With an airy hiss the suction was broken and Rikki scrambled free. Hickok kept pulling, drawing the martial artist up and over the drop-off, Rikki tugging the katana free as he went, and as one they sprawled on the crest, breathing deeply.

"Thank you," Rikki said softly, sincerely.

Hickok made a waving gesture with his left hand. "Piece of cake."

Rikki stared at the quicksand, thinking of the mercenary. "I came close. . . ." He didn't finish the sentence.

"Just one thing I need to know," Hickok remarked breathlessly.

"What is it, my friend?"

"What the blazes were you doing takin' a mud bath at a time like this?"

CHAPTER EIGHTEEN

"So those are airboats?" Blade commented.

Arlo Paolucci nodded, his red hood bobbing. "They are the only practical mode of transportation for navigating in the Everglades. They have a very low draft and can maneuver in shallow water. They're powered by aircraft engines."

Blade was intrigued by the unusual craft. They were box-shaped, a dull, gray metal. There were two flat seats the width of the boat, one a few feet from the prow, the second situated in the center. Immediately behind this second seat was a platform affair, an elevated chair for the person operating the craft. And to the rear of the platform chair was a huge fan or propeller enclosed in a circular housing of wire mesh. Attached aft were the large metal fins used for steering the airboat. Eight of the fifteen airboats secured to the dock had two tail fins, the rest only one.

"It will take us about an hour to reach the Shrine," Paolucci remarked, stepping onto the dock in front of the Warrior.

Blade paused and glanced over his shoulder at the 12 Directors walking toward the dock on the southern boundary of the estate. All 12 were attired in red robes, as was Paolucci.

"Keep going," El Gato directed. Cat and two mercenaries were right behind the giant.

Blade strolled after Paolucci. The swamp stretched to the east, west, and south as far as the eye could see. "Where is this Shrine, exactly?" he asked.

"A man about to die should not be concerned over trifles," Paolucci said. He was holding the Bowies in his right hand.

"Do the Masters live at the Shrine?"

"No. They live elsewhere, on an island deep in the Everglades. Not even the Directors are privileged to know its location," Paolucci replied.

"How do the Masters get to the Shrine?" Blade inquired.

Paolucci looked at the Warrior. "Didn't you ever hear about what curiosity did to the cat?"

"What have I got to lose?" Blade responded.

Paolucci chuckled. "I see your point. The Masters use airboats, just like we do."

"What do the Masters look like?"

Paolucci grinned. "In due time." He halted next to one of the airboats and faced those following. Everyone else stopped. "Cat," he said. "You know what to do."

El Gato reached into his left rear pocket and produced a set of handcuffs.

Blade's eyes narrowed. "For me?"

"I'm afraid so, *amigo,*" Cat said.

"It's standard procedure," Paolucci explained. "The Masters require all prisoners to have their wrists secured."

"They don't like their victims to fight back?" Blade said, baiting the Director.

El Gato reached into the same pocket and extracted a small key. "Your wrists, Blade."

The two mercenaries elevated the barrels of their machine guns.

The Warrior frowned as he offered his wrists to Cat.

"Were it up to me, you would die like a man," El Gato stated. "Not like an animal." He snapped the handcuffs onto the giant's wrists, then handed the key to the Director.

Blade studied the cuffs for a moment.

"We should return shortly after dark," Paolucci said to Cat. "Tell Maria I'll be expecting my supper."

"*Si, señor.*"

Blade gazed at the airboats. On three of them, seated in the platform chairs, were mercenaries.

"Let's load up," Paolucci instructed the other

Directors.

As they had done on many occasions, the Directors stepped onto the airboats, four to a boat, and sat down.

Paolucci indicated the first boat with a jab of the Bowies. "On this one," he said to the Warrior.

Blade entered the boat. Three Directors were sitting on the center seat, and one was in the front. He moved next to the Director in the front and took a seat.

Arlo Paolucci came on board, standing alongside the Warrior. He looked at Cat. "By the time I get back, I trust you will have found the other two Warriors."

"We will find them," El Gato assured him.

"That's what you said five hours ago," Paolucci mentioned. "Inspire your men to perform as if their lives depend on it." He paused. "They do."

"We will find them," El Gato reiterated.

Paolucci, sat, positioning the Bowies between his legs.

"You still haven't told me the reason you're bringing my knives," Blade noted.

"You'll understand when we reach the Shrine," Paolucci said.

"I can hardly wait," Blade quipped.

Paolucci looked at the mercenary in the platform seat. "Let's go."

El Gato and the pair of mercenaries hastily removed the tie lines to the dock and the airboats were shoved clear. One after the other, the three engines turned over, and a minute later all three were bearing to the south at a rapid clip.

Cat watched the airboats fade into the distance, scowling.

"Is something wrong, sir?" one of his men made bold to inquire.

"There goes a man," El Gato replied. "He deserves a man's death."

"What will the Masters do to him?" the guard asked.

"You don't want to know."

"I was told you've been to the Shrine," the guard commented.

"Several times," Cat said.

"What did you see?"

El Gato glanced at the private. "I haven't seen the Masters, if that's what you're wondering. But I have seen their handiwork. It was inhuman."

The mercenaries exchanged looks.

"How so?" one asked.

"I was sent to pick up the Director," El Gato detailed. "He wasn't at the Shrine dock, so I went searching for him. I found an altar, a marble slab—"

"An altar?" one mercenary repeated.

"Yes. And on it were the bones of a person," El Gato said in a low tone. "A freshly eaten person. Strips of flesh were hanging from the bones. It was horrible." He paused, a faraway glint in his eyes. "But the worst part of it was the head."

"The head?"

"*Si.* The Masters had eaten all of the body except for the head. They left it intact." He stared absently at the dock. "I knew her."

"Her?"

"A Director by the name of Carmen Gonzales. She went bad, and they *ate* her," Cat said in disbelief.

"I'm glad I wasn't picked to be an airboat driver," one of the guards remarked.

Cat gazed to the south. He knew the airboats would alter course five minutes from the estate and turn westward toward the Shine. "I never want to go there again," he stated, more to himself than his men.

"Have I got bad news for you!" declared a new voice from their rear.

El Gato and the pair of mercenaries pivoted, beginning to level their weapons. But they were already covered.

"Howdy!" said the one in buckskins, beaming, a pearl-handled Colt Python revolver in each hand and trained on the mercenaries. He stood a yard away.

"Hickok!" Cat exclaimed.

Beside the gunman was the third Warrior, a diminutive man dressed in dirty black clothing, a gleaming katana in his hands.

"I don't think we've been formally introduced,"

Hickok said to Cat.

"I am El Gato."

"The pussycat?" Hickok said. His tone lowered. "Drop the hardware."

El Gato's M-16 was slung over his right shoulder. He gripped the strap, about to lower the weapon to the dock.

His men had other ideas. In unison, they attempted to bring their machine guns into play. Both men had only to raise their barrels several inches; both had confidence in their speed and ability; both believed they could beat the Warriors.

Both were mistaken.

Rikki stepped between them, his katana flashing in the sunlight, streaking to the right, then the left, and with each swing the forged steel slashed into a mercenary's neck, almost severing it.

In the time it took Cat to think, both of his men were dead on their feet, blood spraying over their camouflage uniforms and the dock. Stunned, he scarcely breathed as their forms crumpled into disjointed heaps, their machine guns clattering at their feet.

Hickok wagged his Pythons at El Gato. "Your turn. What's it gonna be? You can lower your M-16, or Rikki here will demonstrate why he always carves the Family turkey at Thanksgiving."

Cat lowered the M-16 slowly. Very slowly. His eyes were locked on the crimson-covered, dripping katana.

"Well, it's nice to see that one of you mangy coyotes has brains," Hickok remarked. He walked up to El Gato and pressed his Pythons against Cat's stomach. "Here's the way it is. We saw our pard being taken on one of these funny boats by those cow chips in the red pajamas. We aim to go after him. *You* are going to take us."

Cat opened his mouth to reply.

"Before you say anything," Hickok cut him off, "there's something you should know. Rikki and I are plumb tuckered out. We're tired of being used for target practice by idiots who couldn't hit a buffalo at two feet with a bazooka. And I'm not in the mood to play footsy with you. So if you don't agree, right this minute, to take us to our pard, I aim to plug you in the jewels. And if you think I'm kiddin', I suggest you take a gander at my eyes."

El Gato gazed at the gunman.

"What will it be?" Hickok prompted.

"I believe you, *hombre*," Cat said. "I will take you to your *compadre*."

Hickok smiled.

"On one condition," Cat added.

"No conditions," Hickok stated.

"I will take you to Blade," Cat proposed, "if you will permit me to help you once we reach the Shrine."

Hickok was confused and it showed. "What are you talkin' about?"

"It is simple. I want to help free your friend."

"Why?" Hickok asked suspiciously.

"I don't know if I could make you understand."

"Try us."

El Gato looked at both Warriors, then sighed. "Once, years ago, I was a man of reputation. A mercenary, but an honorable mercenary. I did not work for just any pig. I picked my employers. If I believed in their cause, I worked for them. If not, I didn't." His lips compressed. "Now all that has changed."

"You're tellin' me," Hickok said. "Now you're workin' for a passel of low-down mutants."

"Don't remind me," El Gato responded, the words barely audible. "I kept telling myself the money was worth it. Even after I saw what the Masters did to one of their Dealers, I deluded myself. I've dishonored my profession." He looked into Hickok's eyes. "Your friend made me see the light. He made me think of things I have not thought about in a long, long time."

"Like what?"

"I have five brothers and four sisters," El Gato disclosed, his voice strained.

Hickok glanced at Rikki.

The martial artist nodded.

"Okay, pussycat," Hickok said. "We'll take you at your word for now. But you don't get a gun until I say so.

And I hope, for your sake, you're not fibbin' us.''

"He is telling the truth," Rikki interjected.

"We must hurry," Cat advised them. "The Directors have a head start."

"After you," Hickok directed.

El Gato stepped onto one of the airboats and climbed into the platform chair. "Remove the line."

Hickok holstered his left Colt and unfastened the tie line. Rikki was busy grabbing the machine guns and the M-16. Both Warriors joined El Gato on the boat.

The gunman glanced over the prow. "This boat is dinkier than I expected. It doesn't sit very high above the water."

"So?" Cat said.

"So what happens if we bump into a big snake?''

CHAPTER NINETEEN

"That's the Shrine?" Blade inquired doubtfully.

"No," Paolucci answered. "That's a small island where we dock the airboats."

Blade scrutinized the few trees dotting the island and the narrow boat dock they were rapidly approaching. The airboat ride was an experience he would never forget. Strung out in a line, with Paolucci's boat in the lead, the three craft had negotiated the swampy terrain with deceptive ease. Most of the hour spent in transit between Happy Acres and the Shrine had entailed crossing vast plains of sawgrass. The airboats had plowed through the grass at terrific speeds, flattening the blades under the prow, the sawgrass and the wind whipping the boat and its occupants. Now, as the mercenary steering the craft killed the engine and allowed the airboat to glide up to the dock, Blade devoted his attention, for the umpteenth time, to his primary concern: escaping. He had toyed with the notion of leaping overboard while en route, but the airboat had been moving at such a great speed that he ran the risk of being injured in the attempt. To complicate matters, the mercenary was armed with a machine gun. And although the Directors were not carrying visible weapons, there was no telling what was concealed under their robes.

The three airboats coasted to the dock and the Directors busied themselves with the lines.

"On your feet," Paolucci ordered the Warrior, rising.

Blade stood. "The Masters must not be here yet," he mentioned. "I don't see their airboats."

"The Masters don't dock here," Paolucci divulged. "They have their own dock on the north side of the Shrine."

"They don't want to share a dock with lowly humans, huh?" Blade taunted.

"Quit wasting your breath," Paolucci advised. He stepped onto the dock and beckoned for Blade to join him.

The Warrior complied, his cuffed hands in front of his body.

Paolucci looked at the mercenaries in the platform seats. "You will stay in your boats until we return. Understood?"

The trio nodded.

"Follow me," Paolucci instructed the giant.

Blade resigned himself to obeying until he could get his bearings and formulate a plan. The twelve other Directors were trailing him as he moved along the dock on Paolucci's heels. A well-worn path at the end of the dock wound in the direction of a large island 60 yards to the west, an island covered with trees and undergrowth.

"There is the Shrine," Paolucci declared, nodding at the other island.

"Why is it called the Shrine?"

"What could be more fitting for the site of the sacrifices our Masters make?"

"You've never told me," Blade noted. "Who or what do the Masters sacrifice to?"

"What do you mean?"

"It should be obvious. Do the Masters sacrifice to a deity? Sacrifices are usually made for a reason. What's theirs?"

"I've never asked."

"You're despicable."

"I wouldn't expect you to comprehend the true meaning of the relationship we share with our Masters," Paolucci said as they wended their way toward the large island.

"I comprehend, all right," Blade stated. "You've enslaved the human population of southern Florida by fostering mass drug addiction, and all for mutant Masters who must view us as cattle. You've sold the human race down the tubes for power and prestige. You deserve to die.''

''How convenient! You've set yourself up as our judge and executioner!'' Paolucci retorted.

They continued in silence.

Blade stared at the Bowies in Paolucci's right hand. His life depended on getting those knives back, but timing would be everything. He must wait for the perfect moment. His gaze shifted to the island ahead, and he scrutinized the grove of trees. One consolation, he mentally noted, was that Hickok and Rikki were free. If worse came to worst, they could fly to the Home, call a meeting of the Federation, and lead a combined military force back to Miami to smash the Dragons.

The party reached an incline at the eastern edge of the island, with willows and myrtles on both sides of the trail. They ascended to the crest of the rise. Beyond was a spacious clearing containing granite pedestals and a low marble altar.

And seven waiting figures.

Blade advanced toward the forms, determined not to betray a hint of trepidation. He wouldn't give the Masters any satisfaction by allowing dread or fear to register on his features. Setting his lips in a thin line, he boldly walked toward the clearing, studying the mutants.

All seven were exceptionally tall, averaging six and a half feet in height. Each projected an ungainly appearance, enhanced by their disproportionately long limbs; their arms hung below their knees, and their legs, while on normal dimensions from their hips to their knees, were thin poles below the kneecaps. Their skin was a sickly, pale gray, with layers of excess flesh forming pronounced wrinkles on their neck. Four of the mutants were males, three females. The males wore red, skintight shorts, evidently made especially for their bizarre physiques. Red halters and short skirts clothed the females.

''Masters!'' Arlo Paolucci called out happily.

One of the mutants came toward him.

Blade received the impression he was watching a skeleton on stilts. The mutant's stride was peculiar, a rolling sort of gait. He noticed that the Master never straightened its legs as it walked; the knees were always bent. But the strangest aspect of all, one that filled the Warrior with loathing, was the bony visage.

Except for the folds of flesh at the neck, all of the Masters possesed thin, partially transparent, and extremely taut skin. Veins and arteries, even bones, could be seen just under the surface. The result was to transform their countenance into a hideous caricature of a human face. Each Master was hairless, their heads resembling animated skulls. Their eye sockets were deep, darl wells, their nostrils were slits, their lips wafer thin.

"Director One," said the approaching Master, its voice gravely.

"Master Orm," Paolucci responded.

The mutant called Orm halted, waiting for them.

As he drew closer, Blade distinguished additional ghastly characteristics. Orm's rib cage was clearly visible, each rib distinct and seemingly pressing against the skin from within. The mutant's knuckles were outsized knobs. And when Orm spoke, he revealed a mouth rimmed with pointed, white teeth.

Orm was returning the Warrior's critical appraisal. "So this is the mighty Blade?" he asked derisively.

Paolucci bowed. "Yes, Master. Delivered as promised."

"You said there were three Warriors."

Paolucci, straightening, his hood only half over his head, blanched. "The other two have not been apprehended."

Orm looked at Paolucci. "This is most unfortunate. We were expecting you to bring all three."

"My abject apology, Master."

"Kiss his feet, why don't you?" Blade quipped.

Orm cocked his head, his dark eyes flat and cold. "Defiant to the last, I take it."

"I'm just getting warmed up," Blade declared.

Orm motioned toward the marble altar and the granite pedestals. "Shall we proceed?"

Paolucci nudged the Warrior. "Get moving."

Blade moved slowly toward the center of the clearing. All of the Masters were watching him intently. The tallest, a mutant who radiated an air of menace, whose expression was baleful, sneered at the Warrior. "Are you the leader of the Masters?" he asked Orm. As he did, Orm stepped past him and he saw one of their backs for the first time.

Orm's spinal column was a knobby succession of bony protuberances extending from the base of his skull to his waist, each knob progressively bigger than the one above it. The spine curved outward, magnifying the repellent aspect.

Disconcerted by his discovery, Blade abruptly realized the mutant was speaking to him.

"—not the leader of the Masters," Orm was saying, "so much as I am the head of my Family."

Blade gazed at the six mutants now six feet off. "This is your family?"

"Yes, Warrior."

The tallest Master took a stride toward the Warrior. "I am Radnor, bastard!"

Blade stopped and clenched his fists, expecting the Master to attack.

"Radnor!" Orm snapped.

"Let me kill him now, Father," Radnor said.

"In due time," Orm responded. He looked at the Warrior. "Radnor is my eldest."

"One big, happy family," Blade cracked.

"You cannot judge us by human standards," Orm stated.

"He has already judged all of us, Master," Paolucci mentioned. "He believes we deserve to die."

Radnor, who was the only Master the equal of the Warrior in height, glared into Blade's gray eyes. "Let me kill him, Father!" he reiterated.

"After we have questioned him," Orm said.

"You'll get nothing out of me," Blade vowed.

"I wouldn't be so certain," Orm responded. "There are ways to force you to talk," he added ominously.

"Give it your best shot," Blade countered.

Orm sighed. "I was hoping we could conduct our business as reasonable individuals, but if you persist in this obstinacy, we shall commence the skinning."

"The skinning?"

"Why do you think we instructed Director One to bring your knives?" Orm asked.

Blade didn't respond.

"Come with me," Orm declared, walking to the east with his hands behind his back.

Blade hesitated.

"No tricks. I promise you," Orm said.

What was the Master up to? Blade, suspicious yet curious, moved to the Master's left.

Orm resumed walking, scrutinizing the trees surrounding the clearing. "It is quite lovely here."

"What are you trying to pull?" Blade demanded. "Why are you being so courteous?"

"What did you expect? Slavering monsters?"

"I don't know what I expected," Blade admitted.

"I repeat. You can not judge us by human standards," Orm said. "To you, we are physically repulsive. Am I right?"

Blade nodded.

"Yet we have hearts and minds, just like you," Orm said. "We can love and hate, just like you."

"What do you know about love?" Blade asked scornfully.

"I love my wife and children," Orm declared.

"But you don't love humans."

"True," Orm confessed.

"Is that the reason you set up the Dragons? Is that why you use drugs to control the human populace? Because you hate us?"

Orm studied the Warrior for a moment. "I will tell you something no other human knows, because the knowledge will go with you to your grave. I established the Dragons to protect my family."

"What?"

"I am serious," Orm insisted. "There is a natural animosity between humans and mutants. When my children were much younger, there was a great danger of being hunted down by your kind. Although I built a hideaway in the depths of the Everglades, I knew it was only a matter of time before we were discovered. I needed a power base, some way of ensuring my family would be protected. The drug war in Miami provided the ideal setting. I offered my services to one of the drug lords, assassinating his rivals. Such a task was easy. Our night vision and strength far surpasses the average human."

"What happened then?"

"Once all the opposition was eliminated, I disposed of my so-called employer."

"No one else in his organization objected?"

"Why should they?" Orm responded. "I promised each of them wealth and power beyond their fondest dreams, and I delivered on that promise. They were eating out of my hand."

"So your . . . children . . . didn't help you take over the Dragons?" Blade inquired.

"No. They were too young at the time. Why?"

Blade glanced back at the six other Masters. "I'd heard all of you were involved."

"There are a number of popular rumors concerning us," Orm acknowledged. "Some we've deliberately fostered."

"You have?"

"Of course. Our principal means of maintaining control over the humans are psychological, not physical."

"What about the drugs?" Blade noted.

"The drugs are part of the overall picture. By legalizing drug use, we've promoted addiction. An addicted population is a dependent population. The people now rely on the Dragons for drugs. They're dependent on us. We are indispensable.''

"You have it all figured out," Blade remarked.

Orm halted. "It hasn't been easy. Solidifying our links with the Colombian Cartel, minting our own money, picking sycophants as Directors.''

Blade looked the mutant in the eyes. "Why do you want to destroy the Family?''

"So that's it!" Orm exclaimed, smiling broadly, exposing his sharp teeth. "The reason you came to Florida! You heard about our plans! How?''

"Forget how," Blade declared. "Why?''

"Because your Family poses a threat to our operation," Orm answered.

"Paolucci said the same thing," Blade noted. "And it doesn't make any sense.''

"Would it make sense to you if you learned the Dragons are planning to expand their market into the Civilized Zone?''

The Warrior's shock was obvious.

"That's correct," Orm said, grinning wickedly. "We have made arrangements with a high-ranking official in the Civilized Zone, one of your allies in the Freedom Federation, to begin distributing drugs covertly. Drugs are illegal there, of course, but that won't stop us.''

"You're going to introduce drugs to the Civilized Zone!" Blade declared in consternation.

"Eventually, we'll introduce drugs, as you put it, into each Federation faction. We'll corner the market. Your accursed Family, though, stands in our way. You're too idealistic, too damn spiritual. We could never foster drug dependence in the Home. And if we can't turn you, then we must destroy you. We're assembling a mercenary unit to pay your Home a little visit.''

Blade raised his hands to his forehead.

"I'd like to know how you found out?" Orm mentioned.

The Warrior appeared to be in a daze.

"Oh, well. I guess it's not important. I'll track down the leak," Orm vowed. "Only the Directors and a few of the Dealers know about our plan to send a demolition unit to the Home. If one of them was indiscreet, I'll find out."

Blade gazed at the ground with a blank expression.

"Don't take the news so hard," Orm said. "It's nothing personal. Business is business, and the Dragons have an opportunity to expand our trade in a big way." He turned and started back.

The Warrior walked alongside the mutant.

"I'm impressed that you got this far," Orm commented. "Once, a few years ago, a disgruntled member of the Colombian Cartel hired a professional assassin to terminate us. We caught him, of course. The assassin was a mutant! Can you imagine that? We cut out his tongue, but allowed him to live." He paused. "You will not be so fortunate. I thought it would be poetic justice to use your own knives to skin you. We relish the taste of human flesh, all except for the skin. It leaves a bitter, salty aftertaste."

Blade was scarcely listening, his mind in turmoil. All the pieces of the puzzle now fit, and a rage was simmering inside him, a fury born of his experiences in Miami. He remembered the boy of six or seven who had begged for coins to buy drugs for his dad, and the 15-year-old girl who hustled men to support her habit, and then he thought of all the thousands of innocent children in the Civilized Zone and the other Federation factions, children whose lives would be forever warped by having the drug life-style forced on them by peer pressure or the manipulation of conniving adults. All because the Dragons wanted to expand their drug market! With each stride he took his rage grew. He glanced down at the handcuffs, at the links connecting the metal bracelets.

"—ceremony was my idea," Orm was boasting. "Humans are easily swayed by elaborate ceremonies. The sacrifices are an excuse for us to indulge ourselves."

Blade looked up. They were 12 feet from the waiting Masters and Directors. Seven of the former and thirteen of the latter. Twenty, all told. Not the best of odds, but he didn't care anymore. He felt like molten lava was circulating in his veins.

"Ahh. Here we are," Orm remarked as they reached the assembled group. He extended his right arm. "The knives, Director One."

Arlo Paolucci began to lift his right hand.

And Blade made his move. His massive arms bunched, his muscles rippling and bulging, as he exerted all of his prodigious strength, his forearms straining outward. For an average man the cuffs would have held; for the herculean Warrior the links were as putty. In the space of a heartbeat they parted with a loud snap, and before the stupefied Masters and Directors could intervene, the Warrior yanked his Bowies from Paolucci and whirled toward Orm.

The mutant leader was reaching for the giant. "Get—" he began.

Blade swept the Bowies under Orm's arms and buried them to their hilts in the mutant leader's chest, his shoulder muscles coiling like steel springs as he lifted the Master on the Bowie blades, surging Orm up and over his head. For a second he stood there, grand and terrible in the sunlight, the mutant upraised and thrashing and screeching.

Snarling and hissing, the other Masters closed in.

The Warrior whirled and flung Orm into the charging Masters, bowling four of them over. But the remaining two, one of whom was Radnor, pounced. Blade felt their bony fingers close on his forearms, one on each side. He dropped to his left knee and wrenched his left arm downward, propelling the mutant holding him to the ground to crash onto its face. Even as he completed the move, he started another. There was no time for needless thought, and there would be no rhyme or reason to this battle. He had to rely on his reflexes, on his honed instincts, and keep moving-moving-moving. If he slowed for an instant, he was dead. Consequently, as the one mutant was crashing onto the hard ground, Blade was already in motion to the right, angling his left knee in a savage arc, ramming the kneecap into Radnor's groin.

Radnor gurgled and released his grip.

The Directors swarmed in, their red robes swirling. Four of the thirteen produced knives, two drew pistols from hiding, and one stepped up to the giant with a sawed-off shotgun sliding out of his left sleeve.

Blade was a whirlwind. He took the fight to them, moving into their midst to limit their ability to employ their guns and knives for fear of hitting one another. His right Bowie took out the Director with the shotgun, the point slicing into the man's right eye, causing the Director to scream, release the gun, and flounder backwards, blood pouring from the ruptured socket as the Bowie came free.

Another Director snapped off a shot from his pistol, but missed.

The Warrior pivoted, slashing and swiping, the keen edges of his Bowies cutting and ripping right and left. The two Directors with pistols were the next to fall, both with crimson crescents flowing from their severed throats. Blade pressed his attack with reckless abandon, parrying a knife strike, hacking off the fingers of a hand reaching for him, and ramming his left Bowie into the jugular of a Director clinging to his right shoulder.

A stinging sensation lanced across the giant's lower back.

Blade spun to find a Director with a bloody knife, and he angled his right Bowie up and in, the blade penetrating the Director's left cheek. The man stiffened and tottered backwards, blood spraying in all directions. Before Blade could press his advantage, a body alighted on his back and a thin, bony arm encircled his neck.

A Master!

Instantly, the Warrior doubled over, upending the mutant, toppling it in the grass at his feet. He saw the Master's upturned, skeletal features, and he thrust downward with both Bowies, both blades spearing into the mutant's neck.

Something pierced his right shoulder, burning and racking him with pain.

Blade straightened. A Director had stabbed him and

was drawing the knife back for another try. But the Warrior was quicker, his right Bowie cleaving the Director's face from eyebrows to chin with a mighty downswing.

A growling Master tackled the giant from the left, bearing the Warrior down.

Blade landed on his back and kicked, flinging the Master aside. He rolled to his right, and there was another Master diving straight for him. His left Bowie whipped around and met the mutant in midair, catching the creature high on the chest. It wailed and fell, and Blade pulled the knife out and heaved to his knees just in time to meet the rush of a Director with a survival knife. He ducked under the knife as it arched toward his face, and retaliated with his left Bowie, planting the big blade in the Director's loins.

The man gurgled and clutched at himself.

The Warrior tugged the left Bowie out and rotated, always moving, always moving, and as fast as he was, he wasn't fast enough, because a mutant leaped on his back and razor teeth tore into the right side of his neck. A clammy substance flowed over his shoulder as he drove the right Bowie back and in, and connected.

There was a cry of anguish and the Master on his back fell away.

To be replaced by a hurtling pair of Directors, one armed with a knife, coming directly at him.

Blade engaged them in a frenzy, fighting on sheer impulse, his blood-soaked Bowies striking in reckless abandon, lashing every which way as quickly as enemies presented themselves. Crimson spurted over the combatants and the grass. He downed the Directors and another mutant, imbedded his left Bowie in the stomach of a third Director, and rotated to the right.

And suddenly the Warrior was alone, standing amidst a heap of bodies, some motionless, others groaning and moaning and twitching. He blinked his eyes rapidly, wondering where his foes had gone, and he spotted several figures in red racing to the east.

"You!" bellowed a voice to his left.

Blade whirled, the Bowies held at waist level.

"I want you!" It was Radnor, standing over the limp form of his father, saliva caking his lips and chin, his eyes blazing his hatred. "Try me, Warrior! Just me! Without your knives!"

The Warrior spied a lone female Master sprinting to the north. He glanced down, astonished at the sight of Arlo Paolucci, dead, a foot away. The Director was lying on his left side, his forehead split open wide. When had he killed Paolucci?

Radnor took a step forward. "Me, Warrior! Try me if you have the courage!"

Blade returned Radnor's glare, his rage rekindled by the repulsive Master. He tossed the Bowies to the ground.

A vicious grin creased Radnor's mouth. "Now you die!" he roared and charged.

Blade met Radnor halfway, their bodies colliding with a bone-jarring impact. Both kept their footing, Radnor delivering a brutal punch to the Warrior's midsection. Blade doubled over, and Radnor locked his hands together and smashed the Warrior on the back of the head.

Suddenly Blade was on his knees, reeling, pinwheels of light flickering before his eyes, his ears barely registering the brittle chatter of machine guns from the near distance. He looked up, squinting, as the mutant swung those cupped hands again, but this time Blade blocked the blow with his left arm and retaliated. His malletlike right fist thudded into the Master's stomach once, twice, three times in all, and Radnor staggered backwards. Blade went after the mutant with his fists flying, landing one blow after another, his knuckles pounding Radnor's face. He swung again and again and again, even after Radnor toppled backwards, refusing to relent, venting his fury on the mutant, straddling Radnor and pounding the Master repeatedly. A red haze enveloped him, and he kept swinging long after Radnor had ceased moving. He was still raining punches when strong hands grabbed his arms, and he surged erect, prepared to take on more adversaries. Dimly, he perceived a familiar voice.

"—enough, pard! Enough! He's dead! Snap out of it!"

Blade shook his head, his eyes narrowing, puzzled. He looked to his right.

"Are you okay?" Hickok asked, holding onto his friend's right wrist. "It's me! Nathan!" A machine gun was over his right shoulder.

"Blade?" said someone to the giant's left.

Blade glanced around, inhaling deeply, his temples throbbing. "Hello, Rikki," he said huskily.

Rikki-Tikki-Tavi peered intently at his friend. "You've been cut. I must tend to your wounds."

"I'm fine," Blade said. "Really." He faced forward, surprised to see Cat eight feet away.

El Gato gazed at the littered bodies, at the dead and the dying, at the pools of blood, the severed fingers, and the slashed throats. He stared at the gore-spattered Warrior, his eyes widening. And then he did a strange thing. He crossed himself for the first time in many, many years and uttered a phrase he hadn't used in ages. *"Madre de Dios!"*

EPILOGUE

They stood at the rendezvous site, awaiting the arrival of the Hurricane.

"—worked my way around to the south side of the compound," Hickok was explaining. "I figured they wouldn't be expectin' me to pull a stunt like that." He chuckled. "I almost bumped into three turkeys on the west side of the estate. Anyway, to make this long story a mite shorter, I went lookin' for Rikki and found him takin' a mud bath."

Blade looked at the martial artist. "A mud bath?"

"He exaggerates," Rikki said.

"Your clothes were dirty until you took a bath in that stream yesterday," Blade remarked.

"He went swimmin' in quicksand," Hickok disclosed.

"That sounds like a stunt you'd pull," Blade said to the gunman.

"What's that crack supposed to mean?" Hickok demanded.

Rikki stared to the south, in the direction of Miami. "What will we do about the Dragons?"

"With most of the Masters dead, the threat to the Family has been removed," Blade said. "And without firm leadership, the Dealers will undoubtedly start fighting among themselves for control of the organization. I don't see the Dragons as a danger any more."

"You still haven't told me what that crack meant," Hickok stated.

Blade glanced at the gunfighter. "Which Warrior nearly ran over half the Family when he was learning to drive the SEAL?"

"Me, but—"

"And which Warrior," Blade went on, "confided to me that he *accidentally* drove a tank into the moat at the Home?"

"Me, but—"

"I could go on and on," Blade said, "but I rest my case."

Hickok looked from Blade to Rikki and back again. "Pitiful. Just pitiful."

"What is?" Rikki asked.

"A couple of teensy-weensy boo-boos and you're branded for life!"